Thank you so much

The Midnight Air

Dear Reina,

Enjoy life each and everyday ☀
I'M so grateful for "All" your support
And continued prayers.

It is "Women" like you that change
our world...

Live life each and every moment ☀

Let go ☀ Let God ☀

With Immense Gratitude,

D. M. Miraglia
XO

D.M. Miraglia

The Midnight Air

~An Adult Historical Romance Novel~

Book interior and cover design by Jean Boles
jean.bolesbooks@gmail.com

Dedication

To my Mother and Father
Thank you for believing in me.
I love you even more...

Acknowledgements

I would like to express immense gratitude to all the people who supported me through this project. It is with their support I was able to write my first novel, continue with my work commitments and complete my dream. The names below appear in alphabetical order.

Jean Boles - A very special thank you for your exceptional work as my creative book designer and for helping me through the book publishing process. I could not have done this without the patience and guidance you showed toward me.

Sandra Breuss, Eternal Flame Ministry - I owe you a very special thank you. You are my kindred spirit who balances me and keeps peace in my life. Your teachings are profound, transforming me into a very gentle strength.

Eileen Dowse Ph.D - I am here today because of your commitment and dedication as my developmental editor. You were able to gently push me past what I believed were my limits, to achieve something I thought was impossible. You believed in me, helped me laugh through the difficult times, and you were able to draw out my deep passion for writing. Thank you with all my heart, Dr. D. – xo.

Margaret Fiskell - You are my dear friend who aided me through this journey, keeping me on track to rise above the challenges and bring my dream to light. Your leadership skills and education shined through during this process.

Julie Lambeth and Bill Ashcraft - My two dear attorney friends whose leadership skills and friendship have carried me to this day.

Ann Marie Nader - I am grateful for you every day. You willingly gave your time and talent to help edit my book. Your experience with your own publications and your keen eye for detail was invaluable. Your knowledge and wisdom is a gift I have treasured through this journey.

Minister Danny Osborne - Thank you for centering my faith and keeping my focus centered.

Katherine Watson - I thank you from the bottom of my heart for illustrating the cover of this book. You are a talented artist, whose time and diligence to create an image for my ideas is treasured.

Chapter One

The rhythmical movement and creaking sound was mesmerizing as Gramma rocked in her rocking chair as she read her book. I slowly lifted my head and looked over to watch her read. Gramma is completely absorbed in her book. Her eyes scroll over the words so intensely that it's almost as if she is becoming a part of the story. I am curious about what she is reading and why this book seems so important to her. I try hard to get her attention. It was no use. The book has her hypnotized, and it seems as if there is no way that I can get her back into this world.

I stare and watch as she slowly goes back and forth in her creaking rocking chair. My curiosity grows deeper as I wonder what she is reading and what kind of magical force this book has over my Gramma Irene.

Finally, I get up the nerve and beg Gramma to watch my favorite television show with me. Gramma keeps reading and never lifts her head. As a young child of ten years old, I do not understand her lack of interest in me, and I start to quietly weep. I am thinking, *Gramma, please just look at me and look how funny this television show is so we could both enjoy it together.* Gramma continues to read.

After a half an hour, I give up on trying to get Gramma's attention and sit back on the large sofa. With both my hands supporting my chin, I sit quietly and listen, and I realize how much I love the sound of her rocking chair as it goes back and forth, making an ever so slightly creaking sound as it glides against the floor. It is late and I know Gramma has no idea of the time. I take advantage of this opportunity to stay up later than my usual bedtime. I continue to watch whatever I want on the television and listen to the rhythmical sound of the rocking chair going back and forth, back and forth. With no conscious supervision I know that I will be able to stay up late, as my Gramma continues to be enthralled in reading her pages. As the night falls deeper into darkness I look over at Gramma. She is reaching for her nightlight and grabbing for her favorite stash of chocolates, which sit on the table next to her. She carefully opens the box, pulling out a chocolate, her eyes never leaving the page of her book. She does not want any noise to wake my Grandpa, who was sleeping in the bedroom upstairs, or wake her sleeping dog, Fluffy, who was lying on the floor next to her.

I stare at Gramma, hoping she will share one of those milk chocolate, caramel peanut-looking clusters with me. I hope she will offer me just one. My mouth waters as I watch her chewing her chocolate, but my craving for the chocolate becomes less important than my appetite for understanding what Gramma was reading and why was it so interesting.

I was surprised when Gramma stood up, approached me and gave me a huge kiss on my forehead.

"You are such a good little girl," Gramma said, as I smiled from ear to ear.

Gramma leaves the room to go to the bathroom. I knew this was my moment to grab as many chocolate peanut clusters from that box as I could. Why not? Gramma likes them and she thinks I'm a good girl. With my heart racing, I snatch three candies from the box. I jump back onto the couch before I hear the bathroom door squeak open and see Gramma walk out of the bathroom. I slowly and carefully unwrap my candies and hide them under the blanket on my lap. I assume with this strategy I will not get caught. Gramma returns to her rocker, and I am happy she is mesmerized by her book and does not notice the time, the missing chocolates or me enjoying my treats.

Even though it is getting later into the evening, I click through the television channels, finding lots of shows that make me laugh. I watch show after show, but my curious mind wonders why Gramma couldn't give me the same attention she is giving her book. I want her undivided attention. I demand to be that book. I want what is in that darn book of hers! As I think more about her book, I wonder what in the world she is reading that is so important that she can't give me any attention. I also begin to wonder about the beautiful lady with long black hair on the front of the book cover. She is wearing a red satin dress, and a heart-shaped locket, with a red stone in the middle, which hangs from a necklace around her neck. The beautiful lady is standing next to a very handsome soldier, who is holding her from behind and kissing her inner neck. What was the story in the book about?

It is late and the house is getting colder and colder. Fluffy, the dog, is asleep and now my Gramma has also fallen asleep in her rocker. I am the only one awake. I eat my third and last chocolate, savoring every bite. I stand up, walk slowly over to Gramma Irene and whisper into her ear.

"Gramma, it's late."

Gramma doesn't wake up, so I cover her with the homemade afghan she made for me when I was a little child. I quietly turn off the light on the side table and walk upstairs to my attic bedroom. I get into my pink heart jammies and climb into bed. Fluffy, who has followed me upstairs, jumps onto the bed with me. My heart and body are racing from all the chocolate I have eaten and I am unable to sleep. My mom always told me not to eat sweets at night because it will make it hard to go to sleep. I guess I just proved that my mom was right.

Now I am alone in my attic bedroom and I look over at my Gramma's bookcase against the wall. I was never really interested in the books Gramma read, but tonight, after seeing how mesmerized Gramma was while reading her book, I begin to wonder what kinds of books Gramma keeps on the bookcase in my bedroom.

Since I can't sleep, I walk over to the bookcase, which holds hundreds of books placed perfectly in a row on each shelf. As my long, ten-year-old fingers slide along the books from right to left, I realize how badly I want to take one of these books off the shelf and open it. I want to get transported to a different dimension by the words of the story. At the same time, I am worried that I might get caught reading something I probably should not be reading.

My fingers stop on one book. From the book's side jacket it looks interesting. I carefully pull it off the shelf, making sure I keep the opening marked so I know where to put it back, ensuring Gramma does not find out that I took it.

On the cover of this book is a beautiful lady, wearing a long, powder blue evening gown. She is layered in old world jewelry. There is also a man in military uniform standing behind her, over-looking a stormy sea view. Looking at the cover of the book, I begin to daydream. I want to be this lady. I imagine the story and the couple on the cover. The scene on the book cover seems to de-pict a story set back in the early seventeen hundreds. I can only imagine this from the types of stories Gramma would tell me about what life was like in those days. Turning the book over to the back cover, I see the lady sitting at a powder dresser stool, taking off her long, pink, shiny pearl necklace. Her hair is in a fancy style, with lace ribbons hanging from it and barrettes holding back parts of it.

I wish I had barrettes to hold back my long, black wavy hair. I wonder if I could ever be this woman one day, all rich and fancy and in love with a military man. As I flip open the book, I notice an old smell. It is a smell that I recognize from the overall smell in my attic bedroom, when the windows have been closed for a long time and the air has not blown through the room. It is a musty, yet comforting smell for me. I know the smell is created from all the old books on the shelf. Not only do I love to read, I also love to write. My mother always encourages me to do both. Slowly, I open the book I hold in my hand. My heart starts to race because I know if my Gramma catches me, I will be grounded for weeks or possi-bly get one of her, "You have been very bad" spankings.

She would tell me when she tucked me in at night or when she put my clean laundry into my bedroom, "Now you stay away from the books, Sarah Marie. You don't want them to fall on you."

When I heard these instructions, I thought, 'okay, I better not go over to the bookcase and disturb her books.' I also thought that if I touched one or two of the books, somehow Gramma would know. For those reasons, I made sure I always listened to Gramma and did not touch her books. But tonight is different. Tonight, as the sugar from the candy rushes through my blood, a new interest is created about Gramma's books. I figure there must be something very exciting and important in these books, and therefore, I should read one. Maybe there is something in these books I should know about so that one day, when I grow up to be a Gramma, I can be as loving and caring as my Gramma is.

I turn to the first page; it said, "Introduction," and then "Acknowledgements." I skip those pages and turn to the next page. All alone on the next page is the word PREFACE, with a short line below it reading:

"With this ring I thee wed. Will you take my hand in marriage?"

I thought 'what kind of a storybook is this?' I turn the page and read the name of the book: *The Night Was Young*.

I read slowly, struggling with some of the words and with the images that come with the beginning lines of the book. Yet I continue to read. I can tell this book did not take place in present time. It occurs in an era that I have only learned about in school and by watching movies. It does not take long before I, too, became mesmerized by what I am reading.

Chapter Two

It was January 1733 in Mildenhall, England, when Colonel Abraham James Langston knocked on Mistress Sophia Cartwright's door, using a brass knocker in the shape of a lion's head. The sound of the doorknocker was direct and solid, with a high-pitched tone. Colonel Langston stood dressed in full uniform as he waited patiently for the massive, dark wooden door to be opened. After a few moments the Colonel heard footsteps, accompanied by deep barking from a dog, coming from the other side of the door. Despite being outside, Colonel Langston could hear the sound of the barking dog echoing off the inside walls and high vaulted ceilings. The door creaked open.

"Good evening, Colonel Langston. Please come in. Mistress Sophia is upstairs and will be with you shortly. May I take your coat?" Thomas had been in Mistress Sophia's and her father's service for eleven years. He never questioned his employer's actions and kept everything in the strictest confidence. For this loyalty, he was handsomely paid and looked after.

"Why yes, Thomas, thank you," Colonel James responds politely to the butler.

Colonel Langston and Mistress Sophia had been courting for almost eight months. Each time he saw her, he fell more deeply in love.

Once inside the home, Colonel James pauses to look at himself in the hallway mirror. He adjusts his uniform and admires his very distinguished and handsome features. He strokes his sandy blonde hair, adjusting it to perfection. He wants to impress Mistress Sophia, knowing the more presentable and dashing he looks, the more he will be able to persuade her.

As Thomas leads the Colonel past the large foyer, his attention is moved away from the mirror toward the large gold and black Great Dane greeting him with a deep bark and a waging tail.

"Astro, sit. Leave our guest alone."

Astro stopped barking and switched to whining in hopes of getting at least a pat on the head from the visitor. Astro gets his wish as Colonel Langston acknowledges his presence.

"Please follow me, sir. I will escort you to the sitting room," Thomas advises. "How was your journey to the estate, Colonel Langston?"

"It was quiet and pleasant. The sun was shining brightly and the wind was mild. Although there is quite a nip in the air, you could still feel the salty air on your face."

"Would you like to sit by the fireplace and warm yourself a bit as you wait for Mistress Sophia?"

"Why yes, Thomas, that would be grand. I will take rest by the fireplace."

"Would you also like a drink, Colonel?"

"Indeed, Thomas. I will have one of the finest scotches this house is known for having."

"Why certainly sir, it would be my pleasure, Colonel."

Colonel James sits by the fireplace, imaging the beautiful image of Mistress Sophia, soon to be arriving at his side. He already envisioned the alluring scent of her fine Parisian perfume and how it would affect and disarm him. He knew this scent well, as he had brought it back for her as a gift from one of his many trips across the English Channel. He chose the Parisian perfume because he wanted it to be a way for Mistress Sophia to always be thinking of and remembering him when he was not in her presence.

"Good evening, Colonel James."

General Cartwright smiled as he entered his sitting room. He respected Colonel James and had no issue that he had been courting his daughter.

General Craig Richard Cartwright, a legendary three-star General of the British Army, and his family, had lived in this house for over twenty years. When Colonel James saw the General enter the room, he immediately rose out of his chair and methodically saluted the General.

Thomas, who was walking behind the General, had his master's regular fine scotch prepared on a silver tray and ready to serve to him whenever he was ready to receive it.

"Shall we enjoy this excellent scotch together, sir?" General Cartwright asks.

"It would be an honor, General," Colonel James replies, intentionally not wanting to become too causal with the General. He was, after all, still the commander he reported to.

As Colonel James sipped his scotch, he thought back to the day he gifted the fine cases of scotch to Mistress Sophia's father. He had brought back several cases of the scotch from his travels to Scotland. It had been a dangerous journey and the General knew it. The importance and urgency of the mission were what caused the General to send out his finest soldier, Colonel Abraham James Langston. Colonel James, who at this point had fallen deeply in love with the General's daughter, thought it prudent to return with a gift that he knew would please the General. During that same mission he had also stopped by France to handle some political matters between the two countries. It was on that portion of the mission when Colonel James bought the French perfume for Mistress Sophia.

Thinking back to that time during the mission, James could remember smelling the perfume shop from blocks away. Perhaps it was because the wind was blowing in the right direction. It was the fragrance of the shop which lured James through the front door, where he was immediately greeted by the salesclerk.

~~~

"Bonjour, Monsieur. May I help you?"

James was grateful the salesclerk identified him as someone who did not speak the native language.

"Yes, please. What is that fine aroma I smell in the air?"

"Aww, Monsieur, bien joué. That is one of our finest scents that we have in our French boutique. This perfume is a combination of bergamot orris, sandalwood, natural gum resin, vanilla and ylang-ylang extract. It is not available year round, and we only have one bottle left to sell."

"May I smell the scent from a closer proximity?"

"Oui, of course you may, sir."

Colonel James held the bottle to his nose and was instantly surprised when the first image appearing in his mind was that of kissing Mistress Sophia's neck. He quickly pulls the bottle away, hoping the salesclerk did not witness the look of raw passion on his face. She did, and no sooner had Colonel James pushed the bottle away, she commented.

"Monsieur, it is not uncommon for men to be transported to a romantic world in their mind and body when they smell this perfume. It has a very potent effect on men."

Colonel James smiled. He was a British soldier and did not want to continue this conversation with the very attractive French salesclerk.

"Is this the bottle it comes in?" Colonel James asks, hoping to redirect the topic.

"Oui."

The perfume was in a small, elegant, dark crystal bottle, with a crystal tincture top. It had an atomizer mister on the side, for spraying the perfume onto oneself. The perfume bottle was accented with a slender black satin fringe cord. Colonel James knew this would be the most special and memorable item Mistress Sophia owned. For that reason, he did not even bother to ask the price of this unique perfume. He knew it would be the perfect gift for the woman he hoped to marry.

"Could I please have this wrapped as a gift?" Colonel James asked the salesclerk.

"But of course, Monsieur. It would be my pleasure," the salesclerk responded, lowering her chin and raising her eyes up toward Colonel James.

The Colonel decided to ignore this obvious invitation. It was not the first time wearing a uniform had caused a woman to swoon over him. Colonel James moved his attention over to the beveled glass counter. There, he noticed a stunning jeweled ivory hair barrette. On one end was a large comb and on the other end an ivory strip with sea pearls and vibrant red rubies, all beautifully positioned. The mastery of the design made it impossible for Colonel James not to purchase this too for Mistress Sophia's long, beautiful, curly black hair.

"I will take this as well. Could you wrap it separately from the other gift?"

"Yes, Monsieur, I would be glad to."

There was no doubt by the salesclerk, that the handsome soldier had a very special woman in his life. A woman he clearly adored.

Colonel James felt the warmth of excitement wash over him as he walked out of that French shop. He knew how much Mistress Sophia would love and appreciate her beautiful gifts. Perhaps she would even reward him for his kind efforts. He could only hope, as any man would. As the Colonel turned back at the French shop's doorway, he read the sign, 'Cherubin Boutique.' *Cherub Boutique.* He could only smile at the irony of the name.

~~~

"Don't you agree, Colonel?" the General asked, snapping Colonel James back to the reality of standing in the General's sitting room.

"I do indeed, sir," Colonel James responds, hoping this would be a correct answer for something he had no idea what was being talked about. The Colonel wanted to engage in conversation with the General, and at the same time, could feel his chest tensing for the love he had for Mistress Sophia. So he waited patiently to see her until she came down from her room. While waiting, the Colonel and the General discussed the fine pieces of art the General had purchased during his many travels abroad. The General not only had a great appreciation for art, he insisted his home be filled with it. Even the high cathedral ceilings in his home had been hand-painted by a well-known artist from Italy. Each ceiling mural was intricately painted with scenes of cherubs playing musical harps, gazing through the blue clouds.

The Colonel and General's discussion was interrupted when Countess Elizabeth gracefully entered the sitting room.

"Good evening, Countess," James said.

"Good evening, gentlemen," she replied, as she curtsied back to the two of them.

The Countess and the General had been good friends for over 20 years—ever since Sophia was born. They had great admiration for each other.

"I have looked after Sophia since her birth, Colonel James, and now she is finally at the age of eighteen. It continues to astonish me that she is being courted by an honorable man like yourself, Colonel."

"Thank you, Countess. I can assure you I have nothing but the greatest respect for Mistress Sophia."

'The Colonel always knows the best things to say to me to calm my concerns,' reflects the Countess.

Countess Elizabeth proceeded to sit on her favorite dark green, velvet, Victorian sofa, the one with large claw feet legs.

"How was your day, your Ladyship?" the Colonel inquired, always hoping to make a good impression on the Countess.

"We had a lovely day," the Countess responds, fanning herself with the ornate silk fan. "We began with tea and biscuits in our garden house, enjoying the aroma of all the fresh roses which had recently bloomed."

"Countess Elizabeth, may, I pour you your favorite champagne, your Ladyship?" Thomas asked.

"That would be splendid, Thomas. Thank you."

Thomas quickly prepares a glass of champagne for the Countess. He knows how impatient she becomes when she did not have a refreshment in her hand while others do. On a silver tray, Thomas presents the crystal flute glass, with a hand-embroidered doily underneath it.

"Your Ladyship, your champagne."

Countess Elizabeth slowly and elegantly sips from her crystal glass; her lips stain the rim with her bright pink lipstick, leaving a lasting impression. She hopes no one can see it but her.

"Colonel, were you wedded prior to meeting our Sophia?" the Countess boldly asked.

She has never been one to mince words, and when it comes to the welfare of Sophia, the Countess believes it is her duty to dig as deep as she can in order to surface anything that might not be acceptable to her.

"I was indeed, Countess Elizabeth," Colonel James calmly replied. "My dear wife passed away several years ago during a difficult childbirth. It was a terrible loss, taking both my child's and my wife's lives."

"I do apologize for your loss, Colonel," the General responds. His heart aching at the thought then moving to annoyance, wishing the Countess had not asked the question.

"Where are you taking Mistress Sophia for dinner this evening Colonel?" the Countess asked.

"I made a reservation at the Grand Lux Hotel on 3rd Street," the Colonel responded proudly, knowing the Countess is protective of Sophia and also curious about her whereabouts. She also wants to ensure Sophia does not visit places which the Countess has not yet frequented.

"Oh, how lovely. Mistress Sophia will adore that. The music there is splendid and the service is excellent. A fine selection indeed, if I must say so myself, Colonel James."

In the distance the Colonel can hear footsteps. Moments later the ravishing Mistress Sophia enters the sitting room, and Colonel James gasps at her beauty. Wearing a pale pink taffeta evening gown, she is an elegant creature. Her light almond skin captivates his eyes, and her slender neck compliments her beautiful and innocent face. Her black ringlets are accented by light pink ribbons woven through her thick, silky hair.

Colonel James stands tall and proud as he walks in a very controlled manner to greet Mistress Sophia.

Mistress Sophia courtesies as she enters the room. She then proceeds to take a seat on the royal blue chaise lounge. Once situated, Thomas arrives with his silver tray and a glass of champagne.

"Champagne?" he asked, offering Mistress Sophia a beverage.

"Thank you, Thomas."

"At last, we are all here and able to toast for the beginning of the new year," the General said in his usual commanding voice.

"What may become of the new year? I wonder indeed," Colonel James replies, looking directly at Mistress Sophia and smiling.

"Do you have any plans or resolutions for the new year, Colonel James?" asks the Countess.

"Why yes, Countess, I do. I plan to travel to the northern part of Italy and acquire a large purchase of wine. It would seem we do not have any battles at this time, and I would like to use my time wisely to expand my knowledge and skills regarding our neighbors. I am also looking for some fine leathers to make new boots and saddles for our men. It has also come time that our men have new uniforms."

Mistress Sophia gives the Colonel a captivating yet adoring stare. She is enthralled with this man. She is impressed with his status, his mannerisms, and of course, his incredible strong features and good looks. Her mind can only focus on how much she wants to kiss him. She has no interest in any other conversation. At 6:00 pm the large wall clock chimes above the elegant fireplace mantel.

"It would seem we must gather our things and be on our way," Colonel James announced, taking a final sip of his scotch, knowing that it is not the scotch that has him exhilarated.

Colonel James walks over to Sophia in a way that commanded attention and stated, "Mistress Sophia, let me help you with your coat."

The long, wool, chocolate brown coat is accented with large silver buttons. It is a simple design, yet obviously very stylish and expensive. Before the couple exits the room Colonel James salutes the General and bids farewell to the Countess. Once outside the house, James is pleased he is finally alone with Sophia. Her beauty and her smell are hypnotizing. It takes all the military training to stay composed and alert, as he knows this is a woman he loves and wants to protect. Their carriage waits for them in the front driveway. Four large black horses, with black leather bridles, stand ready to pull the black coach. The horses' breath can be seen coming from their nostrils as they stomp their hooves on the ground to stay warm. Bernard, the carriage man, opens the carriage door as Colonel James provides Mistress Sophia his hand, helping her step onto the wooden stoop and into their red velvet-lined, enclosed carriage. James follows her into the carriage and Bernard closes the door behind them.

"Ahh, my sweet love, at last we are alone," James said seductively while sliding his body next to her. Sophia smiled as she lowered her chin and raised her eyes, knowing full well this look always excites James.

James smiles back, but not for the reason Sophia might think. He smiles because he recalls how the salesclerk in the perfume shop made the same gesture. It stirred passion in him then as it did now with Sophia. Except now he was with the woman he loved, and now he could release some of that passion on this beautiful woman sitting next to him. Sitting beside Sophia, James moves her wool coat to the side and slides his hand up under her pale pink taffeta evening gown. She does not resist. He kisses the side of her head, admiring the ivory pearl and ruby barrette she is wearing in her hair, the one he bought for her in Paris. It was positioned elegantly, accentuating her beautiful black ringlets.

Sophia's heart races from James's touch. He lifts his hand from under her dress and moves it to gently touch her oval face, first pausing at her breasts for a brief moment before reaching her lips. Sophia becomes more excited. She can feel the sensation between her legs growing and she does not want it to end. Only continue. She draws herself closer to James's lips as they join together and explore pleasures with the movement of their tongues. James becomes more stimulated. His manhood hardens and Sophia smiles. She is pleased, knowing she has the ability to stimulate him. James, realizing he must gain some composure, knowing they will be arriving at their destination soon, leans back to admire Sophia's beauty. His eyes spy Sophia's ivory cameo brooch choker. This was a gift he had bought for her on her 18th birthday this past year. The choker, accented by a black velvet cord that displayed the sensuality of her grace, lay flawlessly on her slender neck.

"Do you love me, Sophia? Do you love me?"

Sophia replies without hesitation. "Yes, my darling, I love you. I love you to the moon and the stars and back."

"I want to know if you desire me the way that I desire you?" James asks, needing to be reassured in order to continue giving himself to this beautiful woman. He could not bear to lose her.

"Yes, my love, I desire you. My heart and soul burns for thee. I believe I am not complete without thee."

"Thank you, Sophia. It may seem strange, but I needed to hear that from you. I needed to understand your level of commitment to me."

The carriage comes to a halt and Bernard jumps down, pulling out the wooden step, setting it onto the pebble stone driveway for the couple to exit the carriage. He then opens the carriage door, ready to serve and be attentive to what he understands is precious cargo inside.

James steps out of the carriage, quickly turning around to assist the woman he loves and cares for. Sophia exits the carriage elegantly, assisted by James's arm. Before entering the hotel, Sophia looks at James and gives a very slight cough, politely indicating for James to adjust his uniform so others will not see his aroused form in his pants, caused by their most alluring carriage ride. He then adjusts his crotch.

Mistress Sophia is amused, knowing her sensual power has caused James to have to walk with perfect posture, despite his hard erection. So far, she is impressed by his performance, although she cannot keep from giggling.

The couple enters through several doors, assisted by servants wearing black tuxedos and bright white gloves. Each servant greets and welcomes the couple as they progress to their final destination. A final set of servants opens the large French doors to the dining room. The music can be immediately heard and is breathtaking. Each instrument was in perfect harmony with others, producing a blissful musical sound to the ear. James extends his open palm upward to his one true love.

"Allow me to escort you to our dinner, Mistress Sophia."

Sophia smiles, feeling like she is in some type of magical fantasyland. As Colonel James and Mistress Sophia walk into the room, their beauty does not go unnoticed. Voices stop. Heads turn. And people wonder who this perfect couple might be.

Chapter Three

The host stood tall, with a controlled smile, as he met his next guests for the evening.

"Good evening, Colonel James and Mistress Sophia," he said, giving each of them an acknowledging nod. "I have your table ready."

The host ushers the prepossessing couple to their table. Colonel James walks proudly through the ballroom as Mistress Sophia tightly wraps her arm through his. The Colonel is well aware that every man in the room has his eyes on Sophia and wishes she was the one on their arm. James smiles with ease, confidently knowing he will own Sophia's heart this evening, and for him, that is all that matters. The host pulls out the large white chair from the table, assisting Sophia with her seating. Colonel James seats himself, indicating to the host with a look that said, "That will be all; your job is complete.'"

James slowly reaches across the table, gently touching Sophia's dainty hand.

"My darling love, I am honored to be with you this evening. You are my love; you are the air that I breathe to keep me alive."

"Oh James, my darling, you are also my true love. I love you so. I cannot imagine my life without you," Sophia responds, unaware anyone else is in the room.

Her fondness and connection with James is like no other. She never knew a person could be so self-absorbed and fastened to another person. With James she felt safe and loved, and most importantly, revered. The waiter arrived at the table, breaking the tender moment between the couple.

"Colonel James, a bottle of our finest French Bordeaux, as per your request."

"Thank you, sir. It only seems right to have a bottle of the finest wine in the house to enjoy with the finest woman in the house," James said, ogling at Sophia.

Sophia shyly smiles and slowly slides her white satin-gloved hand onto the table. Her gloves go above her elbows, with exquisitely embroidered vines trailing from her elbows to her fingertips. She reaches for James's hand and squeezes it, indicating a private "Thank you for the compliment." Sophia then removes one of the gloves, placing it gently onto the fine white linen cloth. Although not intentional, the way Sophia removed her glove was purely seductive. Pulling the satin fabric down her long slender arms would have any man, or woman, wonder what other ways she expresses her sensuality. James attentively noticed and asked.

"May I help you remove your other one, my darling?"

James knows Sophia is all too aware how much he is stimulated by removing her gloves in public. Sophia winks at him and nods approval for him to have permission to remove her other satin glove. James holds Sophia's hand and gently reaches up her arm in what others watching would describe as a tantalizing manner. James is conscious not to be too obvious in this public arena. He still had a public persona to maintain, although his efforts were in vain. Those around the couple found themselves seduced by the simple act of removing a satin glove from a beautiful woman's hand. James found himself excited to *undress* Sophia's arm. He slowly pulled the glove from her elegant and slender arm. Sophia squirmed in her seat, hoping not to be seen by anyone. Again, her hopes were also in vain. When those around saw her squirm in her

26

seat, they could only assume she was becoming aroused, and naturally, they too became aroused. Tonight, in the moment, she was under his seductive power and could feel the hairs on her arm being stimulated as the smooth fabric slowly was removed from her arm. James smiled as he leaned forward to whisper in her ear.

"I love you."

As he came closer, Sophia looked down at his uniform pants. She was not surprised to see his fully erect penis leaving an imprint in the fabric. Sophia turns her head gently to the right and absorbs all the tantalizing sensations of the moment.

"Apologies, my love," James said.

"The pleasure was mine as well, my darling." Sophia slowly raises the corners of her mouth.

"Good evening, sir." The waiter interrupts in an eloquent tone. "Our specials this evening are an excellent roast beef with blue cheese sauce, a stuffed wild bass, or a pheasant, braised in shallots and garnished with a drizzled honey Bordeaux sauce."

Colonel James clears his throat, still recovering from the seductive moment. "Those sound splendid indeed. We will need some additional time to determine our choice."

After the selections were ordered and James and Sophia finished an exquisite meal, they continued to enjoy a second bottle of Bordeaux. Sophia stares at James, wishing everyone in the hotel would be gone and they could be alone. She realized how much she needed his love and the deep passion he has for her.

Part of Sophia's wish was about to come true. James rises from the table and extends his hands, an invitation to join him in a dance. They walk onto the white Italian marble ballroom floor. Sophia waits for James's lead. He holds her right hand, placing his other hand on her hourglass waist. They spin together on the ballroom floor in perfect harmony to the music. Sophia glides across the marble floor as he spins her around. Again, those in the hotel watching become jealous of the undeniable powerful display of love this couple showed toward each other.

The music of the band was magical as it carried their bodies around the ballroom floor. Recognizing the need for more wine, James escorts Sophia back to their table. A server instantly appears at the table, pleased to be the one serving the admired couple.

"Is there anything I can further assist you with, sir?" the server asks, hoping to please this impressive couple.

"Yes, please. Would you be so kind as to bring us two glasses of your finest port," James responds.

Mistress Sophia modestly looks around the ballroom; she is aware her Colonel is very pleasant on the eyes for all those in the room. His refined features and poised stature is by far the most noticeable physical attributes he has. By far, he is the most handsome man in the room. Knowing that, puts a smile on her face. Sophia desires to serve this urbane man.

The waiter returns with two glasses of port. Sophia interprets James's winks as a signal of anticipation for what might happen during the remainder of their evening.

"I suggest, now that we have finished our dinner, that we take a stroll around the water fountain and take in this lovely evening air?" James's statement is actually delivered as a question.

"That would be lovely, James," Sophia said, knowing the more time she can spend with James, the happier she will be.

As they walk out into the grounds, the sounds of their shoes on the cobblestones echo in the evening air. The gentle mist from the fountain lightly brushes their skin as Sophia pulls her coat around her more tightly.

"Can you smell the freshness of the sea, my love?" James asks, with his deep, refined English accent.

"Most certainly I can," Sophia replies, taking notice of the slightly salty taste on her lips.

James guides them down the path toward the garden house. For three generations the Slade family has been raising the finest roses in this garden house.

"I know you have a fondness for roses, Sophia. I cannot remember a time these roses were not considered to be the finest quality roses in the entire area."

Just before reaching the garden house, Colonel James stops in a predominately shadowy area on the path. He gently pulls Sophia close to him, prepared to partake in the most delectable appetizer of the evening—Sophia's lips. A large, lavender lilac tree offers an additional element of privacy as it overhangs above their heads. James leans toward Sophia's inviting and seductive body. He draws her toward him in a graceful manner, almost as though they were performing a well-choreographed dance step. Sophia longs for his touch. She has always been weakened and yet strengthened by James's tender love. In a low but gentle voice, James draws close to Sophia's ear and whispers.

"Kiss me, Sophia. Kiss me in a way that I will never forget you are my lover."

Mistress Sophia parts her lips and kisses James passionately without hesitation. Her soft, moist mouth joins with his as he slowly cups his hand upon her breast. This move also appears as if it is also part of the amorous dance.

"Don't stop my love, please don't stop," Sophia moans and has difficulty speaking.

The arousal of Sophia's voice and moans have James now fully erect. He imagines being deep inside her, feeling every inch of her tight, moist vagina while he visualizes penetrating her, moving in and out and in and out. He knows all too well this will not be possible until they become married. He also knows Sophia will be worth the wait. In James's mind, he continues to envision this intimate scene with this beautiful woman. As James longs to be inside Sophia, making her his, Sophia longs for a lifetime with Colonel James Langston. She longs to live happily in love, forever and ever.

Chapter Four

Waking up in a stupor on the floor of my attic bedroom, I rub my eyes and wonder what time it is. Not sure exactly where I am, I realize I must have fallen asleep on the floor while reading one of Gramma's books. I now become afraid I might get caught by Gramma for doing something bad. Fluffy, Grandpa's dog, is sound asleep next to me and not moving. I can only hope Gramma thinks I am doing well in this bedroom. I start to hear the birds chirping outside. Dawn is beginning. This means the morning sun will soon rise and Grandpa will want me to start helping him with the chores.

As I lay on my back, I stare up at the floral wallpaper's tiny flowers and their leaves that cover the ceiling and walls. I think about what I had read. What does all this mean? What is this story about? I am still unclear about what was happening in this book. I did not understand what allures my Gramma to read these books. All I know is I was starting to have funny feelings in my body.

The next thing I heard is Gramma and Grandpa talking downstairs. I jump into my bed so my grandparents will think I slept in it last night.

"Charles, will you go wake Sarah Marie?"

Grandpa walks up to the attic and greets me good morning. When he sees I'm asleep, he softly whistles for Fluffy, who hops off my bed and walks downstairs with Grandpa. I roll over onto my side and cover my eyes with my pillow. I am tired from being up late reading about Colonel James and Mistress Sophia; I just want to sleep. Grandpa loves his morning walks with Fluffy. When I am visiting, I usually join him on these walks, but not today. Grandpa and Fluffy go alone. I'm tired and my mind is confused. Even though I am tried, I can't sleep because the aroma of coffee and the sound of Gramma frying eggs and bacon on the stove is keeping me awake. Gramma is a good cook. Now the smell of bacon makes my stomach growl with hunger. Gramma begins singing a song; I recognize it from when I was very small. I feel so much comfort in this room and in this house while visiting my grandparents.

The sunlight begins shining in through the window. I could smell Gramma's yummy cooking seeping into my nose. I can hear birds loudly singing their mating calls to each other. The off-tune sounds of Gramma singing her favorite songs from long ago make me smile with comfort. The nice flowery sheets on my attic trundle bed wrap me in a fabric hug. All these things lull me into the state of euphoria. I begin to wonder, is this the euphoria Sophia felt when she was sitting with James next to her. Did she feel calm as all her senses were stimulated by what was around her?

As groggy as I was, I knew my stomach wouldn't allow me to sleep anymore. I knew my Grandpa wanted to visit my aunt and uncle's dairy farm early today so we could help them with all the chores, including caring for the cows. I decide to get downstairs. I cannot take my hunger pains any longer.

"There you are, my sweet little angel," Gramma said lovingly.

Gramma picks me up and twirls me in the room. My legs dance below me. She kisses my forehead, making loud puckering sounds as she kisses me. I melt into heaven as I feel the love she has for me. Gramma loves me and I know that. I can tell by the way she squeezes me hard and hugs me even tighter. I love all this attention, and knowing I have my Gramma's undivided attention is one of the best things in the world to me.

"I'm starving, Gramma. I am so hungry my belly hurts," I say after all the squeezing stops.

I sit down at the kitchen table with my legs crossed, just as Grandpa comes through the back door. Fluffy immediately jumps onto my lap.

"No sitting at the breakfast table," Gramma scolds Fluffy.

Fluffy jumps down and sulks cowardly as he goes to lie in his bed in the corner. He lets out a tiny whimper and looks up with his sad eyes at Grandpa. Grandpa feels bad; his best friend has gotten into trouble. He quietly walks over to Fluffy and slips him a piece of bacon before my Gramma catches them both. I smile back at my Grandpa, knowing how kind and loving he is toward Fluffy.

"See little chic-chic, we must always be kind to others," Grandpa counsels me.

He sneaks more bacon out of his hands and hands it to me under the kitchen table. Grandpa winks at me and I smile back at him.

"How is my little chic-chic this morning? Did you sleep well?"

My heart always melts when Grandpa calls me his little chic-chic. I know little chickens are adorable, and Uncle Johnny has lots of chickens on his large dairy farm. That's how I originally got the nickname, from playing with all the baby chicks.

"How did you sleep last night, chic-chic?" Grandpa asks, with a mouth full of bacon and toast, as he reaches for his coffee cup.

I quickly reply, not wanting to let out my secret about reading Gramma's books.

"I slept okay. My hungry tummy woke me up though." I hope Grandpa wouldn't ask any more questions about last night as I kicked my feet nervously under the breakfast table.

"Well, all righty then, we are going to fix that."

Grandpa winks at me as Gramma is leaning over the stove cooking. The steam from the frying pan is rising up into the air as she prepares to serve us our breakfast.

"It's time to eat; let's say grace," Gramma commands as she sits down and begins a prayer.

After grace, I am offered a small cup of coffee. Gramma and Grandpa will sneak me coffee or espresso at breakfast when I come to visit. It would drive my parents crazy. I think that is one reason why I liked it. The other reason was I thought it tasted good and gave me lots of energy. I knew that having coffee was a treat, and I would behave like a saint just to have more. My favorite part of my breakfast was dunking my overly buttered homemade bread into my special 'I should not have it cup of coffee.' I ate my toast and asked for more espresso. I knew I was pushing it, but my grandparents never say no.

I love my grandparents and especially enjoy being the only grandchild here for this visit. I especially love everyone calling me 'little one' or 'peanut.' Most of all, I love being called little 'chic-chic' by my grandpa.

"Come on, little chic-chic, time to go visit your Uncle Johnny and tend to the dairy cows."

I get up from the table and go over to Gramma to give her a 'thank you' hug for making me the yummy breakfast. Gramma kisses me back and hugs me so tightly I wish I could stay in her arms forever. 'Oh Gramma, I wish you didn't read those darn storybooks at night and you doted on me like this instead,' I ponder while being squeezed.

Grandpa and I walk out the door together to the car. My Gramma trails behind, carrying a few bags in her hands. Grandpa opens the garage door and we all get into the 1965 green Plymouth Fury. It has four doors with a huge back seat. Sometimes the smell of the leather on those seats makes me think I am on the saddle of a horse. Sometimes I think I might love this car more than Grandpa, because I get to sit in the middle of the big back seat and rest my head on my arms on the middle of the back of the front seat. I sit in the back seat with my face between my grandparents in the front seat. They begin to tell me love stories about their younger days. They tell me stories about how they met and how they both thought about what each other was wondering when they first met. They tell me stories about how they would sit on Gramma's parent's front porch and talk after a yummy roast beef dinner.

"Our stomachs were full and we were relaxed and a little sleepy."

"Oh my, he loved that car. He would tell me how the cv joint was broken, and he was so proud that he fixed it himself. I had no idea what a cv joint was, but Grandpa was sure proud he repaired it, so I was happy with him."

For a brief moment I wondered if Grandpa was ever like Colonel James in Gramma's storybook. 'Yuk'... I thought. 'I don't want to think about that.'

"Grandpa, are we almost there? I can't wait to see all the cows and my favorite new chickens and the baby calves," I say, wiggling with excitement in the back seat, as the leather seat squeaked with my every movement.

I think I am feeling the effects of the espresso I had for breakfast. I have a lot of energy and it is hard for me to sit still. I also find myself kicking my feet hard against the back of the front seat, starting to demand more of my grandparent's attention. Both of them start singing the Old MacDonald song. As we get to the part, E...I...E...I...O, I scream the letters out loud. I love that part. Gramma and Grandpa keep me busy for the entire car ride. They point out different things as we drive and have me enjoying the mountain views as we head toward the dairy farm.

I recognize the bend in the road and know we are close to my uncle's farm. I roll down my window, and now I am positive we are close because I can smell the fresh cow manure in the air. Grandpa pulls into the driveway.

"We're here," I call out. "I can't wait to ride the tractor with you Grandpa."

The farm is just south of a very small town in northeast Pennsylvania. My Uncle Johnny owns a few hundred acres of land and is very proud of what he owns. I remember asking, my uncle during one of my tractor rides.

"How many acres do you own, Uncle Johnny?"

I was always full of questions, especially while riding along beside him on his big John Deer tractor. Uncle Johnny was always patient with me and took time to answer all my questions, no matter how crazy or silly they were. I remember asking him once,

34

"Uncle Johnny, why in the morning do you say that your alarm goes off and then you say you turned your alarm off. Shouldn't you say your alarm went on and you turned it off?"

Sometimes some of my questions took a long time for my Uncle Johnny to answer.

Along with all of his acreage, my uncle also owned a farmhouse. It was built in the 1900s and makes lots of different creaking sounds when you walk through it. Uncle Johnny had bought it from Mr. Brookshire, who was an old farmer retiring out of the farming business.

My uncle told me, "Mr. Brookshire was a very hardworking man and helped to employee many people in the area. Mrs. Brookshire was very religious. She was Catholic, like most of the people in this part of Pennsylvania. She was always doing something with the church."

"Mr. Brookshire was always working on the farm. Day and night, this old married couple never stopped working. They never had any children, so I guess they put all their energy into their church work and farm work. Then one day, Mrs. Brookshire got sick and died. Mr. Brookshire was never the same after that. He decided he could not live on the farm anymore because it was too hard for him to live there without Mrs. Brookshire."

My uncle told me this tale as if he was a human storybook.

"Why couldn't Mr. Brookshire live on the farm after Mrs. Brookshire died?" I asked.

"He really loved that woman," my uncle said. "Those two were one of the nicest couples I knew. When two people really love one another, they always want to be with each other. They know they really need the other person in their life to be a complete person. When two people are like this, you could call them soulmates. Two people who were meant to be together for their entire life, that's what Mr. and Mrs. Brookshire where."

When I think about that now riding in the back seat of my Grandpa's car, I begin wondering about the idea of soulmates. People who want to spend their whole life together. I paused again. 'Hmmm, just like Colonel James and Sophia. I bet they were soulmates too.' All this thinking about people being in love

35

and soulmates just makes me more excited to get back to the attic to continue reading my Gramma's storybook. But for now, we continue to drive to my Uncle Johnny's farm.

Uncle Johnny had a love for farming. He was an agricultural teacher and part of the social studies program for the 12th grade students at the local high school. He had always wanted to own his own farm one day. That's why he couldn't pass up Mr. Brookshire's great offer. Mr. Brookshire came to my uncle and offered to give him the farm for a very small amount of money. As much as my uncle wanted to buy the property right then and there, he first had to talk over the decision with Aunt Katherine, his wife. Aunt Katherine also had a love for the outdoor spaces and farm living. She would remind anyone of a typical farm wife. She also loved to care for people. She was kind, yet a stern, strong woman.

Aunt Katherine loved the property the first time Uncle Johnny showed it to her. The decision to buy the land from Mr. Brookshire became an easy one. Being of similar minds on the matter of farming was only more reason for my Uncle Johnny to love my aunt so dearly.

When Mr. Brookshire met both my aunt and uncle together, he felt compassion for them. They reminded him of when he was just beginning his life with Mrs. Brookshire. He thought they surely could use a good start in life, and he knew that Mrs. Brookshire would have approved of his kind and generous decision. Besides, he had no children and he knew he could not take the land with him when it was his turn to go. "There is no U-Haul hearse," he told my Uncle Johnny and Aunt Katherine. Mr. Brookshire decided to pass on the farm to my aunt and uncle and make this young and in love couple very happy.

I was liking Mr. Brookshire more and more, and I had never even personally met him.

I bet reading Gramma's book can teach me a lot about how two people love each other. First, I see how my grandparents talk to each other and about each other. Then, how my aunt and uncle received the land from Mr. Brookshire, a man who loved and missed his wife.

When my aunt and uncle moved into the farmhouse they began to create a home of their own. After four years they had two boys, and the farm became very profitable. Secretly, Aunt Katherine was always sad she had never had a little girl as part of her family. She loved her boys very much, but she knew it would have been fun to dress up a little girl and make pretty dresses for her and teach her to bake. Although sad that my aunt and uncle didn't have a little girl, in a way I was happy about it. I was happy because my aunt and uncle not having a girl made it so they could spoil me rotten. And for me, that was a wonderful thing.

Whenever I came to visit them on the farm, my aunt would always French braid my hair and tie ribbons into it. The ribbons would dangle from the ends of my braids, and they made me feel so pretty. I bet this was how Sophia felt after the Countess fixed her hair. I could imagine my aunt being my Countess. It was fun to pretend like this.

I think my aunt and uncle really loved each other because they were always nice toward each other. I never heard them fight or say mean things to each other. When I was with them, they always made me feel special and safe, as if I were the only special person in the world. Sometimes I even felt as if I were their daughter.

As we pulled into Uncle Johnny's driveway, suddenly the farm dogs came running to greet us. I could see my Uncle Johnny out in the field, driving his big John Deer tractor. I opened the car door and got out as fast as I could. I was a city girl and I was excited to be here so I could finally play with all the farm animals.

"Okay chic-chic, go put your backpack at the front door and then you can head off to see the animals," Grandpa said with a parental tone.

"Whatever you say, Grandpa. I just want to see all the farm animals and play with them."

Dropping off my backpack onto my uncle's porch, I race to the barn. I stop to eat some concord grapes off the grapevine arching out from the side of the red barn. I sat down and began eating handfuls of grapes straight off the vine. I lay on my back after my belly was full and looked at the clouds, imaging different shapes in each one. It was a warm, sunny day, and I could not imagine being in a better place. I am so happy to be visiting my uncle's dairy farm.

By the time Grandpa catches up with me at the barn, I am lying on my back again, looking up at the sky. When Grandpa arrived, I was now looking up at my tall, slender Grandpa, who stretched out his big, strong hand to help me up.

"Let's go into the barn, chic-chic."

The barn was two stories tall and had two sets of sliding red barn doors. I loved hearing those doors open. It was one of my favorite sounds. It was a combination of metal scratching together and wood creaking. Those doors were a signal to me that a world of adventure and fun and cuddling animals was about to begin.

"It's just about time to milk the cows, chic-chic, and your Uncle Johnny will be here any minute to help us."

"Okay, Grandpa. I hope he hurries up."

I could hear the cow bells jingle and the hooves stomping as each cow entered the barn, mooing. Grandpa ensured the huge red barn doors stayed opened as he called for the cows. They came walking into the barn, one by one, as though they were under a magical spell to do as they were told. Grandpa explained to me that the cows had a pecking order and no one ever stepped out of line. He said each heifer knew what stall was hers, as they all lined up like soldiers getting ready for Uncle Johnny. They knew it was time to be milked. Grandpa said the cows had a social order, with ranks and classes. As Grandpa was talking, I was thinking and wondering what the pecking order was between General Cartwright, the Countess, Colonel James and Sophia. I wondered how they knew how to do the right thing.

Grandpa, Uncle Johnny and I stood in the barn. This was an everyday occurrence for Uncle Johnny, but for me, it was exciting. My favorite part of this time was when Uncle Johnny called out each of the cow's name as he secured the leather straps on each of their necks. Each cow went into a stall so they could be attached to a milking machine and be milked. My ten-year-old eyes took in everything, as I roamed freely around the barn.

The baby calves also began going into the barn to be close to their mothers. It amazed me how gentle these huge creatures were. Even with their enormous size, they still seemed to be caring and maybe even loved each other. I began to wonder if all animals need love. My Gramma told me all people need love, so maybe it was the same for cows. Maybe it was a need for Colonel James and Sophia too. Maybe they both needed love from each other. My mind wandered as the smell of oats and sweet alfalfa hay floated through the barn air. My Uncle Johnny let out a loud whistle.

"Betsy, Gertrude, Daisy, get into your stalls."

The cows followed Uncle Johnny's command without hesitation. Grandpa shouted out to me.

"Look, little chic-chic, there are three new calves since the last time you were here."

"Wow, they are so cute Grandpa, can I go over and pet them?" I ask, knowing it is not good to do things in the barn that you were not supposed to do.

"You sure can," my Grandpa said. "Just be slow and gentle."

After all my chores were finished, I walk up to the farmhouse. Along the way I look out at the mountains in the distance and can see the big green corn rows with yellow corn stocks and more unbaled corn plants scattered across the field. I place my foot onto the wooden porch of the beautiful, large, old two story redbrick Victorian home.

It creaks as my foot makes contact with the boards. As I stand beside the five large white pillars stretching from the porch to the rooftop, I wonder to myself if this is what Sophia felt like standing next to James, who was so tall. I bet she looked so pretty wearing her fancy hair barrettes.

"Come on, little chic-chic, let's go inside," my Grandpa calls out to me. At the same time I can hear Gramma's voice also calling me.

"Sarah Marie, come into the house and wash up. It's almost time for lunch."

As I walk upstairs into the bathroom to wash my hands, I was thinking of Gramma's storybook again and how I sneakily read it last night. I wanted to imagine my life being the same as Sophia's.

I imagined living in a big house resembling a palace. It would have a big fireplace room to keep the warmth in it and lots of pretty pictures on the walls.

'Miss Sarah Marie, would you like to dance with me?' my imaginary James asks.

I giggle like a schoolgirl and I race down the spiral staircase into my aunt and uncle's piano room. I slide my fingers down the piano, thinking of the melody that might have been playing while James and Sophia ate dinner. I visualize me dancing and hearing the violins and the piano playing louder and louder. I can clearly see this in my mind as I spin around. I twist and turn and sing as I replay the scenes of the book in my mind over and over again. The music is loud, and I imagine smiling widely back at Colonel James as we dance in the middle of the white marble ballroom floor. I glide like an angel across the piano room floor as my imaginary James looks deeply into my eyes and said.

"I love you, Sarah Marie."

"I love you too," I say, still spinning around on the floor of my aunt and uncle's house. My spell is broken by Gramma, who calls me again for lunch. I eat as fast as I can because I want to get back outside and visit with the farm animals some more.

Chapter Five

C̶ome on, let's go feed the chickens and pigs," Grandpa said, seeing my need to get outside after lunch.

"Okay Grandpa. I can't wait to see the new baby peeps."

I follow my Grandpa out the back door and Gramma takes me in her arms and kisses me so hard, hugs me and said, "Now you be a good little girl."

"Oh I will be, Gramma. I love being on the farm; it's way better than being in the city. I love you, Gramma. Bye."

I open the chicken coop door and all the chickens come running over to me, looking for grain and rolled corn. I shake the grain and corn onto the ground and the chickens race over for their feed. As I am pouring the feed into their feeders, my Grandpa is giving them fresh spring water from the garden hose.

"Look at this one, Grandpa; it's so cute. Is it going to be a rooster or a hen?"

My Grandpa just laughs out loud as he keeps filling their water feeders.

"I want to keep this one, Grandpa. It's so cute and soft. Look at her; she needs a name. Let's name her Pinky because her beak is so pink."

"Okay, let's finish up here. Put little Pinky down and you can help me feed the pigs."

We both walk over to the little red pig barn that has a pitched roof for the snow and rain water to run off from it. My Grandpa swings open the half barn door and I follow him in. I grab the leftovers from lunch and all the old lettuce and tomatoes that Aunt Katherine threw out. I fill the troth with them. All the piggies come running over to me snorting and squealing, excited for their food.

"Here comes the little sucklings, chic-chic. Be careful little one, you know how the mother sows can be when they are feeding their young," Grandpa warns me.

"Yes, Grandpa, I will." I try to pet one of the little piggies on their snout. The baby pig squeals loud and runs under its mother.

"Easy now, just pet the mother pig and stay close to me, chic-chic."

"But Grandpa. I love petting the pigs. They are so cute and their snort is so loud and they squeal like the dickens," I say, still trying to get my way.

"I know little chic-chic, but not today. Let the little ones get bigger and then you can play with them," Grandpa said in his usual kind and patient voice.

I pout a little. Grandpa catches me pouting and said, "Now, now, don't be that way. I will make it up to you, and you can do some other things that you may want to do later."

My grandfather has a heart of gold and he could not hurt a fly. He does not have one mean bone in his entire body. He is always pleasant to be around and he loves me so much. I crave his unconditional love. Plus, I know how to pull on my Grandpa's heartstrings to get extra attention and get more of his love. I know in my heart that I am the apple of his eye.

It was four o'clock and our chores were all done.

"You did such a good job today, little chic-chic. You worked so hard. Now it is time to enjoy life and enjoy the beautiful view of the mountains and take in this pure, Pennsylvania country air and some of the fruits of our labor. Come on over here, chic-chic, let's pick some of these fresh apples off the tree."

My Grandpa lifts me up high onto his shoulders as I start to reach for the apples. With each apple I hand them to my Grandpa, and he sets them into our wicker basket. Seeing some cows in the field, I ask if I can throw some apples to them from up on Grandpa's shoulders.

"You sure can throw them a few apples if you want, chic-chic," Grandpa replies.

I throw the apples as hard as I can as the heifers move toward us. "There you go cows, enjoy."

I squeal with delight from my preferred point. "Grandpa, look," I say, looking out in the field at four large animals. "Why are the three bulls ganging up on the one heifer in the field and jumping on her back?" All the other heifers are further away. "Are the other heifers mad at her? Why are the bulls playing with only this heifer?"

Grandpa lifts me off his shoulders. As I reach the ground, he pats me on the head.

"Aww, good question, little one," Grandpa responds, wondering whether or not he will take this moment as a farmyard teachable moment.

"Little chic-chic, you are right, all the bulls are focused on the one female cow and the other female cows want nothing to do with her."

"But, why Grandpa? It doesn't seem nice. Is she bad?"

My Grandpa slowly takes his time to reply to this question, wondering how my ten-year-old mind might accept what I am about to hear. At that moment he decides on a different response.

"It is like this, little chic-chic. The bulls are thinking, 'why buy the cow if you can get the milk for free.'"

"What does all that mean, Grandpa? The bulls can't milk the cow," I say, scrunching up my nose and my eyes in complete confusion. "The bulls don't want the cow's milk. Right? Only the calves do. Why are the bulls doing this to the cow?"

Grandpa leans over to me, assuming a wise old man position and pointing his index finger at me. "Chic-chic, don't worry about what those bulls are doing today. You will understand it all one day when you get older."

At this point Gramma approaches us after hearing the conversation between Grandpa and me.

"Charles, what did you just tell the little one?" she asks in a horrified tone.

Grandpa laughs.

"I told her something I hope she will never forget for the rest of her life. I told her how it works on the farm and out in the real world for young ladies."

"Sarah Marie, this is an important lesson for you to remember. As you get older you will know exactly what this means. Always remember it and take care of yourself when you are out in the world with bulls."

I am still very confused at this point but it doesn't matter anymore. I just figured I will figure it out when I get older. Maybe one day it will make sense, but today is not that day.

Today, I want to have fun on the farm with my family. I grab Gramma's hand and we walk back to the house. We stop on the back porch so we can sit together on the porch swing.

"Never you mind what your Grandpa said," Gramma said, as we sway back and forth on the swing. Unfortunately, this only reignited my interest and curiosity on the topic.

"But, what does it mean, Gramma? Why would you want to buy the cow if you can get the milk for free? Is the cow for sale? What do the bulls want with the cow's milk?"

Gramma looks over at Grandpa with narrowing eyes and a slightly tilting head. I know this is the look people give someone when they are not happy with the other person. Sometimes Mommy gives this look to my dad and nothing comes out of her mouth, she just gets more red in her face. I know it is not a good look.

Grandpa stares back at Gramma and shrugs his shoulders. I realize, whatever Grandpa said, it must be a big deal because I have never seen Gramma look at Grandpa like this before. All of this silent looking has me very interested now about the cow giving the milk away for free. Gramma grabs my little hand.

"Don't worry little one, it's just a very old saying. It could also be considered rude. One day, when you get older and become a beautiful young woman you will understand what it means," Gramma said, hoping her explanation will put closure to this topic.

"Gramma, please tell me. I have to know right now," I say, pushing her for an answer.

My aunt and uncle join us outside and wonder what the conversation is all about. When my Gramma tells them about what Grandpa had said, everyone starts laughing about the situation.

The adults' response causes my stubbornness to become more agitated. I decide to call my mother at our house. I am certain she will tell me. I now insist on an answer. I walk into the house, leaving the laughing adults outside.

My mother answers after the third ring. "Hello."

"Mommy, it's me. I'm at Uncle Johnny's farm."

"Are you having fun my baby? Is everything okay?"

"Yes, it's great. I am having so much fun on the farm with all the animals. I am working and playing with them."

"That's great, my little peanut. Do you miss me?"

"I miss you and I love you, Mommy."

"I love you too, peanut. I love you to the stars and moon and back."

"Mommy, I called because I have a question. Grandpa and I were picking fresh apples today and there were three bulls and one heifer in the field. The three bulls were all trying to jump on the back of the heifer. The heifer didn't mind; she just stood there. All the other heifers were on the other side of the hill eating the grass in the field."

"Uh-huh," my mom said, secretly hoping this would be the end of my story about what happened in the field with the cow.

"Well, I asked Grandpa why this was happening, because all the nice heifers on the other end of the field didn't want to have anything to do with this one heifer that had all the bulls wanting to get on her back."

My mother asked, "And what did your Grandpa say?" not wanting to take the conversation into any direction it did not need to go. She was not interested in having the bigger conversation about the facts of life, even though this was a potential teachable farmyard moment.

"He said, 'Why buy the cow if you can get the milk for free,'" I said, still confused about the comment.

"What?" my mother gasped. "Oh, my goodness. Put your Grandpa on the phone right now, Sarah Marie."

"But Mom, can't you just tell me what it means? I really want to know."

"Peanut, put your Grandpa on the phone right now please," my mother responds in a very stern voice.

"Yes, Mommy," I say, knowing that when my mother uses that voice there was no way I could do anything but do as she said.

I run to the porch where Gramma, Grandpa and my aunt and uncle are sitting.

"Grandpa, Mommy wants to talk to you on the phone."

"What? Why is your mother on the telephone? Did you call your mother?"

As I nod yes, I turn to look at Gramma, Aunt Kathrine and Uncle Johnny. They are all laughing louder now.

"Yes, I called her," I say, answering my Grandpa's question.

Grandpa walks into the house to answer the phone.

"Hello," Grandpa said in an 'I know what is coming next voice.'

I learned much later, as a grown-up, how their conversation continued. . .

"Daddy, what is going on over there? What did you tell the baby about the cows mating? Why did you make that rude comment without any more of an explanation? You know she will continue to ask questions. You know how intuitive she is. You know how clever she is and how curious she is. She is never going to stop asking all of us until she gets an answer that will satisfy her. I cannot believe you, Daddy. Ugghh!"

"Sonia, calm down. Don't worry. One day when chic-chic gets older she will remember what I told her from the impression I made. When she learns all the other stuff about mating, she will understand what I said. She won't forget my statement."

"Daddy she does not even understand your statement, plus it was rude and sexiest. You may want to make sure she stays safe and does not go out having sex with everyone she meets because you think that's what guys want. But Daddy, for goodness sake, she is only ten years old. She does not even know the first thing about sex, and now you are telling her about not buying a cow and getting the milk for free. Daddy, you are not making my job as a parent easy."

"It's no problem, Sonia. I'm sure she will be distracted by other things on the farm soon. Before you know it, it won't even be an issue. Unless of course, after this phone call, you want me to take her for a walk and give her the birds and bees talk, to help put the whole thing into perspective."

"No, Daddy. That will be just fine. Please do not do that." My mother knows how Grandpa often uses humor to defuse a situation. "I will have 'the talk' with her when she gets home. That way, I can save her from her Grandpa's farmyard life lesson. Besides this question about your comment, is Sarah Marie behaving herself and having fun?"

"She is behaving like a little angel. She is full of energy and life. She does not tire easily, and we are going all day and night with her."

"I know you have to love her high energy, Daddy. She keeps you happy and she can help you with the chores. I also know she loves those farm animals as well as spending time with you and Mom. I love her too, Dad. I miss her. Daddy, please no more major life lessons during this visit. Okay?"

My Grandpa comforts my mother. "We will all be fine. She is in good hands."

"I will see you in a couple of weeks, when I pick up my little innocent one."

"Hon, hold on, Sarah Marie is right next me, let me give the phone back to her."

I had been listening to my Grandpa's side of his phone conversation. I was now equally curious about why this situation made my mother angry. Why does Grandpa think I will need to remember his comment in the future? Would Sophia in Gramma's book know about what Grandpa was talking about when he said 'why buy the cow if you can get the milk for free?'

I take the phone from my Grandpa's hand, deciding to no longer ask any more questions about the cows and bulls.

"Hi, Mommy."

"I love you, Sarah Marie. You keep being a good girl and I will see you in a few days."

"Bye, Mommy, I love you, too."

Gramma takes my hand after I hang up the phone and we walk outside. As we walk around the house, she suggests we go looking for four-leaf clovers in the lawn. I think this is a great idea, unaware that Gramma was more interested in creating a distraction for me than having a desire to find a four-leaf clover. After several minutes of looking in the grass, Gramma said, "Come on, dear. Let's walk around to the front of the house and rock on the front porch swing. Gramma needs to sit for a while."

"I love to swing with you, Gramma."

I run as fast as I can to the front porch and plop my bottom onto the swing. It immediately starts rocking.

"Come on, Gramma, hurry up," I urgently call out.

Gramma sits down on the swing next to me and lets out a faint sigh.

"Do you hear that, Sarah Marie? It's the creek rushing through the fields."

"I do, Gramma. Why is it going so fast? Why is it in that part of the field? Why don't the cows drink from it?" I was always full of questions and Gramma was always there to answer them.

"I love swinging on this swing next to you, Gramma. You make me feel special."

"That's because you are special," Gramma said in a loving voice.

I wish my Gramma always gave me her undivided attention like this and didn't give a lot of it to that darn book of hers. Why does she even have to read that silly book?

As we move back and forth on the swing, we giggle and laugh. Gramma tells me stories about when she was a little girl. I love to hear these stories, 'stories about the good old days' as Gramma calls them. As Gramma talks, she braids my long, black wavy hair.

Having her hand running through my hair is relaxing; I melt into the swing as the French braids are woven through my hair.

"Sarah Marie, you need some new pretty hair barrettes for this long beautiful hair of yours. I think I will buy you some the next time we are at the mall."

"Yes, please, Gramma, I'd love that, especially if they have jewels on them. Maybe they could have rubies and pearls on them," I say, thinking about how I could look like Sophia.

Gramma pauses for a minute. There was something vaguely familiar to her about that combination of stones on a barrette. She just could not remember why. As she aged, remembering became harder, so she let it pass. She also knew that in the spirit of time, at the strangest moments she would remember what the significance was about a pearl and ruby barrette combination. As for now, she would just let the thought pass.

As for me, I knew in my heart I wanted a barrette just like Mistress Sophia's jeweled one. I wanted it in my black wavy hair so I could look and be just like her.

I could hear my Gramma humming a melody as she looks out across the porch while at the same time braiding my hair. I wonder 'what she was thinking about as she stared out at the cow fields and farm equipment. Was Gramma thinking about her book? Would she rather be reading her book than giving me her undivided attention?' When I saw her reading it last night it seemed like she was in a different world. Not a world of Grandpa and dairy farms and farm chores. I wished I could have that kind of magical hold on Gramma. 'What was so special about that book? What is it about two people loving each other that made Gramma go into her own private world?'

Gramma continued to lovingly comfort me, telling me stories. Through her stories she always taught me about love and how to treat others with kindness.

"Gramma, what is that favorite saying you taught me that I love so much?"

"You get more bees with honey in life than you do with vinegar," Gramma said proudly, as if this statement is her life's moral compass.

"Yes, Gramma that's the one. I love that saying. What does it mean again?"

"It means little one, that if you treat others well and with kindness and respect, they will want to be with you more and do things for you. But if you treat others brashly and rudely and make them feel like they are tasting vinegar, then others will treat you the same way."

"I like that saying, Gramma. I want to be more like honey than vinegar. I'm going to remember that. But if I can't, can you keep reminding me?" I said with my ongoing desire to please and learn from my Gramma.

"Of course I can, my dear," she responds with a big smile, knowing that she loves having a positive and hopefully lasting impact on her granddaughter.

Gramma begins to hum again. She stares aimlessly out into the yard. I widen my mouth and let out a big yawn. My eyes become heavy and slowly close. I fall asleep on my Gramma's lap and begin to dream of James and Sophia.

~~~

It was dawn and the morning dew was in the air. Mistress Sophia walked across the field as the hem of her skirt brushed against the blades of the grass, causing it to become damp. Today she was wearing her favorite brown leather boots, laced up just above her ankle. Her boot heels dig deeper into the ground, not only because the ground was moist, but also because her emotions and desires were being transferred to her feet as she moved forward through the field. Mistress Sophia looked down at the wet hem of her dress. Picking up the front of her dress, she begins walking faster through the fields. The sun rises and the colors of the morning sky are breathtaking. Sophia knew the sun would soon become a full ball of fire over the horizon as soon as she reached the high cliff area at the end of the field.

Standing at the edge of the cliff, Sophia looks down. She cannot see the bottom. She does not care. Today she only wants to enjoy all the emotions she is feeling when she looks up at the array of colors lighting up the morning sky.

Sophia's violet grey eyes look out into the sky. She begins to feel the radiance from the sun that warms her body. It touches her face while the dew of the grass cools her feet. She can feel the mist of the morning air wash over her face and hair. Sophia's mind wanders and she begins thinking of James. She longs for her lover. With the morning air upon her, she envisions James's hands touching her and gently fondling her body, while every fiber of her being erupts with uncontrollable passion and desire. 'More, more,' she silently thinks, anticipating that moment.

When she is with James she feels as though she is a fine piece of crystal, one he admires and cares for. She loves him, she needs him. She wants to be with him every day and every moment from this day forward.

'I yearn for thee. I need you inside me, deep inside me to complete me,' she thinks.

Sophia wonders why she longs for James's love so intensely. 'What kind of power does this man have over me? Could he possibly love me as much as I love him? How could I ever know?' Sophia ponders all these questions swirling through her head while the colors in the sky also shift and move, as if there is no predetermined plan for the end result. 'Maybe I just have to let it evolve and happen like the sunrise,' Sophia surmises. 'I must be patient and let my relationship with James evolve, and eventually I, too, shall have the same sense of accomplishment of a sun that has risen high in the sky.'

Searching endlessly for an answer and hoping she can manage her heart pounding, Sophia's thoughts continue to dance around inside her head. She breathes a huge sigh and yells out to the sky and beyond the cliff below.

"Please, if you can hear me James, I love you, with all my heart and soul."

The sun has now moved to a high point in the sky. Sophia begins to perspire. She is not sure if it is because of the warmth from the sun or the feelings she is having in her body because she is thinking of James. 'I love him so,' she concludes. 'I am completely devoted to him.'

"I love you, James," she calls out again. "Please marry me. Marry me, marry me." The words echo against the cliff's stone walls. Sophia slowly sits down on a dark grey rock behind her. She continues to replay in her mind the last time she was with James and how her lover touched her. How her body tingled with sensations for more of his desires.

~~~

As I come out of my sleep, my mind returns to the porch and lying on Gramma's lap. Gramma starts to gently stroke my hair again with her hand. She continues to hum. We swing slowly back and forth on the swing. I try to sit up, but I am too tired, and I gently close my eyes again.

Sleep does not come again. I begin to think about Gramma's book and the story of James and Sophia. I realize now, I am so glad I snuck Gramma's book from the attic into my backpack before I left my grandparent's house. The side of my face continues to rest on Gramma's lap. I can see my backpack sitting on the porch, next to the front door.

"Gramma, I think I want to go inside and play with my horse set in the guest bedroom," I say, thinking about how I can get to a private place to continue reading the story.

"That's a good idea sweetheart, you go right ahead," Gramma said.

I walk through the front door, picking up my backpack before I enter. I am glad Gramma thinks I am playing with something good. I would hate for her to know that I had one of her storybooks in my backpack. If she caught me reading one of these books, I know I would be in deep trouble.

I walk up the spiral staircase to the guest bedroom. I was no longer tired. Instead, I was excited to begin reading more about the love James and Sophia have for each other.

I dig into my backpack, past my hairbrush, the barrettes and some lip gloss I snuck from Gramma's house. I reach past the horse set and find the storybook. I settle onto the bed and begin to read. Chapter Eight, I am one quarter of the way through the book. I can hardly wait to see what happens next.

~~~

James assertively leads Sophia off the path. She does not resist his guidance. One of his arms is supporting Sophia while the other, rests on his hip. His long sword clanks as it moves around in its metal scabbard. Sophia is aroused by the power James's presence commands. He is strong and handsome and looks ever so sophisticated in his military uniform. They enter into a dark, damp, carriage barn. The only light coming into the barn is from the full moon shining brightly on both of their faces. It is quiet, since all the horses are out for the evening. The smell of animals is in the air.

James gently pushes Sophia up against the wall to bring him closer to her again. Their lips touch and their mouths open. James seductively slides his tongue into Sophia's mouth. The sensation of his strong controlling tongue weakens Sophia to a point of bliss. Her knees become weak, but the strength of James holds her up. He wants more and so does she. James removes his tongue from her mouth and kisses her forehead. Then the side of her neck then the spot just between her breasts. Sophia moans with weakness and delight. It does not matter; she is his, for his pleasure. James comes back to her mouth and her lower lip. Sophia knows that he is teasing her, making her beg for his hidden desires and alluring touch. Sophia does not mind. Sophia moans again. As she slowly grinds her waist into his, she feels the large bulge in his uniform pants, and with the little strength she has she said, "Oh James, please don't stop, you have me."

James slowly places his hand on the fabric of Sophia's aroused breasts. Expertly, without issue, he pulls down the shoulders straps of her dress, exposing her young, ripe breast. He begins to tease her nipple with his tongue, licking around her nipple and then gently sucking on it. Sophia moans deeply.

"James, I am yours and only yours."

Sophia is breathing more heavily. Her chin is pulled up and her shoulders are pulled back, exposing her breasts more. James reaches for her other breast as his mouth caresses her nipple ever so slowly in a circular motion. He feels Sophia's knees weakening as he slides his hand up her leg past her garter straps. He reaches the space between her legs and methodically places his fingers between the slit of her legs. He feels warmth and moisture coming from her body. James now slides his two moist fingers between her soft velvety slit. Sophia collapses into his arms. James holds her there, making her take more of his pleasure and hidden desire. James is aroused as Sophia nails clamp into the back of his shoulders, bringing him closer to her. With the little strength she has, she unbuttons his uniform pants. His bulge is relieved by the extra space. Sophia places her hand inside his uniform pants and finds her way to the warmth of his hard, long throbbing shaft. She squeezes it. His moans sound loud in her ear. James kisses her shoulders and around her breasts. He is enjoying her body. He nibbles at her nipples, noticing that with every bite they harden more, as does he. Together, the two of them escape into ecstasy.

Sophia is ready. She is moist with passion between her legs. James gracefully places his two fingers inside her.

Suddenly they are both startled as a carriage pulls up outside. The driver calls out in a deep harsh English accent. "Whoo, ladies. This is our last stop of the day." The horses whinny and neigh loudly as the driver pulls on the leather reins. James removes his hand from between Sophia's legs. Sophia quickly lowers her dress. They both quickly come back to reality, and they did not want to be found in this carriage house. James grabs Sophia's hand. "Follow me. Over here."

He pulls her gently as they run to the other side of the barn, stumbling together in the dark. The ground is uneven and the darkness made it difficult to move quickly. As they approach the back wall of the carriage house, James feels for the sliding door handle. Sophia's heart races. It would be extremely embarrassing to be caught in this predicament. 'What would others say? What would her father, the General, say if he found out?' James carefully slides the barn door open a bit, just enough for their bodies to pass through. They pass through the door as fast as they can, closing it after they leave.

James asks with a heavy and relieved sigh, "My darling, are you okay?"

"Oh, my gracious, James. I was terrified that we would be caught."

They are now hiding behind the closest tree by the carriage house. James holds Sophia's face under the bright, full moonlight.

"Your cheeks are flushed and you are shaking, my beloved Sophia," James said, holding her face between his hands and kissing her forehead, letting her know it will all be fine and they are now safe. "I am sorry I got you into this situation. My intent was to let you know how deeply and passionately in love with you I am. You have made me feel things within myself, Sophia, that I never thought I could feel."

Sophia bows her head. She was not sure if she should feel incredibly complimented or grateful that James took control of the situation and safely removed them from the barn before they were discovered. Sophia decided to feel both.

As they adjust their clothing to make themselves presentable for entering back into a public setting, James and Sophia walk to the front of the carriage house and back onto the path. They were careful to make sure no one saw them emerging from the wooded area. Continuing with their false stroll, they returned to the main walkway. Casually, they walked to their fine carriage. Their driver awaited them.

"Good evening, Colonel. I hope your evening was enjoyable and the delicacies you partaked of were delicious."

"They were exquisite beyond my imagination," James said, smiling, realizing the carriage man was talking about the meal and James was referring to Sophia's nipples and the tastiness of her lips.

James assists Sophia onto the carriage step, following quickly behind her. The carriage man closes the door behind them.

"What a sensational evening, my darling," Sophia said, kissing James's cheek.

"The Grand Lux Hotel is indeed a romantic place, and as it turns out, so is the carriage house," James said, smiling and exhilarated from the evening.

"They certainly are," Sophia said, with a grin on her bashful face.

"The food was delicious but not as appetizing as the sight of you in that dress, wearing the barrette I gave you. It was hard to be a gentleman all night, given the ravishing sight of you, my darling. I had to refrain from my strong desires to touch and kiss and focus on eating my meal," James said, as he begins to cover Sophia with a mink fur blanket. "This will keep you from getting a chill."

"James." Sophia blushes. "I always feel cared for when I am with you. I am beginning to wonder if I could ever live without you. Perhaps you are attentive to my every need because you are in the military?" Sophia suggests innocently and with a slight sense of teasing in her tone.

James slowly moves closer to Sophia and pulls the fur blanket closer between their bodies; he touches her cheek with his hand and looks into her eyes.

"The military has nothing to do with it, Sophia. You are like sweet honey to me. I want to take care of you and savor the taste of your body. I care for you deeply because I love your sweetness."

"I am your honey," Sophia replies proudly, pleased she has such a strong hold over such a controlling and powerful man.

"You are too kind, my love, you are too kind to me," James responds, while pulling the mink blanket onto their bodies and intentionally grazing his hand over Sophia's breast as he brings the blanket to her shoulder. "It must have been the damp barn which caused you to be so cold my lover. I do believe you are much warmer now."

"Yes, my darling, I am. Thank you," Mistress Sophia replies softly, with a shivering voice.

"Sophia, there is something I would like to show you. I have asked our carriage driver to make an extra stop on our way home. It should be a delightful surprise for you," James said confidently and excitedly.

He has always enjoyed showering Sophia with gifts. Perhaps because she was always grateful and excited with what he presented her. That gratefulness would often turn into passion, and that was what James was most grateful for.

"Intriguing. Where are we going, my love?" Sophia asks, knowing that James's surprises have never disappointed her.

James looks into Sophia's eyes in a way that can only mean one thing—he wanted to be inside her and enjoy her perfect body. Sophia lowers her chin, raises her eyes and smiles at James's seductive gaze. Her response could only mean one thing. She wanted him too. Sophia always found herself completely captivated by James. Every inch of her body would become submissive to the overt and subliminal commands he verbally and visually gave her. She yearned for his touch; perhaps she enjoyed and longed to be seduced by him.

James was patient when it came to stimulating Sophia. Now in this carriage he simply held Sophia's hand in the palm of his large, strong right hand and wallowed in the moment of her touch, despite how much he wanted to make love to her right here in this carriage.

The carriage driver slows the four black horses, pulling on the well-worn leather reins. He commands the horses to stop.

"We have arrived," James keenly said in a deep, secretive voice. "Are you prepared to experience your surprise, my darling?" James asks, with a child-like grin, knowing he is about to please Sophia beyond her wildest dreams.

"But of course. As long as it involves you, I am certain it will be wonderful," Sophia responds confidently.

The carriage door opens slowly. James exits the carriage first and quickly leans over to the driver and speaks to him, followed by helping Mistress Sophia down. Sophia looks puzzled, yet certain this is somehow all part of James's surprise. James smiles at Sophia as he leads the two of them forward. He holds a lit lantern in one hand and Sophia's hand in the other while walking with her a short distance down the driveway. James then pauses.

"Aww yes, there it is. I hope you like it, my love!" James glee-fully expresses as he glances over his right shoulder, looking at their new home.

Sophia was drawn only to hearing the sound of the sea waves in the distance as they crash onto the shoreline. This was a sound she had always loved. Therefore, she was not certain if it was the sea James wanted her to admire. The light from the full moon shone down, exposing the confused look on Sophia's face as she replied, "I do not know what you are talking about, James."

"Turn and look over your right shoulder, my darling. Now do you see it?" James instructs.

"Yes, I see it now. It is a house. But I still do not understand."

Sophia has never seen this house before and did not understand what relevance it should have to her.

"It is our house, Sophia. The one I want us to spend the rest of our life in. Together."

"James? Our house? This cannot possibly be true. It is perfect. It is wonderful. It means a lifetime forever with you, and that is a blissful thought," Sophia stuttered.

"Yes, my darling. It is true. This is a surprise I have worked on and been in the process of building for many months. I tried to find you the perfect environment for our home. I knew you would appreciate this spot, overlooking the sea and hearing the sounds of the waves crashing against the shoreline."

As the couple walked closer to the house, Sophia could see it was a pewter-colored plantation style home, with large black shutters. It had a tall, two-story wrap-around porch. The lanterns in the house were lit, distinguishing the array of details easier.

James had clearly thought of every aspect of this beautiful and elegant home, Sophia surmises. Indeed, it was more spectacular than Sophia could ever imagine.

"Oh, James, I cannot believe what you have done. You did this for us?" Sophia squealed with delight.

"I did it for you, my darling," James responded proudly.

"Can we go inside, James?"

"Of course we can." James smiles, now confirmed without a doubt that he has pleased the woman he loves. James walks Sophia toward the wooden staircase leading onto the grand porch.

James had been very methodical when designing this house. He positioned the back side of the house to face the quaint road, so the hired hands and servants could use the rear entrance. He chose the front side of the house to face the magnificent sea view to enjoy with Sophia, along with anyone else she would like to share it with.

Suddenly, Sophia hears the horses whiny, as the carriage pulls off down the road.

"James, did you ask Bernard, our carriage man, to leave?" Sophia gasps in horror at the thought of what society might think of an unmarried couple being left alone together.

"I did," James said confidently. "I also explained to Countess Elizabeth earlier this evening that we would be traveling all night. I told her I wanted to show you a new library building being built three towns over. Since the Countess knows how you adore books, she was more than happy when she heard you would be one of the first guests to see the town's new library. You have nothing to worry about, my darling. I have handled everything for us, even how the General might view this situation."

Mistress Sophia smiles. She was not surprised James had coordinated every last detail. It was something he usually did and it made life much easier for her. It was comforting to know that someone was looking out for her and attending to her every need. To have that person be the man she loved made the situation even more perfect.

Sophia continued to beg James to go inside. Having been dropped off by the carriage driver at the rear of the house, they chose to enter the rear door of their new home. James opened the wooden screen door and placed the large brass skeleton key into the bright shiny keyhole.

"Welcome home, my love. This is yours to keep forever and ever," James said, looking at Sophia with a proud boyish smile of pride.

He places the skeleton key into the palm of his hand and wraps the red cord hanging down from the key around his wrist. They walk directly down the hallway, through the house, toward the front of their home. The pre-lit lanterns illuminated the house in a way that made Sophia feel as if she was in a different and magical world.

"James, you did all of this for me?" Sophia asks in disbelief.

"Of course I did. Sophia, I love you more than even you might realize."

"How did you do all of this without me knowing? This home already looks like we have lived in it for years."

"Because we are soul mates," James confidently and knowingly replies. "My darling, we are meant to be together forever."

Sophia smiles and reaches up to kiss James on the cheek.

"Thank you, my darling. I feel exactly the same way."

"Shall we walk out to your new porch? It has a beautiful view, especially in the light of the full moon."

James opens the French doors, exposing the large expansive sea view. The full moon reflects on the water, creating a path from the front of the house to what Sophia believes to be paradise. The two of them walk out onto the majestic porch.

"Look, my love. Look out across the sea. With the help of the bright full moonlight, you can see out to the sea."

As the waves crashed onto the sand, the sound captivated Sophia's mind.

"Oh James, it's just perfect. I am in complete disbelief. This porch, this home, this view, all of it, is simply magnificent. I am so grateful for what you have done and for what I can only assume is the amount of love you put into building this home." Sophia's voice quivers as her eyes fill with tears of joy and gratitude. How could she be this fortunate to be loved by such a kind and wonderful man, she wonders.

"I love you immensely, my darling, and I love our new home. I will cherish both you and it forever," Sophia said tearfully.

"My love, don't cry. I want you to be happy." James comforts Sophia and rubs her back gently. "There will be no tears today. I want this day to be one of the most memorable days of your life."

As part of his sentence, James bent on one knee and looked up at Sophia. Tears continued to flow down her face. He takes her left hand, and with a warm smile on his face he asks, "Sophia, will you marry me? Will you take my hand in marriage?"

It seemed that the only sounds Sophia could produce were heaving sounds of air coming from her chest. She was barely able to force any words out of her mouth. It took all of her strength, in a state of sheer joy and bliss to cry out.

"Oh yes, my love. Yes, James, I accept your hand in marriage. Without hesitation. It would be an honor to be your wife. Today I am officially the happiest woman in the world." Sophia smiles while experiencing a variety of emotions.

James places his hand into his pocket and produces a stunning engagement ring. It was a full emerald-cut diamond. The stone was set in a 24 carat rose-gold mounting. It was a ring James found in Paris during his last visit there. James places the ring on Sophia's left hand. The ring fit perfectly and looked beautiful on Sophia's long dainty fingers. James was pleased.

"How did you ever know what ring size I wore, James?" she asks, holding out her left hand, admiring the impressive ring from afar. "It is flawless perfection, James."

"I have been studying the size of your ring finger every time I slide your gloves off your beautiful arms. I have the size of your finger memorized, my darling." Then with a wink, he said, "Along with other parts of your body, my dear." James smiles with a sheepish grin.

Sophia extends her left hand out to admire the ring from a distance once again.

"It is the most beautiful ring I have ever laid eyes on." Bringing her left hand across her chest she covers it with her right hand. "I love this ring beyond belief. I love it and I love you, James. Thank you, my darling. Thank you for the many surprises you have showered me with this evening."

With these words, Sophia brings her lips to James's and gives him a long lingering kiss of appreciation.

Chapter Six

After reading the next section of the book, my head was filled with lots of thoughts and questions. I wish there was someone who could answer all these questions for me; however, I did not feel comfortable asking anyone I knew because I was not supposed to be reading this book in the first place. One thing was clear, I knew James really loves Sophia. I begin to think James loves Sophia more than Grandpa loved Gramma. I also hope that one day a boy will love me that much.

As I leave my secret reading place in my aunt and uncle's house and walk downstairs, I see Gramma on the front porch rocking on her porch swing. Peeking through the screen door, I call out, "I'm hungry and thirsty, Gramma."

My Gramma gives me a little smile, gets up from her swing and walks toward the wooden screen door. She pulls it open and it slams shut before we walk into the kitchen to get a drink of ice-cold water. I am aware of the sound of the buzzing of bugs, the birds and the screen door slamming shut. These represent the sounds of summer to me.

It turns out I was not the only one thirsty. Gramma was thirsty also and she was happy for the moment to get some water for herself. I grab my favorite glass out of the cupboard and fill it to the brim with the cold well water. For me, even the water tastes good on the farm. It is much tastier than city water. As I get my glass, I also pour a glass for Gramma. I remember what she has always told me: 'be kind to others.'

"Thank you, little chic-chic," Gramma said with a smile, reaching for the glass and taking a sip.

I can see how much she enjoys the coolness of the glass on her warm lips. As I watch her, I think about the book I am reading. I wonder what is coming next. My head is already spinning from the story. What else could happen? At the same moment, I am daydreaming about the book, I feel my Grandpa's hands picking me up from behind and raising me high into the air. He flips me around to face him and kisses me on my forehead before setting me back down.

"I heard you took a little nap with your Gramma out on the swing, chic-chic. How was it?"

"It was good, Grandpa. I guess I needed it after all the chores we did together."

"You did do a lot of chores; plus, all that country air can make you sleep so well, little chic-chic. That is one reason I like visiting and working on the farm."

"I just love coming here, Grandpa. I love all the farm animals. I learn so much about how to take care of all of them. One of my favorite parts is driving the big John Deere tractor. It's not easy, but it's fun. My arms are also a little sore, Grandpa, from steering the tractor with Uncle Johnny today."

My Grandpa starts laughing out loud as he thinks, 'Good Lord, if I got tired from driving a tractor for an hour, my family would never have had any food on the table to eat!'

"Well, it is good for you, little chic-chic. You could use a few more muscles. You will need them one day to fight off all the boys when you start dating," Grandpa blurts out, realizing these might not be the best words to use given the caution he received from his daughter about 'adult' conversations.

Note to self, Grandpa reflects, no more adult topics for little chic-chic, he concludes.

"I'm not ever going to date, Grandpa," I say, giving my Grandpa a big hard hug. "I want to stay here with you and Gramma forever and ever."

"Ahh, someday, little chic-chic, I know you will meet the man of your dreams and he will sweep you off your feet," Grandpa said, trying to make light of conversation as well as hoping he didn't spur more questions.

As I hear the words Grandpa speaks, I began to think about James and Mistress Sophia. I wondered how they met and if they had been dating for a long time. Was James the man of Mistress Sophia's dreams? Would they be married soon?

The more I thought about these questions, the more I began to put together some of the puzzle pieces to form answers. I figured out how loving someone works. A lady meets a man and they get married. Then they live happily ever after. It was a simple plan, except that plan would not work for me.

"I am not going to get married, Grandpa," I say in a very determined and almost frantic voice. "I'm going to tell Mommy that I want to move in with you and Gramma and live with you forever and ever."

"Okay, little chic-chic, calm down. There is no reason to get upset and tell your mom what we have been talking about. We are just talking here and having some fun and dreaming. Nothing needs to be absolutely figured out right now. At the ripe old age of ten years, you have lots of time to decide what you want to do and who you want to be with for the rest of your life," Grandpa said, with a little worry in his voice as he tries to calm me down.

Gramma looks over at Grandpa and rolls her eyes at him. I am not sure what she was trying to tell him, but I am guessing it was not good, because Grandpa just shrugged his shoulders back at Gramma and sat down in the large, black wooden rocking chair placed strategically beside the fireplace in the kitchen. I sit at the kitchen table, kicking my feet under the table. I seem to do this more and more. My teachers at school are not happy that I am always so fidgety. I know they have been talking to my mom about how to make me control it. I figure, it is just me, and Gramma and Grandpa don't mind my fidgeting and all the extra energy I have, so I am not going to mind either.

"I'm starving. What's to eat, Gramma?"

"We are having dinner real soon, little one. The fresh pork roast is in the oven and will be due to come out shortly," Gramma announces to all of us in the kitchen.

"It smells so good, Gramma, my stomach is starting to growl just from the smell."

I carefully look around the kitchen. I want to make sure no one is looking. I casually get up and walk over to the refrigerator. I quietly open the door and grab a cold biscuit from the middle shelf. My aunt, uncle and grandparents are all talking and laughing. I am sure they have not noticed me sneaking the food when I was not really supposed to. I start to eat the biscuit. I hide it in the palm of my hand and bring it up to my face so my aunt and Gramma do not catch me. Good table and food manners were especially important to my aunt. It was never appropriate to sneak food from the fridge. It was even worse if you were a guest in the house, so sneaking this food in my aunt's house was a big 'no no' and a big risk. But for this yummy biscuit I figured it was worth it.

After I completed eating the biscuit that I snatched from my aunt's refrigerator, I wandered into the piano room, which was positioned just off the kitchen. The room was white with lots of artwork on the walls. White sheer, floor-to-ceiling curtains hung from the two windows positioned along the wall. It was a nice room to sit in. There were lots of things to look at and to do. There was a piano sitting in the middle of this room. I always liked to come into this room and make music on the piano. I never took piano lessons; I just made up the music and let my fingers go wherever they wanted to on the piano keys.

I sit down on the piano bench and slide my fingers up and down the piano keys. I start to think of Mistress Sophia waltzing across the ballroom floor with James, with her beautiful evening gown gracefully moving to the music as they danced. Their attention was not on the music. Instead their attention was spent consumed with staring into each other's eyes and hoping the other was feeling exactly the same as they were. A feeling of immense love.

I get up from the piano bench and start to spin and dance around the room. I dream that I am Mistress Sophia dancing and moving around the white Italian marble ballroom floor, like the dance scene in the book.

"Little chic-chic, come on, it's time to eat," Grandpa calls out, breaking my dream and bringing me back to reality. "It is supper time."

"Coming, Grandpa," I say, running into the kitchen.

I am still very hungry and can hardly wait to eat dinner. The cold biscuit I ate earlier did not do anything to help the growling hunger sounds in my belly.

"What's for dinner, Gramma?"

"Pork roast, along with the diced potatoes, fresh carrots with celery and fresh string beans from the garden. It's all on the table."

Gramma brings over the fresh bread she has just removed from the oven and strategically places it on the table next to Uncle Johnny's spot. We all take our places at the table. Uncle Johnny instructs us to bow our heads, as he starts to say grace. The grace has barely finished with everyone saying 'Amen,' and I can see Grandpa reaching across the table for the bread with one hand and the butter with the other.

Gramma smiles, knowing that if she had placed the bread next to him, it would have been gone by now.

"How was your day, kiddo? Did you have fun today?" my uncle asks.

"I sure did, Uncle Johnny. I loved every second of it."

"What was your favorite part about today, kiddo?"

"Riding with you on your big green tractor, Uncle Johnny. Oh wait, maybe it was feeding the baby calves their bottles of milk. I think I have two favorite things, not just one."

Uncle Johnny smiles at me and lets out a chuckle and wink as he looks at the other adults around the table.

"Kiddo, you are always welcome to stay here and help me out with the chores. It's fun to have you around."

I smile at my uncle. It was strange, I thought. He always asked me the same question about what were my favorite things about the day. And I always give him the same answer. I guess he liked my answer, so he kept asking the question.

But today, what my uncle did not know was that my answer came with less sincerity. Today, as much as I loved being on the farm riding on the tractor and feeding calves, today I wanted to just get back to finishing Gramma's book. I also wanted to read it in the privacy of Gramma's attic. I assumed if I read it there, I would have less of a chance of getting caught.

"Uncle Johnny, I'm sorry but I really want to stay at Gramma and Grandpa's tonight. Is that okay?"

"Oh, sure it is, little one," Uncle Johnny answers, giving me a comforting smile. "And don't you worry, we would love to have you stay here anytime you want. You are never a bother to your aunt and me."

"Thanks, Uncle Johnny. I'll stay over next time. By then the calves will be ready to see me again, and I will be ready to drive the tractor with you again."

As I say these words, I am also planning that I should be finished reading my book before I visit Uncle Johnny again.

"I'll come back to the farm, I promise. Right, Grandpa?"

"Right, little chic-chic," Grandpa said with a smile.

For now, I just want to get back to reading my exciting book. It has become all I think about. Now I understand why my Gramma loves to read it at night. The way the story is written makes you not want to stop reading it. You want to find out what comes next in the story. I decide that Gramma must read at night because she can go into her own world and she does not have to think about me or Grandpa, just about what is happening in the story. Plus, she gets to eat all her delicious chocolates by herself at night.

"Slow down, Sarah Marie, you're going to get a bellyache," Gramma cautions me.

I lift my head and again get jolted back to reality and my location. I am at the dinner table with my family. I know Gramma is right about me eating too fast. It is just that my brain was somewhere else; it was not with all these adults at the table.

"You're a good little eater; you just don't have to inhale your food like a vacuum cleaner, little one. But, from the way you are eating it, I'm guessing you are liking it."

"It's delicious, Grandpa. I love this homemade gravy," I say, as I dunk my homemade buttered bread into the warm gravy.

"What's for dessert?" my Uncle Johnny asks.

"Homemade pumpkin pie with homemade whipped cream and French vanilla ice cream."

"Oh my goodness, I forgot about the homemade pies that are in the oven," Gramma calls out. "Charles, hurry!"

Grandpa runs into the kitchen, carefully taking the hot pies out of the oven. He comes back and joins us at the dinner table.

There is something special about the food you eat on the farm. I think everything tastes better. Even the iced tea is particularly good. My aunt brews the tea bags all day in the warm summer sun on the porch. Then she adds raw sugar cane, which she gets from the local grocery store. Grandpa pours me another glass of this perfect tasting tea.

"Charles, don't give the baby too much of that tea. It has lots of sugar in it, and she will be up for days on end," Gramma scolds Grandpa.

I start to giggle. I know it does not matter what Gramma said, my Grandpa will give me anything I want.

As I kick my feet under the dinner table I think about my Uncle Johnny and how he spoils me more than my aunt does. She is more the matronly type. When I ponder more about it, my aunt can be a little hard on me sometimes, especially when it comes to table manners. She insists on perfect table manners. If you do not follow the rules, she will be sure to immediately tell you what you have done wrong. My Aunt Katherine reminds me of the Countess in Gramma's book. Hoping to change the subject about the tea and about me not having any more, I ask, "Uncle Johnny, what is the school project for your summer students this year?"

Every year Uncle Johnny gives his 12th grade students a project having to do with something on the farm. The students come to the farm and work on their project, experiencing all the chores that have to be done on the farm. I realize they also help Uncle

Johnny with some of the work that has to be done, so it works out well for Uncle Johnny.

"Good question, Sarah Marie. This year we are going to build a large wooden wagon for transporting large items from the farm. The students will start from nothing and after a few weeks they will have created a working wagon. What do you think about that project?"

"That sounds hard. Do all the students get to come to the farm to work on it?"

"No kiddo, that would be too many students. Only my top students, the ones who have earned high marks and showed the ability to work hard. Those are the ones who will get to come. The other thing that helps me decide what students come is if the student has taken a liking to farming and agriculture."

"Oh," I say, as my thoughts begin to wander again.

I bet I can come out to the farm while the students are here. I might meet a boy and fall in love and be just like Mistress Sophia and James.

"As their teacher, when I invite them to my farm, they get to develop their skills and apply what they have learned toward their academics and for their admission to college. It is a good way for everyone to benefit from the project," Uncle Johnny said, clearly weighing out ways he can use his skills as a teacher and as a farmer.

As I listen to what my uncle has to say, I consider, why would I want to go to college when I could stay here and be loved, cared for and receive my family's undivided attention. So far, I do not see any good reason for going to college. Staying on the farm makes much better sense to me.

"Smells like the coffee is ready," Grandpa calls out.

I can smell the aroma of freshly brewed coffee as it finishes its final percolating plops as it sits on the gas stove. My aunt leaves the table to get the pot. When she returns, she begins to pour everyone a cup of coffee. She places the coffee pot on the table, with the assumption that from that point on, everyone will pour their own coffee for the rest of the meal.

"Little chic-chic, would you like a cup of coffee?" Grandpa asks me.

"Of course I would, Grandpa. Thanks." Grandpa proceeds to pour me a cup of coffee. Gramma scolds Grandpa with a large sigh and rolling of her eyes. 'She sure has been doing that a lot to Grandpa today, my mind said to itself.'

Dinner is declared over by my uncle, and Gramma and my aunt get out of their seats, walk over to the kitchen and begin to clean up after dinner. Grandpa and my uncle go and sit in the living room and begin reading the newspaper. I walk over to the big wooden rocking chair in the living room and sit down. I notice the effects of the coffee are starting to take hold on my body. I am feeling less tired and have a bit more energy than when I started dinner. I feel the 'wiggles' coming on; that is what my Grandpa would often call them. The wiggles occur when my brain starts working more and my body starts moving more.

It feels like hours have gone by since my Gramma and my aunt have been cleaning up from dinner. I cannot wait to get back home and read my book, or rather Gramma's book, again. I look into the kitchen and see Gramma sitting down at the kitchen table, pouring another cup of coffee for herself and my aunt. This tells me we will not be leaving soon. Grandpa sees me looking into the kitchen and said, "When those two clucking hens start talking, all they do is gossip and complain. They talk, talk, talk about nothing."

I can hear my Gramma and aunt talking about the next-door neighbor, who will be getting married next month. I do not care what my Grandpa said, I listen with interest about the neighbor, because now I know James and Sophia are getting married. I wonder what their wedding will be like. Will it be like the neighbor's? It is funny to me how this stuff about love and marriage never really mattered to me, not until I started reading this book. Now it is all I think about.

"Katherine, it sounds like your clock is telling us it is time for us to leave and head back into town," Gramma said, smiling at my aunt, knowing how much she dislikes that clock.

The clock was in the shape of a barn. It sat strategically on the wall just beside the kitchen door. It chimed through two cycles, depending on the hour of the day. My aunt believed that was too much chiming. When the top of the hour occurred, a figure of a cow with a rooster on its back came out of the barn-shaped clock. The rooster would then let out a cuckoo sound, based on the number of hours it represented. My aunt told me how she hated this clock; however, my uncle really liked it. The story goes, they had been in a store in one of the nearby towns while out for dinner for their 25th anniversary. My uncle wanted to buy the clock for their farmhouse to remind them that sometimes you just have to laugh and accept that crazy things can happen each hour of the day. He figured that attitude is what helped them survive 25 years of marriage.

On the other hand, my aunt thought the clock was "ugly, silly and stupid." It was a surprise to me to hear my aunt using these words to describe the clock. When I asked her why she kept it and why she hung it in a place where everyone could see it all the time, she gave me a very simple answer. It was an answer that stuck with me for all time. She said, "I keep it, Sarah Marie, because your uncle really likes it and sometimes when you are married, you have to accept and find joy in what is, even if you do not like it. A lot of marriages are like that, little one."

When I heard the clock this evening and remembered what my aunt said to me, I start to wonder what Mistress Sophia was going to have to accept and find joy in, now that she was about to marry Colonel James.

Wanting to speed up our departure, I run over and hug my aunt and uncle. I thank them for the fun day on the farm. While I am hugging my uncle, he whispers in my ear.

"See you tomorrow, little one. I think your Grandpa might take you fishing. Don't tell him I told you."

I pull back from the hug and smile at my uncle. He smiles back at me.

"Come here, little chic-chic, help us carry some of these bags to the car for your Gramma," Grandpa requests.

Gramma and Grandpa wave goodbye to my aunt and uncle. I roll down my window and stick my head out and wave goodbye to them vigorously. I am sure that all that coffee from dinner has reached my hand because I cannot seem to stop waving goodbye. Maybe it is because I am excited to leave and now I can get back to my attic room and read my book. Either way, I wave goodbye with all the energy I have.

"Let's head home," Grandpa said, driving down the long driveway and off my uncle's property.

"Yeah, I agree. Let's go home and see Fluffy. I bet he's hungry and misses us a lot."

"I bet he does," Grandpa replies with a smile.

Gramma begins to fall asleep as she sits in the front seat. I lay my arms over the middle section of the front seat and talk and talk. I tell Grandpa about all the fun I had during the day. I tell him about how quickly I think the baby calves are growing. I tell him about how good the grapes were that I ate by the barn. I tell him how funny I think the cuckoo barn clock with the rooster is. I tell him how smart I think my aunt is for saying that sometimes when you are married, you have to accept and find joy in what is, even if you don't like it. Each time I would say a sentence, my Grandpa would say "Uh-huh." Grandpa is such a good listener, I think. I love my Grandpa.

"What are we going to do tomorrow, Grandpa?"

"Well, little chic-chic, I think we will go sell some produce along the creek road. Maybe we can even go fishing. Does that sound like a good plan?"

"Yes, yes, yes Grandpa! I can't wait until tomorrow."

We pull up to the garage and Grandpa gets out to open the garage door. Gramma wakes up. She does not notice me watching her as she wipes a little drool from the side of her mouth. I did not know my Gramma drooled when she sleeps.

"We're home, Gramma," I say, still containing lots of energy in my body even though it has been a long active day.

"Yes, we are," Gramma said, with a bit of a sleepy voice.

As we drive into the garage we can hear Fluffy barking loudly from inside the house. Grandpa opens the back porch door. Fluffy jumps up and down to greet us all. I can relate to Fluffy. Some-times, when I'm happy, I start jumping up and down too. Grandpa continues to open up the back door and lets Fluffy out to the back-yard.

"I'm not sure if he's happy to see us or to get outside to relieve himself," Grandpa said with a smile. "But I'm sure he has to pee like a race horse since we've been gone most of the day."

Fluffy dashes around the backyard as though he is racing from one side of the yard to the other side. I run outside, too, and run after Fluffy, laughing and giggling as we run around the yard and chase after each other.

"Little one," Gramma said. "It's time for your bath soon. You can have ten more minutes to play with Fluffy and then you can hop into your surprise."

"Hop into my surprise? What is it, Gramma?"

"I bought some special lavender bubble bath for you."

'Lavender bubble bath.' My mind gets pulled back to the book. Mistress Sophia loves the smell of lavender. I remember reading how the Countess would always have bouquets of flowers, with lavender included in the arrangements of flowers that she placed in the large entrance to their home. I remember reading how Sophia would often dry the lavender flower petals and include them in her bath water because she loved the smell so much. I also remember how James made sure to plant lavender bushes along the front porch of their new home so Sophia could enjoy the views of the sea, the sounds of the waves crashing against the rocks and the smell of fresh lavender, as she sat and enjoyed a freshly brewed pot of English tea.

It is weird Gramma got me lavender bubble bath. I wonder what made her decide to get that kind of bubble bath from all the different choices she could have made. For whatever reason, it really did not matter, because tonight I will pretend like I am Mistress Sophia, taking a bath and smelling wonderful.

"Thank you so much, Gramma. This really is a great surprise. I love you so much. I'll be sure not to use all of the bubble bath and save some for you. I bet you will like sitting in the bath, enjoying the lavender smell too."

I see Gramma look off to the corner of the kitchen. I know her thoughts are not about what is in the kitchen. I am guessing her thoughts are about lavender bubble baths.

"Yes, little one, that is a good idea. Maybe I will have a lavender bubble bath tonight too. Now off you go. Go have your bath."

I grab my backpack, which I had leaned against the kitchen wall, and I run upstairs. Fluffy chases after me. He thinks we are still playing tag. I pull the chain dangling from the light centered in the middle of the ceiling. The chain has a fancy gold tassel hanging from it to make it easier to turn on.

I place my backpack onto the floor and go and have my bath.

Mmm, the lavender bubbles smell so good. I can see why Mistress Sophia likes the smell. Between the warm water and the floral aroma, my body is starting to get relaxed. The muscles I used at Uncle Johnny's are reminding me they are in my body because I am starting to feel the stiffness of my muscles relax. I did not even know I had muscles in certain parts of my body where the pain is.

"Sarah Marie, are you almost done with your bath, darling? It's time for Gramma to sit down and read her book, and I don't want to do that until you're finished."

"Just about, Gramma," I say smiling. I am thinking, 'Oh yes, Gramma, I am sure you want to start reading your book, because I am very excited to start reading mine!'

I hop out of the bath and get my pajamas on to go to kiss Grandpa good night. Fluffy follows me like he has become my new shadow. Grandpa is watching television in the bedroom. I hop on the bed and hug him goodnight.

"Thanks for a great day, Grandpa."

"You are more than welcome, little chic-chic. Get some good sleep because tomorrow will be another fun day," Grandpa replies, while facing his eyes toward the television.

I jump off the bed and go downstairs. Gramma is in the living room. She is sitting in 'her' chair. She has already begun to read her book. As soon as I get close, she closes the book and turns it over so the front cover is on her lap. It was like she did not want me to see what she was reading.

'Oh Gramma, I know what you are reading,' I think. 'Now I can understand why your book holds your attention. I can also hardly wait to start reading my book privately upstairs, too.'

"Goodnight, Gramma. Thank you for a great day."

"Goodnight, little one, sleep well."

As I begin to walk away, I slowly and carefully look back. Gramma has flipped over her book and began reading it again. I could see only part of her book cover as I extend out my neck. I realize this was a different book. On the cover of this new book was a very pretty woman with long black hair. The picture was of the woman from her waist up and she was only wearing a black corset. To the left of the woman was a man's hand, holding out some roses for the woman. What was strange about these roses was that they were tied together with a black leather strap. On one end of the strap were fringes. The other end had a handle like you would see on a whip. 'Now why would anyone give someone really pretty and romantic flowers with a whip holding them together?' I decided that some of Gramma's books were very strange. But who knows... maybe that is the book I will read next. When I read that book, maybe I will get my questions answered about why the roses are tied together with a whip.

Upstairs in the attic, I get snuggled into bed. Fluffy situates himself at the end of the bed, as he usually does. I am sure he likes to sleep on the soft comforter as much as I like to sleep under it. I grab Gramma's book from my backpack, open it and begin to read. This has been a perfect day, from working on Uncle Johnny's farm and ending with reading my book.

Chapter Seven

T his evening, my darling, we are going to celebrate. We will celebrate our new home and our new life together." James looks
at Sophia and said these words as though he is officially the happiest man in the world. "As I was building and preparing this house
for us to live in, I only had time to purchase this one settee and a
few other items of furniture for us. I know the rest of our home
needs a lady's touch. However, since we will have a lifetime together, I was not worried about getting more furniture at this
point in time."

"James, everything is marvelous. You did an exemplary job."

"And now for another surprise this evening." James smiling
like a school boy who can barely contain his excitement.

"Oh James, really, this is too much. This evening has already
truly been beyond what I could ever have hoped for."

"Wait for me right here my wonderful lady," James requests,
already walking toward the kitchen.

Sophia watches him walk away. 'Oh, how very dapper he looks
in his military uniform,' she thinks, smiling. She cannot believe all

her dreams are about to come true. She is about to marry Colonel James Langston and live happily ever after.

James returns from the kitchen with a bottle of fine vintage wine and two crystal wine glasses. Sophia is standing in the parlor, looking around the room, appearing radiant, like a goddess. James is mesmerized by her looks and her presence.

"We cannot celebrate this evening without a toast for good luck to our life together and forever," James states, thrilled that he is about to spend the rest of his life with this beautiful, young woman standing in front of him.

"Let us toast to this marvelous house and your skills in making all of this happen, James," Sophia responds, moving her arms around, pointing to the large house and echoing the need to celebrate the many good things she believes will be part of their life together.

James places the two glasses onto the newly purchased end table. The table had braided pedestal legs and was made of fine quality mahogany wood. Sophia takes notice of the slender table and compliments James on his purchase. James proceeds to pour two glasses of wine. The legs of the wine cling to the inside of the glass, indicating its level of quality and taste. As the couple raises their glasses above their shoulders, James clears his throat and said, "You are very special to me, Sophia. I am truly honored you have accepted my proposal to become my wife. I love you, Sophia. Spending the remainder of our lives at each other's side will bring me more happiness than my words could ever express to you. I propose a toast to a wonderful life and the many happy moments we will share together. Cheers."

As the two crystal glasses join together, producing a perfect tone, James bends forward and amorously kisses Sophia on the lips. Their mouths open slightly allowing the tips of their tongues to touch for a brief moment. Sophia then pulls away.

"My affection for you James is beyond expression. I simply cannot image my life without you. You can always be comforted knowing that my love for you is everlasting."

Sophia sits down on the settee. James had searched for many weeks to find a piece of furniture that would serve as a showpiece.

When he could not find what he desired, he hired a local carpenter to craft one for him. The loin-claw mahogany legs he had craved made it clear that the builder of this piece of furniture took great care in his craft.

"Oh, James, the furniture you have chosen for this room is exquisite. I am truly impressed by your eye for fine design," Sophia compliments James sincerely, while secretly amazed by James's good taste.

"I am so pleased you like our new home. I did this all for you, Sophia."

James smiles at Sophia, taking in her alluring beauty. She is all mine, he thinks. No one will ever have her, especially not in the way I desire her.

"It is starting to get a little nippy out. I will start a fire," James said, noticing Sophia's body beginning to coil in to keep herself warm. The fire logs have been prepositioned to light the fire with ease. Even the kindling was perfectly arranged for easy lighting. 'Oh my,' Sophia thought. 'James has thought of absolutely everything for this evening, I can only imagine how living with him will be.'

James strikes the match and flawlessly ignites the kindling. The flame spreads to all the logs and soon beams a roaring fire. He proudly stands up, pleased with achieving a fire with just one match.

As James tries his best to control his erotic desires, he is conscious it is with little success. He begins to feel his glands filling up and his genitalia swelling. He becomes aware that a small amount of pre-ejaculate fluid is coming out and dampening the bottom of his long shirt covering his pubic area. There was not much he could do. His body had spoken and he longed to be inside his soon-to-be wife.

James sits down next to Sophia, carefully adjusting his groin area and taking the wine glass out of her hand. He sets the glass on the end table. Turning back to Sophia, he draws his lips closer to hers and seductively kisses her, trying to further stimulate her with his warm tongue. He teases her with his skill. Sophia extends her chest and moans. James knows it is the right time to caress her breasts. With his hands, slowly and lightly, he touches Sophia's young, firm breasts through her dress. He takes his fingertip, circulating it around each nipple, teasing one nipple at a time. Sophia moans more with what could only be described as a rippling sigh of relief.

"You make me feel desired, James. You make me feel wanted. I am yours."

James gently leans Sophia back onto the settee, moving his body closer to hers. His erotic desires heighten higher in his pants. Even though he knows he is not allowed to touch his Mistress prior to a proper marriage, he is willing to push as close to the edge as possible.

Sophia's alluring presence cannot stop his strong intense feelings. He slowly moves his hand toward her warmth. He slides her gown up past her knees, past her thighs, and now with his two hands, exposes her undergarments. James slides her white, silk chemise undergarment to one side, to moisten his fingers. He feels her aroused area and slowly enters inside her with his fingers. Simultaneously, James kisses Sophia on her mouth. As long as she accepts his tongue, she will accept his fingers, he surmises. Again, he slides his two fingers slowly in and out of her warm vaginal slit. Her sweet innocence of quiet moans drives him mad as he continues to seduce her and make her helpless to resist his tender touch. James whispers seductive words into Sophia's ear.

"Come to me, Sophia. Allow yourself to be with me."

Sophia rotates her hips into his hand, sending a signal that she wants more. Sophia has never before felt like this. She never even knew this feeling was possible. She allows James to pleasure her more. She has no idea how much longer she could continue to feel like this. Her legs are numb with desire and excitement. She feels the area between her legs warm and moist. She feels herself holding her breath, then panting to control the sensations between her legs. The more James caresses her, the more wet, tingly and numb she feels. Then suddenly, as if without warning, Sophia reaches her highest peak, releasing her moist sweetness down onto James's two warm fingers. She is embarrassed. Could she, as a female, possibly release fluids, as a man would do, during intercourse? She was confused and blissfully numb by the wonderful feeling she was experiencing all over her body.

James tenderly kisses Sophia's lips and gently pulls his two moist fingers out from between her legs.

"Ahh, my comely creature. That was exactly how I wanted you to be pleased," James proudly states, as he gently slides back her white undergarments and pulls her gown back down over her knees.

"Please forgive me, my lady, I probably should have been more disciplined and controlled. I should have been more of a gentleman. I do not know what came over me."

Sophia raises her eyebrows and smiles at him with delight.

"Oh, my James. You are indeed a man of many talents. There is no need for you to apologize. You have created desires within me I never knew were possible. You allowed me to trust you, and for that trust I received nothing but great rewards. You have made me feel more like a woman than I ever thought was possible. I am now at your mercy my darling, longing for more of these magnificent feelings you have brought to my body. How is it possible that such a posh woman can also be the luckiest woman to be your wife?"

"For you, my 'posh' lady, I would do anything to please you and meet your every desire," James replies, with a mixture of love and pride in his abilities.

James rises up from the settee; his manhood is still erect. He walks over to stoke the fire, appreciating a moment to settle his own stimulating desires that are now running rampant throughout his body. James turns his head, and looking over his right shoulder, he admires Sophia's appearance and Italian decent. The combination gives her an exterior beauty like none other. 'She is pure sensuality.' James images. A divine piece of artwork. I want to undress and expose her entire naked beauty in front of me, James imagines. 'I desire this beautiful woman. I am barely able to contain myself. She will be my wife and she will be all mine, now and forever.'

As the two of them stare into the fire, their minds become lost in thought. They sit close together on the settee, feeling the warmth of each other's body. James rests his arm around Sophia's shoulders, and she drops her head down onto his shoulder. She is at peace. In this moment they do not feel a need to talk. Just being in each other's presence is enough to bring them both great comfort.

Staring into the fire, James thinks back to the first time he met Sophia. It was a cold winter day; the year was 1732. He saw her from a distance at her father's home. He rode by horseback that day to deliver her father an urgent message. He was immediately drawn toward Sophia's beauty when he saw her at the other end of the room. He knew at that moment he must get to know this creature of beauty. To have her.

From the minute he first saw her, James thought, Sophia's beauty was intoxicating. Once he had the opportunity to spend more time with her he was confused that her presence always caused his brain to work differently. He did not feel like a Colonel. He did not feel like a man who could be logical, commanding and assertive. Instead, he felt like a weak animal who could only be comforted by the presence of Sophia. While he was with Sophia he was indeed an animal, with animal instincts and animal desires. Right now his desire was to enjoy the smells Sophia emitted, explore her body and decide what areas of her body he wanted to devour. He wanted to plan how he could have all of her.

Currently, James was 28 years old. His entire career was spent in the military. He knew no other life. His father was a prominent lawyer and his mother a librarian. This combination made for an interesting home environment. As a child and young adult, nothing in the home could be said unless it was absolutely correct and could be backed up by facts. Debates were common between his mother and father and emotions were never factored into their discussions. James felt that it was a very sterile home to grow up in.

He had a sister and a brother. Each died of pneumonia at a very young age. They died two years apart. This did not make sense to his parents. Simply because it was not logical. This left James as an only child, and therefore, an important child. Although his parents said they had dealt with the grieving process of his siblings, James knew they had not. He knew all they could do was bury their feelings even further. Their feelings had been buried so deep no emotions could surface. They believed exposing themselves made them seem even more vulnerable.

The family lived on a plantation outside Cambridge. They named the plantation 'Bury Saint.' James always thought this was an appropriate name for the property, because it was the right thing to do with a home that created emotional detachments. An emotion was something his parents believed was not able to be proven. It was unable to be justified and therefore should be buried and not surfaced for consideration. 'Bury Saint' represented the metaphor for the tone of his upbringing.

The plantation had been passed down from his grandfather to his father. His father leased the land to farmers for growing and selling tobacco. His father said he felt like he was giving back to the community, even though the money he received was invested back into the farm and used for setting up a form of trust for James's future. James loved, respected and honored his father, despite how others might see his flaws. James decided to invest in his own future and enlist in the military. He wanted to make his father proud of him; however, his father was adverse to this decision. Instead, he would have preferred if James had followed in his footsteps and become a lawyer. James often wondered if his father ever forgave him for making the choice to join the military, a choice he made with the need for his father's approval in mind.

James enjoyed the self-discipline a military career offered. These disciplines were similar to the refined lifestyle he grew up with, although the military accepted the fact that a soldier could experience happiness, sadness, anger and surprise as part of their life. A soldier learned to manage, rather than repress one's emotions.

James was the consummate soldier. He worked very hard over the years to achieve the rank of Colonel. Eventually, his parents came to accept his decision and realized it was, in fact, the perfect career for their son. They were proud of James and told him many times before they passed away leaving him their entire estate.

James believed he was successful because his men wanted to follow him as a leader. They were motivated to complete their operation not out of fear, but rather, out of respect. Being respected and honored was the most important criteria for a leader to achieve, in James's mind.

General Cartwright, Sophia's father, recognized these qualities within James and made the easy decision to continually move him up through the ranks during the time he was General. Three years ago General Cartwright promoted James to Colonel, and he had never been disappointed with that decision.

As James continued to be hypnotized by the flames of the fire, he thought back to the day he met Sophia. It had officially become the most memorable day of James's life. He had been called upon to urgently deliver a letter to the General's house. Everything seemed strange about this request. It was not common for a Colonel to be the soldier delivering a note to the General. It was even more unusual to deliver a note directly to the General's home. For whatever reason, James was summoned for the task. He took his job and the tasks accompanying them seriously and strived to ensure the note arrived promptly and safely. As it turned out, this particular task would offer him a reward greater than he could ever imagine. It offered him his first encounter with the General's daughter, Sophia.

~~~

His horse rode through the crisp, icy air. The frigid weather was made worse by the cool breeze coming off the sea, all which took his breath away. He pulled the horse to a halt and dismounted in front of the General's large home. The four white pillars in front of the house were formidable. Upon his dismount, the stableman approached out of the darkness.

"Sir, shall I unsaddle your horse and cool him down?"

"Indeed, walk him as well, please. Cool him down and give him some fresh water and hay. He just did the better half of an hour riding hard to get here."

James stomped his feet to remove any mud residue from his military boots. He stood tall and straightened his jacket bottom and cuffs. He wanted to make sure he looked presentable when greeting the General. Before walking to the front door, James pulled an envelope from inside his jacket pocket. This was the note for the General. A note that neither James nor the General had any idea about. 'What was so important that I must be the one to carry this message?' James wondered. 'What will I do once the General receives this note? Am I to remain here for orders on what to do next?' James had not had time to think about these questions as he galloped quickly through the woods to the General's house. Now, about to enter the General's home, James had to wonder if the message he carried would somehow affect him and his life, as well as the lives of his soldiers.

James pulled up on the brass mouth of the lion's head door-knocker. He lowered the brass knocker three times before hearing a deep bark from a dog echoing through the hallways. James anxiously waited for the door to open. He was very aware that he was filled with a great deal of emotion, and none of it seemed to be of the positive ilk. As the door opened, James was greeted by Thomas, the butler.

"Good evening, sir, please come in."

"Thank you, sir. I am Colonel Abraham James Langston. I am here to deliver General Cartwright an urgent message. Is he here?"

"Yes, sir, he is in. I will be happy to get him at once. Please wait here, Colonel Langston. The General will be with you momentarily." With that, the butler left to inform the General of the Colonel's arrival.

Thomas knew to knock on the study door when the General was working.

"Enter."

The dark wood and two walls of floor-to-ceiling bookshelves and expensive artwork filled the room. A large mahogany desk sat in the middle of the room. Nothing was on the desk except for a leather desk blotter for writing. The absence of anything on this desk was an obvious sign of power. In the corner of the room sat a well-worn leather chair with a smoking table beside it. This combination served as the perfect spot for the General to rest his glass of single malt scotch. The chair was positioned to see out the window. The General enjoyed reading and then looking up to view his well-manicured gardens through the window. There was only one chair in the room, signifying that the General did not want anyone to join him while he relaxed, thought and strategized. Tonight when Thomas the butler knocked on the door, the General was sipping his scotch in his chair and strategizing.

The conditions in the country were tense and the General needed to think wisely and be prepared to lead his men. Thomas knew that whenever he must disturb the General while in his study, the reason must have great importance.

"Sir, Colonel Abraham James Langston is here. He said it is of an urgent matter. He is here to deliver you a letter."

"I will meet my solider in a moment."

The General was a bit startled by this news. 'Why on earth was a Colonel bringing an urgent message to him this late in the evening?' The General walked methodically down the long hall to meet the Colonel, who was waiting in the foyer.

Standing tall, as was befitting of a soldier, Colonel James looked over his right shoulder. He sensed a presence, but was surprised by the vision he saw. Sitting in a room in front of the fireplace was a young woman. A beautiful woman, who for a brief moment caused James to stop breathing from the shock of her beauty. She sat by herself, reading from a weathered leather book. James was mesmerized by this woman and suddenly realized he had been staring at her for an inappropriate amount of time. He was grateful she had not noticed him. He was not sure how he would explain his rude actions. His gaze was broken by the arrival of the General.

"Good evening, Colonel Langston. I see you found my daughter."

James salutes the General with respect and embarrassment, realizing the General must have seen him captivated by the appearance of his daughter.

As if a regular occurrence, the General brushed over the topic of his daughter.

"My butler tells me you have traveled here with great speed to bring me an urgent message. Thank you for your dedication and service. Now what, dear sir, is this urgent message you have for me?"

With a steady hand, James holds out the envelope for the General. While the General opens the envelope, James looks over at the beautiful woman at the fireplace. She is no longer reading her book. She is now staring directly at him, and the corners of her mouth are raised, forming a mischievous smile. James is taken aback by her boldness, a boldness that he finds even more alluring.

He brings his attention back to the General, who is still reading the contents of the envelope.

The General puts the letter down to his side, takes a deep breath and then exhales—with what James considered was an encumbered sigh. Looking up at James, he said, "Thank you for delivering this message, Colonel. I'll be sure to deal with it swiftly. I will speak to our King first thing in the morning, for I am sure he would not be pleased to be disturbed at this hour of the night."

James's interest in the message was certainly peaked. For a brief moment he found himself thinking about the message instead of the stunning beauty of the General's daughter in the other room.

"Colonel Langston, how was the weather for you as you traveled here?"

"The weather was brisk, indeed, General Cartwright. My horse and I are appreciating this moment of warmth."

"Why not join me for a glass of scotch before you head back on your travels. I would appreciate the company, and I am sure my daughter would not mind if we disrupt her reading."

"It would be an honor, General," James promptly replied.

James was certain his heart skipped a few beats from learning he would come closer to this lovely creature who was sitting confidently in the parlor. Walking into the room, the General turns to the Colonel and proudly introduces his daughter.

"Colonel Langston, this is my daughter, Mistress Sophia Cartwright. She is the young woman in my life whom I love and adore. I cherish her deeply."

Sophia rises from her seat and curtseys. James bows, reaches for her hand and gently presses his lips to her skin. In that instant James's body wanted to kiss more than Mistress Sophia's hand, but he knew that was not possible. As James stands back up, Sophia looks him directly in the eyes. 'Who is this woman?' James thinks. This is not the type of response you would expect from a lady, and yet, I am drawn to her spirit. She attracts me and draws me into her like no other woman I have ever known.

This brief interaction between Colonel James and Mistress Sophia does not go unnoticed by the General. The General was impressed by James's soft, curbed approach to his daughter. The General was also somewhat embarrassed by his daughter's bold actions. He had spoken to his daughter about this type of action before, and yet she continued, as if insisting she was a strong, independent woman.

The General could see himself in Sophia's demeanor. This caused him to worry for his daughter. A woman with this boldest may not attract a husband. The General was well aware of how enthralled Sophia was during this introduction to Colonel James. It was as though cupid's arrow had speared her heart and attached a love line to the two of them. James knew at the moment he stared into Sophia's violet grey eyes that he was going to marry Mistress Sophia. Although this beautiful, intriguing woman was the General's daughter and might complicate the situation, James knew he was up for the challenge of conquering and pursuing Sophia's heart. In all the countries James had traveled, he never had such a strong desire for any woman like he had for the lovely Mistress Sophia.

That first meeting was the start of many more. Over the months, James had earned the General's trust and James felt comfortable approaching the General and asking if he could escort Sophia to various events. James knew the General was protective of Sophia. Having laid eyes on Sophia, James realized the General had good reason. Sophia was an innocent, strong- willed woman, who could be taken advantage of. She had romantic dreams swirling through her head. Or at least that was how the General had explained it.

James was aware he had to prove his good intentions to both the General and to Mistress Sophia. As it turned out, over the months, James had done an excellent job with both the General and Sophia, for now he was now sitting beside this beautiful creature, who had just agreed to become his wife.

~~~

As Sophia sat on the settee in her new home, she was in a state of disbelief. She, too, gazed into the fire, and a magnitude of images, dreams and emotions swirled through her head. She felt her life was almost complete. She had always dreamed of herself married to a strong, dependable, handsome man and giving birth to many babies with him. The courting time with James seemed to happen very quickly. It was just one year ago that her father, the General, insisted she practice her harpsichord lesson in the parlor. Normally, during this time of year, he would send her to Europe to spend time with her relatives, allowing the General to work more with lesser interruptions. It was not easy to cater to the whims of a young woman with a great deal of time on her hands.

The General concluded he had done his best to satisfy the needs of his growing daughter, while at the same time successfully being of service to King George II, King of the United Kingdom of Great Britain.

This particular year one of Sophia's relatives had fallen ill with smallpox, and as such it would not have been wise for Sophia to visit these relatives. Her father could not bear the death of another woman in his life. Therefore, Sophia was required to remain home and entertain herself for the summer.

At times the General grew frustrated with the added responsibilities of caring for a daughter. That should be the job of a mother. Sadly, Sophia's mother had passed away seventeen years prior, leaving the General alone with his only daughter. Sophia had only been one year old when her mother had died.

It had been a daily struggle for the General to raise such an inquisitive, intelligent and attractive young girl. To assist with the needs of helping Sophia become a refined young lady, the General hired Countess Elizabeth and Governess Abigale to assist him. The Countess and Governess were hired to help Sophia with studies, harpsichord lessons and to become fluent in the French language.

The Countess's job was to not only care for and educate Sophia, it was also to run the household. In what little spare time the Countess Elizabeth had, she would enjoy translating books written in Latin into English. When she did not want to tax her brain, she would engage in completing her embroidery or playing the harpsichord. Having known and lived with the General for many years, including prior to the death of Sophia's mother, she was embarrassed to admit that one of her many duties was to intimately satisfy him. Although not required, this 'service' usually occurred during times when the General was extremely stressed from his work and simply needed to relax. Although it was agreed the relationship was purely physical for the General, the Countess justified her actions because she, too, was getting her physical needs met as well. The Countess recognized the General was a man and needed the touch and warmth of a woman's body.

She was also aware because of the General's stature in the community, he could not afford to be seen in a brothel or with a prostitute attending to his physical needs. Therefore, the Countess lived in the house and was 'available' when the General needed her.

The intimate relationship between the General and the Countess was kept extremely secret. Sophia had no idea of their physical relationship, nor did their closest friends. In fact, anyone would have been shocked to learn of this arrangement, mainly because it would not be acceptable to society.

Sophia was now eighteen years old. She had always dreamed of one day getting married to a strong, handsome man. A man whom her father would approve of. However, those criteria's became increasingly difficult to find in a man. There were times she would find a suitor she thought was perfect, but her father did not approve of him at all and made that very clear to Sophia. She was forced to end the relationship, leaving her frustrated and depressed for days. There were times her father would find a man who he thought would be a perfect match for Sophia. His choice was far from her liking and she would humor her father by going to a few public events with the man and then bravely say she did not want to see him again.

The Countess watched this matchmaking drama play out between the General, Sophia and her suitors. She felt sorry for Sophia. She wanted her to be happy. However, she knew her happiness with one man could only occur if her father accepted the man as being absolutely perfect for his only daughter. The General also assumed this man would be someone he had helped choose. Unfortunately, her father was not easily impressed, and this made the situation even more challenging, almost as though she was a character in one of Giambattista Basile's fairy tales.

Sophia sometimes felt like a sorcerer had cast an evil spell on her at birth and doomed her to a life completely absent of romance.

Sophia fondly remembers meeting Colonel James for the first time. He arrived at her home to deliver an urgent message to her father. She was sitting by the fireplace in the parlor after her harpsichord lessons and reading her favorite book by Robinson Crusoe. Oddly enough, Astro, their dog, would bark and act aggressive toward most guests, but not with the Colonel. 'How interesting,' Sophia thought.

Even Astro has taken a liking to this man. As Colonel James entered the large foyer, standing tall and confident, Sophia glanced over. She was drawn to his stature. It was difficult of her to pull her eyes away from the tall, sophisticated, aristocratic man standing proudly in his military uniform. 'Oh my, he is quite a handsome soldier.' It was not because of his high-ranking uniform or the chiseled features on his face, which caused her to have this thought. Sophia paid close attention to her father's mannerism when he spoke to this young Colonel.

After a brief conversation, Sophia overheard her father inviting the Colonel to stay for a glass of scotch. Sophia found herself pinching her cheeks to add a bit of color to them and she adjusted her hair. With just a small amount of time, she did what she could to look attractive for their visitor. She even surprised herself at the desirous response she had toward this mysterious attractive Colonel.

Walking into the parlor, the General introduced his soldier to his daughter. Sophia's heart stopped briefly as her breath was taken away when she looked at the Colonel's face. Now closer to her, Sophia was certain someone had chiseled this Colonel's features into perfect form upon his face. He was handsome from every angle. Sophia found her knees becoming weak as she rose from her seat to say hello. When Colonel James gently took her hand to kiss it for a respectful greeting, Sophia thought she would collapse. 'This man is perfect,' Sophia dreamed. 'This man is the man to have my children with. This man is the man I want to marry.'

Sophia's mind swirled to the point she could not hear the words being spoken to her. The only sound she could hear was the strong pulsing rush of blood pounding through her ears and around her neck.

"Colonel Langston," Thomas said, clearing his throat a second time and coughing.

It appeared Colonel James had also been suspended in time as his hand met Sophia's. He, too, became certain this beautiful creature would be his wife someday, despite the fact that she was the General's daughter.

"I am sorry," James said, turning to the butler.

"Your scotch, Colonel," Thomas said, smiling as he hands Colonel James his glass of scotch.

The General had requested their snifters be filled with the finest scotch. He decided he wanted to impress his soldier. Swirling the aged scotch inside his glass, he spent a moment to enjoy the oak aroma before taking a sip of his drink. This was a scotch to be savored and appreciated for its age.

It became all too clear to the General the instant connection that occurred between Colonel James and Sophia. He had to admit he was surprised the Colonel was willing to allow himself feelings for his daughter. He knew most of his soldiers feared him, especially when it came to socializing with his beloved only daughter. He suspected his soldiers feared the potential wrath of a father's protective spirit. Yet for the Colonel standing before him, if it had not been that Colonel Langston was such a fine and loyal soldier, he certainly would not have allowed the introduction in the first place.

Now that the meeting of these two had taken place, the General sensed that a new set of circumstances might quickly arise regarding their future relationship. He was smart enough to know this first meeting of the Colonel and Sophia would not be their last. As the General picked up the scotch decanter, he refilled Colonel James's glass. Sophia was very notably surprised. She considered this to be a subliminal sign: her father approved of Colonel James being attracted to her. She could only imagine the General was aware that the feeling was mutual. 'Could it be that she had found the perfect man? Someone whom her father approved of and to whom she was immensely attracted to.'

While they all sat in the parlor enjoying each other's company, they discussed the current frosty night air and the difficult ride for Colonel James to the house. In a continuous effort to care and appreciate the service his soldiers provide, the General decided he did not want to increase the risk of Colonel James becoming ill due to the cold, damp air. For this reason, the General turned to the Colonel and made a suggestion.

"Colonel Langston, I would be remiss to increase your chances of becoming ill, due to riding your horse back home this evening. It would be my pleasure if you would consider being my guest at our house this evening. You can stay for dinner and travel back in the light of day?"

"It would be an honor to accept your very gracious offer. General, if it would not offend you, I would be very grateful to partake in an evening meal with you, and I will decline spending the night. I have a duty to my soldiers early in the morning. They have often commented that I demonstrate overly committed loyalty toward them. Perhaps one might consider this a character flaw of mine."

"On the contrary, Colonel. I consider it a very noble trait of a soldier and of a human being. Please enjoy the evening meal with us, and we hope it will help to warm your insides for your return ride home."

Unbeknownst to Colonel James, the offer of staying for a meal and overnight was a test by the General. He had seen how attracted the Colonel had been toward his daughter, and he wanted to test his level of discipline and control along with his intentions. The General was pleased that James had passed the test admirably. In turn, he found himself becoming more fond of this soldier.

As for Sophia, it took every ounce of strength she had to control the muscles in her face and not show the sheer shock and surprise she was feeling. 'What was her father thinking? One of his soldiers had never stayed for dinner before.'

"You must join us," Sophia said, quickly sharing her opinion on the suggestion. She realized she might have spoken too early. If the Countess was in the room she would surely have scolded her for not being ladylike.

James looked at Sophia with a smile as she responded. 'Oh my' Sophia quietly gasped, 'his smile seems to make him even more handsome.'

The General smiled; this soldier was clearly a political master at correct social airs. The General was impressed and approved of Colonel James as a suitor for his daughter.

"Dinner is served," Thomas immediately announced.

As if on cue, James walked over to Mistress Sophia and extended his arm.

"May, I?" he asked, implying he wished to escort her to the dinner table.

Sophia smiled, thrilled the Colonel had taken charge and was not inhibited by her father's presence in the room.

As they walked toward the dining room, Sophia searched for more information on this fascinating man.

"How long have you worked under my father's command, Colonel James?"

"For many years now. I am often not at my post, as the General gives me orders to travel overseas and handle his most important affairs. From my understanding, he has decided to no longer travel over rough seas because he has developed an illness due to his travels."

The dinner was just as one might expect. There was an elegant spread of food on the finest china. The Countess also joined them for the meal.

"Please do excuse my manners earlier this evening, Colonel." Countess Elizabeth comments to James. "I had a dreadful earache. I was out enjoying the garden house earlier today, choosing roses and lavender for our floral arrangements, and I suspect I might have caught a cold in my ear."

"There is absolutely no need to apologize, Countess. I do hope you are feeling better now."

"Much. Thank you," the Countess replied, still a bit confused as to why this soldier was joining them for dinner. She had planned to speak with the General about the dignified handsome Colonel as soon as she had the opportunity, since she could see the joy and romance in Sophia's eyes. The Countess wanted to understand what this man's intentions were and if they were honorable.

The night progressed in the usual way, with the General taking about his work and everyone smiling as if they were interested. Following an excellent meal, everyone retired back to the parlor, where Sophia was asked to entertain the group by playing the harpsichord. Sophia engaged the room with her skilled musical talents. After what appeared to an extended time, Sophia rose from the harpsichord bench, and what could be considered to be quite brash, went over and sat in the chair next to James. Turning to Colonel James, she quietly asked so only he would hear and not the others in the room.

"It would appear you are growing quite fond of me, Colonel. Am I correct in what I say?"

"There simply are some things I cannot deny, Mistress Sophia," James responded, once again illustrating his astute social graces.

~~~

James, while sitting on the settee in their home, breaks Sophia's daydreaming about the past.

From the instant the connection was made during their first meeting, to the lifetime connection they shared now in their new home, Sophia and James enjoyed the sheer bliss of being together.

Chapter Eight

While Sophia stared into the fire, James turned to her, once again admiring her beautiful features. If these were Greek times, she would be the Goddess of Beauty, he surmises. As James covets Sophia's flawless almond skin, his eyes move toward her small firm breasts protruding from her taffeta evening gown. He found himself squeezing the stem of the wine glass harder as his erection grows larger. James imagines himself fondling her breasts. 'Oh how I want my mouth to tease her nipples. I want to hear her moan and beg for more.'

James rises from the settee and adjusts the swelling tissue between his legs. He walks to the fireplace and adds four more logs to the diminishing flames.

"You look cold, my darling. Let's see if this can help warm you up. The fire will certainly help to remove some of the dampness caused by the sea air."

"Perhaps this will be your new home mission, James, to keep me warm. In that way, you can stay here forever with me and never go on your military missions," Sophia teases, with a slight sadness in her voice. The thought of James ever leaving her side after what she considers this perfect evening would now be considered her greatest nightmare.

James smiles as he refills their wine glasses. Setting the empty wine bottle on the fireplace mantel, he walks over to Sophia and again sits down next to her.

"Do not worry, my lady. I will always keep you warm and never allow anyone to harm you. You will always be safe as long as I am your husband, which will be forever."

James makes this statement with great confidence, knowing he is completely committed to Sophia and would never let anything happen to her. His role now is to keep her safe and comfortable.

"No one will ever come between our one true love. I would fight someone to the death if anyone ever dared harm you, my darling. I am the only one for you, Mistress Sophia. I would also like to be clear about my request to marry you. I am aware of your large dowry. You must know I have no interest in your dowry. My interest is solely in you. As I had mentioned to you months ago, I live off my parent's estate, which they left me after they died," James said, while bowing his head in respect for the loss of his parents. "The estate amount is quite large. I can assure you, we will live quite comfortably for our lifetime and our children's lifetime. We will have all the fine carriages you want. We can travel across the seas, and I can show you the most beautiful sights across the countryside. Please know, Sophia, the only thing that matters to me is that you are in my life for eternity."

"My darling James, you can be comforted knowing that you are my one true love. You are the only man I want for the remainder of my life. I love you, James," Sophia responds with so much emotion she can barely hold back the tears.

Leaning forward, James kisses Sophia gently on her forehead. "Wait here for a moment; I shall be back soon to be your groom. I have a very special surprise planned for you this evening."

Sophia agrees, with a surprised and bewildered look on her face. James exits the room, obtaining a bowl of fresh rose petals from the kitchen. He returns to the front hallway and begins to spread the petals on the floor to form a pathway up the stairs toward the master bedroom. Once inside the bedroom, he lights several candles in the room to create the perfect, romantic ambiance. James then reaches for a fresh bouquet of lavender and roses, tied with a pink satin ribbon bow around the stems. He had gathered the flowers earlier that day and placed them on a table in the bedroom in preparation for this evening. He lays the mixture onto the bed. The aroma of the fresh lavender spreads lightly through the air. James walks over to the fireplace, lights another match to start a fire in the fireplace and ignites the pre-positioned kindling, which transfers the flame to the logs. Dusting the dirt from the fire off his hands, James notices they are damp with nervousness. His mind ponders a multitude of significant situations. Yesterday, while at the General's home, he was informed of his next military assignment. The mission meant he must leave the country for an extended period of time. This mission did not surprise James. He had expected it. What James did not expect was that the mission might have him leave next week. A few moments ago he had asked the love of his life to be his wife, and now he must tell her he would be leaving her side on a dangerous mission. James walked back to the sitting room. Sophia's mind was captured by the flickering flames in the beautiful designed room. James was once again inflicted with desire for this beautiful woman sitting before him. James gently places his hand onto Sophia's. Without a word, she rises from her seat and the two walk upstairs.

Sophia had learned to trust James completely. Seeing the rose petals on the stairs, Sophia assumes this can only mean one thing. Sophia pauses for a moment on the staircase. 'How can this be? Does James want to share a bed with me? We are not married yet. What would my father and the Countess say if they knew this union was about to transpire?'

Sophia desperately wanted to run back down the staircase and out the door for the safety of her reputation. At the same time, she also wanted to run up the stairs with James and continue whatever the evening had to offer. James sensed Sophia's hesitation and lightly squeezed her arm.

"You are safe with me, my lady. I can assure you, no harm, nor embarrassment will come your way, nor deduction of social prestige."

The sound of James's deep, comforting voice relaxed Sophia. She smiled a blissfully relaxed smile and continued walking up the stairs to the master bedroom.

Walking through the bedroom door, Sophia's eyes were astonished at what she saw. James had created a beautifully romantic sight. Sophia walked over to the bed and raised the rose and lavender bouquet to her nose. The aroma of the flowers brought her great comfort and an additional feeling of relaxation. James led Sophia to the foot of their bed and they sat down together.

"Sophia, tonight I pledge my love to you and ask you to marry me. I suspect you are already imagining a formal wedding ceremony for your memorable day. However, tonight is the night I want to marry you. I have courted you for eleven months."

Sophia's mind went from excited to confused to concerned. All she could focus on were the words that James wanted to marry her tonight.

"Consent-made marriages have existed for decades, Sophia, ever since the twelfth century. It has been common in England and Scotland for couples to marry this way."

'What was James talking about?' Sophia wondered. 'He wants to marry me. Now. Tonight. How is this possible? What about my father?' Sophia's head was spinning to the point she felt faint.

"Tonight I am purposing we partake in a unique marriage ceremony. It has been passed down by our ancestors through the generations, and it is perfectly acceptable for us. The process is quite simple, my love. If we enter into an engagement of service tonight, whereby I take you to be my wife and you take me to be your husband, we can conduct a 'joining of hands' ceremony. We would become engaged, and by mutual consent we would be married by means of handfasting. This joining hands would allow us to become legally married—tonight. This process of handfasting would be our oath to one another. It would seal our love until we have our Proclamation of the Banns publicly announcing our forthcoming wedding."

"But James, why would we not wait? I imagine this handfasting you speak of would complicate matters. I would also suspect without a doubt that it would infuriate my father."

"Your father and the Countess know we are together this evening, Sophia. The Countess justified our being alone because she assumes our carriage man, Bernard, would be our chaperone for the evening. She believes we are traveling most of the night to see the new Royal Library of Devonshire. So far, for all intentions and purposes, the Countess and your father have no worries about us being together overnight," James responds, hoping to minimize Sophia's concerns. "I was anticipating your concerns. For that reason, I ensured a plan that would account for your resistance. Sophia, I ask again, will you do me the honor, my darling, and become my legal wife this evening? It is important to me that tonight we conduct this ceremony."

Again, Sophia looked confused. Now her confusion was compounded with an even greater concern. 'Why was it so important to James we become married this night?'

"There is another part of my request I must share with you," James said.

Sophia was certain she would faint, as she felt the blood rushing to her head and into her feet.

"My darling, Sophia, I have recently learned that in less than a fortnight I must leave here and venture out on a mission. The thought of leaving you, and you not being my wife, shreds my heart. I plead with you, Sophia. As I leave on my voyage of duty, let me know that Mrs. Sophia Langston is waiting for me when I return home."

Tears were now streaming down Sophia's face. The joy and excitement of becoming engaged to the man of her dreams had become dismantled in less than an hour. 'What should she choose? Should she become James's wife this evening or become his betrothed and wait until he returns from his mission, at which time they would be married, conducted through a proper wedding ceremony.'

It did not take much time for Sophia to return her answer to James.

"Yes, my love, I will become one with you this evening," Sophia said, smiling and blushing while still feeling quite worried.

"Tonight we shall take our vows and be as one, Sophia," James replied with a new level of excitement and relief in his voice.

With those words, the two of them stand up and James places the palms of his hands face up toward the ceiling and extends them to Sophia. In turn, she places both of her hands into the palms of his.

"I pledge my love to you, Sophia. Tonight, do you take me as your husband?"

"I do," Sophia said, with a smile that stretches across her face. "I take you to be my beloved husband and pledge my honor to you. Shall I now ask the same of you?"

James nods yes.

"Tonight, Colonel James Langston, do you take me as your wife?"

"I most certainly do," James said, smiling, and staring directly into Sophia's eyes. "It is done, Sophia. We have completed the required commitment ceremony for us to be married. I am grateful to the lawmakers who devised this alternative for those who must marry quickly, in the event of rapidly needing to leave their loved ones. My darling, Sophia, as of this moment, I will no longer be required to refer to you as Mistress Sophia. Our courting days have come to an end. We have pledged our eternal marital vows by the joining of our hands together tonight. We are now husband and wife."

With that, James draws Sophia's hands closer to his chest and their lips join. Their mouths open and their tongues slowly swirl around as though they were performing a wedding dance of celebration all on their own.

Sophia feels her body swaying. She is weak from bliss, excitement, anxiousness and perhaps dizziness as well from all the wine the two them had consumed throughout the evening.

James was pleased with himself, having implemented the evening's plans perfectly, including marriage to a woman who, from the first day he laid eyes on her, he knew she would be his wife forever. James released Sophia from the connection of their two lips and walked over to the cherry armoire positioned against the wall. He opened the door, reached onto the top shelf, retrieving a package. Turning around, he walked back to Sophia with a beautifully wrapped parcel. Suggesting they both sit down on the bed, James passes the parcel to Sophia.

"Something for my new bride," James said, a noticeably large erection in his groin.

"Oh James, whatever could this be?" Sophia asks, still bewildered from all of the events of this evening—a new house, becoming married and now a present, clearly another part of James's plan.

"My darling wife," James rejoices, enjoying the tone of Sophia's new title. "As I suspect you have summarized, since we have expressed our wedding vows together this evening, it would only seem correct to complete our celebration and my plan with this item I purchased for you. I realized you would not have been prepared to sleep here this evening. After the introduction to our new home and our new life together, I wanted to continue to make you feel special. I wanted you to realize that I am always here to care for you and to take care of your every need, Sophia, my darling. I can assure you that you have already taken care of my needs. The need to be loved by you. While traveling out of the vicinity this past season, I noticed something hanging in the window of a village boutique."

Intrigued, Sophia knew one thing, James had exquisite tastes, and whatever was in this parcel, it would certainly be exceptional. Sophia carefully untied the package's white satin bow and proceeded to unwrap the tissue paper covering the soft pillow-like gift. James sat closely beside her, admiring her beauty.

"Oh my word, James, it is beautiful," Sophia gasped, while gently pulling out the contents and holding up a long, white Egyptian cotton nightgown, beautifully tailored and embroidered with English heather and lavender flowers along the sleeves and bodice of the garment.

"It is your wedding nightgown, my love. I chose it especially for this evening, to ensure everything was perfect as we consummate our marriage."

Sophia blushed at the moment James mentioned consummating the marriage. She had only ever kissed one man on the lips before. For that action she had felt guilty that she would disappoint her father, perhaps damaging her innocence as his daughter. Last night, when James stimulated her, she felt feelings in her body like never before. She was well aware that James touching her in such a way was certainly against all social norms, let alone what would be considered acceptable by her father and the Countess. She knew her amorous acts with James last evening, although wonderful and tantalizing, could discredit her as an aristocrat, to which her father would be outraged and incensed.

James walked over to Sophia, sensing her uneasiness. Without saying a word, he kissed her on her forehead and turned her around. Without invitation nor permission, James slowly and respectfully began to untie the top buttons running along the back of Sophia's taffeta gown. Goosebumps formed over her body and a tiny shiver moved her shoulders ever so slightly. James released four of her corset's drawstrings, allowing Sophia the comfort and ability to undress herself privately in the next room.

"Why not go to the next room, my love, and prepare yourself for us to join together as husband and wife. I will wait here for you as long as it takes for you to ready yourself. When you believe it is the appropriate time for us to become devoted to each other, come join me in our bed."

Sophia silently nodded and walked out of their bedroom and into the attached dressing room. Holding the pure white gown in her hands, she draws it up close to her chest, and a subtle tear rolls down her cheek.

Looking into the dressing mirror, Sophia sees a beautiful 18-year-old woman with her corset partially undone, a beautiful wedding ring on her finger and an exquisite nightgown in her hand. She quietly sits down on the stool in the corner of the room as her head begins to spin. Dropping the nightgown onto the floor, Sophia holds her hands over her face. She wants to scream, but she cannot for fear James will hear her. She wants to run, somewhere, anywhere, but cannot, for she is confined in this small dressing room.

Sophia is convinced she will become ill. Then, as if to take the reins of her emotions, she stops. 'I am about to give myself to a man I love,' she determines. 'A man who cares greatly for me and is willing to grant my every desire. This panic I feel is not warranted. James makes me happy and he excites my body. I will willingly give myself to James this evening. I will apply this cotton garment onto my naked body and know my decision is the correct one.'

Sophia rises off the stool and proceeds to remove all her clothes. Again, she looks into the mirror and this time she smiles. She even feels some tingling in her private areas when she sees herself naked. She can only imagine how uncontrolled James might feel when he sees her naked, pure body. Pulling the nightgown over her head, the fine cotton fibers rub against her already stimulated body as she continues readying herself to consummate her marriage.

In the next room James waited for Sophia at the base of the bed. He was no stranger to having relations with a woman. His status as Colonel made him desirable to many women. He also had more than enough money to afford a brief, yet quality evening with any woman he requested to satisfy his intimate needs as a man. Tonight was completely different. Tonight James was well aware he had gone to great lengths to earn the love of the woman in the next room. The woman he waited for was more beautiful than anyone he had ever been with and whom he loved more than words could express.

Sophia brushed her hair and took one more look in the mirror before returning into the next room barefoot with a single layer of cotton covering her body. 'What have I done? What am I doing?' Sophia's mind continued to race back and forth between logic and lust.

Sophia emerged from the dressing room, wearing her white nightgown and staring down at the floor with embarrassment. James was instantly struck by her innocence. The moment their eyes finally met they remained frozen for what seemed like two to three minutes.

Sophia knew James had legally bonded their relationship by having a handfasting ceremony tonight. He was her husband and she was finally his wife. The void of love she had felt in her life had been fulfilled by her love for James. Still, she continued to feel guilty for the actions already taken this evening and for those which were about to occur. Actions of which she suspected her father and the Countess would become furious once they learn of what had transpired. Yet, at this moment, Sophia did not care. She believed she had made the right decision for herself and her new husband.

James stared at Sophia and became speechless. She is the essence of pure, innocent beauty in its simplest form as she stands there in 'his' purchased nightgown. 'Even her feet are beautiful,' James reflects, looking down at the floor. How can he ensure that he can carefully care for this creature so that no harm will ever come to her? How can he control himself and not thrust himself upon her, wanting to devour her luscious body? 'She looks like a delicate, angelic bird,' he imagined.

James was determined to give Sophia a pleasurable first intimate experience. She deserved nothing less. He decided to be gentle and allow her to feel the true ecstasy her body could produce when aroused in a proper way. For a fleeting moment James's thoughts were brought to Sophia's father, the General. James had resolved that since the General was well aware of the severity of special military assignment, to which he himself commissioned the orders, he would certainly understand and accept the events James had planned for this evening. He hoped!

Both James and the General knew this assignment may cost James his life. It was certainly not without its high level of danger, something James was quite accustomed to. To that end, James had no choice but to do what he felt was correct in his heart, both for himself and for Sophia. What was correct to James included planning the construction of a new home and exchanging their wedding vows this evening—all of this before he left on his mission. Whatever the General thought of the situation, James believed he had admirably and respectfully made his decisions. Therefore, the General and the Countess would have to agree his decision was the right one. Besides, Sophia was a beautiful, grown woman and was of the age where she was ready for a husband to take care of her.

"You are beautiful, my lady. Perhaps we should have a portrait made of you, freezing this imagine of your beauty."

"Oh James, no. This is a nightgown and for private wear and for your eyes only this evening, my love."

Even Sophia was surprised by the boldness in her tone. James was intrigued.

"You look like an angel, my darling," James responds as he begins to unbutton his pants and drop them to the floor. He then proceeds to raise his shirt above his head, exposing his naked body. This was the first time Sophia has seen a naked man. At first she was taken aback. Then she began to focus on the shapes of James's muscles. His strong broad shoulders and his erect penis made Sophia's body draw herself toward him. She had such a strong desire to touch him, caress him, discover him.

James walked toward Sophia. She watched as his well-formed muscles approached her. With one swift move James lifted Sophia up into his arms and cradled her against his body. She did not resist. Carrying her to their bed, James quietly and lovingly stared into her eyes and smiled. He laid her down on the bed, while gently laying himself next to her. Sophia enjoyed James's strong muscles cocooning her body.

"You are mine, my love. Allow me to love you," James asks, requesting one last time for Sophia's acceptance for him to enter into her and become one with him.

Sophia nods her head in agreement as James moves toward her. With his warm lips, the ones she had become accustomed to this evening, he seductively slides his tongue into her mouth in search of an invitation to continue. Sophia does not resist. Instead, her tongue joins in the dance with his. James's hand caresses her body on top of her nightgown, and Sophia feels her pelvis arching forward with delight, an unconscious message for James to continue. James feels her arousal heighten as she begins to moan slightly and move her body in a twisting fashion ever so slightly. His manhood hardens even more. He places his hand under the virgin white nightgown and begins to venture around the perfect skin of her body. His hands travel around her breasts, over the furry mound of her pubis and down her long legs. Sophia moans as she becomes defenseless to any of James's desires. James expertly guides his fingers around her hips, and as though completely natural, between her virginal slit. He has been there before this evening, and again her wetness, along with her helpless moaning makes James want to insert more than his fingers inside her. He inserts just one finger and slowly and masterfully removes his moist finger, tenderly hitting her sweet spot. Sophia arches her back from off the bed and releases an "ohh" in a way that seems to cover a wide range of octaves. James continues this movement, knowing the powerful effect it has on a female.

Sophia feels excited and afraid, yet relieved. It was two weeks ago she had her menstrual cycle; she was relieved she was not having it now. She did not know what would have happened. 'Would they not be able to consummate the marriage? Would James be angry with her?' At this moment in time it was irrelevant. Now she can enjoy the warm rush of sensations flowing through her body, and Sophia wants more. She can feel the warm flow of juices building up between her legs, as her vaginal area swells. She lets out one more moan before she collapses limpness on the bed.

James proudly removes his finger from inside her. He smiles. His conquest is completed: he has given Sophia her first climax of the evening. "You have allowed me to pleasure you. You can feel safe with me this evening. I will do nothing to harm you."

James lifts her nightgown higher and begins to nibble each of Sophia's nipples. He gently teases them one by one, tantalizing Sophia beyond imagination. He moves his mouth around her now hard nipples and sucks on one while deeply massaging the other. Sophia immediately lets out a whispering cry. She calls out while James slowly pulls the nightgown over her head, dropping it onto the floor.

"Oh James, please take me. Please take me."

James is fully aware that he is in control and has decided he is not ready to thrust his hard shaft inside her—yet. Instead, he wants her to beg him for more. He wants Sophia to beg for his seductive acts. He wants to build an excitement within Sophia so she will never forget this enchanted, prefatory evening. James wants

Sophia to never forget this blissful moment their two bodies make love and become one.

"Do you desire my love, Sophia?" James inquires in a commanding way, secretly wanting to control her passions and climax.

"Yes, oh yes, James," Sophia responds, her legs quivering and trembling on the bed sheet. She is barely able to get out the words between her multiple warm moist rushes of peak excitement.

James knows he has satisfied her by his touch, and Sophia did everything he wanted her to do during his soft, tender commands and his loving words.

"Sophia, I am now going to softly enter you and make you mine. Do you want me, Sophia?"

"I want you, James. Take me. Take all of me. I beg this of you. I love you, James. I want you, and I am so happy to be your wife."

Those were the final words James longed to hear. With this affirmation from Sophia, he was ready to consummate their marriage.

Sophia was not sure why, but she began to stroke her hand up and down James's hard, erect shaft, making her lover groan and call out.

"Oh my darling, you know just how to pleasure me so," James expresses in a less than a commanding voice.

'Could it be that I am now in control?' Sophia briefly imagines as she continues moving her hand up and down James's penis. For whatever reason, Sophia decides to squeeze James's penis tightly. He moans. She continues rubbing and squeezing for a little longer. Sophia was surprised by her own actions. 'How did she know to do such things? Was this the normal types of touching wives do to their husbands? Was she more of a sensual creature than she even knew?'

James recognized that it was time. When it came to Sophia, he realized he must proceed slowly when entering her, given this was her first time being intimate with a man. Smoothly and romantically James rolls on top of Sophia, gradually and gently sliding his hardened penis into her virginal, tight vagina. Sophia's warm, moist, femininity, wraps tightly around James's erect penis.

With Sophia's legs spread apart, James accepts the invitation to rhythmically penetrate her. The strength of his muscular lean body allows him to effortlessly and continually thrust his hips against her body.

The two lovers are vividly aware of their gasping moans and fast, panting breath. These sounds further enhance their desires. Peaking in unison, they release the guttural sounds of pleasure as the flush from James enters Sophia. Additionally, Sophia lets out a deep weep. It is with this sound that James knows he has taken Sophia's virginity. 'She is mine now,' he rejoices, rolling onto his back beside her.

In their stillness, with their breathing returning to a normal pace, James turns his head toward Sophia.

"You are mine, Sophia, to have for all of eternity."

"You have made my body feel things I never knew were possible James."

"You, my darling, you have bewitched me in every possible way. I am under your spell, Sophia, and I shall never be the same man again."

Hearing these words, Sophia sits up and smiles. While pulling her long dark hair toward her back, Sophia looks down at the moist stain on the sheets. Along with the juices which have come from James, there was a small amount of blood. Confused by the presence of blood at a time when she was not menstruating, Sophia becomes worried. Seeing the look on her face, James quickly inquires.

"What is it, my lady?"

"I am embarrassed to say, James."

"My love. We are now husband and wife; let us never be embarrassed to share our thoughts and concerns."

"I have damaged our sheets, James. I am sorry."

Confused, James sits up and looks down at what might be causing Sophia great worry. He lets out a laugh and then stops, realizing Sophia is indeed upset.

"Oh, my darling new bride. There is no need for concern. What your body has just told us is that I am the first man to be inside you. I have broken the barrier to your virginity and you are officially my beautiful, yet still innocent of mind, wife. I will take care of you, my darling Sophia, forever. This is a night of celebration and not a night of worry. Come, let us rest by each other's side."

James's comforting words relax Sophia. She also appreciated James picking up her nightgown from the floor and helping her pull it over her head to once again cover her body. Lying back down in James's arms, Sophia falls into the deepest sleep she has ever experienced. James looks over at Sophia's beautiful image. 'I am at peace,' he reflects before he, too, falls into a peaceful and deep sleep.

Chapter Nine

There was a light knock on the attic door.

"Are you okay, little one? You are so quiet up here, Sarah Marie. I saw the light on and you are not asleep. What is going on?" Gramma asks in her caring, elderly voice.

My heart begins racing at the thought of being caught with Gramma's book. I quickly throw the book under my covers and grab my plastic horses off the nightstand.

"Sarah Marie? What are you doing up here?"

Clearly, Gramma hears the shuffling of pages and suspects I am doing something that is not good.

"Nothing, Gramma. I'm just playing with my horses before I fall asleep."

Gramma enters my room.

"You are such a good girl, Sarah Marie. You are my little angel. I just came up to check on you before I continue reading my book. Now, it is very late and you need to turn off your light and get some sleep so you can grow up to be a beautiful young lady."

"I will, Gramma. Good night, Gramma," I respond in somewhat of a rattled voice.

At this point I am petrified I will get caught in the act of reading Gramma's book. 'What would Gramma say? What would she do? What would happen to me?'

I jump up off the bed and run over to my Gramma at the door and give her a big hug and kiss.

"I love you so much, Gramma."

Maybe my message of love was from fear or guilt, or for true love for my Gramma. Either way, I was glad she did not catch me in the crime of reading her book. At least I hope she did not.

"Okay, Gramma, I'll turn off my light and go to sleep. Good night."

"Good night, darling."

Gramma leaves my bedroom and goes downstairs to continue reading her book. The adrenaline from the shock of almost getting caught with a naughty book now has me wide awake. I decide to take advantage of this current energy, along with my natural tendency for being curious and sneak over to my Gramma's bedroom. I decide to play at my Gramma's dresser and inspect what is inside her jewelry boxes. I always love what I can find in there.

I walk out the attic door and sneak down the stairs, making sure Gramma is still captivated by reading her book in the living room. She is. Then, I tiptoe to the television room and see Grandpa fast asleep in his chair, with Fox news playing on the television. I proceed to tiptoe back upstairs into my Gramma's bedroom and sit down at her powder dresser.

One of my Gramma's jewelry boxes is sitting on the corner of the dresser. The jewelry box sits between a silver comb, brush and mirror set. I pick up the brush and begin to brush my long, dark hair. As I pull the brush slowly through my hair, I think about Mistress Sophia and how she brushes her hair every night before she goes to bed. I put the brush down and open up the jewelry box. I wonder where Gramma got such a beautiful jewelry box. Did she buy it for herself? Was it a gift? 'Did someone give it to her and say how much he loved her?'

I began to notice some strange happening ever since I started reading Gramma's book. I realize when things happen in my real life, I start to think about them as if I am Mistress Sophia. I had this thought while I was taking the lavender bubble bath and again in my aunt and uncle's piano room. Now, while I am brushing my hair, I wonder if Gramma also has these same exact things happening to her. Unfortunately, I cannot find out whether she does or doesn't because then she would know I was reading her book and she would not be happy with me.

I open one of the three levels of the tall jewelry box, remove a beautiful barrette, and slide the barrette onto the back of my hair. Wow! It makes me look and feel so pretty. I start to open other drawers in the jewelry box to see what I can find. Each drawer is lined with a piece of red velvet. In one drawer, there is a black satin ribbon with a whitish circle with an old Victorian lady's face on it. I think Gramma once told me this was an ivory pendant. It is so pretty. I wrap the ribbon around my neck and tie it together at the back. I look into the mirror, and I admire how it lays on my neck. 'Is this what Sophia feels like when she is getting ready for a special evening with James? I bet she has a jewelry box just like this.'

I pull open another jewelry box drawer. This one has a beautiful ring inside. It is not silver or gold. The metal is more of a pink color. Wait, I remember James buying Sophia a 'rose-gold' ring. I bet this metal is rose-gold. Positioned in the middle of the ring is a large, square diamond stone. I slide the big ring onto my ring finger and hold out my hand to look at it from a distance, just like Sophia did with her engagement ring. This ring is so pretty; I wish it were mine, and then Mistress Sophia and I could have matching rings.

As I continue to open a few more drawers, my eyes find a necklace with a heart-shaped locket hanging from it. A red ruby stone sits in the center of the locket. I put the necklace around my neck. It hangs very long, between my belly button and my neck. Once again I stare at myself in the mirror. All 'my' jewelry is beautiful. It feels good to be Mistress Sarah Marie. All I need now is for James to love me the way he loves Mistress Sophia, or should I say Mrs. Langston? Not wanting to get caught wearing any of Gramma's beautiful jewelry, I take it off and carefully put it back the way I found it; at least I think I do. I tiptoe across the room and back into the attic, and I turn the light back on so I can continue reading Gramma's book. There is no way I will be able to go to sleep, knowing that Sophia and James just got married. I am sure I can keep my eyes open just a little longer and find out what will happen next in the story. I open the book and begin to read.

The next thing I know I am feeling the warm sunlight on my face coming through the attic window. I roll over on my bed, longing for more sleep. That is when I hear a loud thunk. Something has hit the hardwood floor. Fluffy jumps up off the bed and begins to bark.

"Shhh, Fluffy, you are going to wake up Gramma and Grandpa." Fluffy sits and begins to wag his tail.

Wondering what might have made the sound, I suddenly realize it must have been my Gramma's book. I jump off the bed to find it and make sure I put it in a safe place. I search around the floor trying to locate the book. There, wedged in the corner of the room, the book is lodged between an old trunk and the end of the bed. The trunk fits snugly under the pitched ceiling of the attic bedroom. I grab the book and immediately feel a sense of relief stashing it into my pillowcase. I cannot imagine what would have happened if I had lost the book Gramma owned. The one I should not be reading. Besides the worry of losing the book, I am also filled with lots of questions. 'Why would James put his fingers in Sophia's private parts? And why did she like it?' I know about two people getting together so they can make a baby, but why did James want to touch and kiss Sophia's breasts so much. I guess the biggest question I have after reading this book is when I read about James and Sophia touching each other and kissing each other, 'why do I start to feel strange inside me?' Mommy has told me about men and ladies having sex and my big sister has told me stories too. However, there is something really weird about reading this story of James and Sophia. When I read these parts in the story, I like the way my body feels. My private parts start tingling a little bit. Once, I even touched myself when I was reading that part and it was like I pushed a button for a bomb to explode inside me.

This information is all really strange and I am not sure whom I can talk to about it. I cannot talk to Gramma, because then she will know I am reading her book. I do not think I can talk to Grandpa about it, because he is a man and I would be shy to talk to him. I will have to think more about this later.

Gramma enters the room. "What's all the noise, Sarah Marie. Why is Fluffy barking?"

My cheeks turn flush. I take a big gulp of air before I reply.

"It's nothing, Gramma. Fluffy accidentally fell off the bed. He's fine, Gramma; it wasn't anything too bad, just a light fall. He's a goofy dog."

Gramma calls Fluffy over and inspects his fur and runs her hands under his fur, making sure he is not injured.

I feel bad lying to Gramma. She thinks poor Fluffy might be hurt. I look over at Fluffy and he is loving all this attention he is getting from Gramma. As I look up, I see my Grandpa walking into the bedroom.

"Hon, what's all the ruckus about?"

"It is nothing, Charles. The dog just fell off the bed," Gramma said, making light of the situation and winking at me with ease.

"Come on, let's all go downstairs and I'll make us a hot home-made breakfast," Gramma said.

"Charles, will you put the coffee pot on and set the percolating pot on the stove for espresso."

"Grandpa, I can't wait to have my warm cup of coffee."

Grandpa holds my hand and we walk downstairs together.

"Don't worry, little chic-chic, I will sneak you extra today."

"Aww, thank you, Grandpa. That would be great, because I feel kinda sleepy today. I didn't sleep very much last night."

Sitting at the kitchen table, I feel tired. 'I wonder how many pages I read last night? It's like I am starting to be like my Gramma and reading all night, every night. To make the scene perfect, now all I have to do is sneak some more of her delicious chocolates and eat them while I am reading.'

I wait impatiently for my breakfast. I begin to daydream about James and Sophia. I'm so happy Sophia and James got married and he built her a dream home. My Grandpa sneaks me a cup of espresso. I smile at him and thank him. Gramma places the big plate of sausage and peppers onto a hot plate in the center of the kitchen table, along with a basket of warm toast. She then takes my plate and dishes up some blueberry pancakes for me, followed by pouring lots of warm maple syrup on top of my pancakes.

Grandpa reaches for my plate and puts sausage and peppers on it. I take a piece of toast and dunk it into my cup of coffee, just like Grandpa does.

"I love my breakfast, Gramma. I am so lucky my Gramma and Grandpa spoil me rotten and I can have whatever I want."

"How's the sausage, Sarah Marie?"

"It's delicious. Is this the sausage from Uncle Johnny's farm?"

"It sure is," Grandpa said proudly.

"Little chic-chic, today we are going to pick some vegetables from my garden so we can sell them along the creek road."

"That sounds like fun, Grandpa. I can't wait."

"Now go wash up and get ready, so we can leave soon."

I head upstairs to get ready for the day. Fluffy chases after me. Once in my bedroom, I look at the lump in my pillowcase forming the shape of a book. Oh, I wish I could just read a little more of the story. Instead, I make my bed, ensuring the book cannot be seen. I do not want Gramma to find it. After I finish getting washed and dressed, I run downstairs.

"Give your Gramma a kiss goodbye and let's go," Grandpa instructs me.

I lean into my Gramma and kiss her goodbye.

Gramma kisses me back on my cheek and hugs me tightly in her arms.

"Now you be a good girl. Have fun with your Grandpa today."

"I will. I love you, Gramma," I say as I run out the back door, slamming it closed with a bang. As I land on the back porch, I see Grandpa putting on his favorite baseball team's red cap—the Phillies.

Grandpa takes the bags from my hands and replaces them with vegetable baskets. I am now carrying three wire baskets.

"Let's go to our garden and get some vegetables to sell, little chic-chic."

First, we walk over to the peppers, and Grandpa picks a variety of red, green and yellow bell peppers. He carefully places them in my basket as my fingers grip the metal wire handles of the basket.

"Boy, Grandpa, they smell good. Now I know why Gramma's breakfast was so good this morning."

Grandpa smiles and gives me an affirming 'you got that right,' pat.

We walk down another row of vegetables in Grandpa's half-acre garden. Grandpa picks a few bushels of ripe tomatoes from the vine and loads them into his basket. Finally, Grandpa bends down on one knee, perhaps out of fatigue, but also to reach more tomatoes. I start to giggle at the sight of Grandpa down on one knee. He reminds me of James when he asks Sophia to marry him.

"Oh, Grandpa, are you going to ask me to marry you?"

At first, Grandpa was taken aback by my question. Then, in the true spirit of his playful demeanor, he looks at me and said, "My darling chic-chic, you are such a wonderful young lady. You have brought so much joy into my life."

At this point, he quietly looks around and grabs a tomato leaf off one of the plants. He pokes a hole in the middle and said.

"Little chic-chic, would you take the tomato leaf as a sign of my affection and be my granddaughter for as long as we both shall live?"

I am laughing so hard, I have to put down my basket of peppers. I run up to my Grandpa and give him a big hug.

"I will, I will, Grandpa. I will love you forever."

"Oh good," Grandpa said. "Now can we pick the rest of our vegetables so we can go and sell them?"

"Of course," I say, extending my hand and looking at my tomato leaf ring. I really am becoming more like Sophia, I believe.

Grandpa starts picking fresh cucumbers off the vine and hands them to me.

"Grandpa! My basket is starting to get heavy."

"Okay, little chic-chic, set it down and grab another basket to put the cucumbers in."

After we've picked enough cucumbers, we move on, and Grandpa started to hand me summer squash, basil, parsley and other herbs.

"Okay, that should do it," Grandpa said, standing up and stretching his back.

He proceeds to take off his Phillies baseball cap, while taking a handkerchief out of his pocket. He wipes the moisture off his forehead and puts his cap back on.

"It's gonna be a hot one today, little chic-chic."

"Grandpa, this basket of squash and herbs is pretty light. I can carry this one for us?"

"You bet, chic-chic. I'll carry the others as your big, strong Grandpa."

We walk to the trunk of Grandpa's Plymouth and place the vegetable baskets inside. Grandpa covers them with burlap.

"Why are you doing that, Grandpa?"

"It is to protect them. That way, the vegetables won't roll around. The burlap keeps them safe so they look good for us to sell."

After getting into the car, Grandpa drives down the back alley. Just before the main road, he carefully drives over the old metal railroad tracks. The shocks on the car are not the best and we rock and bounce over the tracks. Two dog figurines in the back car window bob their heads back and forth as if to say, 'yes, yes, let's move on.'

"Grandpa, look how silly those dogs bob their heads. Where did Gramma get them?" I ask, still tickled by the dog's heads moving frantically up and down and side to side.

Grandpa looks in his rear view mirror.

"I don't know, little chic-chic. What I do know is that Gramma bought them just for you. Where she got them, I don't know. We'll have to ask her when we get home."

"I'm so excited for today, Grandpa. I can't wait to talk to all the nice people and sell them your fresh vegetables. Plus, I love spending time with you, Grandpa."

"I know, little chic-chic. We're going to have a good time today and make a little spending money for us, too."

"How long will it take Grandpa, to get to the spot where we sell your vegetables?"

"Not too long, little one. Maybe twenty more minutes." Grandpa turns on the radio to his regular AM station, which is now reporting on the Phillies and Cubs baseball game. I notice when Gramma is not in the car, Grandpa blares the radio to an almost deafening sound. I have no idea what this announcer is saying. All I can hear is yelling on the radio and the crowd is screaming wildly in the background.

"It is a neck and neck game here on May seventeenth, nineteen seventy-nine. It promises to be a great year for the Phillies as they slug it out with the Chicago Cubs at Wrigley Field during the final game of this three game series. If you are just joining this game, you are missing one of the best games ever. Today in the stands, we have almost fifteen thousand fans witnessing this incredible game in Chicago. The crowds are screaming with anticipation. The bases are loaded, and just moments ago the Phillies hit the ball right out of the park. The Phillies are pounding the Cubs. Going into the fifth inning, it was nineteen to nine for the Phillies, and the Cubs fans were not happy. By the end of that inning, the Cubs inched ahead making it twenty-one sixteen for the Phillies. The eighth inning was the showstopper. The Cubs tied the game twenty-twenty-two, and we have been holding there, till what is now the tenth inning. Folks, Phillies are at the bat. The Cub fans are not pleased and seem to believe that screaming at their team will help make them win this series. The crowds are going wild. The Cubs pitcher throws a fast curve ball and the batter strikes out. It's strike one against the Phillies. I'm sure you can hear the screaming crowds all the way to Pennsylvania. The pitcher prepares for his next pitch. He dips his head down, lifts his right leg and throws another curve ball. Ohhhhh! It's strike two. The crowd is out of control. The bases are loaded and the crowd is beside themselves. Could we be going into an extra inning?"

As I sit in the back seat, all I can hear is the announcer, with lots of people yelling and screaming in the background. Grandpa is starting to make grunting noises and begins talking to himself.

Once again the announcer gives an update on the game.

"The next pitch is thrown. It's a forkball and the Cubs pitcher has just struck out the second batter. The Cubs still have a chance. They are still in the game. With two outs, at the top of the tenth, Schmidt steps onto the plate. The pitcher stands ready on the mound. He pulls his right arm back, raises his right leg and throws the ball. Schmidt swings, and it's a hit! I can hear the sound of the ball cracking off his bat from the press box. The ball is flying left center and into the bleachers. This is an epic game! This hit has just won the Phillies the game, twenty-three, twenty-two and given the Phillies their fourth straight National League title. The crowd is out of control! Schmidt proudly touches each base with his bat as he makes it back to home plate. He is waving to the crowds and the crowd is screaming back. The Phillies's team is there to greet him at home base, raising him into the air and carrying him around. Folks, this is a great game here at Wrigley Field. If you are just tuning in, the Phillies have officially won this ball game, and as your announcer, this game was the most entertaining epic game I have ever witnessed."

"Grandpa, what just happened?"

"My favorite baseball player just hit a home run and won the game for the Phillies!"

"Yeah!"

I can tell Grandpa's mood has lifted. He likes it when his team wins. Since Grandpa is in a good mood and the game is over, maybe this is a good time to ask him a question that I cannot figure out about what I have just read about what Sophia and James are doing.

"Grandpa, I have a question for you, because I know you are so smart."

"What's up, little chic-chic?"

Grandpa lowers the volume of the radio.

"Well, I have heard that when two people love each other, sometimes when they kiss, they open their mouths and touch and wiggle their tongues together. Why do they do that?"

I can feel Grandpa taking his foot off the gas, while turning around and looking at me in the back seat, all the while the car still moves forward down the road.

"Why on earth are you asking me this question, Sarah Marie?"

I noticed that Grandpa did not call me 'little chic-chic' in response to my question. I hope he is not too angry with me. It is just that I really want to know why James and Sophia keep kissing this way. 'Is it something people only did in the 18th century or do people do it nowadays too?'

I knew I could not tell Grandpa the reason I was asking this question. If he knew I was reading one of Gramma's books, he would be very mad too. So I had to make up a little fib.

"Some friends at school were talking about it and I didn't understand it. I figured I would ask you, Grandpa, because you are so smart."

"Well, thank you, little chic-chic. The answer is really quite simple, and it has a lot to do with why animals on the farm do all the things they do. It is all part of nature. Kissing that way helps two creatures decide if they are good for each other. When two human tongues meet, the human brain starts to decide if the body's chemicals in each person's tongue are compatible with each other. If the body sends the signal that they are, then the two people will continue to get to know each other more, before they decide if they want to get married."

"Do cows kiss like that, Grandpa?"

Grandpa tried to hide his laugh, but I heard it anyway, and I didn't care.

"No, little chic-chic. They just touch their lips together. Apes and prairie dogs do though. Those animals touch their tongues together. Some people, especially long ago, did not like to kiss that way because they thought it spread germs, especially during the plague of the eighteenth century."

"Wow, Grandpa, I was right, you are really smart."

"Now, little chic-chic, little girls at school don't need to be doing that kind of kissing. You are not grownup enough to do that. So if any boy wants to kiss you like that, you tell him 'no'."

"Okay. Deal, Grandpa."

Oh boy, now I might have started a bigger problem. Now Grandpa thinks boys might be kissing me at school, when all I wanted to do was figure out why Sophia and James kissed that way.

"I got it, Grandpa. I will say 'no' to boys."

I can see Grandpa with a big smile on his face when he looks in the rear view mirror.

"Little chic-chic, we are here," Grandpa said, happy to change the subject from kissing to selling vegetables.

Grandpa starts to slow the car down to make the turn. I can hear the sound of gravel under the car tires as we drive down the side road. Soon after the turn, he pulls the car to the side of the gravel road and parks.

"I'm glad we're here, Grandpa." I hop out of the back seat.

Grandpa opens the trunk and pulls out a portable table, propping it up against the car. He then retrieves all of the baskets from the car and carries them to a spot close to the car. He sets up the table and places the vegetables on top. While doing all of the assembling, Grandpa instructs me to lean our sign by the tire of our car. I remember to place a heavy rock against the sign so it does not fall down.

'Fresh Vegetables For Sale,' reads the sign.

"Chic-Chic, get those brown paper bags out of the trunk of the car as well, please."

"You got it, Grandpa."

Grandpa also sets up two chairs for us so we can sit and wait for customers to buy our vegetables.

"Boy, this strong summer breeze sure feels good this time of year, doesn't it little chic-chic?"

"It sure does, Grandpa," I respond, just happy to be sitting at his side.

We both see the first car pull toward us. We both recognize the older lady and man as they get out of their old two-door red pickup truck. Grandpa greets them with a "Good afternoon, how are you both today?"

"Good afternoon, fine sir. What's for sale today?" the lady asks my Grandpa, as she always does.

"Fresh tomatoes, cucumbers, squash, herbs and peppers from my garden," Grandpa informs her.

"These are beautiful tomatoes. How much are they?"

"A quarter apiece, ma'am," I shout out, before Grandpa gets a chance to respond. Grandpa just smiles.

"Well then, I will take five," the woman said, smiling at Grandpa.

Grandpa fills a brown paper bag with five tomatoes. I notice he also adds one of each of his bell peppers into the same bag as well. Grandpa is one of the most generous and kindest men I know.

"The peppers are free, ma'am. I hope you and your husband enjoy them."

The lady smiles back at my Grandpa, thanking him and assuring him she will be back the next time she sees him parked at this same spot, selling his vegetables.

"Well, little chic-chic, we had our first sale of the day," Grandpa said, reaching over and opening up the old cigar box he uses to collect the money. He places the money inside the cigar box and sits down in his chair, waiting for his next sale.

"I am so happy, Grandpa. That was so nice of you to give that lady free peppers. Why did you do that Grandpa?"

"I did that, little chic-chic, because next time we come here, she will remember those free samples and she may buy the peppers from us. In order to catch a whale in life, you first have to hook the fish. Remember, I taught you that when we went fishing in the creek behind our house?"

"Yes, I do Grandpa, except I am not sure I want to catch a whale when I'm fishing with you. What if it wants to eat us? Or what if we can't reel it in?"

Grandpa laughs, enjoying my innocence.

"Don't worry, little chic-chic, I'll be there to help you."

"Grandpa, I'm hungry."

I see Grandpa take out his shiny pocket knife. He grabs one of the tomatoes and wipes it off with the bottom of his shirt. He cuts into four squares and hands me half of the tomato. I bite it, and juice squirts out both sides of my mouth.

"Mmm, this is the best tomato ever, Grandpa."

Then Grandpa wipes off a fresh cucumber. He peels the skin off with his knife and splits it down the middle. He proceeds to cut those splits into halves and hands one to me. I bite down into the cucumber.

"Yummy. Grandpa, nothing tastes better than Grandpa's home grown vegetables."

Grandpa smiles with pride.

"Look, Grandpa, here comes three more cars."

As the cars pull down the road, we notice more and more cars following them. We begin to get very busy selling vegetables.

I always try to help with bagging the vegetables, and sometimes Grandpa lets me count the money.

"Grandpa, we made three big sales right in a row—$3.50, $4.00 and $7.00. Wow, Grandpa! Our regulars really like your vegetables today."

Grandpa gives me a huge smile.

I notice that the next customer is that nice lady who likes to flirt with my Grandpa. I recognize her fancy car. She parks her car and walks straight up to my Grandpa. She is wearing very fancy clothes and has lots of jewelry around her neck and lots of shinny rings on her fingers. Her hair looks like she just came from the hairdresser. She smells of really nice perfume. Several buttons on the top of her blouse were undone and you could see part of her boobies.

"How much are your big, plump tomatoes today? I need some big ones," the woman asks, with a weird tone in her voice.

Grandpa's face blushes.

For some reason, she really emphasized the word 'big,' and I think that might be the word that made Grandpa blush.

"Ten cents," Grandpa replies. "And I can assure you, these are good tomatoes, because my preference is to produce nice, big firm ones."

The lady smiles, as if there is some secret game they are playing with each other, but I have no idea what it is. Then I realize that Grandpa has just told this lady that the tomatoes are ten cents, and he told the last customer they were twenty-five cents? That's less than half the price.

"I will gladly take seven please. I want to enjoy a whole handful."

Again, the lady smiles with her secret smile.

I watch Grandpa walk over and load the bag into her car. He then walks around and helps her into the driver's seat. I see the lady give my Grandpa some extra money. The car drives away and Grandpa walks back to me.

"Grandpa, I think that lady likes you. She talks different to you than your other customers. Is she special to you?"

Grandpa starts laughing out loud.

"I don't think Gramma would like it if she liked you too much, Grandpa. I think Gramma would get jealous."

"That lady is only a customer, little chic-chic. No need to tell your Gramma anything about her. She is just a good customer."

"I won't tell Gramma anything, Grandpa. I promise. But why did you give her the tomatoes for ten cents when you sold them to the other customers for twenty-five cents?"

"Aww, good question, little chic-chic. It is because this lady tips us, and we make up the difference in the tips and then some. For this lady, tipping a person is important, so we include it in the price. Sometimes in life, you have to learn when to decide what you want to get and what you are giving away to get the same amount or better. You have to give a little to get a little more back in return."

"Wow, Grandpa, you are really smart."

"Little chic-chic, it's called having street smarts. Everything I am teaching you today will help you later on in life. One day, things are going to happen when you get older and you need to remember the things I am teaching you now. 'Street smarts' means you know how to survive in the big world with all the good and bad people you meet along the way. These are the things you can't learn in books. You have to learn them from being in the action on the streets, or in this case, on a gravel road selling our vegetables."

"Thanks Grandpa, for teaching me this. I want to be street smart. It sounds like a good idea."

As we are talking, we see another car pull in. Both Grandpa and I recognize this guy. He's the guy that is always looking for a deal from my Grandpa.

"Grandpa, is that the darn deal man again?" I ask.

"Now, little chic-chic. All customers are welcome. We just have to use our street smarts and make sure he doesn't cause us to lose any money."

"I see you have some vegetables left. Hasn't been a busy day for ya then? How much for all of it?"

"Ten dollars for the lot," Grandpa replies in a strong confident voice.

The man replies quickly.

"I'll give ya six dollars for everything."

Grandpa looks at the man and said, "Make it eight and you have a deal." The man nods and Grandpa walks over and shakes the man's hand.

Grandpa helps load up all the vegetables into brown bags and carries them to the man's old pick-up truck. He waves as the man drives off.

As Grandpa walks back to me, I ask, "Grandpa, why do you always do that when that same man comes around? Why do you always give a higher price than the one he says?"

"Sometimes people like to make a game out of life. They like to wheel and deal. When you are dealing in life, you need to know when to hold them and know when to fold 'em, as Kenny Rogers said. You need to be the one to decide what you are and are not willing to gamble away. You have to learn to make good choices in life, little chic-chic, and once you make a decision, stick with it. For example, I knew I wanted $8.00 for all of those vegetables, but I just let the guy think he got himself a good deal, because he likes to play the game. He's a game-player. Plus, little chic-chic, it's the end of the day and we may not get any more customers, so I would rather sell everything and take the money than load all these vegetables back up into the car and haul them home again."

We both laughed as Grandpa folds up the table.

We put everything into the trunk, including the old cigar box, and pull out two fishing poles, a tackle box and an old coffee can full of live worms. I recognize the can because Grandpa brings the same blue coffee can every time we go fishing. We close the trunk and lock all the doors of the car.

We walk up a small hill. On the other side of the hill is a fishing pond. It is the special pond where Grandpa and I always fish. We call it the G.S.M. pond, which stands for Grandpa-Sarah-Marie-pond. Grandpa opens up the cooler and pulls out two glass bottles of ice-cold soda. I guzzle the first one down because I know my Grandpa will give me as much as I want. Especially when Gramma is not around to scold him or me. Grandpa helps me put a worm on my fishing hook. He then baits his own fishing rod next.

"Grandpa, those worms are gross. I'm not touching those. Yuk."

Grandpa smiles. He is not surprised by my comment.

"Okay, little chic-chic. It's what it takes to get the job done. Now throw out your line and be careful. I don't want you hitting my Phillies cap, especially after the great day that we had today."

"Yes, Grandpa, don't worry. I'll be careful."

I pull my right arm back as far as I can and swing the rod out in front of me, releasing my index finger off the reel. I hear the bobber hit the water.

"Good job, little chic-chic, you got it on the first try. You're getting better and better at this."

"Thanks, Grandpa. It's all because of you. You're a great teacher."

"Now watch your bobber and make sure you keep a steady eye on it or the fish will run with your line."

Grandpa tosses his line out and gets it on the first try.

"Come here, little chic-chic, walk over here with your fishing pole and sit down on the lawn chair, next to me."

Grandpa pulls out a huge bag of my favorite potato chips, and we both keep eating handful after handful. He reaches into the lining of his windbreaker's pocket. I see him pull something out, wrapped in tin foil.

"What's that Grandpa? Is it the sausage from this morning's breakfast?"

"It sure is, chic-chic," Grandpa said, cutting it in half and handing me half a piece of sausage and taking a piece for himself.

"This is like a party, Grandpa. The best party ever."

As I wipe my mouth on the sleeve of my shirt, I see my bobber go down hard into the water.

"Grandpa! Grandpa! I got something."

"Reel your line in steady, little chic-chic. Don't pull too hard or you'll lose the line and the fish."

My heart races as the fish pulls hard. I pull my rod back gently and slowly reel in my line. On the one hand, I want Grandpa to help me, and on the other hand, I am glad he trusts me and believes that I can do it myself. I really want to make my Grandpa proud of me. I start saying my prayers under my breath in hopes of bringing this fish to shore. Sure enough, the fish comes jiggling out of the water, dangling from the end of my fishing pole.

"Hand me your rod, little chic-chic."

Grandpa pulls the line over with his other hand and unhooks the fish. "Nice job. You got a beauty."

"Thanks, Grandpa. Now it's your turn."

I barely finished saying my sentence when Grandpa's fishing line starts to move.

"Grandpa! Hurry up! Look! Your fishing line is moving too. The bobber just went under."

Grandpa grabs his fishing rod and reels in a big fish like a pro.

"That's a big fish, Grandpa. You always make this look so easy."

"She sure is a beauty, and I bet it's going to taste real good, too."

Grandpa threads our fish onto a stringer and plops them back into the water so the fish can stay alive for a little bit longer while we are still fishing. He ties the other end of the stringer to a tree. Another hour passes and we are still alone with our two fish.

"How about we call it a day, peanut?"

"Sure, Grandpa. I think that's a good idea."

I help Grandpa carry the lawn chairs and fishing equipment up and over the hill. Grandpa loads them into the trunk. We get into the car and Grandpa starts up the old Plymouth. The radio turns on. Grandpa tunes in to another baseball game. He is happy listening to the game, and I will be happy when we can get home to read my book. I plan to walk into the house, tell Gramma I need a little rest and I want to play with my horses for a while. What I really want is to find out what else is going to happen between James and Sophia.

Chapter Ten

Sophia's eyes open and she feels her lover's arms wrapped around her body. It is dark out. At this latitude, during the end of fall the sun has not yet decided to rise this early in the morning. Perhaps, like Sophia, it too, wants to be held in a horizontal position. James was still fast asleep, exhausted from pleasing Sophia the night before. Lying in James's arms, Sophia relives the events of the previous evening. She plays every intricate detail over again in her mind. She cannot believe James invested all the time and effort to plan their entire year of courtship right up to the crescendo of this past evening. All the worrying and doubt she had about living with him forever now appeared senseless. James had dissolved her fears of being alone, unloved and without a husband. 'He loves me,' she smiles, in her blissful state. 'He most certainly loves me. How could I have been so foolish to think he was not going to marry me? Now we are married and we will indeed be soulmates for the rest of our lives.'

James begins to move his body as he awakens from his euphoric evening. Sophia begins to feel his hand moving slowly down her left hip as he takes pleasure touching her exquisite soft skin.

Sophia breaths in deeply, at first nervous by what could be considered an invasive touch. Now, as a married woman, this has become a loving touch, a required touch of a wife who wants to please her husband. Her new husband.

Sophia finds her body desiring James's touch. Her body craves him and she does not want him to stop touching her. She moves slowly, as if to squirm, but instead her movements are a signal of her arousal and her desire for more. James gently kisses her left shoulder and then down the back of her neck. His seductive lips peck at her silky, light-almond skin. He knows from the way her body does not resist, she is aroused and ready to be pleased some more. What a perfect way to begin the day, with Sophia as his wife, James rejoices with gratitude.

James slides his fingers between her legs. Sophia accepts his advance without resistance. He slowly wanders his way to her stomach and follows the ready-made path of her slit to her beautiful, wet vaginal lips. The feeling of her wetness and her tender lips excites James.

Sophia can feel his penis swelling and pushing against her back. 'Oh, the delight of this sensual moment.'

Sophia's mind feels disconnected from her body and wallows in all the sensations. She is now without the control of her mind and her body, which demands the ecstasy only James can bring. Her body is ravenous for all the pleasures James can provide. After only one night, Sophia has become a slave to the pleasure James brings her.

James knows his fingers excite Sophia. What he feels excites him as well. He longs for his shaft to be inside his lover. 'She is now mine, all mine, and I will make love to her again and again. There is no end to the pleasures we can draw from each other.' With James's fingers deep inside Sophia, he masterfully rubs on her sweet spot. Sophia feels the warm rush of liquid flow down her leg. Her heart pounds faster. She begs her lover not to stop. James's fingers circulate around her tight moist slit, as he slides them slowly in and out of her vagina. James gracefully rolls Sophia onto her back so the two are now facing each other. He reinserts his fingers deep inside her drawing them in and out, until he feels

Sophia reach her highest peak. He continues to tease her, bringing his penis to her pubis area. He feels her wetness on his hard, throbbing shaft, and the sensation causes him to groan with deep pleasure. She, too, has lost control of her functions. Pleasure has taken over and Sophia moans from a deep place in her throat. James gently moves his hips into hers. He slides his moist wide tip inside his wife, taking her by surprise. He does not go deep. His swallow entrance was intended to be in preparation for his next move. James pulls her body closer into his as he enters her deeply. Arousal heightens for both of them.

"Come to me, my lady, come to me," James calls out his demands.

Sophia's hips melt together with his and they move back and forth to the rhythm of each other's body.

Reaching for Sophia's right breast, James squeezes her nipple with his two fingertips and holds. The pressure of those two fingers force Sophia to let out a large moan. She flushes down onto his hard pivoting shaft and completely lets go of her body. This reaction causes James to know that his lover is experiencing exactly as he would have her to do.

Sophia is helpless with desire as James's shaft pulsates inside her; all the while, her moist vaginal lips hug his insertion. James leads her to follow his every command, given to her through his body language. In another seductive move he pulls her on top of him and grabs her waist and pulls her directly onto his hard erect shaft. Sophia does not resist. He has her. James whispers into her ear with love and cupidity.

"Come, my darling. Show me, Sophia, that I am yours and you are mine."

Sophia heralds a weep, then a gasp, then a long moan signaling the culmination of her experience. Tears of joy roll down her cheeks accompanying her ecstasy. James continues to take her even deeper, feeling her wetness gush down onto him. He knows Sophia has reached her highest peak but it does not matter, he demands more as he continues to penetrate her deeper and deeper, hitting his own climax and flushing his warmth inside her. He consciously chooses to leave his shaft deep inside her, continuing to enjoy the feeling of her tight vagina.

After a few moments, James rolls Sophia onto her side with her back to him and his penis still inside her. James holds his lover from behind, remaining inside her, thus requiring her body to be submissive. He wants to leave an imprint of his presence.

The two lovers fall asleep as though they have been fused together. Each has a dream of a magnificent life of joy and pleasure with each other.

A few hours later James announces, "Sophia, it appears the doves herald a chattering chorus for us to arise from our slumber. It is time for us to travel to the new Royal Library of Devonshire."

"Oh James, is there no rest for the new Mrs. Langston?" Sophia said with a smile.

Sophia rubs her eyes as James opens the sheer curtains stretching from the floor to ceiling. As the curtains open, they reveal a built-in bench, set deep inside the bay window. Sophia beams as she steps out of her bed. Donned in her stained wedding nightgown, she walks over to the window and looks out, taking in the breathtaking views of the majestic sea.

"James, this window seat is beyond splendid. I can do a great deal of my reading from this spot as I wait for you to join me in our bed," Sophia said with a cheeky smile.

"I had it made especially for you, my love. I assumed it would bring you great pleasure."

"Oh, it has, and it will be, my beloved husband. This entire bedroom environment will have me sleeping like an angel. My dearest James, words cannot describe my gratitude."

"The pleasure is all mine, Sophia. I love you. Pleasing you allows me the highest honor in life," James replies as he moves closer to Sophia and kisses her on her forehead.

"How about a spot of tea and some biscuits before our journey to the library?"

"That would be lovely, James, thank you."

James goes downstairs to prepare a light breakfast, as Sophia continues to stare out the window. Surely this is not a dream, she determines. She is certain it is reality, a reality she simply cannot believe is actually happening.

James returns with a doily-covered tray and places it on a small table he had strategically positioned beside the window seat. He pours Sophia a cup of properly steeped tea, accompanied by two shortbreads resting in the saucer next to it.

"Oh James. You planned everything so well, my darling. All of this has taken me completely by surprise. I am content beyond belief."

"I apologize that the cupboards are bare, Sophia. I only had time to gather a few things from the general store."

"James, there is no need to apologize. I am here now and together we can make this our well-furnished and well-stocked home."

"Today we will travel past three villages, as I promised the Countess and your father we would do. I am a man of my word, my darling wife, as I hope you most certainly know to be true."

James found himself enjoying using the word 'wife'. He had hoped that once again he would find one partner to share the rest of his life with. Sophia was that woman, and the term 'wife' did not come close to expressing all the joy and happiness that title brought him.

"Yes, indeed. You are a man of your word, and as I discovered last night and this morning, you are a man of many titillating pleasures as well."

James proudly smiled and although not certain, Sophia thought she might have seen him blush ever so slightly.

"Carry on then," James said wanting to change the subject. "Let us ready ourselves and head out to see the new Royal Library."

Sophia places the same clothes on that she wore last night. She is grateful that the design of her dress could be worn for many different occasions. She also made certain there were no stains lurking on her dress, caused by the activities of last night. After ensuring she was properly dressed, fitting for a General's daughter and a Colonel's wife, she gracefully walked downstairs. Greeted by James in the foyer, he escorted her to the front door. He grabs his sword and metal scabbard out of the umbrella stand and fastens it around his waist. Sophia walks outside, proudly escorted on James's arm.

Bernard, the carriage man, patiently waits, ready to transport them to their destination. Bernard opens the carriage door and James assists Sophia into the finely styled carriage. They ride silently during the hour journey, with Sophia nestled close to James. There was no need for conversation, as each privately reminisced over the blissful events of the previous night.

Upon arriving at their destination, James tightly wraps his beautiful bride in her fur mantle, and they walk nobly toward the front door of the Royal Library of Devonshire.

The entrance of the library had a magnificent massive porch. A large Italian marble statue of Alfred the Great, King of Wessex, stood proudly on the front lawn, welcoming guests to the library. James and Sophia paused to read the statue's inscription. They learned that King Alfred was canonized by the Pope, and was known for using great eloquence promoting the use of English rather than Latin in the country. These accomplishments, along with his admirable negotiation skills and success against barbarism, were compounded by his promotion of education.

"I had no idea he reigned from 871 to 899. I thought it was much later than that," Sophia said, still reading the inscription.

"Leading the resistance against the Viking invasion. I certainly admire what it would have taken to accomplish that massive undertaking. This is quite the epithet," James said, with his military background in mind.

"James, did you know he improved the country's legal system and military structure?"

"Yes, my dear," James said smiling, once again enjoying the innocence of Sophia. "That is one of the first things you learn upon entering the military."

The statue was breathtaking, as the great king held a sword high in the air, addressing his victory to the nation. James was profoundly impressed by his legacy.

"Welcome to the new Royal Library of Devonshire. Please do come in." The doorman, in his black tuxedo and bright white gloves, welcomes them in a dignified voice. He opens the door and James escorts Sophia into the building. Once inside the ante-chamber, James signs the visitor's log as Mr. and Mrs. James Langston. James can only smile as he completes this task.

Entering into the main library, Sophia is taken aback by the grandeur of the sight before her.

"Oh James, this is the most magnificent library I have ever seen. These dark black wood finishings, the tall bookcases and the detailed craftsmanship with inlayed wood on each and every book-shelf is an incredible display of architectural talents. The amount of time and effort that it must have taken to complete this building is beyond comprehension. Each bookcase is marked with gold leaf lettering identifying each bookshelf. It is beyond description. James, I am in awe just being in this room."

Walking across the green marble floor, Sophia inhales the aroma of leather books. In a soft whisper, appropriate for being in a library, with the high ceiling perfect for echoes, she said, "There must be thousands of books here, James. Where shall we begin?"

"It is my wife's choice," James said with a teasing smile.

Sophia responds with a smile as she moves toward the first section on the right.

"Shall we start over here? I would like to explore this section."

James nods in agreement as he glances up to the signage on top of the bookshelf: 'Poets and Poetry.'

Sophia walks freely through the section as James admires her graceful beauty, her refined mannerisms and her elegant gate. He enjoys watching her. 'I thoroughly enjoy the sheer beauty of So-phia's presence,' he concludes. As he sits down on a leather arm-chair, James decides to absorb the vast amount of artwork in the library rather than look at books. The artwork is by far some of the highest quality James has ever seen. He leans his head back and looks up toward the cathedral ceilings. He is astonished by the de-tailed paintings of legendary emperors and kings across the ex-panse of the ceiling, all hand-painted. Restless, James gets up from his chair and walks behind Sophia, who is now staring in-tently into a book. He kisses her on the back of her neck and whis-pers in her ear.

"Darling, are you enjoying yourself?"

"Oh James, not here. Not in the library."

"My darling wife, I am needy for your love and attention. I simply cannot go very long without it."

James places his hands on her hips and pulls her bottom into his pelvis. Sophia lets out a subtle quiet, controlled moan, tilting her head to one side. Her newfound erotic desires have caused her to be oblivious to any other presence in the library.

"I long for your touch and hidden desires, James," Sophia said, looking up to the ceiling while resting the back of her head on James's shoulder.

"I cannot wait to get another divine taste of my new bride," James whispers.

Sophia giggles slightly and again replies in a soft tone fit for a library; however, this time more importantly, realizing her actions and this amorous scene are not fitting for a young woman of her aristocratic stature.

"Oh James. You are making it very hard for me to read, and I want to stay here and marvel at this library."

"Those are my intentions, dear lady. For me, I want to marvel at what is in this library, but it is not about the books. I am interested in marveling at you," James said, in what could only be perceived as a mischievous schoolboy tone.

Sophia steps forward, adding distance between them. She takes her long white glove off, placing it in her other hand. She wants to enjoy the sensual feeling of the book's suede skin. She rubs the soft suede with short up and down motions thinking of how much it resembles stroking her lover. She is fascinated by this book, as she reads out the title to James. *"The Echoing Call Of The Sea,* by Bartholomew Blackburn."

James continues to watch the hypnotic look on her face. Sophia fans through the worn pages. She slowly dips her nose down to enjoy the aroma emitting from the pages. Her heart dances widely inside her chest. James watches her closely. He has always admired Sophia's love for books. 'She is a smart woman,' James thinks. 'She will be an excellent teacher for our many children.'

Sophia gently returns the book to the shelf and walks to the other side of the Royal Library. It was as though she knew her departure will be a tease for James. James remains in the same location.

As Sophia walks further away, James grabs the book Sophia had just been looking at. He makes certain he cannot be seen by Sophia, as he walks toward the counter and requests to purchase it. While the clerk wraps the leather book in tissue paper, tying it with twine, James continues to look over his shoulder, ensuring he has not been seen by his beautiful wife.

"This book is intended to be a surprise gift for a very special lady," James said with a secretive smile.

"Well sir, I can confirm, she is not only a special lady but a very lucky one as well. This is an extremely rare book and will be a treasure to own," the clerk said, in a very controlled, non-emotional way, reminding James of the tone his mother would use.

This was not a memory James wanted to have, not today. He intentionally looks down at the wrapped book instead, focusing his attention on the joy and pleasure this purchase will bring to Sophia. James hides the wrapped book inside his uniform jacket, relieved he has not seen by Sophia.

Rejoining Sophia, he asks if she has completed her visit.

"Oh James, I could stay here for days, I so love this library."

Convincing her it was time to leave, James leads Sophia back through vestibule with Sophia's arm placed properly around his.

"Leaving sir?" the doorman asks, an instruction given to the staff by the doorman's employer. 'Be polite. Make conversation, address our guest's needs.'

"Yes, we are, although it was very difficult to convince my wife to depart."

Sophia blushes, not only for being the one who was singled out for wanting to stay, but also for publicly hearing that she was James's wife.

"Will you be staying in town long, sir?" the doorman asks, as an attempt to make conversation again as his employer requested, due to the prestigious nature of the library.

"I am afraid not," James replies. "Our journey has us here just for the day."

"While you're visiting our village, do you have any desire in visiting an estate sale today?" the doorman asks, unsure what prompted his comment, for even he was surprised by himself asking the question.

"An estate sale?" James replies, confused by the randomness of the question.

"Yes. I have recently learned this morning that an estate sale is occurring at the home of Lady Stephens, who will be moving from our village rather quickly, I am sorry to say. Today is the final day of this sale. Although I am not quite certain why I brought it up, I am in no way implying you appear in need of furniture and home furnishings." The doorman found himself becoming wrapped in his own words with no end in sight, until James rescued him.

"Thank you for the information, kind sir."

"Oh James. Can we go, darling? Please?" Sophia squeals with the excitement at the possibility for purchasing furnishings for her new home.

Looking into Sophia's violet-grey eyes, it was hard to say anything but 'yes, of course we can go.'

"Of course, my darling. I can only suspect that as you admire the many treasures at the sale, I am certain you will find something. I am happy to go because I can admire watching you look around."

"Sir," James said, turning back to the doorman. "Can you give Bernard, my carriage man, the directions to this estate sale, please?"

"It would be my great pleasure, sir," the doorman responds, happy that his random comment resulted in a positive response. "Thank you both for joining us for the opening of the library."

James pulls out the horsehide leather wallet from his pants pocket. He generously tips the doorman for his service. The doorman smiles back, happily accepting the kind offer. James and Sophia drive off in their carriage. James looks over at Sophia, who is staring out of the carriage door window. She is taking her last look at the library as it is growing further in the distance as the horses gallop off.

"How are you, my darling? Are you dreaming of my alluring kisses?" James said, taking her hand and kissing the top of it, not before blowing on her hand to stimulate her senses. By the time James's lips reached her skin, the sound of his lips kissing her was explosive to her ears. Sophia lets out a light sigh of relief.

"Oh, my darling, I love your tender kisses. The tantalizing effect they have on my body has now become an addiction, an addiction with which I have little control nor desire to continue being proper and correct."

Thrilled by this comment, James slowly slides his hand up Sophia's gown, making her shiver at the touch of his large, rough hand. He wants nothing more than to encapsulate all her thoughts so that she will only think and desire him. 'I am going to continue to render her helplessness and seduce her into euphoria,' he thinks. 'I will forever conquer her heart.'

As if without notice, James removes his hand from under Sophia's gown, thus changing the tone and mood within the carriage. If he teases her throughout the day, he thinks, 'then tonight she will be unable to resist my needs.'

James reaches into his uniform jacket and pulls out Sophia's gift. The one he purchased for her at the library.

Sophia is confused, first by being lulled into passionate bliss and now being handed a present.

"This is for you, my beautiful wife. A token of my love for you."

Sophia unties the twine, smiling back at James as she exposes *The Echoing Call of The Sea* from the package.

"Oh James," Sophia calls out with delight.

Sophia immediately dips her nose onto the suede cover and smells the pages of her new book. She gently rubs her hands up and down the suede cover. James is aroused simply by watching her tender hands touching the leather. He reaches tenderly for her face, drawing his lips to hers. Their kiss is long and passionate.

"I love you, Sophia. I intend to strive to make you the happiest woman in the world. I will always prove my love for you through my honor and my word. I promise this for the remainder of our lives together."

Sophia listens to James's heartfelt words as tears stream down her cheeks. James removes a handkerchief out of his pocket to capture her tears.

"No tears, my lady. I shall not allow you to be sad on this first day of our married life together; besides, we have an estate sale to visit."

Holding the book to her chest, Sophia said, "Thank you, darling husband. This was truly a glorious surprise. I will cherish it forever."

Bernard pulls on the leather reins and the horses begin to slow down. "Whoo, ladies. Whoo!"

The carriage comes to a halt and Sophia looks out the window. She admires the splendor of the massive estate. The servants scurry to greet the newlyweds and assist them out of the carriage.

"Welcome to Lady Stephens's estate," the butler said, greeting them in proper form. "Lady Stephens is waiting inside for any guests who will arrive. Please come in and join us."

James extends his arm for Sophia to be guided through the front door. An aristocratic looking woman greets them in the sitting room.

"Good afternoon. Thank you for coming to my estate sale. I am Lady Stephens."

"Thank you, my lady. I am Colonel James and this is my lovely wife, Sophia," James replies, giving a slight bow simultaneously as Sophia curtsies.

"It is a pleasure to meet you, Lady Stephens. We were intrigued when we heard about your estate sale from the doorman at the Royal Library of Devonshire," James frames the context of their arrival.

"Yes, Wentworth is a good man. Please take your time and look around. Everything is for sale, I am afraid," Lady Stephens responds with what could only be construed as sadness in her message.

Despite her dolefulness, she maintains a stiff upper lip as she waves at James and Sophia to convene in the sitting room. They choose to sit side by side on a lavish Knoll sofa.

"I am sorry to hear of you needing to sell all your furniture, Lady Stephens. One can only hope that your reasons are happy in nature," James said, as he attempts to make conversation.

"Unfortunately, the circumstances for the sale are of a very sad nature. My husband had fallen ill a while back and passed away quite suddenly last month. We had thought he had recovered to full health; however, alas, we were wrong."

Sophia's heart dropped at hearing these words. Just yesterday she had gained a husband and today she hears of this woman losing one. Sophia stands up, walks over to Lady Stephens, kneels beside her and she gently grabs her hand.

"I sincerely sympathize with you for your loss of your beloved husband, Lady Stephens. I cannot even imagine such a loss. Please accept our condolences."

James was struck by the warm compassion Sophia showed toward a perfect stranger.

"Thank you, my dear, for your kind words. The doctors did their best to make him comfortable and God decided when he wanted to take him. God rest his dear soul, he is in heaven now, and I am here with the torture of his absence in my life."

Lady Stephens's stiff upper lip could no longer be maintained. She feels her voice quivering and tears running down her high cheekbones onto her aged jowls. Sophia continues to quietly kneel beside her while she, too, joins Lady Stephens with tears running down both of their faces.

"My late husband was heir to a very large fortune. Sadly, I am without any heirs to share these treasures. For that reason, along with the desire to go back to my homeland, I am disposing of everything and moving back to Scotland," Lady Stephens said, very much surprised that she had divulged so much personal information to this couple she had just met.

Lady Stephens justified her actions by intuitively feeling something very endearing about this young couple.

"Please, do have a look around my estate," she said. "Everything is for sale. I can only hope that you have a useful place for it in your home."

"Thank you for your hospitality, Lady Stephens. It will be a delight to look around, however sad, due to your circumstances," James said respectfully.

"Will you be in town long, Colonel?" Lady Stephens asks as she sips her afternoon tea.

Although she had just invited the two to look around, she secretly enjoyed the company and conversation. She had found loneliness quickly entered her life since her husband's death. Ever since her husband passed away, friends opted to not visit her, in fear of experiencing sadness when they came into the house.

"No, your Ladyship, we are only here for the day. The entire reason for our visit was to see the new Royal Library of Devonshire," James said.

"It is a splendid library indeed. Such a shame I won't be staying to enjoy it," Lady Stephens said regrettably.

"Have the two of you been wed long?" Lady Stephens asks, again surprised by her own boldness.

At the same time she realized that in her older age, the loss of her husband and her acquired status in society, she did not have to maintain the air of an aristocrat that might normally be expected at her level of status. At least Lady Stephens had no desire to maintain such expectations. Instead, she wanted to learn more about this lovely couple with whom she had taken an instant liking to.

James and Sophia both stared at one another as Lady Stephens asked what could be construed as very personal question for someone you had just met.

"We are newlywed, your Ladyship," James said looking at Lady Stephens when he responded and then looking at Sophia as he reached for her hand, smiling. "We have been married for twenty-four hours and are now looking to furnish our new home with fine furnishings."

Lady Stephens was stupefied. She had certainly not expected this answer, and at the same time she became more intrigued by the possible story which brought the young couple here today. She asks. "Your rank is very impressive, Colonel. Have you been serving our country for very long?"

"I have indeed. I served under the command of my wife's father, General Cartwright," James proudly said, squeezing Sophia's hand slightly.

A squeeze that did not go unnoticed by Lady Stephens.

"If I am to infer from our brief conversation regarding your life together, you may be in need of many items from my home. Our meeting today may have turned out to be quite serendipitous for both of us. Colonel James, inside my large carriage barn there are two fine carriages for sale, along with the four of my finest black Percheron horses in the pasture. Those are also for sale."

"I see," James replies, raising his eyebrows, knowing that he also wanted to purchase these animals, along with the carriages, as yet another wedding gift for Sophia.

"As far as the interior of the home, the majority of the furnishings have been sold. A few items my husband cherished remain, along with a few furnishings upstairs and in my main dining room. I am with mixed emotions announcing that my home has been sold. The new owners, a lovely family, are moving here next month from up north. I am disparaged I must give up my home and yet pleased that a new family might be able to enjoy it as much as my husband and I once did."

"I can see the sadness in your face when you speak of moving from your home," James said, in hopes that his empathic response might in some way offer her comfort. "We are strongly interested in viewing your lovely furnishings and certainly would like to look at those fine horses you spoke of."

"More tea, your Ladyship?" Theodore, the butler asks, consistently ensuring his exemplary services toward his employer.

"Why yes, Theodore, that would be lovely. Thank you."

Sophia admired the tender grace of Theodore's calm yet elegant mannerisms. It was not often you saw a butler of his caliber in such a small town. He must be paid very handsomely for his services.

"May I walk upstairs and visit the furnishings you speak of, your Ladyship?" Sophia asks.

"Of course, my dear. Theodore, please escort our guest upstairs."

While being escorted upstairs, Sophia finds herself ascending a wooden spiral staircase, feeling as if she is part of the royal family. She is memorized by Lady Stephens's fine tastes and artistic display of priceless works of art throughout the home.

James remained in the sitting room with Lady Stephens.

"James, would you like to join me and perhaps consider purchasing the horses in the carriage barn," Lady Stephens asks, hoping to find a home for these fine creatures.

"I would indeed, your Ladyship. I am very interested in your four fine horses and two beautiful carriages. I have no need to look closely at them, for I can only imagine having deduced by the rest of your fine home and your superb tastes. I am certain your carriages would be of the same caliber. Therefore, I shall take your word regarding your items in the carriage house. Besides, a dignified lady such as yourself does not belong amongst the hay and equestrian equipment. Alternatively, I would take this time to negotiate a price. My intention is to surprise my new wife with these fine gifts as a token of my love for her. A wedding present of sorts."

Lady Stephens is profoundly taken aback by James's fond love for Sophia. She is reminded of her late husband, Henry, and the enchanting love they had for one another. "It is abundantly clear you are deeply in love with your wife, Colonel. My husband and I had a similar love for one another. This is why I am unable to continue living here at our ... I mean my ... estate. I am going back to my homeland to escape the fond memories and constant reminder of my life here with Henry. This estate is also too much upkeep for one elderly woman. All of these decisions and transactions have become daunting. This is one reason why I agreed to accept a relatively low offer from the family who wants to purchase this home."

"I cannot imagine the anguish you must be feeling at selling your home, Lady Stephens," James responds empathically. "I do not think I would be able to stay in a home if I experienced an equally heartbreaking situation, such as the loss of a spouse."

James suddenly became aware of a lump forming in his throat. The mere thought of losing Sophia became a horrific probability to consider. Attempting to graciously change the subject, James asks, "Lady Stephens, would it be possible for us to agree on a price for the horses and carriages before my wife returns with what I can only assume will be a list of items she is certain we must have for our new home. It is conclusive she will be convinced that such items will create a dignified and auspicious feeling in our home."

Both of them smile, since Lady Stephens knows James is probably correct. She gives a light chuckle and surprises herself. She has not smiled or presented any sign of happiness in a very long time. 'It feels good to be happy again, if only for a moment,' reflects Lady Stephens.

James is well aware that relying on a carriage for transportation requires significant wealth. He is prepared to keep Sophia at this level of comfort as part of his commitment to her. "I can pay you handsomely and fairly for these items," James said.

Lady Stephens remains quiet as she briefly ponders a price for her horses and carriages. James waits patiently. He suspects she requires time to think quietly and does not want to be rude and break her concentration. His military training has prepared him well for this moment. 'Be patient. Wait. Let matters transpire for a moment. Gain intelligence about the situation before you make your move.' He could hear the orders being barked in his head from his years in the military.

"Twenty pounds should be an adequate amount."

"Your Ladyship. That is very fair, and if I may be so bold to say, a very low and generous amount. Are you certain it is an equitable amount for your needs as well?"

Lady Stephens was struck by James's honesty and genuine caring for her well-being.

"It is indeed an acceptable amount to me, Colonel. Thank you for your concern. It is a breath of fresh air to meet a man of your caliber. You remind me of my husband when I first met him. His character was impeccable. It is one of the many qualities that drew me toward him."

"I will send my men by in the morning to pick up the horses and two carriages, Lady Stephens. Thank you for your generosity and for keeping this a secret from my wife."

"Colonel James?"

"Yes, Lady Stephens."

"I have decided to also give you all their fine leather harnesses and reins that are part of the horses and carriage maintenance. I will not have a need for them. You might be interested in knowing that these items were made as a special tribute to Henry while he was alive."

"My word, your Ladyship. Thank you very much. I am very grateful for such a gracious gift, indeed."

James could hear footsteps approaching through the foyer. Escorted by Theodore, Sophia walks back into the sitting room. James stands to greet his wife. He takes a new seat, sitting beside her on the sofa.

"Did you find one or two things of interest, Sophia?" James asks teasingly, only too certain that Sophia has surely found enough treasures to fill a caravan of carriages.

"I did, my darling, I did indeed. If this is a good moment, I would like to show them to you."

James and Sophia excuse themselves from Lady Stephens's presence. As they walk up the stairs together, Lady Stephens smiles at the sight of the two love birds walking through her home. 'It is wonderful to see young love bless this house again,' she contemplates.

"This is such a fine home, is it not, Sophia?"

"It is indeed, James. It is perfectly lovely. It is the largest estate I have ever visited. It has also made me realize how much I dearly love our home. I would not exchange it for all the tea in England."

James laughs at Sophia's version to describe how much she admires their new home.

Sophia leads James into one of the guest bedrooms, and said, "Look at this leather high trunk and mahogany powder dresser, James. And look at this fleur-de-lis damask room divider. I do so adore these fine furnishings, James. Also, look over by the large fireplace. There is a matching fleur-de-lis wrought iron fireplace screen as well. James, I think they would look exquisite in our new bedroom."

James enjoys Sophia's innocent young girl enthusiasm. He found it disarming toward any ability or discipline he might have to say 'no'. Ever since he met Sophia, he had this strange compulsion to always please her and give her whatever she wanted.

"I agree with you wholeheartedly, my lovely new wife."

James's mind wanders a wee bit, as he thinks of his wife undressing every night behind their new fleur-de-lis room divider. While envisioning this imagery, he finds himself becoming erect as his desire increases. The thought of her wet, moist parts inflame his passion and lustful desires for her. 'Oh, how I would love to see her at ease, taking off her garments each night before I take her to bed and seduce her with my affections.'

"Did you see anything else of interest?" James said, hoping to force his mind toward a different topic.

"I did see this cashmere wool throw. It would make an excellent blanket as I await for you to return home. It would be sure to warm me up until you can," Sophia said, winking at James.

This act of Sophia winking at him has always been deemed cheeky on her part. It certainly was not fitting for her status in society. However, this wink was definitely a seductive act toward James. It hardened him. Between last night and today he was becoming convinced that his love for Sophia was going to exhaust him. Particularly as a man who continually wants to please her erotically.

"I will be happy to negotiate the purchase of the wool blanket as well with Lady Stephens. Particularly if this blanket will be my competition for keeping you warm at night, then I am certainly glad to purchase it for you," James said, laughing. "Shall we journey back downstairs? Unless of course, you would like to show me something else," James adds, as the perpetual devotee to Sophia.

Sophia ponders for a bit. James is alarmed as to what might be the delay in her response. He slowly approaches his wife to take advantage of this pause.

"Are you needing my attention again, my beautiful wife?"

"I am indeed, my lover."

"Would a kiss satisfy you, my lady?" James asks, boldly joining lips with hers, while at the same time sliding his hands up and down her taffeta gown.

James immediately becomes erect for her. Sophia immediately desires a repeat of last night and all the delicious emotions and feelings her body experienced.

James can no longer resist his desires and urges. He boldly takes Sophia's hand and gently places it inside his uniform pants. He whispers into her ear.

"Please enjoy this, my darling. I do enjoy being touched by you. Please stroke and relish in the delight knowing what your body does to me. Sophia, I need you. I desire you."

Sophia slowly strokes his hard shaft, and James gives a quiet moan, aware he is in someone else's home. Without warning, James removes Sophia's hand and lifts her up in his arms. He carries her quietly to the guest bed, laying her down and laying down beside her. His hand now massages her breast. They must be quick and efficient during this particular carnal fling.

"James, we must not! Not here, James!"

"Shh! My darling," James said, placing a single finger onto Sophia's lips. "You are mine and no one shall ever stop me."

Sophia accepts this request and command.

James slides his hands underneath her gown, reaching for her warmth. He slides his two fingers deep inside Sophia. This naughty act, in someone else's bedroom, causes Sophia to arch back, responding to the swift yet direct penetration of James's fingers. James begs her to moisten his fingers more.

In a more startling act, James brings his finger up to his mouth and sips off her delectable goodness. He reinserts his fingers into Sophia. She grinds her hips slowly into her lover's hand as she moistens his fingers more. James unbuttons the flap on his uniform pants and slips himself deep inside his wife.

"Aww, my darling Sophia, you are so tight and moist. It is special to me to be the one who can stretch you with my girth."

Sophia releases a large moan into his ear. She begs for him to take her. James pumps his hips with a constant rhythm, causing a wet suction sound. All of this instantly swells her nether regions.

James releases his fluid deep inside her, thrusting his hips into hers one last time. He slowly pulls out of her, laying his wet, dripping shaft on top of her soft velvety skin. He takes his index finger and rubs the 'pearl' nestled in her vulva.

Sophia is memorized by this rousing action. James knows how to pleasure her.

He looks at her saying, "My lady, do you think we should also purchase this bed, or certainly at a minimum this duvet cover?"

James and Sophia both laugh. There was a bit of nervousness in their laugh, as they were reminded to survey the area, ensuring no evidence of their amorous escapade could be found.

"Shall we go back downstairs to negotiate our purchases with Lady Stephens?" James said, while tidying up the bed, making it look like no one had ever laid on it.

James and Sophia walk back to the sitting room where they find Lady Stephens sitting and sipping her tea. She detects a different look about them when they enter the room, but she cannot identify its source.

"As you might have suspected, Lady Stephens, we found some items of interest to us upstairs. I would like to inquire about their costs."

"Splendid, Colonel. Before we begin that process, please do finish seeing the other rooms on this floor. There are items in my husband's study and in the main dining room I suspect might also be of interest to you and Sophia."

James nods, honoring Lady Stephens's request. As they prepare to venture out and investigate other rooms, Lady Stephens abruptly remarks, "Excuse me, Colonel James. I do believe I may have spoken out of line regarding the horses and my fine carriages being for sale. When you and your wife went upstairs, my butler informed me that the gentleman who came by yesterday showed great interest in them. I am afraid he has just returned while you were upstairs and has agreed to my terms of sale. I am terribly sorry to disappoint you both. The horses and carriages are no longer for sale."

At first James was surprised by Lady Stephens's news. Then he noticed a very slight wink accompanied by a smile on her face.

"I, too, am very sorry," James said, nodding his head and smiling back at her, impressed by her convincing ruse to make Sophia think the horses and carriages are no longer available for purchase.

James and Sophia venture out to view the other rooms. They come upon the master study. James quickly walks over to the wall, inspecting the superb specimens of muskets and swords hanging on the wall behind a cherry wood desk.

"Darling, these items are priceless. I do not think Lady Stephens should sell them, not even to us."

Sophia sits down on the leather desk chair and listens to the zeal in which her husband speaks of the armor on the wall. She also finds herself rubbing her hand in a circular motion over the top of the desk.

"Perhaps it would be welcomed to mention that to Lady Stephens," Sophia counsels. "On a different subject, I suggest you should purchase this desk and chair for yourself. I believe it would look stunning in your new study."

James slides his hand around the edges of the desk, admiring the intricate details and superior craftsmanship once again. Sophia notes the strength of the muscles in his arms. 'I love how he uses those muscles to slide his hands around my body,' she reminisces, surprised by her sudden and constant interest in coition. 'Is this what married life is all about?' she wonders.

"You have splendid tastes indeed, my dear. I agree we shall purchase this item as well," James responds, pleased by his wife's regard for fine workmanship.

"If we are finished here, shall we walk to the main dining room to view what I believe will be the last room for our shopping trip."

"Of course," James agrees.

The couple walks down the long hallway and enter into what could only be described as a sumptuous dining room.

"James, feast your eyes on this curio cabinet. The fine porcelain and crystal inside is also priceless. These teacups and teapots appear to be rare. Oh... and this cobalt blue bulb pattern china. They could be similar to the King's own personal collection. I believe I recognize this design from reading about them in a volume regarding the King's personal family collections. These are such fine silver servers. And James, look at these spectacular vases. If we purchased these, my vases would be finer than the Countess's vases."

Again, James is stimulated by the excitement Sophia expresses over an item she likes and cherishes.

"They are splendid indeed. I shall show a strong interest in them when we negotiate prices with Lady Stephens."

"I'm so grateful to you James, for your kind generosity and your willingness to indulge me in these purchases. So as not to stretch the limits of your generosity and recognizing we have an empty house to fill, I suggest we purchase this dining room table as well. I do find it most agreeable to our home."

"We could certainly use this in our dining room, one of the many rooms in our house that is completely empty at this moment." James smiles as he pulls out one of the heavy wooden dining armchairs, upholstered in emerald velour. He motions for Sophia to be seated.

As Sophia sits down, her interest has peaked by the high quality and comfort of the armchair.

"James, you must sit down on one of these chairs. They are extremely comfortable."

"I feel more great comfort looking at you, Sophia, and your elation for all these furnishings."

Sophia bows her head and blushes.

"Of course, we will purchase the dining room suite as well. Althhough I must say, that for a day that was designed to include a trip to a library, we have managed to put a rather large dent in my wallet. For which, my dear, I am only too happy to do so for you."

"Thank you, my love. You are not only my husband, but a treasure as well."

James escorts Sophia back to the sitting room where Lady Stephens is waiting for them and finishing some of her embroidery.

"Colonel James, did you find anything of interest in my husband's study or my dining room?"

"We did indeed, Lady Stephens. We most certainly did. However, I would like to discuss the items upstairs first, if I may? My wife and I are very interested in the leather trunk, the fleur-de-lis room divider and matching fireplace screen and the powder dresser. We think it is prudent to purchase the guest bed and duvet cover as well, if, of course, it is still for sale."

James chooses not to look at Sophia while making this comment, in fear of giving Lady Stephens an indication of their escapades upstairs.

"I would like to offer fifteen pounds, as what I believe to be a fair price," James's offer is made as not to insult the value of Lady Stephens's belongings.

Lady Stephens accepts the offer without hesitation. Sophia smiles as she speaks directly to Lady Stephens.

"Thank you, your Ladyship."

"You are most welcome, my dears."

"As far as your husband's study," James continues. "I would like to offer you ten pounds for the desk, chair and the stained glass lamp."

He remembers Sophia's sitting at the desk, her eyes admiring the tasseled strings dangling from the lamp as she twisted her fingers through the satin tassel.

"That, too, sounds very agreeable. I shall accept your offer, Colonel," Lady Stephens said, pleased with the number of sales this visit has resulted in. "I must say, Colonel, I am surprised that you have not shown interest in my husband's wall hangings."

"Lady Stephens, I have immense interest in your husband's prize possessions. However, I do not feel it is appropriate for me to make you an offer."

"And why might that be, Colonel James?"

"They hold great value, and I would be fearful my offer might be too low."

"My husband always advised me that nothing would be gained if you did not first attempt to try. On that advice, Colonel, I suggest you make an offer, knowing that at worse, all I can do is decline. I can assure you, I will not be offended."

James politely smiles back to Lady Stephens, appreciating her bold approach to these negotiations.

"Lady Stephens, my fearfulness also comes from the fact that since you have been so gracious to us today, I would be concerned in harming our newly found friendship."

"Colonel James, if I must say so myself, you are a very chivalrous man indeed. My dear late husband would be proud to know a man of your character. With that being said, I am of the impression that you, in fact, would cherish his prize possessions for a lifetime, more than anyone else I know."

"I would, indeed, your Ladyship. Perhaps we can hold off on these items for a moment and discuss some other items that we are interested in. For example, I would like to give you an offer on the dining room table and chairs."

"Did you and your wife see the fine porcelain, silver and crystal displayed in my curio cabinet?"

"Yes, Lady Stephens, we did. We are interested in those items as well. However, we do have some concern on their value, as my wife feels they may be from the King's personal collection."

"What an astute observation, Sophia. You are correct on this matter. My late uncle, on my father's side, was a third cousin to the King, and he willed them to me."

Sophia and James could barely imagine how to respond. They were amazed by Lady Stephens's link to the King of England.

"Please forgive us, Lady Stephens, for showing such fond and in-depth interest in your personal and sentimental items. We apologize if you find our behavior offensive," James said, recognizing that conversation had extended deeper than what was normally customary between people of this level in society, especially for those who had just met.

"Not a bother at all, Colonel James. Many people have shown interest in my husband's possessions and my fine collections as well. I have strongly refused everyone's offer because no one has shown me a character that I would determine worthy of their ownership. I admire people who have a kind heart and an altruistic nature, particularly since these items were most dear to my husband's heart and mine. For these reasons, I want them to go to a lovely home and to someone who will cherish them the way my late husband and I have cherished them over the years. For me, I want them going to a home with owners who have an appreciation for personal belongings, and more particularly, not valuing possessions over people."

"I most assuredly agree, your Ladyship. Most assuredly," James replies, looking Lady Stephens directly in the eye to support his comment.

"On that note, did you both happen to notice the hand-painted mural behind my master bed? My master bedroom is on the first floor."

"No, your Ladyship, we did not. I am sorry. We did not enter your master bedroom. It did not seem appropriate to enter into your private space," James said.

"You may have wondered why my master bedroom is on the main level of my home, certainly not a usual location for such an estate. In the last few years, I have fallen ill with pain in my knees and hips. Old age comes with its own set of challenges. Managing the stairs with my knees and hips has become an ordeal, and I decided to accept this annoyance and create a lavish master bedroom on this level."

Once again, Lady Stephens was quite impressed they did not have the gall to enter her master suite without first asking for her permission. She had very quickly become immensely impressed by the way James handled himself throughout all these financial transactions.

"I must say, I have become quite fond of the two of you. In the short time we have gotten to know each other, it is clear to me you love each other immensely. This is obvious and quite rare. You both remind me of Henry and myself. We, too, had the same deep-seeded love for one another. Our many years together was a lifetime of tremendous amounts of joys, accomplishments and blissful memories, dear to my heart. It is these memories I bring forward with me to grant me the strength to continue on with life."

Sophia begins to weep over the pain she can only imagine Lady Stephens must be feeling. The thought of losing James, even after what would be considered a short period of time together, would be devastating, compared to what Lady Stephens is experiencing.

While continuing to maintain eye contact with Lady Stephens and at the same time trying not to appear rude, James pulls a handkerchief from his pocket for Sophia. He passes the handkerchief to his opposite hand, which is resting on top of Sophia's thigh. James nonchalantly places his handkerchief under Sophia's fingers, resting on her thigh. His actions were an offer of support for her tears. Being dually concerned for the emotions of Lady Stephens over the loss of her husband, as well as Sophia, now tearful, were more emotions than James had felt at one time and in one place. He did his best to manage both of their needs, still unsure how he got into this predicament.

"Please do not cry, my dear," Lady Stephens comforts, looking at Sophia while again impressed at James's compassionate nature. "Henry was an astonishing man indeed." Lady Stephens attempts to compose herself, although her teary voice is evident. She continues to speak. "Please do excuse me for my display of emotions. It appears speaking of Henry and talking about his prize possessions has opened up a Pandora's Box of hidden emotions for me." Regaining her composure, Lady Stephens continues. "If I may, I would like to present you both something. Colonel James, how much will you offer me for the dining room table and chairs?"

"Your Ladyship, I am prepared to offer you thirty pounds, with the hopes this possible low amount does not offend you."

"I shall accept at once," Lady Stephens responds quickly.

James nods and smiles as Lady Stephens rocks gently in her elegant black and gold wooden rocking chair.

"Colonel James and Sophia, I ask for your kind attention. I want to present something to you both. As a grieving widow, I will refuse to take 'no' for an answer."

Intrigued, James and Sophia nod in agreement to Lady Stephens's request.

"On the behalf of my late husband Henry and myself, we are going to give you my prized possessions of all the fine porcelain, silver and crystal in my curio cabinet."

James and Sophia find themselves taking a gasp of air, as their heads jolted back and one hand covered their mouths. Their actions were in unison and caused Lady Stephens to smile at the sight. She could imagine she and her husband doing exactly the same choreographed response to surprising news.

"Oh, my gracious, Lady Stephens. We cannot accept such a precious gift," Sophia said, attempting to gather her words while expressing her shock and appreciation for the generosity.

Lady Stephens abruptly stops Sophia in mid-sentence.

"I insist. Neither of you can refuse my wedding present. Particularly as a newly married couple. I simply will not take 'no' for an answer."

"Your Ladyship, your offer is generous beyond words. I have determined that during our brief time together, you do not seem like a woman who, once she has decided upon something, will take 'no' for an answer. For that reason and knowing your prized possessions will be going to a loving home, we gladly accept your wedding gift with the greatest level of appreciation. You can be assured they will be cherished during our lifetime together."

"Theodore, come here please," Lady Stephens said, calling for her butler.

"Yes, your Ladyship?"

"Please bring us a bottle of our finest champagne. We are going to have a celebration. It is time for there to be some joy in this house again."

Theodore quickly returns with a server tray of glasses and champagne. With his right hand, he pours the champagne, while his bright white gloves protect the crystal he is holding.

"Shall we?" Lady Stephens said holding up her glass. "Let us make a toast to our new friendship and for a wish for many more fond memories to come. Cheers."

Again, quickly changing the subject, Lady Stephens asks, "Sophia, do you like to read?"

"Why, yes, your Ladyship, I am quite fond of reading. In fact, just today my husband surprised me with a new book from the Royal Library entitled, *The Echoing Call of The Sea.*

"Oh," Lady Stephens said, raising her eyebrows. "That is a rare and fine book indeed. Reading enriches the soul and it keeps our mind sharp as a whip. I, too, am a reader, and I am happy to hear you have the love for reading as well."

James stands up from his sitting position on the Knoll sofa and retrieves the wallet from his pocket. He is grateful he carried extra money in his billfold today, knowing that he would be at the library, and one never knows what donations are required at such openings. James totals the amount he owes Lady Stephens, remembering to include the amount for the four horses and two carriages.

Lady Stephens eyes the total amount with keen attention. She notices James added in the extra money for the four horses and both carriages and is pleased.

"My husband would have been very proud to have met such a fine man as yourself, Colonel. I am sorry he is not here to enjoy your company."

"Thank you, your Ladyship."

"The honor is all mine, Colonel. In addition, I have a small favor to ask the two of you."

"But of course, Lady Stephens, I would be more than happy to extend any amount of kindness to you, as a sign of our appreciation for the generosity you have shown us today," James said with the greatest of sincerity.

"I recognize that my request might seem bold; however, as I have learned in my later years, it is always worth asking if you want something. As you already know, I will be traveling back to my homeland and I prefer to leave few possessions and obligations as part of my departure." She pauses, points to the far right in preparation to assign instructions. "Colonel James, please close the French glass doors for me."

"Of course," James replies, intrigued by her request.

Sophia is equally captivated. She is already amazed at what has transpired today. 'What could possibly occur now,' she surmises.

"It has occurred to me and is with great concern that my butler, Theodore, would prefer to stay in England. This decision is due to his strong families ties in this location. I must agree with his desire to remain here, and sadly, I must honor his decision. As his employer, I believe it is my duty to arrange for Theodore to serve in a home that will welcome his outstanding talents. Again, I am aware I am making a bold request; however, I wish to ask if you have any interest in hiring him and acquiring his services?"

"Your Ladyship, as you already know, we are newly married and we have not even given the hiring of a butler a thought," James said, without looking at or speaking to Sophia. He looks only at Lady Stephens. "My wife and I would be honored to accept your suggestion and graciously hire Theodore."

"Splendid news, indeed. You both will never know how much this means to me. I can discuss his wages with you when I depart next month. I shall ensure he is well acquainted with requests often before I even make them. Upon your departure today, I will ask him to join you and your wife in your new home. A home, which after today's purchases will be furnished with items he will be familiar with." Lady Stephens smiles at her own cleverness.

As James and Sophia leave Lady Stephens's home, they are dumbfounded by the events of the day. In their wildest dreams, they could not have presumed they would meet a woman who would help furnish their home, provide them with a priceless wedding gift, coordinate an excellent butler for their hire, and without her knowing, provide a secluded bed for James and Sophia to share a sensual moment.

"This was an excellent first day of marriage, do you not agree, my beloved wife?" James concluded.

Chapter Eleven

"Dinner is ready, little chic-chic," Gramma calls out loudly for me, as I roll over in bed onto my side.

I realize I must have fallen asleep while reading in my room. I step out of bed, stand up tall and stretch, and I walk downstairs to the kitchen.

"There you are, peanut," Gramma said, greeting me with a hug.

"How long did I sleep, Gramma?" I ask, rubbing my hands on my eyes, trying to clear my blurred vision.

"You slept quite a long time. It must have been from all the fresh county air you got today when you were out with Grandpa."

"Yeah, Grandpa and I worked hard today. I'm starving, too. What's for dinner, Gramma?"

"Homemade cheese raviolis with meatballs and homemade sauce with baked garlic bread, tomatoes and cucumbers in a red wine vinegar dressing."

"Mmm, that sounds delicious. I can't wait to eat it. How much longer until dinner?" I ask, finding myself always hungrier after I have been outside all day.

"Dinner will be ready in about ten minutes. Can you go out on the back porch and tell Grandpa to start getting ready to come in."

"I sure will."

I walk out the back door, slamming the screen door behind me.

"Don't slam the screen door," Gramma calls out, but it was too late. The loud sound of screen door hitting the wooden doorframe had already been created.

"How are you, my sleepy chic-chic?"

"I feel great now, especially after my nap, Grandpa. Did you rest too?"

"In a way. I've been sitting out here listening to another ball-game on the radio. Come on over and lets count up all the money you made today."

I carefully watch as Grandpa opens the old cigar box we used while selling our vegetables. First, we sort the money into different denominations. Then we count the total amount. After adding up all the coins, I call out, "We made thirty-three dollars today, Grandpa. That's awesome."

"Yup, all from Mother Nature and from keeping my garden healthy. See, little chic-chic, you can always make money in life. You just need to be real clever about it and use your good' ole common sense."

"What are we going to spend it on, Grandpa?"

"We aren't going to spend it, little one. We are going to save it. However, depending on how the night goes, we might use it to play a fun card game."

"Yeah," I say with great excitement.

"Tomorrow, little chic-chic, we will go by the bank and deposit whatever money there is into your bank account. Saving money is very important in life. By you saving this money, you will be able to buy your own car one day."

"Grandpa, you really are kind to me. Thank you for wanting to give me this money and taking care of me. You are like those husbands I read about who take good care of their wives."

I was clearly thinking about James when I made this comment, although I definitely did not want Grandpa to know that.

"On one hand that is true, little chic-chic. On the other hand it is important to remember that caring in a husband and wife relationship goes both ways. Just as a husband does his best to take care of his wife, it is also a wife's role to help take care of and make her husband happy."

"How do wives make their husbands happy?" I ask innocently, and at the same time wanting to hear what Grandpa has to say, especially after what I've been reading about with James and Sophia.

I suspect I know how Sophia makes James happy, with all that lovey-dovey stuff. Of course, Gramma and Grandpa would never do that sex stuff. That would be too gross.

"Well, little chic-chic," Grandpa said clearing his throat. "Wives have different ways to make their husbands happy."

I am not sure why, but I see Grandpa moving a lot in his chair, like he is uncomfortable about something.

"One way, is by being kind to their husbands. Another way is they can look pretty and the third way...." Grandpa pauses.

"Dinner time," Gramma calls out.

Grandpa must have been happy that the food was ready, because he sure looked relieved.

"What's the third way, Grandpa?"

"Huh?" Grandpa said, forgetting he was in mid-sentence before Gramma called us in for dinner.

"The third way, little chic-chic, is to help the husband have children so that his children can have children and he can go out and sell vegetables and go fishing with them." Grandpa smiles at me, hoping I will understand that the wives help make husbands happy by creating a legacy and eventually bringing them grandchildren to make them happy.

"Let's go in and eat before Gramma gets mad at us," Grandpa said, hoping to move the conversation along.

As we walk into the kitchen, I can smell the combination of different foods cooking.

"Dinner smells good, Gramma."

As we all sit down for dinner, Gramma said, "Okay, now let's all say grace before we eat our dinner."

We all bow our heads and say grace together.

"Gramma, this is the best cheese ravioli I have ever had. They are so darn good. I love your homemade meatballs too."

"Your Gramma is a great cook. It is one of the many things I love about her," Grandpa said, giving a cheeky wink and a smile to my Gramma.

Gramma returns the smile with a bit of an 'I cannot believe you just said that' shake of her head and look at Grandpa.

I can tell how much my grandparents love each other. I could see it in the way they talk and behave toward each other. 'But how did they get this way? I know how James and Sophia met, but how did my grandparents become so much in love?'

"Grandpa, how did you and Gramma first get to know each other?"

"Well, coincidently it was over food, little chic-chic. I worked as a John Deere salesman. Beside my work there was a little ice cream shop. On hot days, after work, I would go next door and buy myself an ice cream cone as a special treat for making a lot of sales that day. One day, during the summer, I walked into the shop and there was a new young lady behind the counter. Oh, Sarah Marie, she was a beautiful lady too."

At that moment I could hear my Gramma quietly giggling as she, too, listened to Grandpa's story.

"I started talking to this good looking ice cream lady. I just couldn't get enough of her. I even found myself going to the store more often, just to get a look at her and talk to her. She wasn't very talkative, so I begin to loosen her up by telling some jokes to get her laughing."

"What kinda jokes, Grandpa?"

"Knock, knock!" Grandpa quickly responds, happy to be the center of attention.

"Who's there?" Gramma and I both asked.

"I scream."

"I scream who?"

"I scream tastes cool on a hot day," Grandpa concludes, as Gramma and I groaned.

"What's another one, Grandpa?"

"Well, have you ever watched the television show, *Sesame Street*?"

"Sure I have; when I was little I did," I answer, wondering how this will relate to Grandpa's joke.

"Well, one day Bert and Ernie were talking on Sesame Street and Bert said, 'Do you want any ice cream, Ernie? Ernie replied, 'Sherbert.'"

Again Gramma and I groaned.

At this point Gramma breaks in to continue with her side of the love story.

"Even then I didn't find Grandpa's jokes that funny, but I did become less shy, and I began looking forward to Grandpa's daily visits at the ice cream shop. I even found myself looking out the window of the ice cream shop to see if his convertible roadster was driving by, or even better, parking in front of the store, which meant he would be coming into the store. Over the summer, we started talking about more things and he began telling fewer jokes. We would talk for hours in the store. Only when there was no one else there.

"Grandpa had become my friend, and our talks were really nice. He would tell me about things that happened at his work, and I would tell him about what happened during my day at high school. At that time, I was only fifteen years old and this was my summer job. Grandpa was twenty-five years old. We knew there was a big age difference between us; however, it did not matter. We really enjoyed each other's company. Then one day Grandpa asked me to go out with him on a date. I knew my parents would not want me to go because Grandpa was a lot older than me, but I did not really care. I just told them I was going out on a date, but I did not tell them who I was going with. Your Grandpa picked me up in his white convertible roadster. It had a leather rumble seat in the back. I use to love seeing this car as Grandpa would drive by. During our first date, I was finally able to ride in that car, instead of just watching it drive by. Grandpa decided it would be romantic for our first date to go on a picnic. We went near the pond where you and your Grandpa sold vegetables today. We had lots of fun that day."

Again, Gramma and Grandpa looked at each other and smiled. They smiled in a way like there was more to this story. Like the two of them shared a secret about that day.

"I had come to really like Grandpa. And don't tell anyone, Sarah Marie, but I was starting to fall in love with him."

I look over at Grandpa. He was bringing his fingertips over to his mouth, blowing on them and then shrugged the area between his shoulder and his neck. I laughed. I am not sure I had ever seen my grandparents act this way before. They seemed more playful than usual.

"After that first date, we went on a second date and then a third. After about one year later, Grandpa did something very romantic."

"What? What?" I asked, now on the edge of my seat, wanting to hear more and not caring that my dinner was getting cold.

"Grandpa walked into the ice cream shop carrying an old half gallon container of Blue Bell ice cream. The minute I saw him, I was really confused. I could not figure out what he was doing. But you know Grandpa, he is always full of crazy surprises and silliness. He walked up to the counter and waited for the person in front of him to complete his order. Then, when it was Grandpa's turn, I looked at him and asked, 'How can I help you sir?' I had to ask him this because he was still a shop customer, and my boss, who was standing in the corner, did not want me to treat people coming into the shop any different from any other person. After I asked Grandpa the question, he raised the container of ice cream toward me. I was very confused now and could not for the life of me figure out what Grandpa was doing. Grandpa instructed me to open the container. Before I did, I looked over at my boss, because I was worried I was going to get in trouble. My boss nodded that it was okay for me to open the container. Everyone in the shop had stopped talking and was now looking over at me. I had suddenly become the center of attention in the shop. I opened the ice cream container and inside was a small, black velvet box. A ring box. I looked at Grandpa in complete shock.

'Open it,' he said. I opened it and inside was a beautiful engagement ring. As I take it out and put it on my finger, Grandpa said to me, 'Irene, will you marry me and make me the happiest man in the world?'"

At that moment Gramma turns to Grandpa at the dinner table and grabs his hand. Looking at him she said, "Of course, I will."

After a short pause she said, "Charles, I hope I have made you the happiest man in the world, after all the years we have been married together."

Grandpa, who was a mushy kind guy and a man who could also be sarcastic replied, "Hon, I am the happiest man in the world, especially when you let me go fishing with Sarah Marie."

Gramma smiles and Grandpa winks at me.

I am having so much fun listening to Gramma and Grandpa's stories and laughing with them. I know I am really lucky to live in such a loving family. Gramma has always told me that in life, love is the most important thing.

'You have to love others and love yourself,' she would always say to me.

Grandpa turns to me and said, "Do you want play cards tonight, little chic-chic. I know it's your favorite."

"Yes. Yes," I quickly reply.

Gramma removes all the dishes from the table and Grandpa slides the heavy coffee can, filled with all the coins from the sale of our vegetables that day, into the center of the table.

"Grandpa, how much do I need to count out for each of us to play?"

"Count out five dollars in nickels and dimes, little chic-chic."

"You bet, Grandpa. What are we playing tonight?"

"Deuces wild, no peak, black jack and queens and what follows. Oh, and five card poker," my Grandpa said.

"Okay, Grandpa."

I count out the change for everyone, thinking how great it is to have the nicest grandparents in the world. I slide my change over to the side as I twist the metal cap off of my little glass bottle of soda. I take a big sip. I am really glad Grandpa lets me have sugary drinks at night. Between the long days with Grandpa selling vegetables and going fishing, even the days working on my Uncle

Johnny's farm, I get tired in the evenings. Now, when I stay up late reading Gramma's book, I find myself really tired during the day.

Grandpa shuffles the deck of cards and Gramma sits down with a large bowl of popcorn for all of us to enjoy. Gramma and I slide ten cents into the center of the table as our ante. Grandpa, the dealer, slides in fifteen cents into the center of the table.

"Little chic-chic, cut the deck," Grandpa said, handing me the deck of cards he has just shuffled.

I cut the deck in half. As we continue to play more and more hands of cards, the time passes and there are lots of screams, laughter and groans from one person's hand beating another person's. I am almost out of money and Grandpa and I are getting tired of playing cards.

"Would it be okay if we stop? I think you wore me out from all the fun I had with you today and yesterday," I say to my grandparents.

"No problem, little chic-chic. I think this is a good time to stop. Besides, it is late and it is bedtime for you," Gramma said, as she nods in agreement.

I am happy Gramma and Grandpa are willing to end this card game, because I really want to get up to the attic, not to sleep, but to read my book some more.

"Okay, Charles. I am going to read and rock in my rocking chair for a little while before I come to bed," Gramma said with an anxious voice.

I can only guess that her voice is anxious because Gramma is as excited as I am to get back to reading about the characters in her book.

"Sounds good, sweetheart," Grandpa said lovingly.

I can tell Grandpa really loves my Gramma a lot. I can also tell Gramma can be kinda cold toward Grandpa when she wants to read 'her' book. I wonder why that is.

I walk upstairs and I open my attic bedroom door. I can smell the old book scent from all the books in the room. I reach under my pillow to get my book. 'I need to find a new hiding spot for it. I wonder where I can hide it.'

I look around the attic room, trying to find the perfect spot. 'I can't put it in the old trunk against the wall, because I'm not strong enough to open it. Plus, my Gramma told me that leather trunk is old and important to her. Her parents brought it over here from Europe when they moved to the United States years ago. I know this trunk is Gramma's pride and joy and I would be smart not to touch it.'

I look over at the wall opposite my bed. I see a bunch of shoe-boxes stacked in the corner. I begin to open up all the shoeboxes. They all have shoes in them except one box on the bottom. This box has a bunch of old photographs in it, along with some old letters. 'I need to see if my book fits inside this green shoe box.' I slid the book inside. 'Yeah, it fits. This will now be the new hiding spot for my book.'

I carefully put back the other shoeboxes along the attic wall so they look like they did when I found them. My plan is to put the green box on top of the other boxes so it will be easy for me to get to it, and hopefully, it will not be discovered by Gramma or Grandpa.

I jump up on my bed with my book in my hand. I pull out the red fringe bookmaker, placed to remember where I was in this book. I begin to realize I have become addicted to this book. 'I am not sure I have done this much reading during a summer vacation ever.'

My eyes zero in to the correct page and I begin to read.

Chapter Twelve

James and Sophia's carriage comes to a halt outside the front entryway of Sophia's father's estate. Sophia quickly removes the engagement wedding ring from her finger and places it into the wristlet purse she carries. She does not want her father, or the Countess, to see the ring on her finger before she and James share the news that they are married. After they make the announcement of their handfasting ceremony, she has decided it is then she will slip the ring nonchalantly onto her finger.

The carriage driver sets the wooden step on the ground to assist in exiting the carriage. James departs first and then helps Sophia step down. There is a sense of nervousness washed over her face, and James tries to calm her tension with a smile and a squeeze of her hand.

Sophia was obviously worried about how she and James were going to share the news that they were now married. Last night the idea to wed seemed brilliant. Today, as they are about to walk into her father's home and announce the news of their marriage and consummation of such marriage, the brilliance of their decision did not seem as apparent.

Thomas, the butler, waits for them at the front door. James escorts Sophia, his new bride, into the grand foyer of her father's home.

"Good day, Mistress Sophia. Colonel James. How was your trip?"

"Very pleasant, Thomas. It was very pleasant indeed," James replies.

Thomas could not understand why James placed great emphasis on the word 'very.' It seems strange, yet it was not his job to question.

"Is the General and the Countess home?"

"Yes, Colonel, they are both home enjoying this fine day. The General is in his study and Countess Elizabeth is reading upstairs in her quarters."

"Thomas, could you please tell General Cartwright I would like to meet with him in private."

"Of course, Colonel James."

Thomas walks away, his back to James and Sophia. James turns to his new wife to steal a kiss.

"Wish me luck, my lady. I suggest you wait in the sitting room for me. Why not sit on your favorite settee, the one where I first laid my eyes upon your beauty. That way, I can picture you there, as I announce to your father our marriage and the reason for our decision to perform the handfasting ceremony. I shall return to you as soon as I have finished sharing the news with your father."

"My darling James, I love you so," Sophia said.

'It seemed strange, returning to this house as a married woman,' Sophia thought. This was no longer her home. She had her own beautiful home, with an incredible husband and a butler and dishes to use—dishes that were once the King's. Her life was better than she would ever have imagined. Certainly it was better than the life of anyone else she knew.

Thomas returns to the foyer after announcing Colonel James's request for a meeting. He escorts James to the study for his meeting with the General, his leader, and his new father-in-law.

"Good afternoon, General Cartwright," James respectfully greets the General.

"Well, good day, Colonel. What can I do for you on this fine day?"

"Sir." James clears his throat, realizing he is actually more nervous than he thought he was. "General, you and Countess Elizabeth are well aware that I have been courting Mistress Sophia for more than a year."

The General, who had been focused on other pertinent matters relating to his work, listened impatiently. He did not have time for lollygagging. He needed the Colonel to get to the point.

"I have become very fond of your daughter as we spend more time together. I can imagine providing well for her and allowing her to live in a manner in which she is accustomed."

"Bloody hell man, get to the point," the General barks, now fed up with this gibber gabber the Colonel was spewing from his mouth.

"Sir, it would be our honor if we could have your blessing and I accept Sophia as my wife."

"Accept Sophia as your wife. Did I hear that correctly Colonel? What exactly does that mean?"

"General." It was with great consideration and forethought that James pauses before continuing. "You must excuse my hasty judgement. My heart has grown very fond for Sophia over our time together this year. I am certain you are aware of my wishes to move beyond courtship into a more permanent relationship."

At this point, James finds himself reverting back to his military role as Colonel—a role of justifying his strategic actions and expanding on the operations to achieve the results.

The General had now fallen silent, as suppositions creep into his mind. 'What on earth could the Colonel possibly be alluding to, other than the fact that he had courted Sophia for the appropriate amount of time and the next logical step would be to arrange for a marriage.'

"I have agreed with your and the Countess's requests to complete my one year of courtship, as would be deemed proper in our circles. I have spent the last five months designing and building a large and distinguished new home for Sophia."

"A new home?" the General, shocked, rumbles sternly.

"Yes, General. A majestic and resplendent new home, one that I built for your daughter and myself to live in, sir."

The General was becoming more agitated by James's lack of willingness to address the issue head on and not get directly to the point. He knew that James was trying to ask for his daughter's hand in marriage. 'Let us hurry past this part of the conversation,' he thought, 'so we can go off and celebrate your engagement with champagne.'

"Is it your intention, during this discussion to express your wishes to engage my daughter and ask for my blessing for her hand in marriage?"

"Sir, I am proud to provide for Sophia with my family's entire estate. The estate pays high dividends. Indeed, over 13,000 pounds a year. I can buy her all the fine carriages and horses she could ever dream of. I can have her live in a home with the greatest of comforts."

"What the devil are you blabbering about, Colonel. Your estate, carriages, new home, accepting her as your wife? Are you asking for my daughter's hand in marriage or not, Colonel?"

"Sir, I will continue to love your daughter with all my heart and soul. Nonetheless, your agreement for our engagement is not required at this time. As of last night, I became wed to your daughter through a handfasting ceremony."

James had fought and won many battles in his life in the military, but, by the look of outrage on the General's face, he was certain this might be marked as one of his greatest crusades.

"You did WHAT?"

The General's voice could be heard throughout the house, despite the fact that the study door was closed. Sophia leaped when she heard her father shout in the distance. The pleasures and desires of the night before now seemed indecorous. Her mind began to wander. 'What would her father do to James? What would her father do to her? Would she ever be allowed to step in this house again? Would her name and reputation be smeared across the town so that she could no longer walk down the street with respect? Would her father discharge James from his army?' Sophia's head was spinning as she sat nervously on her settee waiting for

James to exit from her father's study, hopefully, still alive from sharing the news of her marriage with her father.

James thought it was important to continue to supply the General with information that might comfort him with the surprising news he had just shared.

Determined it was prudent to continue sharing details of their marriage, James continued to supply the General with details about how he could support Sophia. He could only hope this approach would help the General be more comfortable about his decision to wed Sophia last night.

"Recognizing that you have asked me to head out on an important mission, a mission you wish for me to depart in a fortnight, I thought it would be imperative that I vow my love to Sophia formally."

"What exactly does that mean, Colonel?" the General asks, confused, concerned and desperately trying to control his temper along with the desire not to strike James out of anger. "Are you telling me you wed my daughter last night?"

"Yes, sir. Your daughter and I are now wed and I vow to honor, be loyal and provide her my unconditional love as long as we live. What I ask from you General, is not only your blessing of this marriage but your recognition that the decision for us to marry last night was not made frivolously. It was made so I could ensure Sophia will have a good and noble life, deserving of her family lineage and her kind and gracious spirit."

General Cartwright fell silent. He stared at James for what James thought was more than ten minutes with his head shaking, he proceeded to walk over to his bookcase and the serving cart positioned beside it. He reached down and tightly gripped a bottle of fine scotch positioned on the cart. James stood tall. Based on the General's silence and walking to the cart he still did not know what to expect. James stood his ground. He was determined to maintain Sophia's honor and help the General understand what he did was the correct thing.

James takes a deep breath, simply because he had not been breathing very well the entire time the General was walking to the cart. The General pours one glass of scotch... and then another. James feels his shoulders relaxing slightly.

The General hands one of the glasses of scotch to James. Again, James begins to hold his breath. The General raises his glass of scotch into the air and with a smile on his face he spoke.

"Cheers, my new son-in-law. I welcome you to our family. I bless this marriage between you and my daughter. Although I cannot say I am pleased with your approach. I can say, I probably would have done the same thing if I were in your situation. I am proud that Sophia is married to you. I am very confident you will be an exceptional husband for her."

The two crystal glasses filled with scotch join together in a toast. The men hear Countess Elizabeth enter into the master study.

"What is all the commotion occurring in this room?"

Her eyes focus on the smiles on the two men's faces and the empty glasses in their hands.

"A celebration, I see? Your evening must have gone well, Colonel James?"

"It did indeed, Countess," James responds, a bit shocked by the Countess's form of the question. 'Had she overheard the discussion between him and the General?'

"Is Mistress Sophia wearing her new beautiful engagement ring?" the Countess asks.

Now James had become completely baffled. 'How did the Countess know about the marriage and the ring?'

"Why yes, Countess Elizabeth, she has it with her."

He remembered that Sophia took it off and hid the ring before entering the house.

"I proposed to her last night."

"How wonderful, indeed. I suspected as much when I heard you two were off to the Royal Library of Devonshire last night," the Countess said, very proud of her fine detective work. "It can be a large wedding with the finest of decorations and music. I now know why you were both celebrating. An engagement is a great cause for celebration. Come, let us all adjourn to the sitting room and begin to plan out the wedding. Oh, it will be grand. Grand indeed."

Countess Elizabeth continues rambling on about planning for the wedding. James and the General both looked at each other, as brothers in arms. Who would be the one to share the news of James and Sophia's marriage—not engagement—for which they are celebrating?

"Countess, I am afraid there will be no need for a wedding. It is true last night I asked Sophia to marry me. She accepted my pledge of honor and loyalty while we visited the new home I have built for her. Immediately after the engagement, we completed a handfasting ceremony and became wed. I am afraid your Ladyship, we are already married. We are now officially Mr. and Mrs. Langston."

"MARRIED!" the Countess calls out loudly.

That level of shrill, even the General had not heard from her before this evening. Again Sophia hears high-pitched voices coming from her father's study. This time it was the loud voice of the Countess. Sophia's mind continued to be distressed. 'Would she ever be able to look her father and the Countess in the face again? Was she doomed to a life of abandonment from her family?'

"General Cartwright," the Countess said in a very stern voice. "This is certainly not an arrangement we would agree to. Surely, you can do something to undo this. Sophia's reputation is at stake. She must be married in the proper way. Oh, dear God, did the two of you consummate the marriage? Did you take away this perfect young women's innocence?" The Countess asks James personal questions with a look of horror on her face.

"Yes, we did consummate the marriage, Countess," James responds maintaining his composure. "We did because we had officially become married."

A loud scream was heard from the study. This one even louder than the Countess had made prior. 'What is occurring in there?' Sophia imagines. 'Will James be able to leave the room unscathed?'

The Countess feels faint. She is determined to continue to resolve this appalling situation.

"Colonel James, what were you thinking? What are your wishes for Sophia? Did you wish to intentionally discredit her?"

"My intentions and my love for Sophia are good and pure, Countess," James retorts, speaking in a calm and confident voice, in hopes of defusing this situation. "Discrediting Sophia would be the furthest thing from my mind."

"Well then," the General blurts out. "Countess Elizabeth, I ask that you, too, bless this union and extend fond wishes for a happy life for James and my daughter."

The Countess seemed oddly taken aback by the General's firm request. "At your insistence, General, I will."

"I am afraid I know why James was forced into this strategic marital decision. I am aware of James's most recent orders. Ones which I gave him prior to this engagement and handfasting ceremony. It is clear to me why James made this honorable decision and chose this tactical approach for my daughter."

"I do not understand, General. He has violated the wedding protocol expected of us. This is disgraceful and not satisfactory," the Countess rejoinders, bewildered by the General's easy acceptance of this entire situation.

"Countess Elizabeth, there are many matters between my Colonel and myself which you are not be privy to. With regards to this situation, I can tell you, Colonel James is due to leave in a fortnight. I have asked him to lead an important and urgent mission for our military. He is the only soldier qualified to carry out such an assignment for me. Due to the Colonel's utmost loyalty and honesty, he is the only person I can trust to lead this dangerous mission. More notably, this assignment cannot wait."

"My goodness," the Countess said, changing her tone. "This sheds an entirely different light on this situation. We must not tell Sophia of the severity of this mission," the Countess recommends as she begins to weep. "Sophia will be devastated. Her heart would be shredded with fear over James's safe return."

James hands the Countess a new handkerchief. He smiles to himself, aware of the number of handkerchiefs he had needed to distribute to women today. It seemed to be the theme today, and he was pleased with himself that he had brought extra handkerchiefs for all the weeping ladies he encountered. Countess Elizabeth blows her noise quietly and politely into the handkerchief. Before bringing the cloth to her nose, she reads the monogrammed letters AJL, in black, stitched onto the handkerchief.

"It is not our role to tell Sophia at this time. It is the role of her husband," the General announces turning to James. "He will tell her when he is ready. As for now, we must make this the finest day for Sophia. A special day which she deserves. I know, for a fact, she has dreamed of being married her entire life. And today, she is now Mrs. James Langston," the General said proudly.

Once again he fills his and James's glasses with more scotch and raises his glass into the air.

"Cheers."

"Thomas," Countess Elizabeth calls out. "Come into the master study, please."

Sophia became aware that the screaming has subsided and Thomas has been called into the room. 'Could it be that Thomas is being asked to escort James and herself out of this house, never to enter it again?'

"Yes, your Ladyship?"

"Please bring us the finest bottle of our champagne and please arrange for it to be sipped in our sitting room. We are going to celebrate the marriage of James and Sophia."

Thomas was convinced his jaw had just dropped to the floor. His position as butler did not allow him the privilege to ask additional questions about this unfathomable news of Sophia's marriage.

"Of course, Countess, at once."

Before exiting the study, Thomas approaches Colonel James and shakes his hand.

"Congratulation, Colonel James. Sophia is a fortunate lady to have you as her husband."

"Thank you, Thomas. I know how caring and protective you are of the lovely Sophia. I can assure everyone I will do everything in my power to keep her safe and happy."

The General, Countess and James now walk into the sitting room. Sophia is waiting for them, sitting nervously on the settee.

Her worried face looks at them, fearing the worse and expecting to be immediately removed from her family home. She stands as they get closer. Her hands, in the prayer position, rub up and down with trepidation.

"Sophia, you have had a busy past twenty hours," the General pronounces.

Sophia's heart was still not in a place of relaxation. She had no idea if she was about to face the wrath of her father and the Countess, or if they would genuinely be pleased for her happiness. She then turned to James and saw a smile on his face. Once again James had brought comfort into her life, and she knew at that moment that all would be well.

"Oh, my darling Sophia, the day has finally come," Countess Elizabeth rejoices. "Although the General and I were quite surprised by this news, in retrospect, we realize you have married an upstanding and honorable man. Now dear child, please allow me the opportunity to see what I can only assume is your stunning engagement ring."

Luckily, Sophia had already slid the ring back on, now thrilled by her decision to marry James last night without her father's consent. She gracefully lifts her hand to show the Countess her full emerald-cut diamond, set in a 24-carat, rose-gold mounting.

"It is superb, my sweet child. I must say, James has exquisite taste."

"James told me he purchased it in Paris," Sophia said with glee in her voice.

"Clearly, he is always thinking of you, even while he is off on his missions," the Countess said, with some sadness in her heart, knowing James is about to embark on another mission, this time a more dangerous journey.

The Countess cannot bear to imagine the thought of James not returning and Sophia left a widow after being married for only two weeks. The Countess forces a smile and continues.

"We are going to celebrate this memorable day in honor of my beloved Sophia and Colonel James."

James's eyes happen to wander up at the mural on the ceiling. He sees the cherubs playing their musical harps. 'I hope this is a sign that the angels will watch over us as Sophia enjoys our life together,' he prays quietly to himself.

"Is everything okay, my darling James?" Sophia asks seeing him staring up at the ceiling.

"Oh yes, my wife," James said intentionally, hoping everyone will begin becoming used to Sophia's title. "I was just thinking how the angels are already watching over us." James is aware he has altered the truth and does not want Sophia to begin worrying about his departure. Certainly not on this day of celebration. He is the man who must now manage all the concerns regarding the relationship. As the four toast to a long and prosperous life, the Countess breaks in with her need to coordinate.

"General, I insist. I must begin to plan a public wedding ceremony at once. We shall have it in the courtyard and it will be a wedding like none other."

"A wedding?" Sophia asks. "But James and I are already married," she responds with great confusion in her voice.

"Why yes, Sophia, a public ceremony must occur. We cannot allow any rumors to emerge about your handfasting ceremony last night. It simply cannot happen. It could damage your prestigious reputation, along with the reputation of your father. As your Countess, it is my duty to protect your every need, and I intend to do just that."

Looking in the direction of her butler, she continues. "Thomas, please call for Governess Abigale right away and send for all my servants at once. I need to give everyone instructions so we can produce a wedding that will be talked about for years to come. Hurry please!"

No one could say they were surprised by the Countess's response to the situation. She was always the one who wanted to be perceived well in her social circles. A wedding for the General's daughter would be her greatest accomplishment.

As excited as the Countess was to plan this wedding, she was also burdened with the news of the perilous mission James was about to embark upon. Sophia watched the Countess give directions to Thomas. She could also sense some sadness in her eyes. Sophia could only imagine it was because she did not follow proper protocol in announcing her engagement and then allowing an adequate amount of time to a plan a memorable wedding.

With the room full of activity, Sophia gazes across the room and sees James staring out the window. He has a look of concern on his face as well. 'What could he possibly be concerned about? We are married. The marriage has been accepted by the General and the Countess and we will live in a beautiful home together. Once James returns from his mission, we will be able to spend hours together, making passionate love to each other.'

James realizes Sophia might have seen the concerned look on his face. In no way does he want to alert her to the seriousness of the mission he is about to lead. He quickly smiles at her and blows her a kiss. Sophia catches the imaginary kiss flying through the air and brings it to her heart.

After returning back from her meeting with the staff, the Countess enters the sitting room. With complete disregard for anyone talking in the room, she is only focused on her own mission, the mission of planning the perfect, most memorable wedding.

"May I have your attention please? We have a wedding date," the Countess blurts out. "The wedding shall be next Sunday at 3:00 pm, December 13th in the year of our Lord, 1733. This means we will only have two days to plan a wedding."

Looking directly at James and Sophia she continues. "I shall immediately announce your Proclamation of the Banns publicly and announce your forthcoming wedding. We still have a lot to do; however, I am certain this will be a publicized event in all of society's circles. After all, the General's daughter is getting married."

Sophia was struck by the notion that the Countess seemed to have forgotten that she and James were already married. Clearly the production of this wedding was extremely important to the Countess.

As the Countess spoke, James did not listen. Instead, he could not control himself from staring at Sophia's firm breasts as he sipped his scotch. Sophia's shape reminded him of their recent erotic encounters. 'I want her,' he thinks. 'I want to fondle her breasts and nibble her tender pink nipples until they harden and she craves more of my affections.'

James quickly excuses himself in hopes that being absent from the sight of Sophia will help the raised situation in his pants. James's bulge in his military pants has begun to enlarge, for which James had no control. Even the sound of Countess Elizabeth rambling off wedding plans could not reduce the area continuing to grow between his legs. He must leave this room. He cannot look at his beautiful Sophia any longer. 'This is not the home in which to be spotted with a bulging groin,' he thinks.

While exiting the sitting room, the General meets him in the hallway and invites him back into the study. This time, under much better circumstances, James surmises.

"Did I mention we were able to hire a butler, General?" James said, hoping to prove to the General that his daughter's well-being should never be in question.

"How did you find one so soon?" the General asks, rather surprised by this news.

"We had the honor to meet a recently widowed woman named Lady Stephens. We learned she was having an estate sale while we were attending the opening of the Royal Library of Devonshire."

"Her name sounds familiar, but after all these fine scotches, all names sound familiar," the General chuckles. "This is excellent news, my son. Sophia will need support while you are handling the important affairs for our King."

"Indeed, General. It might also be of interest to you, while at this sale I also was able to purchase Sophia a lovely wedding gift, four black Percheron horses and two fine new carriages. Sophia does not know about this present yet. I am having them delivered first thing tomorrow morning to our new home. I was thinking, perhaps we could use them on our wedding day."

The General had always been impressed with James. Upon hearing this news and reading into the discussion of how his daughter would be living in the way to which she is accustomed, he was dumbfounded. James was not only an impressive soldier, he was, in fact, the perfect husband for his daughter.

"Using your horses and carriage for your wedding is an excellent idea," the General said, ready to pour more scotch to dull the pain of the unexpected events of the day.

"After purchasing several rare and unique furnishings from Lady Stephens, she decided to gift us with a wedding present," James adds.

"A wedding gift, from a stranger whom you had just met the very same day?" The General seemed even more confused by the turn of events of this day.

"To me, Lady Stephens presented her husband's prized possessions of trophy muskets and battle swords. To Sophia, she gave all of her fine porcelain and silver, passed down to her by her uncle. What is even more astonishing is that these treasures came from the King's personal collection."

"Good Lord, man. Are you serious? It is unheard of for someone to be so kind and generous. I must repay this woman and thank her for the generosity displayed to you and my daughter."

"Sophia and I tried to offer her funds for the items, but Lady Stephens would not hear of it. What we did arrange, in exchange for her more than generous gifts, was to accept her request to hire her long time butler, Theodore. We will acquire him after she departs from her estate and moves back to her homeland of Scotland."

"You must invite her to our home, Colonel. She sounds like a remarkable woman, and I would like to personally thank her."

"I most certainly will, General. It is also my hope to convince her to relinquish the services of Theodore earlier than our arranged time. In that way, I can depart for my voyage knowing Sophia's needs will be addressed and she will not want for anything."

It was now time for James to leave the General's home. Tonight he would return to his and Sophia's house alone. It was decided in an earlier discussion that it would be not be acceptable to have the two of them be seen alone together for the duration of a night, especially since in the eyes of the public they are not yet married. For this reason, the General declared that it was now time for James to leave, and for him to leave alone.

Sophia was allowed to visit with James at their new home from mid-day till sundown, at which point, Morgan, the carriage man, would return her home to her father's estate. The instructions were clear, strict, well-defined and uncompromising, despite the fact that Sophia challenged her father on these conditions. She was not certain she could last two days without spending the night in James's arms. In the end, after much disquietude, Sophia agreed to accept her father's constraints.

The next day Sophia waited for Morgan, to transport her to James, who was eagerly awaiting her at their home. Sophia paced the sitting room, glancing out the window to see if Morgan had arrived. The waiting seemed an eternity, even though she had spent extra time preparing herself in front of the mirror to look just right for James. Her hands cradled her new book from the Devonshire library. Sophia had been unable to read it up until this point. She had only been able to enjoy its aroma.

The carriage pulled up to the front entrance. Morgan prepared the wooden step for easy access to enter the carriage, and Sophia ran out the door, passing Thomas, the butler, who was coming to announce the arrival of her carriage. She flew passed him, calling out, "Goodbye, Thomas. I will see you later today."

As Sophia hurried out the door to enter the carriage, Thomas could do nothing but smile at the sheer joy exuding from Sophia's entire body.

"Enjoy your day, Sophia. The Countess requests you return home before sundown," Thomas calls out, unsure if Sophia had heard him.

Morgan had always admired Sophia's free spirit. A spirit that was similar to the one her late mother had. Morgan had the opportunity to watch Sophia grow into a young woman over the years of working for her father. He found it refreshing that she still kept her childlike sense of wonder, joy and appreciation for what could have been considered the insignificant things in life by others.

Morgan was a good man and one whom Sophia also admired. He had been like a father to her, especially during the times when her own father was regularly absent on one of his many voyages. Similarly, Morgan had the upmost respect for Sophia and thought of her as if she were his own daughter. For this reason, Sophia knew that whatever her actions were, Morgan would hold them in the greatest of confidence.

The carriage transporting Sophia pulled up to her new home, and she was again impressed by the auspicious look of this house. 'James has made me a very happy woman,' she determined.

Sophia exited the carriage and was greeted by James, who offered his arm and escorted her into their home. He had decided to be very proper with his actions in front of Morgan, in fear news of frivolous or inappropriate public gestures might be referred back to the General and or the Countess.

"Good afternoon Mrs. Langston. Welcome back to your new home," James said with a smile on his face.

James places one hand around her waist and the other behind her knees whisking her up into his arms, spinning her around in their large foyer, like an angel who had just arrived into heaven and was about to have a lifetime of bliss and blessedness.

"I love you, Sophia," James pronounces as he carries her through the house and out to their porch to take in the views of the sea.

James is well aware of Sophia's fondest for the sea. He strategically and gently places Sophia down on the porch swing to overlook the water. The smell of the fresh sea air is calming and refreshing to Sophia.

"Let us sit here and enjoy some afternoon tea," James expresses, looking down at the pot of tea, along with prepared biscuits and nibbles. The arrangements sit perfectly positioned on a silver platter.

"Tea?" James said, looking at Sophia, with the teapot in his hand, ready to pour the first cup.

"Yes, please. And may I note, Mr. Langston, that I am aware you have thought of and prepared everything perfectly. You have made it too easy to love you and want to be with you every minute of the day."

James smiles. He enjoys doting on Sophia, while secretly wanting her to crave his fond attentiveness, in hopes she will be willing to reward him with her intimate affection afterwards.

"James, this view is breathtaking. I am beyond the feelings of love and gratitude for you. At this moment I am feeling marvel. I love you and need you more than I could have ever imagined."

As James looks at Sophia, her face is peaceful and blissful. This makes him feel content as well.

Sophia sips her tea and stares out to the sea with daydreaming eyes. Her mind is comforted being in this home and being with James. She begins to recollect the events of yesterday, realizing just how generous Lady Stephens was to the two of them.

"How can we ever repay Lady Stephens, James? How can I ever thank her enough for all the kindness she displayed to us yesterday?"

Not certain where Sophia's mind had wandered while staring out at the sea, James replies, "I suggest we invite her here for dinner. She can dine in our home and on her dining room table," he remarks, smiling. "Yesterday, your father suggested I extend this invitation to her. If you agree, I will send word right away to Lady Stephens and extend her such an invitation."

James finds himself also captivated by the view and stares out at the sea. His lips are warmed by sipping his tea. He appreciates this moment of bliss because it may soon end. He knows that this afternoon he must tell Sophia the somber news regarding his pending departure on a dangerous mission.

As the couple rock slowly on the porch swing, James gently turns Sophia's face toward his. Sophia could only assume James wants to kiss her the way he did last night. 'Oh, how wonderful her body felt during those times of ecstasy.' She was convinced, if she could, she would lie in bed with James for the rest of her life, making love with him all day long.

"My darling, my dearest Sophia, I must tell you something. Something that will most likely not be pleasant to hear, yet as my wife you must know."

Sophia places her teacup down on the table, observing the concerned look on James's face.

"This matter is of the utmost importance to our country, and for that reason I want you to remain calm and focused on our country's safety. I must share this information with you because it affects you and it affects us."

Sophia now shares the same look of concern on her face as is on James's. 'What possible news could James have to tell her about our country?'

"Your father shared additional news about my mission with me last night," James declares in a controlled voice, holding Sophia hands tightly. "I must leave next week to manage urgent political matters with the King of Portugal. It would seem your father, in his role as General, has determined that I am the only man he trusts to accomplish this task. A task that must be achieved swiftly. What I am telling you, Sophia, is that I must leave you for a short time, as I go off to serve our country."

"Oh James, you mustn't go! You cannot leave me! We have just become married." Sophia pauses. "We are about to have a wedding and become publicly married. I do not want to imagine how I can be here without you at my side. I do not believe my heart will have the capacity to yearn for you for such a long length of time. I will be broken with the pain if you are not here with me. I will not be able to breath without my love near me. Please James, please, ask my father to send someone else," Sophia pleads as she responds to this unsettling news from her lover. She begins to breath faster as her entire body appears as though it is being shocked. Little twitching movements begin all over her body.

"It is my duty to follow your father's direct orders; you must know that, Sophia. This is a matter of my service to our country. You must recognize that I am a Colonel in our King's Royal Army. It is my job and duty to serve our King."

Sophia knew James was correct. Secretly, she wished it was James's job to serve her with endless love in their life together.

In his usual commanding way, James stands, extending his arm for her to follow. Sophia stands up from the swing, sobbing uncontrollably. James picks her up into his arms and carries her upstairs to their bedroom, laying her on their bed. Sophia immediately rolls herself into a ball on the bed and continues crying.

"Don't cry my love. Allow me to wipe all those sad tears away for you."

James walks over to the ceramic water pitcher against the wall and rinses his hands. He reaches for a woven towel and brings it to

Sophia, who has now stretched herself out and is lying on her back. James lovingly hands Sophia the towel.

"Here is something for you to wipe away those tears, my darling. Consider keeping this towel nearby, as you might be needing it for other fluids that will be flowing soon onto this bed." James was clearly talking about having coitus and Sophia knew it. She also knew James was wonderfully talented at cheering her up along with teasing her with his salacious comments.

Sophia lies on the bed, smiling from James's comments, while James, rather quickly, removes his uniform and undergarments. He drops the clothes onto the floor. This act was intentional. At this moment he wanted Sophia to see that his uniform and job did not matter. Instead, his love for her and her happiness was his only concern. James stands naked before his wife, fondling his own groin. Sophia had not seen this from James before and for some strange reason she found herself excited by this action. He was hoping to allure his wife to the possibilities which were about to occur.

"My Sophia, let us get you out of your mantua gown, so I can enjoy my wife's beautiful body, as well."

Sophia, now distracted by these venereal pursuits, stops crying and slowly begins to unbutton the front of her low-neck silk mantua gown. James gently kisses the nape of her neck and begins to see and recognize the red silk corset she is about to completely expose. He recalls this is the corset he bought for Sophia during his trip to Paris last summer. He remembers sneaking to her bedroom in her father's home the day of his return and begging her to try it on. She was mortified he was in her room and frightened by the possibility of being caught by the Countess, her Governess or even Thomas, the butler. James vividly remembers that day well. He was beyond control as he watched Sophia model the red silk corset for him while he sat on the edge of her bed. On that day he fell even more madly in love with Sophia as he set his eyes on her beautiful body in that corset. He was also thrilled that the woman he had fallen madly in love with was willing to take exciting risks. James had never forgotten this unforgettable and exhilarating moment.

Now they were in their own home, although still aware there were restrictions on the times they were able to meet and be together. James wanted to ensure he made good use of this precious time, as he continued to peck at the nape of Sophia's neck.

With his bold, moist lips, he slowly and seductively unties each string of her corset, becoming more stimulated as the garment drew closer to falling off her body.

"I see you have worn my favorite corset, my darling wife. It is unfortunate that you won't have much need for it to stay on you for very long, simply because I have decadent plans for you while it is off."

"Ohh, James." Sophia moans and relaxes, by James's arousing comments and insinuations.

James continues to unfasten each string, exposing Sophia's flawless, soft light almond skin. He celestially kisses down her back. Sophia can feel the swelling in his groin pressing against her buttock's cheeks. Intermittently, James would nudge her with his groin, moving himself from side to side, to seduce Sophia even more. The seducing seemed to be working, as Sophia let out a sound that could only be described as a groaning sigh. She was titillated as she feels the tip of James's penis beginning to moisten and leaving a faint line of fluid across her buttock.

'I want to be in her,' James thinks. 'I want to move her against the bedroom wall and deeply penetrate her. I want to go deeper and deeper inside my wife, until she can moan no more.'

James grabs Sophia's bare bottom with both hands, and kneeling down, he begins to kiss her behind. Sophia's hips begin to rock. She realizes her feelings and desire have taken over her body, and she can no longer use her mind to think. James gently turns around her naked body. He is now facing her frontal beauty as he kisses his way down toward her legs, which he has masterfully spread apart without Sophia even realizing it. He targets the warmth between her legs and with his lips and teeth, nipping at her vulva.

Sophia is astonished at what is occurring and how it stimulates her passion. She had no idea that kissing another person's private area was ever done during a couple's intimate moments. Now that she knows about it, she will be certain to urge James to do it more often.

James does not stop performing these, what can only be described as luscious acts. He continues by inserting his finger inside Sophia to feel Sophia's warm, moist, alluring pathway, one he perceives as heaven. With his other hand behind Sophia, James grabs her bottom again. This time his grip squeezes her bottom even harder. With one hand holding and squeezing her bottom, James moves Sophia's front closer to his mouth and slides his warm tongue between her slit. He then places his finger deeper and deeper inside her. Sophia moans with each gentle touch of his finger. She flushes down onto his moist finger. James savors each divine lick as he tastes her sweetness in his mouth. He looks up at her from his kneeling position.

"Ohh, James, my lover, please don't stop. You have me. I am yours. Please take me. I beg you."

James picks Sophia up in his arms and carries her from the bed to the chaise lounge, where he lays her naked body down. He kneels on the wooden floor beside her and slowly slides his hands up and down her legs. James's hand moves toward the warmth between her legs again. She is filled with desire as he slowly opens up her willing legs. This time he places three fingers deep inside her tight warm vagina.

"Moisten on me, Sophia. Come. I will not stop until I can tell that you have gushed with arousal for me."

James gently moves his three fingers in and out of Sophia, teasing her with one dominate hand. He moves his other hand away from her buttocks and onto one of her nipples. He swiftly squeezes her hard, pink nipple. Sophia arches her back, enraptured by the excitement her body is feeling. James places both of his hands on her breasts, pushing her nipples toward her ribs. He moves his muscular hands in a circular motion and then, without warning, pinches both of Sophia's nipples at the same time. Sophia starts to weep and moan with rapture. James begs for her to release again. Sophia arches her back from the chaise lounge. Her body is kindled with the desire for more passion. James moves away from her breasts and penetrates her vagina even more with his fingers, knowing she is going to peak soon. He lifts her off of the chaise lounge and carries her to their bed. Before laying her down, he removes the ivory barrette holding back her hair. This causes her hair to fall gracefully onto her shoulders. James is stimulated by the sight of her uninhibited look, her naked body and her long flowing hair now lying on the bed. As James straddles Sophia, her legs tremble with desire. James leans forward and begins to suck hard on her right nipple. His teeth graze its tip and then he proceeds to nibble it in his mouth with his teeth. Sophia releases with a gush.

James moves his mouth to her left breast, pecks at it even harder. Again Sophia lets out a spurt of her female come. She had no idea her body was capable of such erotic feelings.

James opens her legs wider and thrusts the head of his bulging tip quickly inside her. His girth expands further from the desire Sophia has created within him. He pulls his penis back out and rubs her clitoris in a circular motion with the head of his penis. Sophia moans uncontrollably.

When James thinks Sophia is ready, he thrusts his throbbing penis deep inside her again, moving it in and out rhythmically. She is his and unable to resist his desires.

Sophia moves her hands toward his body. James stops her, holding her two hands firmly over her head. He does not release his grip. He watches her naked body squirm and wiggle slowly. Sophia becomes surprised by this stimulant, this philter of James holding her hands down and restraining her. Again James thrusts into her. Nothing will stop him. Not even Sophia. He, too, has lost control and wants only to explode with pleasure inside her. Sophia lets out another loud moan, as James takes her even deeper. Her new tightness stretches by his girth as he continues to moisten her even more.

"My darling wife, I can feel inside you," James utters on the edge of orgasm, moving his hips harder and harder into hers.

"Please, James. Please stay inside me," Sophia's voice calls out, begging for more.

James finally has heard the words he desired to hear.

"Come, Sophia. Come for me as your lover," James commands in a direct tone.

James generates a loud moan, as his animalistic urges surrender him to his biological needs.

He bucks his hips and finishes inside her, releasing Sophia's hands from behind her head. At the same time, Sophia gushes onto his shaft, both reveling in satisfaction.

James rolls over to rest beside Sophia. As he does, he looks over and sees tears rolling down her face.

"Please do not weep, my beautiful wife. This experience was meant to bring us both pleasure and joy."

"I am not weeping with sadness, my love. I am weeping because of the sheer bliss I am feeling. Words cannot describe the deep passion, love and desire I have for thee."

"As your husband, the truth bares out to me as I make love to you, dear one. Truth be told, I have wanted you for a long time. You are the most beautiful creature I have ever laid my eyes upon, and now you are mine."

"Oh, James. I love you so. You make me feel things I have never felt before or could have even imagined myself feeling."

James holds Sophia tightly in his arms, dispirited, knowing that she must leave soon and return back to her father's home for the evening. She will leave him alone in their new home. 'This home will be empty without her,' he broods.

Due to the short amount of time before his departure, James has decided to work only part of the day at his post, leaving the afternoons for making love with Sophia. At least he can be comforted knowing he has this precious time with her.

Meanwhile, Morgan, the carriage driver, continues to wait outside in the driveway, tending to the carriage. During the last hour and a half he could hear the screams of intimacy from the open window above him. He could only smile, knowing his job as a driver included maintaining confidence regarding the actions of all family members. Although he wished he could share with others what he had heard and assumed was the perfect intimate experience, he had to remain silent. He did, however, have a new respect for the 'attribute' of Colonel James Langston.

The next day, the sun rises on James and Sophia's new home. James dreams about how prefect it will be once Sophia is filling their home with her wondrous presence.

Today, he anticipates the arrival of Sophia's wedding present from the estate of Lady Stephens. He busily prepares himself for the long day ahead.

The scheduled time has arrived once again. Morgan drives the carriage up to their home and James hurries outside to greet his lovely wife.

"Good morning, my lady," he said with a grin, immediately thinking about the pleasures of yesterday and hoping for more today. He kisses Sophia on her right cheek.

"Good morning, Morgan. Thank you for ensuring my lovely wife arrived safely to our home."

Morgan gives an acknowledging nod. James escorts Sophia to the porch so they can both look out and enjoy the view of the sea once again.

"Sweetheart," James said lovingly. "I need to give some instructions to William this morning. I must leave you here for a brief moment and go to our carriage house. I realized I neglected to inform William which saddles and bridles need polishing and shinning."

"William?" Sophia asked, confused by whom James was referring to. "Who is this gentleman you speak of?"

"I hired him last week as our stable man and grounds keeper. He will be assisting us both with all of our needs."

"I must say, James, I am entirely impressed with all the coordination and arrangements you have made, not only for the ease of running our home, but in making my life happier," Sophia said, leaning over and kissing James, almost as if she is rewarding him for his good work.

James was pleased by her response and motivated to do more.

"While you go and talk with William, I think I shall take a stroll down by the sea."

"Excellent proposition. And you can be assured you can have no fear, knowing I will be missing my beautiful wife while she is gone," James responds in a teasing way.

Sophia proceeds down the long wooden steps of the house, out to the grounds and onto the shoreline. As she walks along the beach area, her shoes leave heel prints in the fresh sand. This is a private area and it is clear that no one has walked this shoreline for many years.

'This is the most magnificent view I could have ever asked God for,' Sophia reflects. 'It is as though the sea is speaking directly to my heart and soul.'

Sophia pauses for a moment, listening to the waves and enjoying the experience of the salty air spraying onto her face. She becomes mesmerized by the sound of the sea as the waves crash against the shoreline. Walking along the shoreline, with the warmth of the sun shining on her face, she accepts the gift of being completely at peace. Wanting to capture this moment forever, she decides to search for a shell, one that she can bring back and place in the reading nook located in her bedroom. 'In that way, when I hold it while reading, I can be brought back to this moment in time,' she daydreams.

After what seems like an extensive long time of searching, Sophia glances down and finds a beautiful pink iridescent pearl-colored shell. She decides it will be the perfect shell to create a tangible memento and lifts it up from the sand and holds it to her ear. Instantly, she can hear the echo of the sea coming from the shell. 'Oh, the wonders of this world,' she thinks.

After Sophia had left the porch, James gathered the tea tray and returned it to their kitchen. He smiled to himself, realizing at his status in the world, he was performing the duties of a butler. "I look forward to our new butler, Thomas, being in our service. I am certain I make a better Colonel than a butler," he chuckles as he said these words out loud in the empty kitchen.

James then proceeds to walk to the carriage house to greet William, his new stable man.

"Good morning, Colonel."

"And to you, William," James returns the greetings with a nod. "I am here to alert you that today we will have four black horses and two fine new carriages arriving as a surprise wedding gift. They will be arriving shortly. I ask that you manage their arrival discreetly so Mistress Sophia does not see or become aware of them."

James intentionally chooses to identify Sophia as Mistress, respecting the Countess's request that the first public announcement of the couple being united will be after the wedding.

"I recognize you have just been here a day, yet I would still like to ensure the guest house is satisfactory for your living arrangements?"

"It is indeed, sir. It has every comfort I could have hoped for. I am very grateful to you and your soon-to-be-wife for such accommodations. She is a lovely lady indeed from the brief imagine I saw of her walking along the shoreline."

James smiles, thinking, 'Oh William, if you only knew about this "lovely lady." What you believe is my soon-to-be-wife, and what we have been doing in our bedroom, might surprise you. Do not assume her ladylike innocence so quickly, sir. I have had the pleasure of learning my wife is a wonderful erotic creature.' James continues to smile, as his mind wanders, and his drifting look does not go unnoticed by William.

As if typical of any hired staff, William maintained his role of preserving the confidentiality of his employer. It would not be his place to search for any additional information on what he suspected was only a piece of the story being shared by James about Sophia, his soon-to-be-wife.

"You can be confident that all will be managed well, Colonel James."

"Thank you, William. I need a strong lad like yourself keeping a close eye on all my prized possessions. I am intentionally counting on you to bring me peace of mind while I am away on my military assignment. I am choosing to pay you handsomely, William, so that you will guard my possessions with your life."

"You have my word, Colonel," William responds with a dutiful voice.

William's loyalty is partially due to his personal character, but more recently it is due to his gratitude. William had become eternally loyal to James ever since his personal time of need when Colonel James had rescued him. It was a time when no one would hire him for a job. It was the Colonel who stepped up and provided him employment.

Six months prior, William had moved to England from Prussia. He arrived hoping to escape the sorrow experienced in his homeland. It was exactly six months to this day that William had stood at the English port, and William remembered again the loss of his wife and unborn bairn in a tragic carriage accident. The loss of his family left him an empty man, with no purpose in life. Running away from his meaningless life in Prussia seemed like the only logical thing to do. William believed starting a new life in a new country would help him forget his sorrows, and with any luck, reduce his anguish. With this goal in mind, he had gathered up an ink drawing of his wife, a few items of clothing and a wooden cross he had made for his wife as a wedding present and packed it all into his shoulder bag. He had booked passage on a small cargo ship bound for England, hoping for release and escape from his misery.

His dreams were not achieved as easily as he had hoped. As his vessel landed in the midst of a dreary day, not uncommon for England, William stepped onto British soil for the first time in his life. It was then he was struck by the realization that he knew no one and had nowhere to go. He immediately set out in search for employment. Unfortunately, no one would hire him due to his lack of ability to speak perfect English. His ability to convince people that he was a capable man did not seem to be possible. As the weeks turned into months, his standards for the type of employment he searched for lowered, along with his spirits.

While living in Prussia, William was a serf. He considered himself fortunate that his sovereign lord allowed him to marry. He farmed the land and worked hard for it to become profitable. Then, the accident happened, and on that night he lost everything. Nothing was of importance or of value anymore.

After six months searching for employment in England he attempted to become a tosher—a sewer hunter. He had learned that these men, in their velveteen coats, old shoes and a bag on their back, would wander the sewers of London for miles collecting scraps washed down from the streets. It was not uncommon to find bones, bits of metal, cutlery and coins during a day's work. It was a filthy job; even finding dog feces was valuable, since it could be sold to tanners and used to cure leather. Even in this level of employment and pleading for work he could not be accepted for a job.

It was on a warm day in the summer William wandered the countryside, continuing to look for work and for food. To his astonishment, he came upon what appeared to be a military post. In the distance he could hear the sound of many horses. The sound of their hooves was like thunder on the horizon and music to his ears, as he loved working with these majestic creatures. Out of curiosity, William began walking in the direction of the noise, deciding to inspect what was occurring and perhaps take a closer glimpse at the horses. As William approached, he could see the horses were being worked by men of the British Army, who were practicing their maneuvers. Amidst all the activity one man stood out. His smile was disarming. He was a Colonel, William could tell from his uniform. As William stood still, in awe of the scene before him, the Colonel walked up to what he described later as a 'crestfallen man' and shook his hand. William immediately stood up and firmly shook the Colonel's hand. It was as if life had been breathed into him again.

With the English William had acquired from living with his British wife, the two men had a brief conversation about why William had come to England and about his work experience. Much of the conversation was through acting out the words, yet the information appeared to be interrupted correctly.

The man introduced himself as Colonel James Langston.

James saw in William a loyal man, a man of conviction; through their conversation, he could tell he took pride in his work. He also seemed to have a natural physique for work with horses and in the fields. William's tall stature and wide build made him appear as sturdy as an ox. In fact, this is what drew James to say hello to him as he saw him standing alone on the edge of the post. As large as William was, James could tell there was a gentle giant inside this hardened exterior of a man.

As conversation continued, a runaway horse came galloping toward the two men. The horse had broken lose from one of the soldiers. Colonel James had his back to the charging horse and was not aware of the imminent danger he was in. William lashed out at the horse, and with his giant hand he was able to grab hold of the horse's leather reins within seconds before the horse would have impacted the Colonel. After recovering from the shock of what had just transpired, it was immediately evident to James that William had risked his own life to save this Colonel he had just met. William's valor instincts and abilities impressed James immensely.

Having just had the conversation about how William was looking for employment, James decided to offer William the position of his personal stableman and groundskeeper right there on the edge of the military post. William was shocked and humbled by the offer. His current reduced level of confidence made him unsure if he should accept the offer of this prestigious position. James pushed, reminding William he required a strong and loyal man and that he would be perfect for the position. After much discussion and more hand signals to help with the communication, William accepted the offer of employment and began working the next week.

Today in the carriage house on Colonel Langston's estate, William still looks back at that time as one of divine intervention. Perhaps there might have also been a little help from his deceased wife, who he believed was now an angel in heaven.

After speaking with William about the arrival of the horses and carriages today, James returned back to the porch. Surprisingly, Sophia was not on the porch. He immediately called for her throughout the house. No response. He called out for her amongst the grounds. No response. Running down to the beach, James spies Sophia in the distance. Relieved, he runs toward her, annoyed that his military boots were slowing him down.

"Sophia! Sophia!" James calls out, not wanting to waste any time to be at his wife's side before he departs for his long mission.

Sophia looks up and sees James running toward her. She smiles at the sight of the powerful Colonel running like a child who had just lost and now found his mother.

"My love, at last, I found you. I thought you had gotten lost."

Sophia smiled again thinking, 'Oh my, James is more concerned about my whereabouts than my own father.'

James wraps his arms tightly around Sophia and kisses her fondly on her lips. The kiss grows to become more passionate. Sophia is both stimulated by James's kiss and by the sound of the waves crashing beside the two of them.

Picking Sophia high up into the air, James swings her around with jubilation. Her feet dangle below her, as they both laugh out loud. He places her feet back down on the beach, then with his hands scooping under her legs, James picks Sophia up and cradles her in his arms.

"I love you more than you can imagine, Sophia. I shall always love you. I give you my heart and my soul, my dear and precious wife. We are two hearts, one soul."

As James said these words, he realizes that his mind has become, once again, heavy with the thought of his expected and extended departure.

"Shall we head back to our house? There are a few things I want to talk with you about before my departure as you prepare to run our estate."

At that moment it suddenly occurred to Sophia, as James's wife, that this would be a required role dictated by her wealth and status in society. Unfortunately, Sophia knew nothing of running a household, except from what she had learned from observing the Countess.

"Oh, my, James, I had not thought about my role in performing these duties."

"I am certain you will be just fine, my darling, my new and precious wife. I have coordinated, in advance, as much as possible, to make your task easier."

"James, again I must say how grateful I am for all you do for me. Now, most importantly, I require you come home safely from this mission, one which my father has you going on. I love you so much James and I need you more than you can imagine, so please come home safe."

James could indeed imagine; simply, he knew he equally need-ed Sophia. She had infused endless levels of joy within him. He could not imagine life without her.

As the two walked hand and hand toward the house, William approached to greet the couple beside their home. Greeting them, William first nods to James and then to Sophia.

"Hello, sir. My lady."

"Mistress Sophia," James said looking at Sophia. "This is Wil-liam our stableman and groundskeeper."

"It is an honor to meet you, my lady," William responds with a gentlemanly bow.

"And to you as well, William. Thank you for your service."

William, who was tending the grounds, waiting for Colonel James's wedding gift of horses and carriages to arrive, was imme-diately struck by Sophia's beauty. He was also impressed by her graciousness and caring spirit. 'She reminds me of my late wife,' he surmised. A memory he thought he had conveniently placed away in his heart. Seeing Sophia before him, he was once again reminded of how much he missed his late wife and unborn child.

"Sir." William turns to address James. "You have guests."

"Thank you, William," James responds with a knowing nod.

"And sir," William said, about to share additional news which he imagines James is not expecting. "There is a lady asking for you, sir. She has chosen to remain in her carriage as she awaits your presence."

"Thank you, William," James responds in a tone indicating that he is indeed confused by who this mystery lady might be. It was certainly no one he was expecting.

Strolling toward the carriage parked in the driveway, James sees Theodore, Lady Stephens's butler, stepping out.

"Good afternoon, sir. My lady," Theodore said, looking directly at James and bowing to Sophia.

Sophia responds with a nod, surprised and confused as to why Theodore is at their home. The black carriage door swings open and Theodore assists Lady Stephens down from the carriage step. James bows and Sophia courtesies, both with shocked and sur-prised looks on their faces.

"Good morning, Lady Stephens, what a very pleasant surprise. It is an honor to see you and to have you here at our home," James said, still confused by Lady Stephens's presence.

"Good morning, Colonel James, Sophia. By the look on your face, Sophia, I can see your husband still has not told you of your surprise."

"Why, no Lady Stephens, he has not," Sophia said, looking at James and wondering what on earth is going on.

"Well, I decided, my dear, to get out of my house for a bit and enjoy a journey to your home on this very fine day," Lady Stephens said in a much jollier voice than they had heard her use when they first meet her at the estate sale.

"Welcome to our home," James said again. "My darling, Lady Stephens is here to deliver your wedding present. While at Lady Stephens's estate sale, I purchased the four fine horses and two carriages she had for sale."

"Ohh, James you did not, you must not. I can only imagine they are exquisite and quite expensive, and I simply do not think we are worthy of such an extraordinary caliber of horses and carriages."

"Nothing is too fine or too great for you, my dear," James replies in a loving and caring manner.

In hopes of changing the topic of money and worthiness, James asks, "Lady Stephens, would you like to join us for a cup of tea after your journey?"

"That sounds marvelous, indeed. I would very much like to visit and see your new home."

"I suggest we sit on the porch for our tea, in that way we can take in the sea views, Lady Stephens."

"Brilliant suggestion, Colonel, I do enjoy lovely sea views," Lady Stephens replies in an almost giddy tone.

Once on the porch Sophia announces, "Lady Stephens, I have exciting news. We have set our wedding date."

"A wedding date? Excuse my old mind for sounding daft, but I thought you spoke of already being married?"

Recognizing how easily the situation could appear confusing, James steps in to clarify the circumstances.

"Yes, Lady Stephens, you were correct in what you heard; we are married. My wife and I handfasted the night before we met you. Sophia's father accepted my intentions and actions yesterday, along with Countess Elizabeth, who also lives with Sophia. Although we are legally married, with all the rights and privileges that bestows, Sophia's father, General Cartwright, and Countess Elizabeth requested that we hold a public ceremony and adhere more to the social norms of two people joining together forever."

"Our wedding is set for tomorrow at three pm," Sophia broke in, wanting to change the subject away from the acceptance of a handfasting ceremony and the need of having the public think well of her.

"Lady Stephens, we would be honored if you would be a guest at our wedding," James requests.

"Oh my, now I am the one humbled by a sense of worthiness. Thank you, James, for your very kind invitation. But I must not be in the way of your special day. I would not want to impose on the two of you."

"Oh nonsense, Lady Stephens. For all you have done for us and all your generosity, it would only seem right for you to be in attendance at our wedding. In fact, Sophia and I would be delighted if you would stay at our home until the wedding tomorrow. That way, you will not have to make the long journey home today. Our home is certainly not as elegant as yours, but we will do our best to make you feel comfortable and treated as a dignitary."

"Good gracious, Colonel, you are quite the protagonist," she said in a wry manner. "How could anyone turn down such a gracious offer? I accept your request and would certainly be delighted to witness your public marriage. In addition, and with no intention of being brash, I noticed as we walked through the house, it is a bit sparse in respect to furnishings."

"You are not perceived as brash at all, Lady Stephens. You are correct; our furnishings are sparse. That is why we were so grateful to attend your estate sale. We needed to purchase furniture, and I believe your furnishings will look quite lovely in our new home," Sophia said proudly and with a sense of gratitude.

"I am comforted to know they will have a good and loving home in which to reside," Lady Stephens responds with a smile of contentment.

Lady Stephens settles into her cane chair as the midday sun shines down on her. She begins to rock back and forth on the wood plank floor of the porch and thinks about how enjoyable it has been to have met such a lovely young couple. It reminded her of how she and Henry used to be when they were first in love.

Theodore, instantly assuming his duties as a butler, steps out onto the porch and serves each of them their afternoon steeped tea.

"I hope it is not a bother," comments Lady Stephens. "I asked Theodore to begin his role as your butler and bring in all your wedding presents from the carriage. I also requested he start to tidy up your home with your new furnishings."

"Oh my word, Lady Stephens, that is a lovely request," Sophia responds with immense kindness and appreciation.

"I would also like to share a wee bit of bad news with you both," Lady Stephens announces. "I am afraid I will need to leave a tad bit earlier than I had originally planned. This means Theodore will need to assume his duties for you sooner than we had expected. It is my hope this change will work well for both of you?"

"It most certainly will, your Ladyship. We would not only be delighted to have Theodore come work for us earlier than planned, we would also be honored to have him as an employee," James quickly responds.

Secretly, the news comforted James. He now knew Sophia, his new wife, would be cared for while he was away on his mission.

"Why the sudden early departure, your Ladyship?" Sophia asks boldly. She was aware that requesting personal information from an older woman could be perceived as rude.

"The family who has purchased my home has informed me they will be arriving sooner than they had expected. They have requested an earlier occupancy of my home. I said I would be willing to accommodate their request and depart sooner."

"Lady Stephens, may I suggest another alternative. I have recently learned that James must depart on an important military mission next week. Since Theodore would be coming to work here as our butler, why not you come live here as our guest. In that way, you will not feel rushed to move back to your homeland."

"What an intriguing offer, Sophia. Allow me to ponder it throughout the day, if you would."

"Most certainly," Sophia answers politely.

"On a different note, I must say this view of the sea is breathtaking and your new home is remarkable. Colonel James, you are to be commended on your stupendous efforts."

"Why thank you, Lady Stephens. I searched this area for a long time until I found this particular view. Once I laid my eyes upon it, there was no doubt I must instantly purchase the land. Once I began to build on the property, my only hope was for Sophia to also feel the same way about this property and this view as I did. As luck would have it, she was thrilled by my selection."

James looks lovingly over at Sophia, as if to convey the thought. 'I did this all for you, my love.'

"Your arrival today is very timely, Lady Stephens. As Sophia has already mentioned, I was informed by General Cartwright, I must depart next week on an important mission. I need to handle some political matter with the King of Portugal. As you might imagine, my wife's safety and well-being is of the utmost importance to me. Your desire for us to engage Theodore's services earlier than expected will work out very well for us indeed."

Lady Stephens detected the concern in James's voice as he spoke about his mission, as did Sophia. Both the ladies chose not to comment on his obvious tension.

"I am glad these new arrangements will work out well for all of us, Colonel James."

"Lady Stephens," Sophia interjects. "Since you will be staying with us this evening, I invite you to please join us for supper at my father's home."

"That sounds splendid, my dear. It will be a delight to meet the father of such a lovely young lady. If, of course, it is not a bother."

"Theodore," Lady Stephens calls out. "My evening plans have changed, and I will be attending dinner this evening at Sophia's father's home. Would you please follow my instructions we discussed in the carriage while traveling here?"

"At once, your Ladyship," Theodore responds.

James and Sophia look oddly at one another. They wondered what those instructions might be. They chose not to ask, and instead were simply left to conjecture the numerous possibilities swirling around in their heads.

During the short thirty-minute carriage ride to the General's house, the three of them talked about Lady Stephens's early years of being married to Henry. Theodore stayed back at the house to follow Lady Stephens's instructions. Lady Stephens regaled the young couple with tales of meeting Henry, purchasing their first home and acquiring pieces of furniture throughout their lifetime together. James and Sophia listened intently. They were sorry when the carriage arrived at the General's home, as they were enthralled by the stories they were hearing.

Once at the General's house, the three gathered in the sitting room. The General entered the room and James and Sophia immediately stood to greet him. Lady Stephens remained sitting.

"Good evening, Father; I would like to introduce you to Lady Stephens. She came by our home today to deliver another wedding present from James, impeccable carriages and four Percheron horses."

"Yes, Sophia, I am aware. James informed me of this gift yesterday."

"It is a pleasure to meet you, Lady Stephens," the General said, with a huge smile. He was struck by the beauty of this older woman.

Upon hearing the General's greeting, Lady Stephens stands and curtseys to the General.

"I will assume you are here to accept my invitation and join us for supper, Lady Stephens. We are delighted you are able to share a meal with us. I would also like to extend my gratitude for your kindness and generosity you bestowed upon both Sophia and James. When I heard about all the lavish home furnishing and gifts they acquired from your estate sale, I must say, I was taken aback. Thank you for what you have done for them."

"General, let it be known that I am not someone to be trifled with. Yet, I could tell from the moment I met both Sophia and James, their hearts and intentions were pure. That is why I was, in your words, kind and generous. I was more than happy for my belongings to be passed on to them. They personified the true meaning of love. In addition, they remind me of my late husband Henry and myself."

Everyone in the room could see Lady Stephens becoming saddened as she spoke about her late husband.

"I am very sorry for your loss, Lady Stephens. Please accept my sympathy," the General answers with sincerity.

During the conversation, Lady Stephens was equally surprised to learn the General was not married. For some reason she had assumed he was. 'Perhaps this evening will be more enjoyable than I expected,' she thinks.

Thomas, the butler, walks quietly around the room with his silver serving tray of champagne, and Lady Stephens gladly accepts his offer—particularly after learning the General was widowed like herself.

While laughing and gaiety ensued in the sitting room, Countess Elizabeth and Governess Abigale join the rest of the group. Introductions are made and all the ladies gather together and begin to discuss the plans for tomorrow's wedding.

James looks at the ladies and then turns to Thomas. His mouth forms one word. 'Scotch.' Thomas instantly understands and brings him a glass of scotch along with refilling the General's glass.

"I suspect the discussion about wedding plans might require us to have a scotch in our hands," James said to the General, who wholeheartedly agrees.

"Are you nervous about your wedding tomorrow, my son?"

"No sir, my concern is more about leaving your daughter for an extended period of time."

"I can certainly recognize how that would be concerning for you."

"I know Sophia's heart is breaking, knowing I must leave her soon after tomorrow. She is also aware that she will be left to manage the important affairs of our home. These are valid concerns, as she is not well prepared for these duties. For that reason I am concerned for my departure and for my wife."

"I, too, have been in your place, son, when my wife, Sophia's mother, was alive. Your heart is torn, as you love my daughter and you also have the duty to serve your country."

"You are correct, General. At least I can gain some level of solace knowing Sophia has come from a military family and has experience with these types of departures. As a husband in the military, it pains me to witness the anguish and torment she experiences."

"Perhaps, my son, it will bring you comfort knowing Sophia will be in good hands during your departure. We will ensure she is taken care of."

"Thank you, sir. That thought does provide an great amount of consolation."

Upon saying these words, James lowers his head. His eyes become moist. A tear escapes from his eye. The General notices James's pain and decides to end the topic. James quickly regains his composure and hopes that no one in the room has noticed his, however brief, emotional moment.

The General notices Thomas entering the room and is relieved by the distraction.

"Ahh, it looks as though our supper is ready for us," the General comments.

"Tonight, supper will be served in the main dining room," Thomas announces to the guests.

James approaches Sophia and wraps her arms under his. He proudly walks her down the long corridor and into the dining room. Sophia pauses before sitting on the chair James has just pulled out for her.

"I love you, James," she whispers in James's ear.

"I love you even more," James whispers back with a smile.

The General insists Lady Stephens sit at the head of the table. This spot had been left vacant ever since the day Sophia's mother passed away.

"I believe it is only right that Lady Stephens assumes this seat at our table. After all, she has managed her large estate and she certainly qualifies as the lady of a house. Please, Lady Stephens, honor us by sitting at the opposite end of the table to myself."

Suffice to say, everyone else at the table was shocked by the General's request for Lady Stephens to sit in Sophia's late mother's assigned place, including Thomas the butler. At the same time, no one in the room dared to comment or challenge the General's wishes.

The events of the evening were most enjoyable, with everyone telling anecdotes and exchanging stories of similar experiences. The wine flowed freely and everyone ate until their stomachs were full.

As the end of the evening approached, comments began about leaving, and Sophia mentioned she was excited about riding back to the house with James and Lady Stephens.

"My dear," Countess Elizabeth said sternly. "Must I remind you that you are not allowed to sleep overnight in that house until you are publicly married and all of society can see that you are wed."

"Countess," Lady Stephens interjects, feeling compassion for Sophia and also recognizing that Sophia and James were in fact already married. "If I am staying the night in their house, would it not be publicly acceptable that I assume the role as chaperone. In that way, all would be well and the two will have the opportunity to spend time together before James leaves on his mission."

This recommendation places a huge smile on Sophia's face. It put erotic fantasies into James's head. And it places a grimace on the Countess's face. She knew Lady Stephens's suggestion was a good one, but was still annoyed by Lady Stephens being offered a seat at the head of the supper table in her, or rather her employer's home. She was not inclined to agree with Lady Stephens, simply out of spite.

"That is a splendid idea," the General said, knowing James and Sophia could benefit from having extra time together.

It was settled; James and Sophia and Lady Stephens would all travel back to the newlywed's—yet not publicly wedded—house for the night.

The ride to James and Sophia's house was a quiet one. Everyone was content due to food and alcohol they had partaken at the General's house. Each of their minds drifted off with very different thoughts.

As the black carriage stopped in front of James and Sophia's home, Theodore and James assist the ladies down from the carriage. They all walk toward the newly built house.

"Before retiring, shall we have some tea and fresh sweet cakes? I have heard they are your favorite, Lady Stephens," Sophia said with a smile, pleased by her knowledge.

"Theodore must have released my secret. I do indeed have a weak spot for my sweets," Lady Stephens replies, with a slight chuckle. "Tea and sweets would be a perfect end to this evening. Thank you. I would certainly enjoy such a treat at the end of what has been a most enjoyable day."

"Let us sit on the back porch and enjoy the sound of the evening sea while Theodore prepares our dessert," James suggests.

"Your father is an excellent host, Sophia," Lady Stephens said, changing the subject.

"Thank you."

"What will become of your governess now that you are married, Sophia?"

"My father has suggested that since James will be departing on his mission soon, my governess will continue to live at my father's estate and visit with me five days a week to help me with my studies and music lessons."

"I see," Lady Stephens responds.

"Your Ladyship," Theodore interjects. "Your instructions have been completed as per your requests."

"Thank you, Theodore," Lady Stephens responds with a nod of her head.

The confused look on James and Sophia's face is evident.

"I hope the two of you don't mind," Lady Stephens pronounces. "Before we enjoy our tea and sweets, I took the liberty of having Theodore and your groundskeeper, William work together in what was indeed a short period of time, to produce what I can only state is perfection."

"Lady Stephens, of what do you speak?" James asks inquisitively, still puzzled by what Lady Stephens is referring to.

"Let us go inside and I will explain myself."

As they walk inside, Lady Stephens continues.

"I noticed when I arrived today that your home was empty of furnishings. Knowing that I wanted to present you both with another special wedding gift, I took the liberty...."

With this last word, Lady Stephens paused as Theodore slid open the two pocket doors to the parlor. As the doors opened, Sophia gasps with amazement at what she saw. The room was entirely furnished. It was only this morning this room was completely empty; now it looked like someone has been living here for quite some time.

"My word, Lady Stephens. We cannot possibly accept these most generous gifts," Sophia said, with stupefaction, well aware of the cost and fine quality of these furnishings.

"Unfortunately, I am afraid to inform you, Mrs. Langston," Theodore pipes in. "Lady Stephens is not known for taking 'no' for an answer. She can be very persuasive in her thoughts and opinions."

"That is correct," Lady Stephens announces in a dominate voice, one Sophia and James had not heard before. "I can assure you, Theodore has known me for a very long time and he speaks with experience and accuracy."

Lady Stephens's comments make everyone laugh and breaks the tension in the room. Sophia turns to the marquetry and veneer harpsichord. It was hand-painted, with gold accents and brass lion claw feet. Sophia gracefully sits down in the accompanying chair and begins to play several notes.

"This is the most stunning harpsichord I have ever seen, Lady Stephens. And its tone is perfect. It plays so well."

James looks down at the beautiful scene of his wife at the harpsichord. He notices the massive handwoven rug underneath it.

"My darling, look at the rug beneath your feet."

"Lady Stephens, all of these furnishings are exquisite. We will be forever grateful for your acts of generosity," Sophia declares, with great sincerity in her voice.

"You are more than welcome, my dear. I am comforted to know these treasures of mine will reside in a loving home."

"And now Mr. and Mrs. Langston, may I escort you to your main dining room?" Theodore announces, leading the group on a tour of majestic proportions.

Upon entering the dining room, Sophia immediately recognizes the curio cabinet, filled with all her wedding gifts of fine porcelain and silver, heirlooms from the King's family.

Lady Stephens turns their attention to the left of the room, where there was once a huge open wall, now hung a large mural of cherub angels, dancing in the sky merrily, holding musical instruments in their hands.

"It is heavenly, both literally and figuratively. You have splendid tastes, Lady Stephens," James states, in awe of the fine furnishings now occupying his home.

"I must say," Lady Stephens remarks. "I chuckled when I looked up at your father's cathedral ceiling in his sitting room, Sophia. I saw a similar image in this home as well. Clearly you were meant to have this tapestry in your home as a continuation of life in your father's home."

"Since I was a little girl, Lady Stephens, I have always been very fond of cherubs. This is why my father had the cathedral ceiling hand painted to my liking."

"Your father is a very kind and loving man," Lady Stephens pronounces with a smile.

"I do believe these dining room furnishings will fit perfectly in your new home. Again, I must say, I hope you do not think me too presumptuous in furnishing your home without your consent."

"Oh, course not," James immediately responds. "If you detect any hesitation from Sophia or myself, it is most assuredly not from our dismay but rather astonishment at your generosity."

"Lady Stephens, allow me to add, I believe you have the most wonderful and kindest heart in all of England," Sophia declares, approaching Lady Stephens and hugging her.

"Lady Stephens, you have completely showered us with your gifts today. Thank you for your munificence. We are so appreciative," James declares.

After the tour of their newly acquired furnishings, the three of them returned back to the porch to finish their evening tea. "Lady Stephens, may I be so bold as to ask, what was your husband's employment?" James asks.

"My husband was one of the finest bank owners in all of England. His high-level position did not come easy. He was able to attain such a rank with the support of my late uncle and the acceptance of the King. I am afraid it all started with Queen Anne's war between England and France. If that war had not begun, my late husband may not have taken a path into banking and made exorbitant amounts of money, more money than he could have ever imagined making. Despite the fact my dear Henry came from a very affluent family, he did not expect this type of large fortune to come our way."

"My word, what an incredible story, your Ladyship. As I can attest, you are correct; war can be quite costly indeed," James affirms.

"So, I am afraid, this is how banking started in England and how my husband became involved. In was a strange twist of fate; sometimes the outcome of war can be a positive to some and devastating to others. In this case, Henry and I are the benefactors of those destructive times."

It was evident that fatigue had settled upon Lady Stephens. She was, after all, an older woman and had a full day of travels and social gatherings. Sensing her fatigue, James makes a suggestion to the ladies.

"I propose it is time for all of us to get some rest, since tomorrow is our wedding day and we will be busy indeed. Please allow me to show you to your guest quarters, Lady Stephens. We are aware it is difficult for you to manage ascending our long stairwell due to your health."

James opens the door to the guest bedroom and Lady Stephens is instantly impressed by what she sees before her. The room is more comfortable than she would have expected. James also points out to Theodore his living arrangements.

After saying their pleasantries, James and Sophia walk upstairs to their bedroom. As the door closes behind them James grabs Sophia and begins pecking at her neck.

"At last, my darling lover, we are alone again."

Sophia does not resist his advancements.

"I am very grateful for Lady Stephens to be here this evening. It is because of her, I can hold you tightly in my arms all night long."

"She really is a lovely, almost motherly figure," Sophia responds, with a certain level of comfort in her voice as she walks behind her new fleur-de-lis room divider and begins to undress.

James sits on the chaise lounge, watching the top of her head moving and her body forming shadows from behind the screen. The crotch of James's pants rises as he observes the silhouette of Sophia's body.

"Lady Stephens has quite the political circle around her, does she not, James?" Sophia said, knowing that she is teasing her lover with her shadowy image.

"She most certainly does, my love. However, it is not Lady Stephens who I wish to focus on right now. Do you require my assistance Mrs. Langston?" James asks in a teasing voice.

"Why, yes, Mr. Langston, I do. Would you be so kind as to please come and help me untie my corset," Sophia requests in a flirtatious voice.

James finds that his legs have become weak, as all the blood seems to have rushed into his groin and swelled his organ. He rises from the chaise lounge and walks behind the divider to join Sophia, approaching her slowly. With Sophia's back toward James, he pecks at the back of her neck, then gently slides his hands up and down the skin under her arms. His hands move under her breasts, massaging each one in a rhythmical motion. Sophia lets out a girlish moan. James pulls her closer as he begins to gently squeeze her nipples, one by one. He teases them to both harden and accept his desires as he continues to kiss the curve of her neck. Sophia, immensely aroused, once again feels the erotic yearning she has newly experienced over these last two days. James moves his lips toward her ear, whispering.

"I want to be inside you, Mrs. Langston. No one will ever be inside you but me."

Sophia continues to weaken by his touch, as James slowly pulls off her corset, dropping it to the floor. James picks Sophia up into his arms and cradles her close to him as he walks toward the bed. He lays her gently onto their bed, kissing her forehead and playing with her hair, twisting her curls in between his fingers. Tenderly, he slides his tongue into her mouth. Sophia reciprocates with her tongue. James, hungry for more of this luscious woman, moves his mouth toward Sophia's hard nipples. He opens up his lips and nibbles on her left nipple for a brief moment before moving to the right breast. Sucking a little harder, he masterfully arouses both nipples, one with the curve of his mouth and tongue and the other with his hand.

James releases his hand from Sophia's left breast and tenderly caresses her inner thigh. Sophia finds herself helpless, completely submissive to James's needs. James, aware of his power over Sophia, slides his middle finger up inside his lover, penetrating her. Sophia does not resist. Instead she lets out a deep and long "ohhh." James, ever so gently, places his hand over her mouth, saying, "We must be quiet, my darling. We have a visitor, and I would hate to imagine she thinks we are doing something naughty in our bedroom."

Sophia can no longer concentrate; her body has taken control and she wants more. She wants that feeling of ecstasy only James can provide her.

James, now fully erect, cannot believe he will be leaving soon. 'No. I must not think of that, not when this beautiful, helpless creature is in front of me. I want to implant my seed in her, in hopes of conceiving our first bairn tonight. I will share my love with her and know while I am gone that I can return to my lover and enjoy capering around with her in our bedroom.'

James stands up from the bed while Sophia lies helplessly, heavily breathing. He removes his clothes. Sophia's eyes enjoy the appearance of his lean, naked muscular body. The candlelight creates a shadow on the floor of his erect penis. Sophia smiles at the sight. James has chosen to stand sideways on purpose. He wants to expose his enlarged penis to Sophia. Sophia's eyes are mesmerized and glad her lover is allowing her to stare so long at this erotic sight.

James turns slowly and walks toward Sophia, and the speed of her breathing increases. He climbs into bed and under the cotton sheets with Sophia. With a swift act, James turns Sophia's body onto her side so her buttocks are facing his front. He spreads her legs, one leg up and the other on the bed. He guides the tip of his penis into her vagina thrusting into her while her tightness seals around him. James wants to feel all of her. He moves his hips rhythmically with hers as he slowly guides his penetration before giving the final hard thrust with his hips and releasing inside her. With his strong force, their wetness collides and they collapse together.

"Oh James, I shall bare you all the bairns you shall ever desire as long as we can continue sharing this method of loving each other."

James did not hear Sophia's words; he had already fallen into a deep and blissful sleep.

Chapter Thirteen

Opening my eyes, I realize I must have fallen asleep after reading the last line of the chapter. I am glad Gramma did not come into my room to wake me up and find the book resting on my chest. Fluffy lies next to me, with his floppy ears tickling the side of my face. I suspect it is time for me to wake up. I leave the book on my pillow, planning to hide it later. I walk downstairs with Fluffy following beside me, his toenails making a tapping sound on the old hardwood floors. Reaching the main floor, I see Gramma in the living room, intensely rocking in her rocking chair and reading her book.

Hearing me, she lifts her head and lowers her book onto her lap.

"How did you sleep, little one? Are you ready for some breakfast?"

"I'm starving, Gramma. I'm always starving in your house. Maybe because you are such a good cook or because I have so much fun all day with you and Grandpa."

"Well then, let's fix you some breakfast," Gramma said, smiling, walking into the kitchen and placing her book onto the counter. Following her, I am able to sneak a peek at the book cover. The author's name reads, Anaed Eiram. I know that name. It is the same author who wrote my book. I smile; now I know why Gramma keeps wanting to read her book, just as I do. I am hardly sleeping on this vacation because I cannot stop reading my very interesting book.

"Here you go; I poured you a bowl of your favorite cereal."

"Thank you, Gramma. I love 'Special G' cereal. That's 'Special Gramma' cereal."

"That's correct," Gramma said, smiling, as if I just gave her the best gift ever.

"Maybe we should change the name to 'SGG' cereal. Super Great Gramma."

"Even better," Gramma said, laughing.

After making sure I do not need anything else, Gramma grabs her book off the counter, returns to her rocking chair in the living room and begins to read. I can hear the sound of her rocking chair over the crunching sound of cereal in my mouth. Her chair rocks back and forth repeatedly. Fluffy walks over to Gramma and lies down beside her. He is used to having his own spot as Gramma reads. Gramma chews another piece of candy. She does not like to share her 'adult candy,' as she calls it. I am not sure why; I ponder this while sitting at the kitchen table eating my cereal. 'I wonder what her story is about? Do they do that sex stuff in her book too? Is it old fashioned, like my book? I can start reading it when she puts it on the bookshelf in my attic bedroom.'

"Gramma, I'm going to play with my horse set upstairs."

"Okay, little one. Have fun and be good," Gramma said, without lifting her head up from the book's pages.

I am usually a good kid, except when I do things like sneak into Gramma's room and start reading one of her books. I know I am breaking the rules, but in this case I cannot stop secretly reading her book. Besides, every adult I know says it's good for kids to read books.

On the way to my attic bedroom, I decided to walk into my Gramma's bedroom, and I sit down at her powder dresser. I reach over and pull the tassel cord, turning on the old fashion light. I am sure Gramma would not be happy with me doing this, but I want to pretend I am Sophia. I grab Gramma's purple glass perfume bottle. With the mister, I begin to spray the perfume onto my neck. I feel fancy with the fragrance surrounding me. Sitting in front of the mirror, I pretend I am getting ready for my wedding day, just as Sophia has done in the book. As I twist the knob on the back of the jewelry box, the metal pieces inside move and begin to play, "Here comes the bride."

'Hmmm, what necklace should I wear for my pretend wedding day?' I asked myself. I open the drawer of the jewelry box and find a long strand of pink pearls inside. I put them around my neck, and I find the matching clip-on earrings and clip them onto my ears. I pin up my hair with a big hair clip and slide two jeweled barrettes into my hair. Looking into the mirror, I see how pretty I look. I find some bracelets and some rings and put them on too.

Another necklace catches my eye and I put it on around my neck. It is beautiful and looks very special on me. From the necklace, hangs a locket in rose-gold, a heart-shaped locket with a red ruby heart placed in the center. I slide the necklace over my head and the locket hangs between my belly button and my throat. Dressing up like this makes me wonder how I will really look on my wedding day.

Suddenly, I hear the bathroom door shut downstairs. I run downstairs, wondering if Gramma or Grandpa are making plans to go out and do something fun. It must be Gramma who is in the bathroom because no one is in the living room. I decide to take advantage of this moment alone and hurry over to Gramma's chocolate box. I grab two pieces of candy and place them in my sweatshirt pocket. I hear the bathroom door creak open.

"Sarah Marie? Did you come back downstairs, darling?" my Gramma asks.

"Yes, Gramma."

"I see you got into my jewelry box."

I shamefully lower my head, realizing I forgot I was wearing Gramma's jewelry. Now I am caught wearing Gramma's jewelry and I have her chocolates in my pocket.

"Your hair looks very pretty like that. You should wear it up more often. I can also smell you found my French perfume," Gramma said calmly and in a controlled manner.

I could tell she was not pleased with me and did not want to get angry.

"Yes, I did Gramma. I'm sorry. I was just pretending I was getting ready for my wedding day."

"Your wedding day? Oh, little one, you have many more years before that will happen. I am sure when it does happen, you will be a beautiful bride and it will be a special day for you. Maybe I will even let you borrow some of my jewelry for that day; however, not today. Please go upstairs and carefully put all my jewelry back where you found it, and no more playing with it unless you ask Gramma first. Okay?"

"Okay, Gramma."

"All right, now upstairs you go while Gramma finishes the last few pages of this chapter in my book."

"Okay, Gramma."

I run back upstairs, playing tag with Fluffy on the way. I take off all my Gramma's jewelry and carefully place it back into the correct drawers. While putting away my Gramma's jewelry, I hear my mother's voice. "Is she here?" I run downstairs hoping to find my mother talking with Gramma.

"Mommy! Mommy!" I shout out her name as I run down the stairs again.

My Gramma quickly comes out of the main floor laundry room.

"Oh, my goodness, Sarah Marie, are you all right?"

"Is Mommy here? I miss Mommy."

"No darling, it is just you and me in the house this morning."

My bottom lip begins to quiver.

"I want my Mommy. Gramma, I want to go home."

"Okay, don't cry, little one. Just minutes ago, you were happy and imagining. Well how about you imagine this? Guess what we are going to do today?" Gramma said, trying to change the subject and get my mind off my mother.

"What?" I ask, still shivering with sadness; however, slowly forgetting about missing my mother and being homesick.

"I'm going to take you shopping and buy you some new hair barrettes."

"Really?"

"Yes, we will find some and make you look as pretty as you did when you were wearing my jewelry."

"Will I look as pretty as if I were getting married today?"

"Oh, Sarah Marie, what is with you and all this talk about your wedding day? Today we will be sure you look pretty, and I will make sure you look pretty on your wedding day, too. Now, do you feel better?"

"Yes, Gramma."

"Okay. Go take your bath so we can go shopping."

Gramma grabs the laundry basket full of clean clothes and heads upstairs first. I watch her as she climbs up each step. I begin to panic.

'Oh, no! My book is on my pillow and Gramma is about to bring those clothes into my bedroom.'

I run for the stairs and closely follow Gramma, who walks directly into my bedroom and heads straight for my dresser, carrying the laundry basket of clean clothes. I jump on my bed and sit on my book. I begin to rattle off questions to Gramma.

"What time are we leaving, Gramma? Where did you get that dresser, Gramma? Do you think we will be able to play cards tonight, Gramma?"

Gramma patiently answers all my questions. Although the more questions I ask, the more her tolerance level decreases.

"Hurry up now, little one. Please go back downstairs and take your bath. We are going to leave soon."

"Okay."

I slip the book into the pocket of my hoodie, which was lying on my bed, next to my pillow. Then I placed the hoodie deep under my covers, shoving it to the bottom of my bed. Gramma has her back to me, filling the drawers with my clean clothes.

"Don't worry, Sarah Marie. I will make your bed."

"It's okay Gramma, I'll do it. Thanks anyway."

I make my bed, ensuring you can hardly see the small book bump at the bottom of my bed. A bump that is hiding the most exciting book I have ever read. I know that if Gramma found out I was reading her book, I would be grounded for life.

I hurry downstairs to take my bath. I wash faster than usual, so I can go shopping with Gramma. Then I dart back upstairs to get dressed. Gramma is in her bedroom and sees me passing her room.

"Get dressed, little one. We are going to be leaving in ten minutes. First, I need to take the rollers out of my hair and style it, then we can go into town."

"Okay," I say, holding my pink terry cloth bathrobe close to my body.

Walking into my bedroom, I start to feel ill by what I see. The sheets and comforter from my bed are gone. More importantly, my book is gone. I try very hard to control my panic. I call out to Gramma.

"Gramma, where did my sheets and comforter go?"

"Oh, I decided to strip your bed today. I am washing everything so it will be nice and clean for you."

'Washing everything,' I think. 'Gramma, you are washing my book. Right at the part where James and Sophia get married.' With my robe still on, I run downstairs. I can hear the washing machine running. I see my sheets on the floor but do not see my comforter. I tear through my sheets lying on the floor. I find my hoodie rolled up in a ball in the sheets. My book is still securely tucked into the front pocket. I let go a huge heavy sigh of relief. I hold the book close to my chest. 'I have saved it. I get to continue reading it, and most importantly, Gramma did not discover I am reading her book.' I put my hoodie on over my pink terry towel robe. I zip up the zipper, making sure the book is positioned inside the hoodie pocket. I return to my bedroom, walking past my Gramma's bedroom. She sees me wearing a hoodie and a bathrobe.

"Sarah Marie, I want to wash your hoodie. Please take it back downstairs. It is going into the washer next."

Thinking fast, I respond,

"Okay, Gramma, but first I'm going to get my clothes on."

Gramma nods, as I attempt to walk calmly to my attic bed-room. My heart is racing and my throat is dry. Looking around the room, I reach for the green shoebox, my secret hiding spot for my book. I stash the book safely inside and arrange the boxes neatly so that it does not look like I have disturbed them. I finish getting dressed and carry my hoodie back to the laundry area.

'Whew. I do not know what I would have done if I had gotten caught with Gramma's book. I must make sure that does not happen again.'

The panic feeling slowly leaves my body; however, the memory of Gramma almost finding out I was reading her book sticks with me for a very long time.

Gramma and I soon leave for our shopping trip. She buys me a new dress and some shoes, and of course, some new hair barrettes. As we begin to exit the store, we walk toward the aisle that sells books. Gramma turns the cart around. I watch her pick up a book off the store shelf. She is unaware I am watching her. I can see the book's cover and the author's name. I am familiar with the author. It is Anaed Eiram, the same person who wrote my book about James and Sophia. This time, the picture on the cover of the book has a box of chocolates on it. In the box, there are a few chocolates, but there is also a pair of very thin, very pretty, red lace panties and a bra. The bra looks like it was only one quarter of a bra, because there is not enough cloth where the breasts would go. 'Wouldn't you be worried your boobies would fall out of your bra?' I wonder. Gramma secretly places the book in the shopping cart, under the new dress she is buying for me. We proceed to the checkout counter to pay for our purchases.

When we arrive home, Gramma tells me how tired she is.

"I need to take a break, little petunia, and finish my book."

"No problem, Gramma. I am going to go upstairs and play with my horse set. I love you," I say, as I walk up the stairs.

Oh yes, Gramma, I really love you. I love that I can take this time to read about James and Sophia's wedding day.

I remove 'my' book from my secret hiding spot in the green shoebox. With my new barrettes in my hair, just like Sophia would have them, I sit down on my bed. Before I begin to read the pages, I think, 'Thank you Gramma and Grandpa. This has been the best summer vacation ever!'

Chapter Fourteen

W ake up, Sophia. It is Sunday, December 13th, in the year of our Lord 1733. It is your wedding day," James announces.

The two prepare and get dressed for their public wedding before taking their new carriage, the one from Lady Stephens, to the General's estate. Both were delighted for this day to happen, particularly since it meant they could soon enjoy their life together in a way that would be socially acceptable by the aristocratic level of society.

The Countess was thrilled the winter weather had cooperated for them on this day. It was sunny, yet slightly nippy for an outdoor ceremony in the estate courtyard. Sophia was amazed the Countess was able to coordinate such a beautiful social event in such a short period of time. She was also surprised that 125 people made themselves available to attend her wedding day. Standing under the wedding arch, covered in pine boughs, James and Sophia stare into each other's eyes and begin sharing their vows, with the assistance of their longtime friend and local victor, Reverend Paddington.

Following the formal ceremony, the guests adjourned to the house where food and spirits were served. The Countess insisted James and Sophia circulate around to each of their guests and thank them for coming. As the festivities continued, the General approached James and pulled him away from socializing to discuss a thoughtful decision he had made.

"Son, once again I want to say congratulations to you. I know you and Sophia will be a good match for each other."

"Thank you, sir."

"I want to let you know, I took the liberty of asking Lady Stephens to stay here this evening. I thought you and Sophia might want to be alone in your home tonight," the General said with a wink.

"Yes indeed, sir," James replied with a respectful nod, grateful for the General being empathic to his masculine needs.

From the corner of the room, the Countess was heard announcing it was time for the couple to depart. As the crowd gathered outside, the newly married couple rode off in their new luxurious black carriage while their guests applauded.

"Mrs. Langston, it is official in the eyes of the ever-judging society; we are indeed married."

Sophia smiled, followed by her eyes filling up with tears.

"I am extremely joyful to be your wife, James. It is simply that my heart aches when I think you must leave again soon. I am barely able to breathe, knowing you will be gone and not by my side."

"Oh Sophia, do not ache. I will return to you. For now, let us focus on the rare opportunity of having two wedding nights alone for marital pleasure."

Sophia smiles, appreciating the shift to more positive thoughts. .James forces a smile, hoping Sophia will not be able to detect the intense concern he has with respect to the safety for his trip.

The remainder of the carriage ride to their home was in silence, with Sophia snuggled in the nook under James's arm. When the carriage stops in front of their house, Theodore greets them by formally congratulating the official Mr. and Mrs. Langston. He then pauses, prepared to assist Lady Stephens with her footing out of the carriage. James, sensing the pause, informs Theodore.

"Lady Stephens will be staying at the General's house tonight."

Theodore responds with a subtle surprised look on his face. "I see."

"Theodore, Mrs. Langston and I plan to go upstairs and remove our wedding clothes. We then plan to sit on our porch to enjoy some champagne and listen to the sounds of the sea while enjoying the midnight air."

"Oh James, I do so love the midnight air."

"We will be downstairs in a short while, Theodore. Thank you."

James and Sophia enter their master bedroom. Sophia purposely sits down in the armchair by the fireplace. She reaches her arm out, indicating to James the need to assist her in taking off her long, white satin gloves. James happily complies, removing a glove saying, "You know me well, Sophia. Taking off your gloves, brings me great stimulating pleasure."

Sophia laughs. She stands up and walks over to the room divider, signally for James to help her unfasten the first few white satin buttons flowing down the back of her wedding gown. James then moves away from the room divider, allowing Sophia to finish undressing. After removing her wedding gown, Sophia reaches for her light cotton sleeping gown and covers it with her night coat. James also undresses, putting on more comfortable clothes for the rest of the evening.

As Sophia emerges from behind the room divider, James again is struck by her natural beauty. However, tonight something is different. Tonight Sophia's sheer beauty is accentuated by what could only be described by James as a glow. It was a radiant glow, one he had never seen on Sophia before. 'It must be a wedding glow from the day,' he thinks.

"What is it, James?" Sophia asks, noticing a trance-like look on his face.

"When I look at you, Sophia, I have never experienced such beauty in all my life. You are glowing this evening. My heart has stopped beating. This vision is one I will never forget."

Sophia smiles, with a look of complete peace radiating across her face as she takes James's hand to walk downstairs to enjoy the midnight air on their porch. Theodore has prepared chilled champagne for their arrival. He pours each of them a glass. The couple sit on their porch, telling stories from their day and about the guests who attended. Recognizing the chill in the air, Theodore goes inside and returns with two warm blankets to help the newlyweds stay warm on this December evening in England.

"Thank you, Theodore, we appreciate your attentiveness," James acknowledges.

"You are more than welcome, sir." Theodore then positions himself near the door leading to the house, in case his services are needed again. He intended to be close enough to pour the champagne, but not too close as to seem intrusive.

After enjoying the sounds of the majestic sea and breathing in the midnight air, James suggests they retire to the bedroom.

"Theodore, can you see that the house is closed up for the evening?"

"Of course, Colonel Langston," Theodore responds, acting as the ever-dutiful butler.

Unable to control his passionate desires, James taps Sophia on the bottom as they walk up the stairs. Sophia giggles with delight.

Walking into their bedroom, they notice the logs in the fireplace blazing and the room is warm.

"Theodore is an excellent butler. He is clearly aware of meeting our every need," James said, thrilled that he has been able to provide Sophia an excellent butler to serve her.

To enhance the atmosphere in the room, James begins lighting numerous candles he had positioned around the room earlier. Sophia sits at her dresser, enjoying the shadowy view of James's muscular body as he moves around the room.

"Sophia, my love, how strange it is that over one year ago, we first met in your father's home. When I first laid my eyes upon you, I knew I must have you for myself."

Sophia giggles, pulling the ivory comb barrette out of her hair and placing it on her dresser. James recognizes the barrette.

"I see you chose to wear the barrette I bought you in Pairs on our wedding day."

"I did. I love it and wanted to wear it for everyone to see. You should know I received many compliments on it today."

Walking over to Sophia he removes his clothes as he stands behind her and reaches his hand over her shoulder, placing it on her breast. He begins to circulate his two fingers around her nipple. Sophia's response is not heard by James. Instead, he is fixated on her nipples rising up from the outside of her nightgown. Sophia has become familiar with this action, as she likes it. Without permission, James pulls Sophia's nightgown over her head and lays it on the dresser. She rises from the bench, turning her naked body toward him. Again James marvels at Sophia's beautiful naked body. Taking each breast into his hands he begins to fondle them while Sophia arches back her head with pleasure. Moving his mouth toward one breast, James nibbles around the firm yet buoyant gland. Sophia bends down and reaches her hand between James's legs. Her hand grips his naked, long penis.

Astonished by Sophia's audacious gesture, James moans with pleasure. Stroking her lover up and down, she squeezes her hand tighter into her palm.

"Harder my love, harder. Please continue."

"Release for me, James. Please release in my hand."

These words thrill James as much as the movement he is feeling. Sophia can feel the throbbing vibration going through her hand as his tip moistens. Enticed and surprised by his wife's invitation, James releases a few more drops of moisture, making it easier for Sophia to continue rubbing up and down. Completely letting go of himself, James squirts his warmth into her hand. Sophia reaches for the towel on the dresser, one which James had warned her she would need.

"You have begun performing as though you are an experienced sensual goddess, Sophia."

Sophia smiles, equally astonished by her natural abilities.

In their erotic state, James and Sophia amble to the window seat. Sitting together in each other's arms, the full moon shines through the window and reflects onto their naked bodies. James leans Sophia back so he can see her entire body. The combination of the moonlight, the view of the sea and Sophia's beautiful body, makes for an extremely erotic scene and heightens James's desires even more. He lifts his body off the window seat and kneels down onto the floor, while at the same time turning Sophia around to face him. He spreads Sophia's legs open, as her head rests on the windowsill. Sophia cannot imagine what is about to occur and does not resist.

"My hidden desires run deep for you, Sophia. Allow me to pleasure you. Close your eyes, lie still for me and trust that what is about occur will bring pleasure to us both."

James gently tucks Sophia's hands under her head and places a pillow behind her back.

"I want you to keep your hands behind your head at all times, Sophia. Will you agree to do that, my darling?"

"I think so," Sophia said, a little surprised at what might occur next.

James has planned for this moment. He unfolds the blanket lying next to them on the window seat and exposes a black leather horsewhip. He had placed the whip there earlier this morning, before their wedding ceremony. Sophia looks down and sees the whip.

"James?" she shutters, bringing her hands down to her sides.

She was not quite sure what question she wanted to ask, as her head was filled with confusion.

"Shhh, all will be well, my dear," James comforts her. His hidden dark passions run deep. "I asked for your trust and I promise you pleasure. Now place your hands behind your head and enjoy what you are about to receive."

With that, James cracks the whip on the floor. Sophia, now concerned, wonders if this is still a kind, gentle, caring man she thought she married. 'Or has he been replaced by a devilish twin relative?' No matter what she was thinking, she obeyed James's request and kept her hands behind her head and her legs spread apart on the moonlit window seat. James could no longer hide his fantasy from her, and begins slapping the leather whip against the floor. 'She is mine,' James muses 'and she will do as I say as I pleasure her with my fantastical commands. I shall take her body to the unknown.'

As James tightly grips the leather whip, his foreskin draws, allowing his penis to harden and expand in length and girth. He lowers his face toward the V formation between Sophia's legs and blows lightly onto her vulva. James proceeds to slide the leather straps of the whip across her pink wet clitoris.

Sophia moans and moistens. 'Is it possible this could feel so stimulating?' she considers. James proceeds to drag the straps of the whip down the inside of her legs, bringing it back to further arouse her slit. In a surprise action to Sophia, James lightly slaps the leather fringe across her slit. He repeats the action, only this time strikes the whip a little harder. Sophia feels a stinging sensation and releases a loud moan. A moan that James has not heard from her before. She arches her entire body and widens her legs as if to naturally beg for more.

Amidst the intense erotic pleasure, Sophia is astounded James would do this to her. 'How could he know she would become so aroused by the leather touching, slapping and tingling her skin?'

James then takes the whip handle and proceeds to walk and rub it around Sophia's aroused lips. Even in the moonlight, James can see how much her lips have swelled. Her bulging labia signals her deep pleasures and the desire for more. To satisfy her need, James places the handle around her vaginal opening. He inserts it a few centimeters.

Sophia moans a euphoric, "Ohhhhh!"

'I can do more to her,' James thinks, pulling the leather handle in and out of her vagina quickly with short, swift gentle movements. He stops and again slaps the whip on top of her vulva. Her pleasurable moaning does not stop. Her clitoris is now fully erect and almost purple with intense stimulation. James looks down; he sees his enlargement begging to be inside her.

James gently swishes the whip across each of Sophia's nipples. She calls out in what could only be perceived as an animal sound. This level of arousal surprises her.

Sliding her buttocks to the end of the window seat James brings his mouth to her wet vulva and savors the sweet taste of her.

"Come for me Sophia, let it out for me."

Sophia feels her body has taken over her mind. When she hears James's request to come, he merely needed to touch her clit with his tongue for her to explode again.

James lifts Sophia off the window seat and lays her onto the blanket, which is now lying on the floor. He enters her. The tightness and wetness of his wife's vagina makes him want to penetrate her more. Straddling her, he raises the whip into the air, struck by her moist scent on the handle. His passion bolts through his hand, as he slaps the whip onto the floor, demonstrating his control. Sophia moans as her body squirms. He draws the whip into the air and whisks her breasts several times with it.

James looks down at himself inside Sophia while holding the whip in the air. He falls onto her, grinding his hips deep into hers, letting out a hard, long cry of hedonism. Sophia joins him, as they both release together. Collapsing with exhaustive pleasure next to Sophia, he concludes. 'I have performed my ultimate fantasy on my wife.'

"James, your heart is beating so fast," Sophia notices, with some concern in her voice.

"That is true and you should know it beats only for you, my love," James responds, with a weary yet loving smile.

After a few moments, they return to their bed and sleep heavily, as the moon sets and the sun rises.

In the morning, there is a heavy knock on the front door, which echoes through the foyer's vaulted ceiling. Theodore opens the door, finding Lady Stephens and General Cartwright waiting on the front stoop.

"Good afternoon, Lady Stephens, General Cartwright, please come in."

The couple enters, laughing from a previous conversation they were having. Theodore, quite surprised by what appears to be a close connection between the couple, who had only met two days prior, offers to take their coats.

"Theodore, is James and Sophia in? We have a little surprise for them," Lady Stephens said, looking at the General and giggling.

Theodore is most baffled by Lady Stephens's giggling. He has not seen his previous employer this happy in a very long time.

"They most certainly are, Lady Stephens. They are still up in their master bedroom, I suspect fatigued from a wedding day and wedding night. I shall go and alert them to your presence."

Lady Stephens was struck by how quickly Theodore had transferred into his new role as James's butler.

"Thank you, Theodore. We will wait here in the drawing room. Perhaps we could have some tea while we wait for the newlyweds. In addition, this opportunity will allow me some more time with the fascinating General. Oh, how I did have such a marvelous time with you last night, sir. Shall we sit, General?"

Theodore departs, shaking his head. 'What on earth has happened to his previous employer,' he wonders?

When Theodore knocks on James and Sophia's bedroom door, there is no answer. He knocks again. Again, there is no answer. Theodore carefully opens the door slightly and finds the couple spooning in bed. It was indeed a lovely sight to see such pure love. He clears his throat, hoping to wake the couple and make them aware of his presence.

"Sir, I am terribly sorry to bother you, sir."

Sophia, suddenly becoming aware of Theodore's presence, begins to rub her eyes. James rolls onto his back and stretches his arms above his head, exposing his muscular body.

"Good day, Theodore."

"Sir, I am very sorry to disturb you and Mrs. Langston, but I thought you would want to know that Lady Stephens and the General are downstairs and requesting your presence."

James and Sophia immediately sit up in unison, as if strings had been pulled by a puppeteer.

"Here? Now? What time is it?" James fires off questions to Theodore in his groggy state.

"Yes, sir. They are downstairs, and it is two pm, sir."

"Oh my. I am surprised how long we have slept. Please tell them we will be downstairs shortly."

"Yes, sir."

As Theodore turns to leave the room, he notices the pile of clothes and a horsewhip by the window seat. 'How surprising,' he reckons. 'These new employers are similar to my previous employers, Lady Stephens and Sir Henry.'

After thirty minutes, James and Sophia join the General and Lady Stephens in the library room.

"Well, good afternoon, Mr. and Mrs. Langston," the General said, standing by the bookshelf, smiling.

"Hello, Father. I am very sorry we kept you waiting. We were resting and recovering from a very busy last few days."

"Not a worry at all, my child. I have brought you a wedding gift, my dear."

"A gift? Father, no. You have already been too kind."

At that moment Theodore enters the room, leading a one-year-old, tan-colored Great Dane at his side. The dog runs directly over to Sophia and sits properly in front of her, waiting to be noticed. Sophia smiles and begins to pet the lovely animal.

"Oh Father, she is precious, and the pink bow around her neck is the perfect wrapping for such a perfect wedding gift."

"She's our dog, Astro's sister. The breeder said she is the finest pick of her litter and the finest pick for you, my dear."

"Oh, thank you, Father. She does have many similarities to Astro. I can see that."

"Astro and she have been playing all morning. That is also why Lady Stephens and I have remained overnight at my estate—to help me with the two dogs. We had a marvelous time playing with them in the yard today. Did we not, Lady Stephens?"

"We most certainly did, General," Lady Stephens said with a titter.

Sophia becomes perplexed. 'My father was playing on the grounds with a dog? My father, who rarely speaks to anyone, especially someone of the caliber and vast wealth of Lady Stephens, had invited her to stay overnight at his house and joined her on his grounds to play with the dog?' These thoughts posed quite the conundrum for Sophia. Her father was a private man, who rarely expressed emotions, all of which were necessary for his stature as General. 'My father does seem happy,' she thinks. 'I must say, I am pleasantly surprised.'

"What name do you think I should give her?"

Some names were suggested by the group, but Sophia did not listen.

"I think I will call her Hannah."

"That is a perfect name. Now Sophia, James and I are going to take Hannah for a walk, we shall be back in a little while," the General announces.

Sophia was surprised that her newly received gift was to be taken from her this quickly. However, she knows better than to argue with her father.

James was less surprised and yet more alarmed. He had become acquainted with the General's tone over the years, and this particular tone meant the General has something of great importance to discuss.

"I shall be sure to take good care of Hannah, my darling," James comments to Sophia, trying desperately to mask his worry.

Unfortunately, his efforts did not work. Sophia could tell something was not right.

As the two men closed the door, they were treated by the views and fresh air of the sea. The General promptly began to speak to James.

"I have some rather important matters to discuss with you, James. I have received word this morning from our King. He wishes the political affairs with Portugal be handled immediately. I have sent word back to him that you would be able to depart in two days."

James was certain he felt his stomach fall onto the beach. 'Two days? I was supposed to depart in a fortnight,' James argued within his head. 'Now I am torn. Who shall I give my loyalty to, my King or my new wife?'

"Yes, sir, I am at your and my country's service, sir," James said with a heavy heart.

"This is a very difficult day for both of us, my son. I must send one of my best men out on an extremely dangerous mission, and I must witness, what I suspect, my daughter dissolving at this news. I can only hope Hannah will help ease her heart's burden while you are away."

"Yes, sir," James responds, no longer aware of his surroundings. His mind had already moved onto how he would tell his official wife of twenty-four hours this news.

Sophia and Lady Stephens sat quietly on the porch. There was no need to talk as they took in the beauty of their surroundings. Sophia's mind wondered back to the life of a General's daughter. Never did she expect she would fall madly in love with a Colonel. Her father had always wanted her to marry a prestigious doctor or an attorney. He wanted her to be well cared for and to continue living in a lifestyle to which she was accustomed.

From the first moment she saw James in her father's house, she knew he was the person she would marry. Now she was a happily married woman, sitting outside her home and waiting for her husband to return from walking her dog. 'I cannot believe my life could make me any more happy,' she thought, and smiled, while gazing out toward the sea.

James and her father soon returned with her new puppy, Hannah, who had suddenly become very tired after her long walk on the beach.

"I hope you had a lovely walk, gentlemen. It is indeed a perfect day for such an activity," Sophia remarks.

"We did," the General said, stretching the truth. "We were able to discuss some important matters while watching Hannah become startled by the splashing of the waves. I am certain this dog will bring your many smiles and offer you much love, Sophia."

Sophia smiles at her father's comment. She also deduces that there was more behind his comments. She was just not certain what it was.

"If you do not mind," Lady Stephens interrupts, rising from her chair. "I am ghastly tired from the events of the last few days. I think I might retire for a bit and have a short nap."

"Of course. Is there anything else you need?" James offers.

"Oh no. Just a moment to lie down in your very comfortable guest room. Thank you, James."

"I, too, must be heading back to my home. I have many issues requiring my attention today," the General said, taking Lady Stephens's hand and kissing it. "It was lovely spending time with you, Lady Stephens."

"And with you, sir."

James and Sophia were not quite sure what had transpired between Lady Stephens and the General, but the two of them had certainly formed a close connection in just a few days.

Lady Stephens leaves to retire to the guest bedroom as James and Sophia walk the General to the front door. When the door closes, James suggests they retreat upstairs to the bedroom.

"Fantastic idea," Sophia said. "I could benefit from a nap myself."

"Napping is not what I had in mind, Mrs. Langston," James said with a wink.

James picks up Hannah into his arms and the three of them venture upstairs to the bedroom.

"James, I have something for you," Sophia said, opening her dresser drawer.

"I thought you gave me my wedding gift last night," James said, with another wink, pointing to the whip still lying on the bedroom floor.

"No James, this is my wedding gift to you."

Sophia presents James with an embroidered handkerchief. All four corners of the cloth were drawn together and a silk ribbon tied the corners together to form a pouch. The handkerchief had been sprayed with Sophia's perfume.

"A handkerchief? Thank you, my dear," James replies, wondering why it was so important to present this simple gift at this particular time.

"Open it up. Look at what is inside the pouch."

James unties the ribbon, exposing a gold pocket watch with an ornate gold chain attached to it. Engraved inside the cover of the watch are the initials "AJL with love, SL."

"This is a unique treasure. Thank you, my love. This indeed is something I will carry and remember you always." James walks over to the armoire, reaches his hand into the drawer and removes two packages.

"And for you, my lady, I also have a few gifts."

"Oh, James. At one level, I cannot say I am surprised. At another level, I am fascinated. Which one shall I open first?"

"Open the largest one first, my love," James said, smiling, always enjoying seeing his wife become excited from opening his gifts.

Sophia unties the ribbon of the largest package, unfolding the tissue paper away from the gift. Inside the paper she sees a beautiful dark burgundy, crushed velvet cape.

"James! This is lovely. It is perfect. I shall be protected from the cold winter air."

Sophia places the cape over her shoulders and pulls the silk-lined hood onto her head.

"You look like a princess, or Little Red Riding Hood, only with a burgundy cape."

"I feel like I am living in a fairy tale, so this cape is appropriate. My life hardly seems real, James."

Sophia begins to pull the green ribbon off the second package. Upon opening it, she gasps. Inside the paper is a rose-gold, heart-shaped locket, with a red ruby heart positioned in the center. The locket hangs from a delicate rose-gold chain. Sophia opens the locket and sees the engraving, "SL love, AJL."

"It seems we both had the same idea, darling. As you wear this locket, know that you have all my endless love. I am yours completely, Sophia. You have my heart."

"Oh James, your kindness and generosity overwhelms me," Sophia said, as James approaches her from behind, placing the locket around her neck. "I will always wear it, James. I promise I shall never take it off."

James proudly smiles, watching Sophia admire the heart-shaped locket in the mirror. She is secretly surprised to find that the locket hangs past her cleavage line.

Sensing her slight dismay, James informs her, "This heart is intended not to be seen, my love. It is to be worn close to your heart, as a reminder that you are always close to my heart."

Sophia begins to weep at James's thoughtful and romantic gift.

"We have a special bond, Sophia. We have been united as one, and it is that conviction I want you to remember as I share some news with you."

The two return to the window seat. James positions the brocade silk pillows behind their backs. He sits beside Sophia, holding her hands tightly in his lap.

"Sophia, my darling, while walking on the beach this afternoon, your father brought me some disheartening news. I cannot imagine how best to share this information with you in a way you will not become upset."

Sophia pulls back her hands from James's grip and tightly grabs her new heart locket.

"I have been informed of new military orders. The orders require I leave earlier than expected on a mission for the King."

"How much earlier, James?"

"In two days."

Sophia falls forward onto James's lap. She weeps as James places his hand on her head and strokes her hair.

"Our love is strong and will keep us together through this time, Sophia. Our hearts will infiltrate the burden of this space. No matter how far I am away from thee, nothing shall keep my love from thee." James comforts her while continuing to stroke her long, curly hair.

"I cannot hear it, James."

"You can and you will, my lady. You are a Colonel's wife now. In addition, your father and the Countess will be here to assist you, along with our staff."

"James, I must rest. My head is troubled by this distressing news and my heart is in arresting pain."

"Of course, my love. Let us lie together, nap and rejuvenate ourselves. When we arise, we can visit more with Lady Stephens."

It did not take long for Sophia to fall asleep, although her rest was neither rejuvenating nor restful. Instead, it was filled with dreams of fear and torment.

After everyone in the house completed their naps, Lady Stephens and Sophia sat in the library room reading while James prepared for his departure. There was a tension in the house that everyone noticed; however, no one spoke of it.

Supper was served and again everyone ate in silence, besides the occasional proper request of, 'please pass the vegetables' or 'please pass the potatoes.' When the meal had finished, once again, the ladies returned to reading their books while James continued preparing for his trip. Night came and with it the evening air brought uneasiness wafting throughout the house.

In the morning Lady Stephens joined James and Sophia on the porch for tea. The couple was holding hands and staring out at the endless expanse of water, while listening to the trashing waves.

"Am I interrupting something?" Lady Stephens asked.

"Oh no, not at all. Please join us."

"Sophia and James, I have been thinking all night about the situation presented to you both. I recognize it is not easy to have James depart so quickly after your wedding. I also believe it might be difficult for me to work as swiftly as would be required to prepare and complete all my finances in order to depart for Scotland. I would like to propose a possible solution that might just work out well for all of us. If, of course, it is not much of a burden, I would like to extend my stay here as your guest a while longer."

James immediately recognizes the wisdom of Lady Stephens's proposal.

"Most certainly, Lady Stephens. It would be our pleasure to accommodate you. It is the least we can do after the generosity you have extended to us," James responds, smiling directly at Lady Stephens and extending a look of warm gratitude.

"Oh, Lady Stephens, how wonderful it would be to have your company instead of being here all alone in this big house."

"Splendid. Then I will have Theodore coordinate everything at once. I must have everything moved out of my house this week for the new tenants to assume ownership of my property."

Following Lady Stephens's suggestion, the mood on the porch instantly shifted. Suddenly, there was much more gaiety in all of their voices and the topics being discussed centered around the lovely surroundings and the possibilities of planting different varieties of blooms in the garden. Lady Stephens was pleased with herself for her ability to lift the burden of the imminent departure of James from Sophia. She, too, was deeply saddened by the ill news of Colonel James's sudden departure. Her hope now was he would return home safely.

Chapter Fifteen

The midnight air rolled in from the sea, swirling around the room and brushing against James and Sophia's naked skin. Lying silently awake in their bedroom, they treasured being wrapped in each other's arms, and they cherished these final hours before James's departure later today. The curtains swayed from the soft air entering the room. 'Peculiar,' Sophia thought, 'I had always enjoyed the mystique of the evening air, yet tonight this midnight air levitating over me is ladened with the murk of trepidation. How am I to live in this house without James? Will he return from his mission unscathed? If James does not return, could I ever love someone else?'

The midnight air also caused James to drift away and contemplate. 'How funny it is, while lying here with Sophia in my arms, the air, which usually feels like a blanket that a mother might use to make her infant feel more snug, does not serve that purpose for me. No, tonight the air seems to carry with it a message of foreboding. Tonight, the midnight air heralds a warning, a cautionary alert. "Do not let thy armor down," it says as it wafts into the room.'

The midnight air continues to softly blow whispers upon the couple. James slowly rubs his warm hands along Sophia's skin while she looks up at him with an unsettled look of fear on her face. He tenderly kisses her neck and forehead, as if to say, 'it will be all right,' despite his own tremendous fears.

"I need to be inside you, Sophia. Deep inside you. Please allow me this moment to connect with you on the most intimate level I know how."

"Of course, my darling."

Sophia worries as she stares into her husband's eyes. She does not see joy. Rather, she sees consternation. Sophia closes her eyes. This is not the manner in which she wishes to remember James when he is absent from her and on his mission. James enters Sophia with a craving he has not experienced before. He forces himself deep inside his lover. They come in unison, showing the true testament of their love.

James removes his penis, dripping with both their juices. He finds himself aroused again by the sight of his wife. Moments later he enters Sophia once again, coming a second time inside her.

"Bloody hell woman, what have you done to me? You have possessed me with your beauty and your love!" James calls out, surprised at his own virility.

"I love when you are inside me, James. I hope this is a feeling you will remember when you are gone."

"My love, this is a feeling that would be difficult for any man to forget," James said, smiling at Sophia.

Sophia can feel James's chest rising and lowering from the intensity of his breath. She continues to rub his chest, enjoying the area of hair amongst his muscles. 'This is the most special memory I shall have of the midnight air in our bedroom. A memory that includes the euphoric feeling of James next to me while surrounded by the air caressing me into a state of blessedness.'

The daylight rises and James knows what lies ahead. He steps out of bed, putting on his uniform. His heart is weighted by his somber and conflicted emotions. He can only hope he has done the right thing by not telling Sophia about the severity of this mission. He did not share the extent of her father's warnings regarding the extreme concern the General had for the voyage and what James might encounter once he begins his negotiations with the King of Portugal.

The General trusted 'no one' but James to have the skills and strength to complete this mission. As part of James's duties, the General explicitly requested the letter, now sealed with the British coat of arms, be hand-delivered to the King by James himself. He was also insistent that James remain in the King's presence to witness him opening and reading the letter.

James pulls on his uniform jacket. The final button signals one of the final tasks he must undertake before he begins to depart his home. In his hand, he holds a letter. This one is not the one the General wants him to deliver to the King. No, this sealed letter is written to his precious wife, Sophia. This one is marked with a black seal stamped with a heart. James places the letter for the King in his uniform pocket and quietly walking over to their bed, he once again reads the outside of the envelope. *"To My Darling Lover. I Shall Return. AJL."* He places the letter under the pillow, so only a small portion of a fibrous corner of the envelope is exposed.

He looks over at Sophia peacefully sleeping in their bed. James was careful not to awaken her; he could not bear to see the forlorn look on her face, caused by his departure. A tear escapes from James's eye. 'I am a Colonel now, there shall be none of that,' he determines, as he quickly gathers his composure. James leaves the safety of their bedroom and walks downstairs.

"Thank you for your service, Theodore. I trust that my home, my wife and my guest will be well cared for in your service," James said, as he bids his farewell to Theodore.

"Indeed it will be, sir," Theodore replies, surprised about the sadness he feels at the Colonel's departure.

Walking to the barn, with a commanding look to his step, James calls out. "William?"

"Yes, sir," William responds, sticking his head outside the barn door.

'Funny,' James thinks. 'This blonde hair, blue-eyed German man seems out of place in my English barn, yet I could not imagine anyone finer for this job. I trust William implicitly.'

"I want to have a conversation with you."

"Of course, sir."

"I am in need of leaving my home with my peace of mind intact. I want you to watch over my wife and guard and protect her under all circumstances. You have my full permission to protect her and all my prized possessions in any way you see fit. Is that clear?"

"Yes, sir. It is a duty I will take very seriously. Sir, I am indebted to you and you can be assured I will watch over and protect Mrs. Langston with my life. I will also protect your estate, sir. You have my word, Colonel James."

William is immediately drawn back to the loss of his wife in Prussia. He would not wish that pain and anguish on any other human being, especially the Colonel, whom he respects.

James smiles with relief and shakes William's hand.

"I know I can depend on you, William. I know you are a man of integrity and honor, and that is comforting to me. I will see you upon my return and then we can celebrate my arrival with a fine pint of ale."

"I would enjoy that, sir," William said, surprised by the Colonel suggesting a friendly moment together instead of acting only as his employer.

'Why would the Colonel deem it necessary to celebrate his return? Is there something more about this mission I should be aware of?' he surmises.

James walks back toward the house to gather his sword and leather bag. In the distance, he sees Sophia walking on the beach. For reasons unknown to Sophia, she turns back to the house and sees James standing on the grounds.

'I cannot leave without saying goodbye and kissing my wife one more time,' he thinks.

James runs quickly toward the beach. Sophia freezes and stares at him, crying. She cannot regain her composure. Reaching his sobbing wife, James wipes her tears away with his handkerchief and pulls her close to him for comfort.

"Please do not cry my love. Please do not cry. I shall be back. I shall return safely to you and we will lie in bed for days and make love and hold each other close."

With the hem of her gown wet from the splashing of the sea waves, Sophia begins to shake from the dampness of the morning air.

"Your hands are freezing, Sophia. Your entire body is freezing. You should not be out here in this damp and chilly weather."

"I must clear my head and gain comfort from this sea, James."

"Sophia, you look pale and weak. I must take you back to the house at once," James said, now extremely concerned for his wife's health.

James can see Sophia's eyelids begin to lower and her legs begin to buckle, no longer able to support her weight. James catches Sophia in his arms before she faints.

Carrying Sophia's limb body, James runs to the house, calling for Theodore and William.

"I have you, my darling. Speak to me, Sophia. Wake up," James yells, panicked by how lifeless Sophia feels in his arms.

Reaching the porch, James is met by Theodore, Lady Stephens and William. James carries Sophia into the drawing room and lays her down on their settee.

"Oh, my gracious. What has happened?" Lady Stephens cries out in a flustered voice.

"I was on the beach, she became pale and then she simply fainted into my arms."

"Theodore, bring some cold water and some towels. William, quickly ride off and return with the doctor. Hurry at once!" Lady Stephens shouts orders, immediately assuming the role of the person in charge.

"Lady Stephens, I am torn. I must leave as my duty requires, but I cannot leave my wife here under these circumstances."

"James, look at me," Lady Stephens commands in an authoritative voice James had never imagined she could possess. "You must leave on your mission for our King. That is your required obligation. I shall stay here with Sophia and ensure her well-being. I will not depart for my homeland until you have returned home safely to your wife. You have my word as your friend."

'Your friend,' thinks James. 'Those are incredibly comforting words at this moment in time.'

"Thank you, Lady Stephens. I will be forever in your debt."

"Do not think twice about it, Colonel. Now off you go, or you will miss your ship, and for all I know, if the King does not receive whatever message he is due to receive, our country may be in peril."

James kneels down next to Sophia. He can feel the pressure of his King's letter in his uniform pocket. He places his hand on the protrusion in his jacket. 'I am shredded by two duties, that of a husband whose wife has been taken ill and that of a Colonel', James ruminates as he rises and exits the drawing room.

Lady Stephens continues to place cool towels upon Sophia's forehead. Reaching the room door, James turns to take one more contemplative look at his wife. His face is that of a man who has already been to war in his mind. Lady Stephens sees his look of worry and wishes these were not the circumstances to which he must depart. Sophia awakes abruptly.

"What happened?" she asked, confused and groggy.

"Oh, my darling," James declares, immediately returning to his wife. "You are awake. You cannot imagine the fear you placed in all of us. You collapsed into my arms. William has gone off to retrieve the doctor."

"Take a sip of these bitters and water my dear. It will help settle your sickness," Lady Stephens said comfortingly, handing Sophia the glass while James raises her head and Theodore places additional pillows behind her neck.

"I felt a wave of dizziness and nausea come over me on the beach."

In the distance James can hear the carriage pull onto the driveway. He knows he must depart and is frustrated by the anomalous and frantic events of the last thirty minutes. James notes that Sophia's paleness continues.

"Sophia, I love you more than the stars in the sky and the fish in the seas. In the evening when you look up at the sky, think of me, for I will be there in your thoughts. I promise I shall do the same while I am gone, my love. You will always be near to my heart. You, Sophia, will be my strength," James said, holding back his own tears while embracing Sophia tightly. "I love you, Sophia. Wait patiently for me. I will return to you and then we can continue our love-making in the bedroom and perhaps throughout our house," James whispers into Sophia's ear.

Sophia listens to James's whisper while at the same time releasing several tears from her violet-grey colored eyes. Lady Stephens can no longer hold back her own tears. Her cheekbones also become moist. Theodore feels a large lump in his throat and turns to look away in fear of bawling like a young child in front of his employer.

"I shall wait for thee, my love. I promise to watch the stars and breathe in the evening air every night and think of you. I ask of you, that you promised me, that you will remain safe," Sophia said.

"I promise," James replies kissing her softly, uncertain he will be able to keep his promise.

Again, he does not want Sophia to perceive any indication of the extreme danger of this mission.

James rises, pulling himself away from Sophia and intentionally throwing back his shoulders and lifting his chin as he walks out of the sitting room. He does not look back. He knows he cannot, for if he did, he would not have the ability to leave Sophia.

James's mind was now on his mission and his duty to his King. He places his hand on his sword hanging along his leg, unaware the other's eyes are all staring at this hand on his sword.

Sophia can hear the horse's hooves trotting briskly away. She is certain she is about to faint once again. 'How can she continue without her lover? How can she live without James at her side?' She lies lifeless on the settee as tears roll down her face and her chest heaves from her sobbing.

"My dear, do not cry. Everything shall be fine. Theodore and I are here to help you manage through this temporary absence."

Sophia suddenly realizes, since James has left, 'I am the Lady left to manage a new estate and... I have a butler and a wise woman at my side.'

"Oh, Lady Stephens, I would be lost if you had not decided to extend your stay with us. I am so appreciative of your presence here."

Lady Stephens is impressed by Sophia's ability to turn away from delirium, toward management of the situation. She gently slides the back side of her hand down Sophia's cheek.

"All will be well, my dear," she responds, looking down at Sophia and suddenly sensing a wonderful glow about the young girl, despite Sophia's ill feeling. 'How strange that Sophia should look so beautiful when she has just been queasy and worried by her husband's departure.'

Both women hear the arrival of two horses. Their eyes turn toward the front door. "It must be William and the doctor," Lady Stephens announces.

Theodore opens the front door as the two men, William and Doctor Hadley, enter the house, both rushing into the drawing room.

Doctor Hadley, an elderly man, was wearing a very proper black suit. He had been a doctor for many years and was the doctor who brought Sophia into this world. He was also the physician who tended to the General's wounds after every battle. Sadly, he was also the doctor who tended to Sophia's mother during her dying hours. Observing the very flushed looking Sophia lying on the settee, his mind conjured all sorts of memories regarding the medical care of this family.

Lady Stephens, assuming command of the situation now that Colonel James has departed, said, "Doctor Hadley, thank you for coming so quickly. We are most appreciative."

Turning her attention to William for a moment, Lady Stephens delivers William directions.

"William, please tend to yours and the doctor's horses. I can only imagine their flanks are still moving quite briskly from your ride. Once you are done, come inside and Theodore will prepare a hardy meal for all of us."

Theodore takes his cues from Lady Stephens and leaves the room to begin preparing food for everyone. William leaves to tend to the horses and is very impressed that Lady Stephens is aware and concerned about the horses' flanks. 'She must care for the fine creatures as much as I do,' he reckons.

Doctor Hadley stands over Sophia, looking down at her.

"Sophia, what have you done this time, my dear?" It seems Doctor Hadley had often been called to the General's house to address a variety of medical needs of this strong minded, adventurous young lady. Lady Stephens answers for Sophia, not appreciating the doctor's flippant tone.

"She became pale and dizzy while walking on the beach this morning. She collapsed into her husband's arms."

"I see, and how and where is Colonel James?" the doctor asks.

He had attended their public wedding, and the General had confided in him regarding the handfasting ceremony held by James and Sophia previously. Doctor Hadley was surprised that the Colonel was not in charge of this situation today and wondered why Lady Stephens felt it was her duty to assume the role.

"The Colonel was required to depart on a mission today. I am here upon the Colonel's request to assist Sophia with matters of the estate and her well-being," Lady Stephens confidently replies, aware Doctor Hadley is leery of her presence. "This has been a very busy few days for Sophia. She has been constantly fatigued and seems to become nauseous at the sight of food and at other odd times."

As Lady Stephens describes Sophia's symptoms, it was as though the prognosis entered the doctor's and Lady Stephens's mind at the same time. To confirm the look the two had just given each other, Lady Stephens adds, "And today, as Sophia lay on this settee, I could sense a lovely glow about her."

The doctor gives Lady Stephens an affirming nod. Sophia is completely unaware of what these two people leaning over her are implying. 'Is something horribly wrong with her and she will not be alive for James's return? Has she been cursed with a terrible, deforming disease?'

"My dear," the doctor retorts. "Although it is too early to confirm, I would surmise, based on your symptoms, you are going to have your first bairn."

"A bairn, but how is that possible?" Sophia sits up forming a very distinctive 'L' position with her body on the settee.

"I suspect the 'how' has been explained to you, Mrs. Langston," the doctor responds with a cheeky grin. "I will coordinate a midwife to come pay you a visit, as you prepare for a joyful next nine months."

Sophia begins to cry tears of joy.

"Sophia, what wonderful news. You are going to be a mother," Lady Stephens said, trying to hide her own sorrows of not being able to conceive and become a mother herself.

Sophia, overwhelmed by the news she is carrying her husband's first bairn, touches her stomach and smiles.

"Theodore, please prepare us some tea," Lady Stephens instructs.

"Let us be sure it is not Pennyroyal tea, Theodore, as that would induce an abortion," the doctor advises strongly.

Suddenly Sophia was struck by this urgency of any additional knowledge she must gain in order to secure the well-being of her child.

After everyone enjoys their tea, followed by an invitation to the doctor to stay for supper, Sophia retires to her bedroom. Theodore, diligent in his duties, had prepared a fire in the room for Sophia to be more comfortable. She reluctantly climbs into bed, for what she can only assume will be a restless night. It does not seem tolerable that she must lie in this bed by herself. She misses the smell, the touch and the voice of James. Hannah, her new pup, lies on the carpet next to her. As a puppy, she has already assumed her role as a guard dog.

'It has been quite a day,' Sophia thinks. She rubs the area in the bed where James sleeps. Perhaps she can do as Aladdin had done in *One Thousand and One Nights* and rub her ring against the sheets for James to reappear.

While making large circular motions on the sheet, Sophia notices an envelope near James's pillow. She holds up the envelope and reads.

'To My Darling Lover. I Shall Return. AJL.'

At first Sophia thinks this must be a dream. 'Perhaps I am like Aladdin.' She realizes the envelope is, in fact, real, when she sees the black wax seal stamped with a heart on the envelope. It was as though James sealed this letter with his heart. Sophia moved her fingers slowly over to the wax heart shape. Carefully, she opens the letter, ensuring she does not disturb the heart seal, beautifully carved into the wax. Sophia began to read the words on the page.

My Darling Love,

I am a man of ardent desires.

For which my dear, you've lit my internal fires.

You feed my heart, you feed my soul.

Without you, my love, I am not whole.

You are my one true love, my beautiful wife.

Your love brings me comfort during my military strife.

Do not weep nor long for me,

As I set out on the treacherous sea.

Though I travel without thee for this endeavor,

I shall be with thee forever and ever.

Fondest Love, James

December 15, 1733

Chapter Sixteen

At the breakfast table, all I can think about is the fact that Sophia is going to have a baby and James does not even know because he is away. 'That is awful.'

"You are awfully quiet this morning, Sarah Marie," Gramma comments.

Trying not to let Gramma know I was worried about what I was reading in her book, I ask, "When did you know you were pregnant with Mommy, Gramma?"

Gramma, whose back was facing me while she washed dishes in the sink, immediately turned around with a sharp jerk to her neck. She looked at me with her eyebrows raised and her eyelids hidden. It was as if her eyeballs were sticking out.

"Oh my, I did not expect that question from you today, little one. Let me see, I guess the first time I knew I was pregnant was when I was with your Great Gramma in my mother's kitchen. We were having coffee and she said I looked different. I looked happier and brighter and there was a sparkle in my eye. I said I didn't know what she was talking about, because that morning I felt faint and wanted to throw up."

"Did Great Gramma think you had a glow on you?" I asked, not completely aware of the concept I was referring to.

"Yes," Gramma responded, even more confused that I knew about 'the pregnancy glow.' "Great Gramma looked at me and said, 'Oh heavens, you're pregnant, darling!' After that I went to the doctor and he confirmed Great Gramma was right. I was indeed pregnant with your mother. Why do you ask, little one?"

I had to think fast about my answer. I did not want Gramma to know I was thinking about Sophia.

"Ahhh, I was just thinking, because Uncle Johnny thought one of his cows might be pregnant and I was wondering how he knew."

"Well, pregnant cows are different than pregnant women. They don't glow, they just keep mooing," Gramma said with a smile, turning back to continue washing the dishes.

Moments later Grandpa walks into the kitchen.

"Good morning, little chic-chic. How would you like to do something special today?"

"I always love doing special things with you, Grandpa."

"I've just cleaned my BB gun. Would you like to try it out and see if it works okay?"

"Really, Grandpa? Will you really let me shoot your BB gun?"

I can see Gramma standing at the sink, shaking her head in disbelief.

"You bet, little chic-chic. Come outside with me and let's leave Fluffy in the house with Gramma."

Once outside, Grandpa sets up three large blue coffee cans in the dirt at the end of the garden. He puts them in a straight row and tells me about how this is a good position for them, because nothing is around that could accidentally get hit.

"It is important you learn how to handle and shoot a gun properly, little chic-chic. It is better you know about gun safety now. Guns are no joke; they are not for silly play. It all begins with safety first." He continues with a very serious look on his face. "You know how Grandpa keeps all his guns locked up in the house? That is for safety. With this BB gun you can only touch it when I take it out. Do you understand, little chic-chic? This is very serious and very important for you to remember."

"Yes, Grandpa, I understand."

I don't know how, but Grandpa had instantly turned this fun and exciting activity into a stern and serious moment. He was not kidding around, and I knew it.

Grandpa grabs his mason jar filled with copper BB pellets and loads them into his gun. He then pumps the chamber full, getting the gun ready to shoot.

"Watch me closely as I eye my target," he instructs me. "Always hold the gun here on your shoulder. Keep your right eye steady and aimed on the target. Hold your arms steady, now gently squeeze the trigger."

The BB gun instantly lets out a 'bang' followed by a 'ping' from the pellets hitting the coffee can. Then in a millisecond, there was the echoing sound of the original gunshot.

"That was loud, Grandpa," I call out, surprised.

"Yes, it was. Now it's your turn, little chic-chic."

"I'm scared, Grandpa."

"Sarah Marie, you can do anything you put your mind to. Don't you forget that, young lady. Now put on these goggles for safety and let's shoot. Let me help you brace the gun on your right shoulder. Let your left arm stay straight out. Hold her steady. Focus on your target by closing your left eye."

Grandpa guides me from behind. He holds my two arms steady, as I pull the trigger gently. I hit the cans.

"Nice shot, Sarah Marie. Good job for you! We can shoot for a little while longer, then Grandpa has to go do some chores."

After we finished shooting, Grandpa shows me how to put the gun safely away.

"Thank you Grandpa, that was really awesome."

"You are welcome, little chic-chic. Now tell ya what, come help me get some baskets and pick some vegetables for dinner."

"Sure."

After we pick the vegetables, Grandpa carries our heavy baskets over to the outdoor faucet and washes the vegetables, one by one. He hands me the first batch to bring into the house.

Walking into the kitchen, I see Gramma reading her book, with a half-drunk cup of coffee beside her. The book cover is different from the one she was reading yesterday, the one with the roses and the whip. The book I see today is the one Gramma bought yesterday at the store when we were shopping. It is the book with the cover that has the box of chocolates and the underwear on it. Gramma quickly, yet very controlled, turns the book upside down on the kitchen table. She looks up at me and said.

"How was shooting the BB gun with Grandpa?"

"It was so much fun. After shooting, we picked some vegetables for dinner. Here they are, Gramma. I'm going to go back outside to help Grandpa."

"Okay," Gramma said.

I continue helping Grandpa in the yard and then he asks me to help pass him tools while he does some work on his truck. After what seems like a long day, it was time for dinner.

I go inside to help Gramma set the table and pour iced tea into our drinking glasses. Gramma places her homemade spaghetti sauce on the table while Grandpa slices some of the sausage he had just cooked for us on the grill. We all bow our heads, as Gramma said grace.

After dinner, the kitchen is cleaned up and Grandpa goes off to watch television. It does not surprise me when Gramma walks over to her rocking chair, picks up her book and begins to read. I look forward to reading too. I have been waiting all day to get back to reading.

"Gramma, I'm going to go upstairs and play dress up with all the old dresses and shoes you gave me."

"Okay, that's a good idea, Sarah Marie. Come give Gramma a hug before you go."

Looking back, I see Gramma with her face in her book. Smiling, I proceed up the stairs.

Once in my bedroom, I retrieve my book from the green shoebox. Placing it on my bed, I notice my room feels stuffy from the warmth of the day and the cooking smells from dinner. I crack my bedroom window open to bring in some fresh air. Staring out into the darkness of my grandparents' yard, I begin to think and dream about Sophia. 'So much is happening in her life. Life in the 18th century is really different from living now,' I contemplate. 'Maybe this year in school, I will get to do a project on the 18th century. I sure would have a lot of information I could write about after reading this book.'

I decide to scatter some of Gramma's dress-up clothes around the room, so it looks like I have been playing with them. Then I clip in my new sparkly hair barrettes and start to brush my long, black curly hair. I also tie my new fancy ribbons into my hair. Looking into the mirror, I am certain I look just like Sophia. I am excited about being a grown-up; I could read books all the time like my Gramma does.

Lying down on my bed, I remove my bookmark indicating the page I had last read. I can feel the midnight air blowing onto me from the yard, or should I say, from the estate. I rub the texture of the sheets, as Sophia would have done. I feel the barrettes in my hair—my long, curly hair—and in this moment, I am Sophia. This book has definitely put a spell on me. I look over at my door, making sure it is closed and locked. I lie back onto my bed and begin to read.

Chapter Seventeen

Captain Taller's tall ship begins to set sail. Everyone on board had acute concerns regarding the conditions of the rough seas. James places his feet firmly on the deck, looking at the white caps on the waves. Although not a sailor, as his military rank came from his years of service in the British Army, he did, however, have a keen interest in predicting the weather. Before boarding the ship, James noticed the weather vanes on the houses were all pointing eastward, a sign of changing weather. He had also been checking the barometer in his master study to determine if the atmospheric pressure might be conducive for this journey. He was most thankful to Torricelli for inventing such a great device almost 100 years prior. His barometer had indicated the weather on the following days would be fair, and for that, James was grateful.

For hours the ship jostled amongst the swells and waves crashed over the side of the Royale Darrick. It was December 15th, 1733 and everyone on board could not wait for this day to be over and for smooth seas to return. The salty water sprayed against James's face as Captain Robert Taller approached with a limp. He wanted to greet his ship's visitor.

Captain Taller was a man of height with gray hair. He spoke in a gruff voice from one side of his mouth, with the other side being used to rest the end of a long clay pipe filled with sweet Virginia tobacco. It was obvious the Captain intended to impress his passengers with his ability to access products from the Colonies. James was not impressed. The bowl end of the Captain's pipe bobbed with the waves as he spoke.

"I understand General Cartwright has requested I help you obtain a safe passage to Portugal, Colonel. General Cartwright and I have helped one another quite a lot over the past twenty years."

As Captain Taller speaks, he takes another puff of his pipe, blowing out the sweet tobacco aroma into the air.

"The General was always willing to take in my soldiers when we needed a place to stay for a night or two. I was his ship and he was our port in the storm, so to speak." The Captain smiled, impressed by his simple naval analogy.

James had always been impressed by the General's political abilities. He sensed the General may have also used those abilities with the Captain. During this conversation with the Captain, James could hear the General's counsel in his head.

'You must act like a Roman. Roman leaders embraced and partnered with as many groups as possible. The creation of an ally was instrumental to their rising. In my military role, I choose to do the same.'

"How did you originally meet the General, Captain Taller?" James inquires, suspecting it was most likely the General who sought out to meet the Captain.

"Ahh, yes. It was a day I shall never forget," Captain Taller replies, looking off to the right, as if he was about to relive a pleasant day. "We were in heavy battle against a French ship. I am saddened to say I believe we were about to lose the battle that day. I pushed my men to their limit as the pressure from the French ship continued to bludgeon our ship. Some French soldiers had boarded our ship, while others remained and kept firing upon us. Although my right leg had suffered several stabs, it was my sheer will and desire to protect my men that kept me fighting."

That would explain the Captain's limp, James thought.

"In the distance, I could hear a horn echoing off the water of the sea. I was certain these were the trumpets of heaven calling me to my final home. The horn could have also been the signaling of help on the way. Either way, I kept fighting and was proud my men did the same. Fortunately for us, the sound was not the angels' trumpets, but rather a vessel with General Cartwright and his men. When they reached my ship, they came charging on board. That was the day General Cartwright saved me and my men's lives. The French ship retreated and the General immediately tended to my bleeding leg. He had the quick wit of a physician. If it were not for the General's timing and medical knowledge, I would have lost my leg that day. In addition, me and my men would not be here to transport you on this voyage, Colonel James."

"What a benison that brought General Cartwright to your aid that day," James said, mesmerized by the intensity of the Captain's story.

"The General had been returning from a political mission for our King. It was providence that during his mission, he had purchased a large amount of military supplies. It was the availability of those supplies that saved our lives."

"That is indeed quite the story, Captain. The General is a courageous and wise man indeed."

"You appear to view him with great fondness," the Captain responded, interested to hear the Colonel explain his connection between the General.

"I most certainly do, Captain Taller. I am one of his most loyal soldiers. He claims I am his most trusted soldier."

James immediately can hear another one of the General's lessons emerge in his mind. 'Trust no one.' The General reiterated these words to James before he departed. James heeded this lesson and chose not to discuss he was the General's now son-in-law. Instead, James chose to change the direction of the discussion with the Captain.

"I count thirteen days for the completion of our voyage, Captain."

"If she holds the water steady, we can gain a few days and arrive sooner than we had expected," Captain Taller replies, intentionally wanting to provide additional information to demonstrate his advanced nautical knowledge. "It would also be advantageous to mention, we must always be alert to enemy ships in these waters. I am confident my men are prepared for battle and an extra pair of military eyes and arms would be welcome if battle ensues."

James's mind drifts out to sea. The thought of entering into battle with the possibility of never returning to his beloved Sophia was unbearable. The mere thought sickened him. Oh, how he longed to hold Sophia in his arms, his beautiful Sophia.

"The sea holds many dreams and secrets, does it not, Colonel?" the Captain asks, noticing James's mind drifting off to a different place.

"It does indeed," James replies, again offering only a limited response.

"And how many years have you served and looked out to the sea?" James asks, once again diverting the attention away from himself.

"Thirty-five years. I was but a boy of sixteen when I enlisted. I was a troubled young bairn, and my father enrolled me in hopes the military would set me straight on the right path."

"Did your father achieve his goal?" James asks.

"Shall I invite you into my quarters for a whiskey, Colonel? We can continue our conversation there and not on this public deck."

"Of course," James responds, surprised by the abrupt diversion to the question and with an invitation to a less public location. There was something about the Captain that James did not trust. His senses were on high alert for the man who was to be transporting him safely to Portugal.

Once inside the Captain's quarters, two larges glasses of whiskey were poured. Captain Taller swilled back the first glass effortlessly.

"Sounds like you were a handful for your parents," James commented, eagerly edging the Captain on for more details about his past.

Captain Taller refills his glass, taking another large swig of whiskey, for the purpose of numbing his feelings. 'It would appear I have hit a sensitive nerve,' James reflects. The consumption of vast amounts of whiskey had reached the Captain's mind, causing him to become tipsy in both stature and speech.

"I was always in and out of some sort of trouble. I was arrested a few times for theft, only because of the types of people with which I associated. My parents attempted to curb my actions; however, it was futile. Trouble seemed to always find me. Finally, I recognized and accepted the fact that I was destined to be in constant trouble. I was cursed by trouble. I am Captain Trouble. That is what they call me, Captain Trouble," the Captain said, slurring his speech and weaving from side to side. Taking his final swig of whiskey, the Captain sets his empty glass onto his table. He looks forlorn.

"You need to go now, Colonel. I must review some important documents."

The abruptness of the Captain's request surprises James.

"Of course, Captain," James said, rising from the bench seat. "Thank you for your hospitality."

While departing, James grabs on to the rail tightly, saying under his breath, 'I certainly hope trouble does not follow him on this trip.'

After several days, James notices himself becoming thin. His diet of heavily salted cured meat and dry biscuits and beer was not enough to sustain his weight. The only thing that brought sustenance to James was the gold pocket watch he carried in his pocket. Each day, he would regularly open it carefully and imagine his time with Sophia. Oh, how he wanted that time together again. Oh, how he wanted to smell her long, black curly hair, feel her soft, light almond skin and feel the rush of being inside her. Standing on the deck of a ship, packed with smelly, crass sailors, did nothing to help remove the aching, absent feeling he had. 'Oh Sophia, I hope you are well and waiting for me, my love.'

~~~

One day after James's departure, Sophia waits in her music room for Governess Abigale. She is scheduled to visit today and lead Sophia through her harpsichord lessons. Sophia suspects the Governess has arrived, as Hannah barks at the sound of a carriage approaching the house. She hears Theodore receive the visitor at the front door, but the footsteps are not those one would expect of a governess. No, instead Sophia hears her father's heavy leather military boots walking through the house.

"Father?" Sophia said, surprised by her father's presence. "To what do I owe this pleasant surprise?"

"Not a surprise, Sophia. Purely a visit from a concerned father. I was just informed that you had fallen ill yesterday and the doctor came to your aid. This visit is to ensure my only daughter is in acceptable health."

Before Sophia could answer, Lady Stephens enters the room, followed by Governess Abigale. Hearing the General's question, Lady Stephens politely clears her throat.

"General, may I suggest we all take our seats."

"You may not, Lady Stephens," the General retorts, looking directly at Lady Stephens, and speaking in a tone that indicates he is not the type of man who takes orders from just anyone, especially a woman.

"Father, Lady Stephens means no harm. In fact, I would be happy if she would answer your question about Doctor Hadley's visit."

Sophia was accustomed to her father's dominance, although she was not in favor of it. In this moment, she was proud of herself for standing up for Lady Stephens and against her father. Lady Stephens was not fazed in the least by the General's comments. 'Oh sir,' she thought. 'Clearly you have not been in a room filled with arrogant bankers. You, General, have not experienced dominant men.'

"The doctor presented Sophia with some delightful news, General. Sophia is with her first bairn."

The General's demeanor instantly changed, as he walked over to embrace his daughter. "Sophia, this is splendid news indeed. James must be elated."

Sophia's face drops, along with her shoulders.

"No father, he does not know. His carriage came and he left before I received this news."

The General's stomach sours. 'I have sent a soldier, my son-in-law, on a dangerous mission without knowing his wife is with child.' A feeling of guilt overwhelms the General. As he looks at his pregnant daughter, he is suddenly in agony. He can only imagine the anguish she must be feeling with James not here.

After some conversation about the pregnancy, it was suggested by the General that the harpsichord lesson be cancelled, based on this news. Lady Stephens insisted it should be continued, and while it is occurring, she and the General should go for a walk on the beach. The General agrees to the suggestion and Governess Abigale sits next to Sophia at the harpsichord. The moment Sophia places her hands on the keys, Abigale covers one of Sophia's hands with her own.

"Congratulations," she said with the happiest of grins.

"Thank you, Abbey. I hope this bairn will not mind hearing all my mistakes as I continue to learn from you."

"Of course not," Abigale replies. "Of course not."

The next morning, Sophia greets Lady Stephens in the foyer.

"Shall we head out to the garden house while the sun is shining and enjoy the posies," Sophia asks.

"That would be lovely, my dear."

As the two ladies enter into the garden house, they are greeted by William. He was excited to see their interest in the flowers and the new blooms.

"Your gardening skills are exquisite, William."

"Thank you, Lady Stephens."

Still in her role of head of an estate, Lady Stephens begins issuing directions to William.

"I think we shall go into town today. I would like you to purchase some paint and give this new garden house its first coat of paint. I would also like you to build Sophia more working tables; she will need space for her herbs and an area to cut her fresh roses for her vases. Do you not agree, Sophia?"

"I do, Lady Stephens. I most certainly appreciate your instant willingness to help advance 'my' home to such a stately level. I am grateful for your presence here as our visitor."

Sophia was instantly aware her lessons from Governess Abigale were being channeled through her at that moment. 'Ensure you graciously establish your presence in the room. The aristocrats have a way of establishing power. You must not lower yourself to them; simply remain at their level,' she would advise.

"I think the fresh air from a carriage ride shall do us both some good today," Lady Stephens said, encouragingly.

"William, will you prepare our carriage for transport and inform Bernard, my carriage man," Sophia said.

"Yes, my lady, it would be my pleasure. I will have it ready at once."

"Thank you, William."

Lady Stephens is pleased Sophia is showing less melancholy this morning. It is apparent she is attempting to keep her mind away from the absence of Colonel James.

The carriage arrives in front of the town's shopping area. Its elegance does not go unnoticed by those walking along the cobblestone street. Theodore was also asked to accompany the ladies. It was thought he would be helpful, especially with Sophia, in her fragile state.

Theodore escorts the ladies into Franklin's Linen Store. Sophia's bustled gown creates a flowing affect as she walks toward the linen section. She explores the fabrics, sliding her hand over the different textures and colors.

"Have you found something to your liking, my dear?" Lady Stephens inquires.

"I suspect these fabrics will be perfect for a blanket for our bairn. I can also decorate the room with these two other colors over here."

Lady Stephens notes that life and excitement has been breathed back into Sophia. What a tremendous relief, she concludes. "Sir," Lady Stephens calls for the clerk. "We shall take a roll of each color."

Lady Stephens quietly hands Theodore the money, telling him to pay for the purchase.

"Sophia, I suggest we look at the shop next door. Perhaps we may find some additional items for your bairn's room."

"Brilliant," Sophia responds with glee. "First, I must purchase my selection."

"Nonsense, my dear. I have arranged for the transaction to be settled. My gift to you."

"Oh my. Thank you so much," Sophia answers with sincere gratitude.

Theodore proudly walks the two fine ladies into the next store, the package of purchased fabric resting under his arm. Sophia's spies a white bassinet. It is hand craved, with a detailed inlay of hand-painted cherubs accenting the border.

"Oh my gracious, it is magnificent! This is the bed for my bairn," Sophia immediately blurts out, not appropriate for her refined stature.

Lady Stephens chuckles. Sophia rocks the bassinet back and forth, soothed by the motion.

"I wish to purchase this item," Sophia tells the clerk, who had been hovering over them, waiting to assist. Sophia dreams of the moment she will tell James the news of their bairn growing inside her. 'He will be elated by the news and most assuredly be a proud father.'

"Sophia," Lady Stephens beckons. "Come look at this clothing. I suspect you are in great need for many of these items, my dear. Let us fill up that bassinet before we leave." Once again, Lady Stephens advises Theodore to purchase the items from the clerk.

Sophia's insides race with joy. 'What a perfectly lovely day this has been.'

"Your Ladyship. I must not allow you to continue to shower my bairn with all these new and wonderful gifts."

"You must," Lady Stephens insists. "As you find great joy in selecting these items, I find great joy in purchasing them for you."

"My heart is gladdened you have chosen to stay with us. Today, I have especially realized my need for your moral support during my husband's absence."

Over in the corner, Sophia's eyes are drawn to an outdoor table and chair set. The clerk, aware of Sophia's interest, draws the chair away from the table and motions with his hand for Sophia to have a seat. He then does the same for Lady Stephens.

"Ladies, this is a bistro table. It arrived into our shop last week."

Sophia massages the hand-carved walnut table with her finger-tips.

"These hand-carved artisan tiles, inserted into the table top, have also been hand painted by Jobear. He is quite a local famous artist. If you look carefully at the end of the table, you can see his name inscribed." The clerk points to the autograph on top of the table.

Lady Stephens gives Sophia what she hopes is an unnoticed nod, indicating the aristocratic stature of the artist.

"I do think this would look lovely in my garden house. In fact, perhaps Lady Stephens, we shall have afternoon tea on it tomorrow. Sir?" Sophia said, turning to the clerk. "I shall pay you now and send my stableman, William, later today to retrieve it."

"Of course. I shall have it ready for him to take."

As the ladies and Theodore leave the shop, Lady Stephens suggests stopping by the Grand Lux Hotel for high tea.

"I would welcome that, Lady Stephens. Additionally, the last thing I would want to do is have another fainting spell because I am feeling too weak. I find I am famished every hour of the day while in my condition."

The host welcomes Lady Stephens. She is disappointed that he is not the gentleman she has become accustomed to. This man is smaller in build and his clothing looks like it is the first time it had been worn, or had not yet formed to his body.

"Will you ladies be joining us for high tea?"

"Yes, please," Lady Stephens acknowledges as they are shown to their table.

Theodore waits with the carriage to secure the purchases.

"My late husband Henry and I came here often," Lady Stephens said to Sophia. "We have both always admired this white marble ballroom floor. Henry's business clients and associates would often stay in this hotel."

Sophia smiled. "Your Ladyship, James and I frequently visited this dining room during our courtship. We dined here several more times after that as well."

"There are coincidences in yours and my life Sophia, after which I am constantly being made aware of."

Lady Stephens notices the host walking nervously over to their table. He turns to Lady Stephens and politely said.

"Lady Stephens, please excuse my ignorance. The staff has just informed me of your relationship with our hotel. They also expressed you are the finest guest we have ever served. I am sorry, my Lady, I was not aware. Also, please, accept my sincere sympathy, for the passing of your husband, the late Mr. Henry Stephens."

Lady Stephens and Sophia desperately tried to contain their giddiness at the clumsiness of the host's apology. He was fraught with fear at how this gaffe might affect his employment.

"Apology accepted, young man. Now let me introduce my guest, Lady Sophia. I suspect you will be seeing more of her in the days to come."

Lady Stephens smiled at Sophia. She realized the host assumed she meant Sophia would be visiting the hotel, when in fact she was referencing Sophia's growing belly.

After what could only be considered the finest high tea in town, Lady Stephens indicated she would like to show Sophia something of significant importance. As the two ladies walk through the foyer, almost everyone they encountered greeted Lady Stephens by her full name. Turning the corner, Lady Stephens stops and points at the black marble plaque positioned on the wall. Sophia reads the gold lettered inscription. "In commemoration of Mr. Henry Stephens." It was clear Henry was an influential man. What a life he and Lady Stephens must have had.

"Let us venture outside and sit by the fountain in the gardens. I want to share a story with you, Sophia," Lady Stephens suggests.

Sophia nods in agreement.

"My late husband, Henry, made his first banking transaction in this building. Ever since that day, all of his business transactions were fruitful and extremely profitable. Even Henry could not explain how easily his good fortune fell upon him. Between his business and his large family inheritance, we wanted for nothing. For that reason, Henry decided to make an anonymous donation to the building fund for the new wing of the Grand Lux Hotel. Despite all of his wealth, Henry was a humble man. He wanted to be remembered in his life for being a good and honest man. To our great surprise, Henry once again received public recognition. This time for the kind act of his donation. If there is one thing my Henry taught me during our blissful life together, it is to be compassionate and generous. I am the woman I am today because of the daily lessons Henry graced me with. Oh Sophia, I miss him so. No matter how many riches you have, you always miss your true love when he is no longer in your life."

With those words, Lady Stephens held her hands to her face and began to sob. She did not care if she was seen by others. This was the first time she had publicly shown how she truly felt about her deceased husband and she could not stop the tears.

Sophia sat on the bench beside her, placing one arm over her shoulder to comfort her. Tears also rolled down Sophia's face. 'The loss of a husband is unimaginable pain. How could she ever live without James?' Sophia's warm tears rolled down her cheeks as she looked over at Lady Stephens.

~~~

Captain Taller proudly greets his passengers as they exit his ship on December 28, 1733. He had always enjoyed this Portugal port, finding the food, wine and women most enjoyable and entertaining. Colonel James took his turn in line to walk down the plank. The Captain was impressed by how smartly the Colonel's uniform appeared after such a long journey.

"I shall return tomorrow at this time to take passage home. I hope this shall still coordinate with your plans, Captain?" James confirms, shaking the scraggly Captain's hand.

"Indeed it does, Colonel James. I shall see you here tomorrow on December 29, 1733," the Captain responds proudly, pleased he had remembered the date. He also thinks the Colonel should really learn to relax a bit more and get his fill of wine and women while on this foreign soil. There is much to enjoy in Portugal. The Colonel's stiffness did not impress the Captain, who was anxious to set out and enjoy the excellent wine Lisbon has to offer.

"I suggest we meet at the Seafarer Inn, beside the tavern. I will either be resting in my room or enjoying myself in the tavern. Hopefully, you will be able to join me for a drink before we depart on our thirteen-day journey. I await your return from your mission, Colonel."

James nods and moves on to locate the carriage man who had been assigned to deliver him to King John V's palace.

Ensuring the sealed envelope was inside his uniform pocket, James prepares himself to deliver the message to the King and leave immediately following their private meeting. While the carriage transports James to the King's palace in Lisbon, a nagging feeling keeps occurring about Captain Taller's eyes, particularly when James shook his hand while departing the ship. James had taken notice that the Captain looked down at the ground and not into his eyes while shaking his hand and saying he would await his return. This positioning concerned James, as the Captain knew very well James would be risking his life delivering a message to the King. James required loyal and trusting colleagues surrounding him. He did not need to associate with people who believed trouble followed them wherever they went, trouble like Captain Taller.

James continued to replay in his head the conversation the two men had during their voyage. One comment in particular, bothered James the most. It was when Captain Taller said to him, 'You seem to think very fondly of the General.' There was something about the Captain's tone which made it sound as if he was questioning his loyalty to the General. James decided to stay aware of his concerns for Captain Taller. For now he would place his efforts and thoughts on this mission and his meeting with the King of Portugal.

Upon arriving at the palace, James was escorted to the King's meeting room. He was instructed to sit in a chair and await the King. Looking around the room, James was intrigued by the unique architectural finishes of the room, something the King was known for.

James was intrigued to meet the man who ruled with complete power over the land. He wanted to gain insight into the King's reputation for searching out and building relationships with other European countries. 'What type of character did he have, to produce such a reputation? Who did he not show interest negotiating with? How did he engage people?'

James did know the King's political approach helped him gain territories and branch out into India and America. 'But how did he do it?' James wondered.

It was obvious from the King's office he was a religious man. A painting of Pope Benedict XIV hung over his desk, as did many Christian artifacts, including crucifixes, rosaries and statues of saints.

King John V entered the room and as such, James bowed.

The King was James's age, 28 years old, but somehow he looked much older and much less happy. Perhaps it was his wig or all the medals and armor he wore. James was not certain of the reason; he just knew that this was not a contented King.

"Your Majesty, I am Colonel Abraham James Langston, sent of the behalf of the British Army and General Craig Richard Cartwright."

"Good day, Colonel. Welcome to our fine city of Lisbon. I trust your journey was uneventful."

"Indeed it was, your Majesty," James responds immediately, pleased the King attempted to put him to ease.

"I have been instructed to present this envelope to you and await your response." With those words, James presented the sealed envelope to the King.

King John V reads the letter while James patiently waits for his reply. "I see," said the King, sitting down behind his desk.

"It would appear your King would like to come to an agreement with me and stop this bickering between our two countries. If you and I can reach an arrangement today, I do believe an agreement can be formalized. Colonel James, do you have the authority to engage in such a discussion?"

"I do, your Majesty."

James was aware of the contents of the letter. He was also prepared to use his negotiating skills to finalize an agreement with the King.

The General had continually complimented James on his excellent negotiating abilities. 'You have a skill that cannot be learned, James. It is part of your character and mind. It is a natural talent of yours,' the General would say. James hoped that today he would be able to use his skills to negotiate an agreement in a timely manner so he could quickly board Captain Taller's ship and return home to his new wife, Sophia.

"I suggest we discuss this matter over a meal, Colonel. Will you join me? I am certain my palace will provide you with much better food than you might have received on the ship which brought you here."

James knew the King was correct. He was famished from his long voyage and a meal in his belly would be the perfect remedy for his empty stomach.

"Yes, your Majesty, that would be most welcomed."

Once in the dining hall, the servants delivered lavish food and wine to the table. James noticed that the King specifically asked the alluring, large bosomed, female servants to stay in the room. On several occasions, while serving food, these same female servants would brush softly against James's uniformed arm. James had to admit, the touch of a female felt exceptional after being fourteen days out at sea. He consciously dismissed each one of their advances.

"I notice these fine ladies have taken a fancy to your strong masculine frame, Colonel James. I have all the finest ladies a man could ever need for his pleasure. I have my Queen, my three mistresses and any one of these servants for my own male needs and fantasies."

After making this statement, the King looks down and continues to consume his food. James does not comment. He is well aware of the trolling tactics the King is attempting in order to gain negotiating and political power.

"Perhaps you did not hear me. I have many fine ladies, Colonel James. Do any of these voluptuous women fancy your interest?"

the King repeats, this time with his mouth filled with half chewed meat, whose juices drip down from the corners of his mouth. "I said, I am certain your male appetite must be strong after your voyage. You may have as many of my women as you would like."

"Thank you, your Majesty; however, my focus is on our negotiations and what is best for our two countries."

"We shall negotiate soon, good Colonel. I just want to assure you, I can send in as many women as you would like. You are welcome to stay as long as you like and enjoy yourself with as many women as you would desire. A man must get his fill by eating at the table and eating in the bedroom." The King then laughs, as if the two had been old friends from childhood.

"Thank you for your generous offer your Majesty, but I must refuse," James responds, repulsed by the King's devious tactics.

"I am offering a feast of these beautiful women, Colonel."

"Your Majesty, I appreciate your kind offer and again decline. The issues between our countries are such that this is where I must place my attention at this time."

James is well prepared for this strategic manipulative tactic. He had heard how the King uses divisive maneuvers for his quest for power. The General had warned him well.

"Well Colonel, you obviously enjoy working more than you enjoy playing."

The King flicked his fingers at one of the servants, indicating for her to approach James. As she walks over to him, she bends down and her breasts rub across his earlobe. She then slides her hand across the back of his neck. Lowering the shoulders of her gown, she presses her bare breasts into the back of his head. The King nods his head to her.

James, who has only pretended to sip his wine, is watchful, alert, and appalled by these unscrupulous tactics.

"Once again, your Majesty, I appreciate your kind offer and I must decline. Shall we talk about 'my' King's request?"

Disgusted and frustrated, the King slams his golden goblet down on to the table.

"What is wrong with you? Have you no passionate desires?"

James rises from the table. An unconscionable act, as one should never rise before a King has risen from his seat.

"Your, Majesty," James exerts with confidence, looking at the King, who at this point is in shock by the bold and arrogant move made by a Colonel. "As I stated earlier, I decline your very kind offer."

During his statement, James can only think about one thing. 'Now King John V of Portugal, I have you exactly where I want you for these negotiations—reduced in power.'

The King waves his hand, dismissing the servants, for he had determined a man of the Colonel's caliber would be difficult to bribe and negotiate within a way that benefits himself.

"Colonel James, as far as our negotiations go, have you brought with you ample amounts of gold and silver?"

"I have brought enough to negotiate a fair and equitable agreement, your Majesty."

Colonel James reaches into his leather bag and removes a heavy leather pouch, filled with valuable gold and silver coins. He places the pouch on the table near the King. King John V removes the leather drawstring and dips his hand into the pouch. He is aroused by the feel of the coins against his fingers.

"Is this all the coins you have, Colonel?"

"It is, your Majesty," James said, lying, while looking directly into the King's eyes.

"Bring me three more of my finest mistresses," the King calls out, looking directly into James's eyes.

James's other pocket held another pouch of coins. This second pouch of coins was even more valuable than the first. It was intended to use only if the negotiations required further persuasion.

Three women enter the room, wearing their finest silk skirts. Their perfect naked breasts have been dotted with diamonds.

"These mistresses, Colonel, are from my personal collection. No one has bedded them but me."

In his entire life, James has never seen such alluring women. He steadies his manhood. These women are by far impossible to decline.

"Three women at one time would be a stimulating fantasy and empower any man to say 'yes', would you not agree, Colonel?" King John V said, nodding his head for the women to swarm around James.

All three mistresses aggressively fondle and rub their naked breasts around James's body. They strip off each other's skirts and dance nakedly before his eyes, while rubbing and touching one another and James.

James continues to stand straight, a position assumed by a soldier. Oh, how grateful he is for his military training at this moment in time, he determines.

"Your Majesty. I have presented you with what is considered a fair amount of money. I ask that you see this amount as equitable and sign my King's document for the completion of this agreement and of this negotiation."

"Are you a damn eunuch, man!" the King shouts out.

"No, your Majesty. I am Colonel James Langston, a soldier to my King in the British Army."

"Well, you are the most obnoxious negotiator I have ever experienced."

Upon hearing these words from the King, James knew he had won. James removed his gold pocket watch, opened it and observed the time.

"I suggest this is a good time to sign the document before I retrieve my coins, take my leave and become disappointed that an agreement was not reached."

King John V sits down at the table, turns his head to spit on the floor and signs the document, along with writing a small note back to the King of England. He calls for his aid to bring his seal and an envelope. The silence in the room was heavy and thick.

James had held his ground and the King felt as though he had been strung on a cross, upside down, for all the world to see. Handing the envelope back to James, he looks directly at him saying, "I wish you were on my side, Colonel. I could use a good man such as yourself."

"I will take that as a compliment, your Majesty." James bows.

"As it was intended, Colonel." The King nods.

James leaves the King and the palace, not without thinking, 'Thank you, Sophia, for engraving those letters into my pocket watch. If it had not been for that reminder of your perfect love, I might have failed at this negotiation and had the most fanciful night I could ever have imagined.'

The carriage pulled away from the palace. James tapped the letter in his pocket and smiled. He then removed his watch to confirm the time. His timing was good, for he had hoped to sleep at the Seafarer's Inn tonight and be ready to depart first thing in the morning.

James replayed the events of the negotiations with the King over again in his head. He understood now why the General wanted him for this mission. Most men would have surrendered to these temptations of beautiful women and failed for their country. As James continued to recount the day, he suddenly feels the carriage make a swift turn. He did not remember such a turn on his way to the palace. Immediately, he adjusts his sword and prepares for the unknown. He stashes the unused small leather pouch of precious gold and silver coins into a hidden compartment inside his jacket. The compartment was positioned behind the breast pocket of the jacket and was designed for hiding valuables, along with making them difficult to discover.

The carriage man pulls on the reins, bringing the horses to a full stop. James carefully slides back the black curtain to look out the window. He sees two men on horseback. He easily identifies them as highwaymen, thieves with their faces covered with black handkerchiefs and holding their swords high in the air. In a surprise and swift move, James barrels out of the carriage, swinging his sword high into the air. The carriage man follows James's lead, jumps down from the carriage, runs toward one of the men and cracks his whip onto him. The highwayman slices the carriage man across the throat and he dies instantly. While keeping the two men on horseback in sight, James positions himself next to the carriage's horses. Simultaneously, the thieves approach James. Their horses stop a king's foot away from him. Holding their swords up high, one man speaks loudly.

"Dar-nos o seu dinheiro."

James looks confused. He does not know Portuguese, but does recognize the word 'dinheiro', meaning money.

"Dinherio ou morre." *'Money or die.'*

"No!" James shouts back.

The message is received by the thieves.

"Voce no palacio. Tem dinheiro." *'You at palace. Have money.'*

James ascertains these highwaymen saw him leaving the palace and believes their King gave James money. 'They are here to rob me,' he deduces.

"Palacio yes. Dinheiro no." James attempts to communicate, desperately trying not to be distracted by the dead carriage man lying near him.

"Dinheiro ou morre." *'Money or die.'* They call out again.

"No dinheiro," James repeats, in the most convincing voice he can muster and frustrated that he only knows a few words in Portuguese.

In that instant, the two men turn to each other in an effort to confer what to do. James takes advantage of the attention no longer on him and briskly grabs the leather strap of one of the carriage horses. He slides his sword between the horse and the strap, slicing it to release the braces and free the horse. James quickly jumps onto the massive bay horse, turning it toward the two thieves. He is now staring directly at them, eye level. James charges toward the men, raising his sword high and slicing the smaller man across the throat, killing him instantly.

"That is for my carriage man and his family," James said, not sure if the thief, who is still alive, understands what he just said, but James felt relief from the revenge.

"Meu amigo." *'My friend,'* the bandit calls out in horror.

"Morre, Morre, morre, por meu amigo." *'Die, die, die for my friend.'*

James kicks his horse's ribs aggressively, forcing the horse to charge without fear, directly toward James's enemy. The bandit raises his weapon, meeting James's sword high in the air. A battle for life and death had begun.

James clips the bandit's arm with his sharp sword, enraging the thief even more. He returns a strong, swift stab in James's heart area, but the sword does not pierce through. Instead, a strange medal sound is heard, not by the thief, but by his horse, who becomes startled by the sound of coins inside the lining of James's jacket—precious coins, which in that moment saved James's life. The thief's horse also becomes startled and rears up into the air, causing the thief to fall to the ground.

James rides his horse over to the man, who is now lying flat on his back and aware his end is near. James points his sword down toward the man.

"Fool," James said to the man. "No dinheiro and your amigos is dead. You are a stupid fool. I could have killed you with my sword today, if I had so chosen. Instead, I have decided to let you live, to remember the value of your mercenary acts. You will have to live with this agony forever, as I continue to live with pride."

James shakes the reins of his horse and trots forward while the thief runs away in the opposite direction.

Chapter Eighteen

As the cold, hard rain falls heavily onto James, he travels down a dark road. He can feel the horse's warmth rise up from its steaming body. Yet the horse's mane and thick winter coat do little to help James keep warm as he rides bareback down the dirt road. Reaching a break in the road, James looks out into the distance. He hopes the light he sees afar is not his imagination. He is well aware he must find shelter and gathers his bearings. He proceeds toward the hazy light in the distance, pleading it is a light of refuge, one to help ensure he reaches Captain Taller's ship in adequate time before it sets sail tomorrow. He is aware that caution, along with his sword, are critical weapons at this time. A saturated soldier wearing a British Army uniform, riding aimlessly along a road was a definite target in this foreign country.

As James approaches the light, he begins to make out the outline of a house. The closer James trots to the light, the more he can make out the sound of a barking dog, most assuredly warning of an intruder's presence. With one hand, James taps the lump created by the gold and silver coins, located in the secret lining of his jacket. With the other hand, he feels the agreement letter signed by King John V next to his chest. He is exhausted, vulnerable and in need of refuge. Yet, he must take his chances and trust his wits, since at this point it is all he has.

The sheep dog draws closer to the legs of James's horse, weaving in and out, as if herding the animal. James rides closer to the small granite stone farmhouse. A young bairn opens the door of the house and steps onto the porch. He steadily holds a flintlock pistol and aims it directly toward James's chest.

"Nao se mexa!" *'Do not move!'* the boy calls out to James.

Immediately the boy identifies James's British military uniform.

"I need help," James calls out, trying to make his exhausted, weak voice be heard.

Another figure emerges from the door. This person also points a flintlock pistol at James; however, this figure is that of a woman.

"Who are you? What do you want with us?" the woman asks in perfect English.

"I mean no harm to you or your family. I was attacked and injured by highwaymen," James said, using the last of his strength to explain the reason he is at their door in the pouring rain.

"We have nothing for you. Leave at once!" The woman said, shaking the pistol in a way that implies the direction she wants James to move toward.

"I need a moment to rest. My horse and I need water. I beg ·you, please help me. I believe I am injured."

It is at that moment the woman focuses in on James's clothing. She identifies him as a British soldier. James slides off his horse and looks at the woman. In what could only be described as a pitiful, distressing voice, James once more pleads. "Help me, please!"

The woman signals to the boy to assist James into the house, while she maintains her pistol locked into position and pointed directly at James's chest. As the boy brings James onto the front step, it is evident to them both that James is severally hurt.

"We need to lay him down near the fire," the woman instructs her son.

James drifts in and out of consciousness as the young bairn and woman remove his boots, socks and jacket.

"I need water," James requests weakly.

The woman gathers blankets from around the house to create a makeshift bed for James in front of the fire. The boy lifts James's head and helps him drink water from a cup he holds. He then goes outside to hide James's horse in the barn and give it some hay and water.

James gives in to his exhaustion, falls asleep and dreams heavenly.

"Sir, can you hear me?" the women shouts at James while at the same time shaking his shoulder.

James struggles to become responsive. Slowly, he opens his eyes and looks at the woman, confused and unaware of his surroundings.

"My name is Colonel James Langston of the British Army. Where am I? What country am I in?"

"You are in my home in Portugal," the woman responds in a loving voice and with a British accent.

"Portugal, but you speak perfect English," James said, absolutely certain he is still in one of his dreams.

"I am Grace. This is my only bairn, Byron. I speak English because I was born and lived in London until a very handsome Portuguese soldier convinced me to marry him and move us here to this home in Portugal. Our son was born here. For the past three years I have been a widow after my husband died on the battleground protecting our country."

Grace was not certain why she was rambling off so much information at one time. Perhaps it was nerves, or perhaps it was because there was something about this soldier she liked.

"Your bairn is a good protector. You have raised him well," James said weakly.

"His father taught him and myself how to use a pistol. He wanted us to remain safe while he was away on missions."

"Your husband was a smart man," James said as his eyes close again.

Grace walks toward the stove. She begins warming some biscuits and preparing some tea, as the torrential rain continues outside.

James awakens again and immediately realizes his jacket is hanging on the chair next to him. In an attempt not to be noticed, he checks to see if the King's signed agreement is still where he left it. It is. He then checks to see if the leather pouch of coins is still there. It is.

Grabbing the coins out of his jacket pocket, James presses the pouch down into the toe of his boot.

Grace turns around. She has not seen what James has done.

"Colonel James, do you think you have the strength to sit at our table and have some biscuits and hot tea?"

"That would be excellent. Thank you," James said, sitting up from his bed on the floor.

For the first time, Grace notices a downward line of blood drawn below James's vest.

"You are bleeding, Colonel James," Grace calls out, with panic in her voice.

She helps James to the table and gets him settled into a chair.

"Colonel, if I may be so bold, we must remove your vest and shirt so we can find the source of this bleeding. As a widow of a soldier, I can assure you I have cared for my fair share of wounds. May I?"

"Please." James smiles, believing divine providence must surely be on his side today.

"I would appreciate your assistance, Grace. I am afraid those bandits may have inflicted more harm than I had first thought."

Grace removes James's red uniform vest, exposing a bloody circle on his white cotton shirt. Carefully, she removes his shirt, as James attempts to conceal the excruciating pain he is experiencing. A large opened wound is exposed on James's muscular chest.

"I was stabbed with a sword," James said, almost apologizing for the gaping gash.

"It is very deep, James. You are fortunate, because the wound's location is by your heart. If the bandit's sword would have pierced you any deeper, I am afraid we would not be here talking. You would be dead."

At that moment James realized the pouch of precious coins in his jacket pocket had saved his life. 'Those coins were indeed precious,' James thinks. 'They allowed me to stay alive and return back home to Sophia.'

"I do not think the sword pierced any of your organs. I believe I can sew up this wound and then we must ensure it does not get infected."

James recognized he had no other choice than to accept Grace's counsel. James places his hand in his pocket and pulls out thirty reis. He planned to spend this Portuguese currency on meals and lodging during his trip. He presents Grace with the handful of reis.

"Please take these as a token of my appreciation. You have been very kind to me and I am very grateful for your help."

"James, I cannot take them. You are a British soldier, a soldier from my homeland. It has been an honor to assist you."

"Grace." James looks at her as though declining his offer is not an option. "It is an honor to be assisted by you. I am certain there are many more homes along this road that would not have been as hospitable as you have been. Please, I ask that you accept this money with my gratitude."

Grace places the coins on the table and proceeds to gather supplies to care for James's wound. She would decide later if she would take them or not. For now, James needed mending.

While James was sipping his tea, Byron enters the room and James looks up to greet him. 'I am sure this must be strange sight for a young lad, a wounded, shirtless stranger in his kitchen.'

"Do you speak any English?" James asks, although weak from his wounds and loss of blood.

James had a fondness for bravery in children.

"My mother is making me teach." Byron stumbles with his words.

"Learn," Grace calls out from the stove, where she is heating the water.

"My mother is making me learn," Byron said, smiling, acknowledging that at least he is trying.

"It is a good skill to learn another language," James said, praising him. "Your mother is a wise woman."

Grace returns to the table with a bowl of boiling water, clean towels and a sterilized needle. She threads the needle with black thread. "I am afraid I do not keep any alcohol in the house, James. I have brought you this wooden spoon to bite down on, in the hope it will help you manage the pain."

James was aware Grace's message was meant for Byron. He felt certain the boy had not seen this level of home surgery before now.

"Byron, help me clear this table. We will lay James down here. I suspect it will be easier for him to manage the pain I am about to inflict on him if he is lying down."

Everyone gets into their positions for the home-style surgery. James lies on the table, biting down on a wooden spoon. Byron holds down James's shoulders so he will not move while his mother stitches him up. Grace holds a needle in her hand, thinking that this morning when she woke up she had no idea by evening she would be hand sewing a British soldier's chest in her kitchen in Portugal.

"Are you ready, James?"

James nods yes as Grace pierces James's skin with her needle. James growls, trying to manage his pain. Grace carefully stitches the long and large wound closed, cleaning the blood away as she works.

Upon completing the last stitch, Grace looks up and sees Byron vomiting into a bucket in the corner of the room.

"I reckon my son will not become a doctor," she said, smiling at James, hoping to lighten the mood. "I have closed your wound the best I could, James. At least I have stopped your bleeding."

"Thank you, Grace," James replies, dizzy from the pain and grateful he is lying on his back.

"Now, allow me to help you sit up and put my husband's shirt on you. I will then wash and repair your uniform vest and shirt."

"I can leave when they are dry," James weakly responds, wanting Grace to know he has no intention of being a burden. "I am very grateful for all of your help, Grace. I must ride to the port in hope of securing my scheduled passage back to England."

"James," Grace replies in disbelief. "You are weak. I am concerned you are not capable of venturing out on a day's ride to the port. I do not think your health could sustain that journey."

"A day's ride! How could that be, Grace? I was only a half a day's ride before I was attacked."

"I believe you must have ridden your horse in the opposite direction of the port. The storm was not in your favor. It took you further out of your way and in the opposite direction of the port."

James's pain increases, not only from his wound but now from the thought of missing his voyage home with Captain Taller.

"I shall rest for a moment Grace and determine what should be my best course of action. Thank you again for your assistance. If it is not too much of an inconvenience, I would like to lie back down on the bed by the fire and take a moment to regain my strength."

~~~

"Good morning, James. Good to see you are finally awake."

James shakes his head, hoping to engage his brain to start working again.

"After I repaired your wound, you collapsed from the pain, and I suspect from the massive amounts of blood loss. You have been asleep for the better part of a day."

"A day!" James said, sitting up in surprise, but stopped by the sudden throbbing pain in his chest.

"Yes. I sewed you up on December 29 and it is now December 30, 1733. Clearly you were exhausted and you needed time to heal. Byron and I have assured your horse was well cared for, and we regularly checked to see if you were still breathing and not suddenly expired on us. In addition, your boots have finally dried and are ready to be worn. Byron rubbed mint oil over them so the leather would not crack. I repaired, cleaned and folded your shirt and vest and placed them on the chair next to you. Fortunately, I was able to remove most of the bloodstains from your shirt. James, it is very evident to me that you were near death when you arrived at our door. I am still surprised you are alive after all you had to endure."

The Midnight Air

James was still in shock about hearing he had slept an entire day. For that reason he heard little of what he perceived as Grace's ramblings.

"You have my endless gratitude. With that said, I have important obligations requiring my immediate attention. Grace, I must write two letters and send word immediately to my General and to my wife. If it is not too much of an inconvenience, once I am finished, would it be possible for Byron to ride into the nearest town and deliver my letters to the post-boy? I am hoping if these letters are mailed on January 1, they should both arrive within fifteen days."

"Most certainly, James. It would be an honor to do a service for the British military, and I cannot even imagine how worried your wife must be. As a widow of a soldier, I am emphatic to your wife."

"Thank you, Grace. My wife and I had only been married for two days before I had to leave on this assignment. I would like her to know I am well."

Grace assists James to the kitchen table; he is weak from his injury and not moving for two days. She sets parchment paper, a feather quill pen and two envelopes onto the table then moves away to give James his privacy. James is well aware these may be the final words he ever communicates to Sophia. He knows the prognosis of surviving potential complications from his injuries is not in his favor. He knows he may never see his Sophia again in this lifetime as he dips the quill pen into the glass inkwell and begins to write.

His first letter is to the General, informing him of his current circumstances. This letter includes his success in negotiating an agreement with the King, the subsequent ambush by the highwaymen and the grave condition of his health. James then writes a second letter to his wife.

My Beloved Sophia,

I confess all my love to you. I am yours and yours only. Your love is my strength and it shall sustain me till the end of my days.

I am blessed because you are my wife. I seal this letter with my heart. Let this heart be a symbol of our love. I want you to touch this etched heart and know that my fingerprint was placed upon it as a token of my endless love for you. If for some reason I do not return, you must continue your bountiful life without me and be comforted knowing my love for you is forever.

I love you immensely, James
December 30, 1733

Chapter Nineteen

As the early morning light begins to reflect on the sea, Sophia sits on the porch, with Hannah resting at her feet. She stares out into the distance, pressing the heart locket deep into her chest. Sophia is well aware it has been almost a month since James left. She is concerned it is one week after the date James promised he would return and hold his arms around her. 'Something is wrong, terribly wrong.'

"Are you all right, Sophia?" Lady Stephens asks as they sit together. "You look as though your mind is somewhere else this morning."

"Today is January 16th and James should have been home on January 11th. I am worried for his safety. I am worried for my bairn."

"You should trust him as a fine soldier. Also, you can be comforted knowing God will protect him. Each day we shall ask this from Him in our prayers."

Lady Stephens can see the anguish on Sophia's face as she tries desperately to ease Sophia's pain and help her believe all will be well. "Perhaps we should visit your father today."

Sophia begrudgingly agrees, feeling incapable of deciding anything at the moment.

Upon arriving at her father's estate, Sophia walks directly into the house and proceeds toward her father's study. Thomas greets Lady Stephens, who walks with him into the drawing room and explains the reason for Sophia's torment.

"Father," Sophia said in a strong voice, one which causes her father's head to instantly rise up from the papers he is reading. "Something is terribly wrong. I just know it in my heart. You must believe me."

"What is it, my child? Are you and my new grand bairn not all right?"

"My bairn is fine, Father. My concern is for James. He has not yet arrived home from his mission. I know something is wrong, Father, something is very wrong."

Sophia feels herself panicking the more she speaks of James's absence.

The General ponders this news. He had lost track of time as to when James would return. Now he was forced to assume two roles, one of a loving concerned father and one of a General, a General who had just learned about the absence of one of his men. He methodically lowers the gold rim glasses from his face and places his large sun-beaten hand across his mouth. The General decides to assume the later role, that of a General.

"Thank you, Sophia for bringing this to my attention. It is indeed concerning news."

Sophia recognizes this typical polished response of her father. It indicates to her that the General was also concerned.

"I can assure you I will take immediate action based on this news."

"Thank you, Father. My heart aches to imagine my life without James. It tears apart every fiber of my being," Sophia said, raising her hands in a motion of helplessness. Sophia lowers her head, turns toward the door and leaves her father's study.

Sophia joins Lady Stephens, and recognizing there was not much more she could do at her father's house, the two ride silently back to Sophia and James's home.

The General immediately clears his desk of all his papers and selects a clean piece of linen paper on which he begins to write Captain Taller a letter. He demands a prompt update to the whereabouts of Colonel James. In his letter, he writes. 'I want you to expeditiously learn of Colonel James's location and if he requires any assistance. I want all resources made available for his immediate return to England. I trust from the urgency of my tone, I make myself clear,' the letter concludes.

The General seals the letter with his official waxed stamp and asks Thomas to ensure the letter is delivered to the Captain on the next ship bound for Portugal. It will be the duty of this new ship's Captain to locate and deliver this important message to Captain Taller.

Within minutes of sealing this letter, there is the sound of galloping hooves heading toward the front of the house. The General promptly walks to the front door and finds Thomas opening the door. The General, unaware of what was occurring, could only assume this soldier was bringing urgent news.

"General Cartwright," the young soldier said, saluting nervously at the General, with Thomas standing at his side.

"Yes, Private."

"I have been instructed by my Sergeant-Major to bring you this news, which he believes will be extremely important to you."

"Proceed," the General instructs the fretful private.

"The other privates and myself overheard some soldiers talking in our town's tavern. They were talking about Captain Taller. These soldiers had just returned from Portugal and were amused by the stories Captain Taller regaled while they were drinking at the tavern with him. They said they overheard him speak about certain dangers in Portugal. More particularly, the story was being told between Captain Taller and a highwayman about attempting to rob a British soldier as he traveled back to the port after being at the King's palace. Captain Taller assumed the British soldier was one of his passengers, a certain Colonel James Langston. The soldiers in our tavern continued the story, saying the highwayman was bragging about his skill, remarking how he killed the carriage man by slitting his throat. He was able to badly injure the British soldier, who unfortunately retaliated and killed his friend. The highwayman regaled to the men in the tavern that he was a Portuguese hero, that even though he did not get any money, at least he survived the fight and severely wounded the British soldier."

"Did Captain Taller confront this bandit and gain additional information regarding what happened to Colonel James?" the General asked, dazed and panicked by this horrific news.

"Apparently, Captain Taller did nothing, General. He did not want to create a scene as a foreigner in the country. Assuming the story he heard was about Colonel James, he did not know where he was, how he was, or when he would return. To the best of our knowledge General, Captain Taller is still waiting at the arranged location of the inn, near the Lisbon port, and Captain Taller is still attempting to locate Colonel James."

"Good God, man!" the General calls out, his throat swelling with alarm and his heart sinking deep into his chest. "Thank you, soldier. I want you to not say a word of this to anyone, and inform the other privates and your Sergeant-Major to do the same. This information could be dangerous in the wrong hands. Do I make myself clear?"

"Yes, sir."

"Off you go, Private. I have much to think about. Thank you for your service."

The soldier salutes and the General offers a quick salute in return. Mounting his horse the soldier rides off, realizing the severity of the situation. His Sergeant-Major was correct in commanding him to inform the General immediately.

Turning to Thomas, the General has a look of complete shock on his face. "We shall not tell Sophia or Lady Stephens of this news, Thomas. I cannot imagine what this news, although limited, would do to my daughter. I simply do not have the strength to bring this level of heartbreak upon my daughter." The General continues to shake his head. "Although I am a General of the British Army, I am also a father, and I tell you tonight, I will be hard pressed to send my son-in-law, my most valued soldier, on an overseas voyage again. It is my job to protect my men. It is my job to see that the Colonel returns home safely, back to my daughter. I cannot bear the endless sordid agony of destroying my beloved Sophia and her bairn if her husband did not come home."

The General lowers his head as he returns inside the house and back into his study. 'It is time to contemplate my strategy,' he realizes. 'Certainly it will be a long night.' The General pours himself a glass of scotch, keeping the bottle next to his side.

~~~

On January 16, the morning sun shines through the General's study window, and a beam of light alerts his swollen eyes to open. Hunched over his desk, after a long night, he hears a knock at his door. It is Thomas, alerting him to presences of the post-boy at his front door.

"He has a letter and he insists it must be handed directly to you, sir," Thomas said, observing that the General must have slept at his desk.

The General rises, suddenly happy to stretch his stiff legs. He walks to the front door and sees a small lad with a large leather satchel swung over his shoulder.

"General, I have been told to give this letter personally to you, sir," the post-boy utters, shaking with nerves from being in the presence of someone of such high authority.

"Thank you, post-boy. Given the events of these last few days, I suspect this letter is of the utmost importance to me."

Recognizing James's handwriting on the front of the envelope, the General, said, "Please remain here, post-boy. After reading this letter I may also need your services to deliver a message."

"Yes, sir."

The General proceeds to read the letter, right there on the doorstep.

Dear General Cartwright:

This letter is intended to inform you of my situation in Portugal. Upon returning from the King's palace, I was ambushed by two highwaymen. A skirmish occurred, resulting in my carriage man and one of the bandits perishing. I was also injured, taking a blade to my chest, resulting in a deep wound. I was able to ride to safety with the signed agreement by the King, along with the additional bag of precious coins intended only for use, if necessary.

A rainstorm took me off my path, causing me to take refuge in a country home, one owned by a British citizen, a widow of a Portuguese soldier and her bairn. The woman's name is Grace and she has been very kind to me.

I am a day's ride from the port and I must remain here for a few more weeks to heal. I can only anticipate my health will soon improve as I make my way back to the Seafarer Inn, which is where Captain Taller and I arranged to meet.

I would be remiss if I did not say, I am not certain if I will survive my journey home. I am weak from the loss of a great deal of blood. My fever would indicate an infection is settling into my body. Although not fitting for a letter, I feel it is important to recommend that you be very leery of Captain Taller and his word. I have found him to be a deceptive drunk and therefore not a person to be trusted. Despite that observation, I must depend on him to bring me home.

I will wait at the Seafarer Inn, in an attempt to coordinate my return trip home to England.

Colonel Abraham James Langston
December 30, 1733

The blood drains from General Cartwright's face. He cannot believe what he has just read. The General immediately turns around and walks directly to his study, leaving the post-boy muddled.

General Cartwright sits down at his desk and begins to pen a letter. This letter is to his army, requesting five elite soldiers for a mission. He then returns back to the front door and requests the post-boy to deliver the letter immediately.

"Here is a pence for your troubles."

The General pulls a coin out from his pocket and tosses it to the young boy, who cannot believe his good fortune.

"Thank you, General," the post-boy said, bowing and heading back to his horse.

The General is filled with alarm. 'Good God, what have I done? The guilt of James possibly never returning home would destroy us all. I take full responsibility for anything that happens to James. He was there under my direct order. I must reach Captain Taller. With the Grace of God, my correspondence will help bring James home alive. I must also heed the warning from James to be cautious in my approach.' With that the General returns to his study, pulls a quill pen and paper from his desk drawer, and begins to write a letter.

Dear Captain Taller:

I have recently learned of the situation regarding one of your passengers, Colonel James Langston. I have been informed that he was ambushed by highwaymen and has taken refuge in a country home with a British citizen and her son. He has been injured, and as a true soldier, has mustered the strength to make arrangements to meet with you at the inn by the seaport, as the two of you had previously agreed. I urge you to remain at the inn until you are both together. I will see that you are rewarded handsomely for all your efforts when you bring Colonel James back to England safely.

General Craig Richard Cartwright

January 16, 1734

A few hours later there was a knock on the study door.

"Enter."

"Sir, there are five soldiers here. They have said you asked to see them."

"Ahh, yes, send them in. And Thomas, I wish for you to say in the room as well."

"Yes, sir," Thomas responds, thinking 'How odd, the General has never requested me to stay in the room with his soldiers before.'

Five smartly dressed soldiers enter the study and salute the General, who tells them to stand at ease.

"What I am about to tell you all is of the utmost importance and secrecy. I am about to send you on an urgent mission, one that must be held in confidence and with the highest political protocol. Let me begin by asking, do you all understand these expectations?"

"Yes, General Cartwright," the soldiers responded in perfect unison.

"Thomas, my butler, is here because he is aware of this situation and I want him to witness my wishes."

The soldiers turn around and nod at Thomas, who is still confused as to why he is in this room at this time.

"I have recently been informed that Colonel James Langston has been wounded in Portugal and is in grave danger. His health is failing and Captain Taller, the soldier hired to sail him back to England does not know of his whereabouts. The only thing Captain Taller and Colonel James know is they should meet each other at the town's inn, next to the tavern near the port. I want all five of you to immediately board a ship for Lisbon, Portugal. I want you to find Captain Taller and give him this letter I have just written. The letter outlines Colonel James's situation and my instructions for getting him back to England safely. Then I want you to find our valued soldier, Colonel James Langston. You may find him at the inn or held up at a country home with a British citizen named Grace. I tell you this in trust. Colonel James needs our immediate assistance. I am depending on you soldiers to travel there quickly, locate Colonel James and bring him home alive. Do you understand?"

"Yes, sir." The soldier's voices were strong, despite their disbelief.

Thomas escorted the soldiers to the front door for their exit. He returned back to the General's study and left the door open.

"Sir."

"Yes, Thomas."

"May I inquire as to why you wanted me to be in the room with your soldiers during that discussion?"

"Thomas, I wanted you to know the details of Colonel James's condition. I also want you to know that I do not want Sophia to know anything about this strategy. I am afraid if she asks me about James, I will become weak and fraught with worry. I am counting on you, Thomas, to change the subject and redirect me from what I can only assume will be my panic-stricken state."

"Of course, sir. In all my years of service, you know you can depend on me."

The General continues to sip his scotch, thinking, 'Captain Taller will not expect my elite soldiers, and if there are any untrustworthy actions occurring, he will begin to have his guard raised.'

The General still did not know why James felt it necessary to warn him of Captain Taller's devious nature. He knows the Captain could be motivated by money. Perhaps the reward he offered Captain Taller will help dissuade his deceit.

The fatigued General takes his last sip of scotch and slides the letter from James into the sleeve of his leather desk blotter. He departs his study to retire to his bedroom, although sleep will not come easy for him.

~~~

'Talk to me, my love, talk to me. I hold your bairn deep inside me. Please come back to me, James, I love you.'

Sophia watches the sea move as her heart aches. 'This was once a beautiful sea, now it may be holding my husband's body,' she thinks. Her sobbing drowns out the knocking from the front door. Hannah barks and Theodore greets the soldier standing smartly on the other side of the door.

"Good morning. May I help you?" Theodore asks.

"I am Sergeant Calvin Harvey Gideon. I am here on behalf of General Cartwright. He has ordered me to stand post and remain here until Colonel Langston returns from his voyage. Is Mrs. Langston present? I was told to inform her of her father's request myself."

"Please follow me, Sergeant Gideon," Theodore said, recognizing the delay in Colonel James's return may suddenly be cause for concern.

Theodore leads the Sergeant into the drawing room and instructs him to wait for Mrs. Langston.

"Good morning, your Ladyship," the Sergeant greets Sophia as she walks into the room.

"I am Sergeant Calvin Harvey Gideon. I am here upon the request of your father. He has asked me to stand post until Colonel Langston returns home safely to you."

Sophia looks at this tall, handsome soldier. His buoyant charm does not go unnoticed by her.

"Perhaps you will remember me, your Ladyship. We met briefly at your wedding."

"I do remember you, Sergeant. As I recall, you were dancing with several women that day."

"That is correct," the Sergeant replied, grinning like a school boy who had just been caught doing something he knew was bad, however, was very proud of. "I did indeed enjoy myself that day. I am unmarried and found the ladies attending your wedding quite enjoyable to spend time with."

Again, the Sergeant smiles, adjusting his dark auburn hair. His bright blue eyes move toward Hannah, who has just walked into the room.

"And who is this, your Ladyship?" the Sergeant asks, bending down to greet Hannah with his hand extended.

"Her name is Hannah. My father bought her for me as my wedding gift."

Hannah wags her tail rapidly as the Sergeant rubs her head and ears.

"Hannah appears to enjoy your attention, Sergeant. She is not often fond of new guests. You must have a way of calming tense animals," Sophia said innocently.

Lady Stephens, hearing a visitor in the house, joins them in the drawing room.

"Oh Lady Stephens, this is Sergeant Calvin. He will be standing post until my James returns."

"It is a pleasure to meet you, Sergeant," Lady Stephens said abruptly, and in no way could it be perceived as being sincere.

"Shall we all have some tea before you begin your post outside, Sergeant Calvin?"

"That would be delightful, Lady Stephens," the Sergeant responds in a cocky accent. This accent does not go unnoticed by Lady Stephens, who is not pleased that a man of lower stature would be charged with guarding Sophia.

The group sits down at the dining room table, and Lady Stephens finds herself staring at the young Sergeant as he boastfully flirts with Sophia during teatime. Sophia smiles and laughs as she talks about her father. Lady Stephens is determined to stay vigilant and keep close watch on the Sergeant, whom she believes to be a leech.

William enters the room, excusing himself and asking to speak with the Sergeant.

"Sir, may I speak with you for a moment?" William asks, holding the Sergeant's leather bridle in his hand.

"But of course. Ladies, I shall return." The Sergeant nods, looking only at Sophia with the most charming smile.

Soon after leaving the room, Sergeant Calvin quickly snaps at William.

"What is it? Can you not see I am busy?" the Sergeant admonishes him, in a surprising switch of character.

"Sir, I noticed your leather bridle has a tear in its leather. The bridle could have given way at any time while you were using it."

"Let me see that bridle," the Sergeant demands angrily, grabbing the bridle from William's hand. "I had not noticed this before. We have stablemen to handle these duties for us. And, before you found this fancy new position with Colonel James and his exceptionally beautiful wife you did not have the privilege to work at their estate."

William feels the anger boiling up within his body. He was determined to maintain his composure and control himself. What he wanted to do was flatten the Sergeant right there on the foyer floor for speaking about Mrs. Langston in such a way. Instead, William remembered his promise to Colonel James. 'Watch over and protect all my prized possessions with your life.'

William tightly grabs the back of the Sergeant's neck with his massive left hand. It appears he was not able to control his anger after all. He asks the Sergeant to join him for a walk, as he pushes him out the front door.

"Allow me to show you Colonel James's fine new horses," he said, squeezing on the Sergeant's neck even harder. "And allow me to inform you that I am here to protect everything the Colonel owns and loves, especially his wife. I have given the Colonel my word. And I am a beastly man of my word. Do you understand me, even with my German accent, Sergeant Calvin Harvey Gideon? I warn you, stay as far away as possible from getting too close to Mrs. Langston. She is a wonderful and gracious lady."

"William," the Sergeant responds in a carefree and unimpressed voice. "I believe you are speaking out of order here, my good man. You have no rank on me. You have no right to tell me what to do. In fact, I should be telling you what to do. And you, good sir, should attend to your chores and fix my leather bridle at once. Lovely chatting with you, stable boy."

The Sergeant's response was intended to be disparaging. He released himself from William's grip and walked back into the house to enjoy Sophia's company once more. Returning into the dining room to finish his tea, the Sergeant stated he would begin his duties immediately.

"I will begin by surveying the perimeter of the property," the Sergeant announces before taking his leave outside.

Walking along the white sandy shoreline with the warm sun on his face, Sergeant Calvin begins to fantasize about Lady Sophia. 'She is the most adoring creature I have ever laid my eyes upon,' he contemplates. 'A plan is needed to make this woman mine. I must have her. If Colonel James does not return home, I could beg her father to allow me to marry the widow because it might be difficult to find a husband for someone who is already married. Yes, I could be the soldier who helps the struggling, lonely and saddened widow. I can easily win Sophia over with my charismatic charm. I will make her fall in love with me. I believe this is a plan that will work. When I marry the General's daughter, it would be certain I would move up in rank. Then I would live in this lovely home, ride in these fancy carriages and enjoy spending Lady Sophia's wealth, which I am certain she has.'

The Sergeant believed it was providence he overheard the General talking to Doctor Hadley at the wedding reception about the combination of Sophia's wealth combined with the fortune from Colonel James's family estate.

'Easy and instant wealth,' the Sergeant thinks, smiling proudly at his conniving abilities. 'All I have to do is be charming and Sophia will fall madly in love with me. Then my life will be secure.'

~~~

Sophia turns the page of her book, as she enjoys the sea air rolling onto the porch.

"There you are, my dear. I could not find you in the house," Lady Stephens said, while sitting down in one of the wicker chairs next to Sophia.

"I came out here as a distraction," Sophia replies, greeting her. "Reading alone in my bedroom only makes me think of James more. I pray, Lady Stephens, this is the day my beloved returns home to me."

Once again Sophia grabs her heart-shaped locket hanging around her neck.

"Where is Hannah?" Lady Stephens asks, seeing Sophia gripping the locket tightly and attempting to change the subject away from James's absence.

"Sergeant Calvin has gone down to secure the shoreline and Hannah followed him. I saw him throwing a ball to her. She really likes the Sergeant."

"Where you acquainted with the Sergeant prior to his arrival yesterday, Sophia?"

"Oh no, Lady Stephens. The first time I met him, like you, was at our wedding. I am however, thoroughly enjoying his company."

"I suspect he is becoming quite fond of you as well, Sophia. Perhaps a little more than a soldier, who is supposed to keep guard, should be."

"He is here to protect us while James is away. I must believe he is a good soldier. Why else would my father have sent him? Perhaps what you are seeing is that he is lonely. He is unmarried, and I am certain he is enjoying some female company."

"The young Sergeant is not married? I was not aware of that. Does he have any family or personal wealth?"

"I do not believe so," Sophia responds innocently. "He seems to live alone. He has not said much regarding financial status. Lady Stephens, is there something you are alluding to with your question?" Sophia asks candidly.

"Sophia, I have become quite fond of you and James. Theodore has as well. Because of that, I want the best for you. From a wise old woman and someone who cares deeply for your well-being, I strongly urge you to not trust a man we know little about. I also speak of what I believe are his carnal desires as well. I sense he is not a prudent man and will do anything to get what he desires, despite the consequences. I apologize for my frankness, my dear Sophia. I feel it is necessary to speak what is on my mind and through my intuition."

"Lady Stephens, I do so appreciate your comments and concerns. I value and honor your opinions. I must say, I can also assure you, I have taken heed to your words and will stay alert to any unprincipled words or actions of Sergeant Calvin."

The ladies finish their tea and decide to stroll to the garden house.

"Shall we go and see how my new bistro table fits in the freshly painted garden house?" Sophia asked.

"Splendid idea, Sophia," Lady Stephens responds.

Upon entering the garden house, Sophia leans down to smell a vibrant pink rose. Her rose-gold heart locket swings out from her gown. The luster from the heart-shaped ruby catches the sunlight and reflects onto her hand. 'Perhaps I can perceive this as a message from James. Perhaps he wants me to know he is well and his heart still beats for me.' This thought creates warm goose bumps down Sophia's arms. She holds the ruby heart tightly in her hand and whispers under her breath.

'Please come back to me, James. My heart needs to be with you.'

~~~

In the little farmhouse, far from the Lisbon port, James holds his gold pocket watch tightly in his hands. Something unknown forces him to speak out loud and say,

"I am here, my love. I am well and I shall return to thee. My heart needs you so."

Upon saying these words, James feels an odd sensation running down his arms. 'How strange,' he thinks. 'It is as though I can feel Sophia's hand upon me. How comforting.' Once again James drifts off to sleep, as his body continues to heal.

~~~

"These roses are lovely, Sophia. William is indeed a very talented gardener," Lady Stephens comments.

"The yellow ones are my favorite. This particular bloom, yellow with just a dusting of pink, is entitled 'Dream Come True.' I am not certain if I like best the look of it or its name," Sophia chuckles.

"Your tea, Ladies," Theodore said, placing the tray down on the bistro table.

The two ladies sit down, surrounded by the sweet aroma of blooming roses.

~~~

On his way to the house Sergeant Calvin spies the post-boy carrying a letter for delivery. "I will take that envelope, boy."

"Yes, sir."

The Sergeant notices the envelope is addressed to Sophia and written by James. 'I need you dead and forgotten Colonel,' he thinks, looking at the envelope and ripping it into several pieces. 'I will burn these pages in the fire so Sophia does not know of your state. It is time for you to be out of her life and for me to play a central part in it.'

The Sergeant places the torn pages of James's letter to Sophia into his pocket and proceeds to walk to the garden house, where he sees Sophia sitting at a table. The door to the garden house opens and Sergeant Calvin enters, approaching the two women with his charming smile.

"I am not certain which is more beautiful, you lovely ladies or these fine roses," Sergeant Calvin said with a smirk.

Smiling back, Sophia accidentally spills her tea. Sergeant Calvin comes running to her aid, rubbing up against her body as he attempts to squeeze between her chair and the bench holding some flowerpots. The contact between Sophia and the Sergeant's groin area was almost more than he could manage.

"Sophia, have you burned yourself? Allow me to help you."

Pulling his handkerchief out of his pocket, Sergeant Calvin gently wraps her hands, then holds the handkerchief in place. In a move surprising both Lady Stephens and Sophia, the Sergeant bends down and gently kisses the hand that is covered by the handkerchief.

"My mother always taught me that if you kiss a wound, it will instantly make it better. I hope it has that affect for you, Lady Sophia."

"It sounds like your mother was a very caring woman," Sophia said, trying to redirect the awkwardness of their situation.

William, who was trimming a large wisteria branch draped over the entry of the garden house door, witnessed Sergeant Calvin's actions. He saw the Sergeant brush up against Sophia and then kiss her hand. He instantly becomes angered, protective, and borders on the brink of wanting to snap the Sergeant's neck.

To ensure the Sergeant is aware that his actions have not gone unnoticed, William positions himself in front of the garden house window in clear view of the Sergeant, but not of Sophia and Lady Stephens, whose backs were both turned away from William. Looking like some character out of a tragic Shakespearian play, William holds a sharp pair of garden shears raised in his hand. He slowly mouths the words with exaggeration to the Sergeant. "I am watching you and I will kill you."

Sergeant Calvin clearly receives the message and is not fazed by the threat. He smiles back at William, making it seem as though he is smiling back at the two ladies. The challenge has become greater in the eyes of Sergeant Calvin. He is more determined to win his prize. He is certainly not interested in dealing with the likes of a poor stableman.

Out of the corner of her eye, Lady Stephens sees William standing in the window with the garden shears. She excuses herself, saying she has forgotten something in the main house and will return momentarily. Taking notice of the opportunity of being alone with Sophia, the Sergeant decides to seize the moment.

"Your Ladyship, I am glad I was here to protect you from the hot tea harming you. Please know I am always willing to help you."

"Thank you, Sergeant Calvin," Sophia said politely, well aware she could have managed the situation on her own.

"May I say, Sophia," the Sergeant expresses, intentionally choosing to be less formal by using her first name. "You have the most beautiful eyes. I find myself drawn by your beauty."

Sophia is quite taken aback by the Sergeant's boldness. In fact, she is a little shocked.

Sergeant Calvin takes Sophia's injured hand with one of his hands and rubs his other hand against her cheek.

"I must return to my duties of securing your safety, Sophia."

With these words, Sergeant Calvin leans down and softly kisses Sophia's forehead before walking away silently.

Sophia is aghast and embarrassed that she had done nothing regarding the Sergeant's advances. 'I must not tell anyone of his bold behavior,' she surmises. 'They would certainly wonder why I would agree to let him continue his duties. Lady Stephens warned me of his intentions and she would most assuredly scold me if she knew of the inappropriateness of his actions today.'

Lady Stephens returns to the garden house as Sophia busies herself admiring the blooms. "Is the Sergeant still here?" she asks.

"No, he left to continue his duties."

"Sophia, you promised your father we would visit him today. I suggest this is a good time for us to depart."

"Most certainly. I am anxious to hear if my father has heard any word from James."

~~~

The ladies arrive at the General's estate and are greeted by Thomas, who escorts them into the drawing room.

"There you are, my beautiful darling daughter and the lovely Lady Stephens," the General rejoices at the sight of both women. "How is my daughter and her bairn feeling today?"

"Much better Father, thank you. More importantly, have you received any word from James?"

"Your timing is perfect, Sophia. Just hours ago I did receive word."

"Where is he, Father? Is he well? When will he be home? Has he sailed back yet?" Sophia spouts out, barely able to contain her level of joy and excitement.

"He is fine, Sophia. He sends his love. He misses you dearly. Unfortunately, on his trip back from the King's palace, the carriage man was unclear of James's directions. He traveled in the opposite direction, causing him a great delay and complications for his voyage back," the General states, finding it extremely difficult to lie to his only daughter, but he continues to believe it was the correct thing to do at this time.

"I am so glad to hear he is fine, Father."

The General takes a large sip of scotch and steadies himself against the mantel.

"When will he return, Father?"

"That is not clear, my dear. I suspect he will be able to give us a better indication of that in his next letter."

"Please let me know as soon as you know. Thank you, Father. As for today, we are only here for a brief time. Lady Stephens and I are going to gather some clippings from your garden house so William can begin to have them flower in my garden house."

"You are always welcome to visit, Sophia."

With that, Sophia joins Lady Stephens outside, and the two ladies gather their clippings and head back to Sophia's home.

The General is not pleased with himself about lying to his daughter. He justified his actions with the intention of protecting his daughter and her growing bairn from additional worry and agony.

Outside the Langston estate, Sergeant Calvin walks toward the stables, calling for William.

"I require my horse ready to ride, stable boy," he demands, intentionally using a degrading tone in his voice. "I have an important meeting with the General today, so please hurry."

William deliberately takes his time with the leather strapping, hoping to aggravate the Sergeant, who has begun pacing the barn floor in his polished military boots. William holds the horse as the Sergeant mounts the gray gelding.

"I would be careful riding today sir, if I were you," William warns, with a smirk.

Sergeant Calvin cautiously looks William in the eyes and asks. "And why would that be, William?"

"Leather can be troublesome at times. I would not want your saddle or bridle's leather strap to come loose. I remind you of the deep crack I found in your leather bridle when you first arrived at this home. I simply wish you good luck and suggest you stay alert on your ride, Sergeant."

"Ignoramus," the Sergeant calls to William, as his crop whip taps the gelding on its rear and rides off. As he departs, the Sergeant hopes his journey will be uneventful.

~~~

Traveling down the road in their carriage, Sophia continues to read her book. Lady Stephens stares out the carriage window and notices Sergeant Calvin trotting past. Their eyes lock and she feels a sense of disgust at the sight of the scoundrel. Sergeant Calvin is concerned the old woman will get in the way of Sophia falling in love with him.

Arriving safely at the General's estate, Sergeant Calvin hands over his horse to the General's stableman, Horace. The General, who happened to be walking out the front door, greets the Sergeant.

"Good day, Sergeant."

"Good day, General," he said, immediately saluting the General. "I am Sergeant Calvin Harvey Gideon. I am the soldier who received your orders to protect your daughter in the absence of her husband. I am sorry for my delay, General; I was deeply concerned about my riding gear."

"Safety first," the General replies.

"Stableman. Check my horse's riding gear. It felt a little loose as I was riding over here," the Sergeant demands.

"Thank you, Horace. We would certainly appreciate you checking the Sergeant's gear," the General breaks in, not at all pleased at how the Sergeant addressed his stable hand.

"Yes, sir," Horace said.

"Horace is one of the finest stablemen in the area. He has an excellent way with caring for horses," the General said, wanting to let the Sergeant know his horse was in good hands. "Before Colonel James's departure to Portugal, he had ensured Horace and his stableman William, were well acquainted. The two spoke in German together and their common language quickly bonded them as fast friends." The General continues, "Please join me in my study, Sergeant. I have some news to share with you."

"Of course, General."

Once situated, the General begins to share the information which brought the Sergeant to this meeting. "I am afraid I have some terrible news, Sergeant. While on his mission in Portugal, Colonel James was ambushed. He is injured and it is unclear if his condition will allow him to return home safely. This is the cost a soldier pays when he accepts his duty, as I am sure you are aware."

"Yes, sir of course, General," responds Sergeant Calvin, both shocked and ecstatic by learning this news.

"I also am sharing this information with you in confidence. I do not want my daughter, Sophia, to learn of this news. I do not want to upset her. Do you understand Sergeant?"

"Yes, sir."

While the General continues to talk, greed oozes throughout the Sergeant's veins. 'My plan is forming,' he concludes. 'Little does the General know that Captain Taller and I are cousins. Cousins, who are tired of these aristocrats always obtaining all of the wealth. It is my cousin and I who arranged the ambush against Colonel James. An ambush I have now learned was successful. All we have to do now is make sure Colonel James does not return home, and I will enjoy spending my days counting money and making love to Sophia.'

"Sergeant Calvin, are you listening to me?" the General asks in an abrupt tone.

"Yes, General. I was reviewing your plan in my mind. Please do excuse me."

"As I was saying, Sergeant, I am awaiting word from Colonel James and Captain Taller. I offered Captain Taller a handsome sum of money for the safe return of Colonel James."

"It is good to see you are very generous with your funds, General Cartwright," Sergeant Calvin replies, a comment very unsuitable to make directly to a General.

"The happiness of my beloved daughter is important to me. Colonel James is the finest, most loyal soldier I have ever known. He is irreplaceable to me and my family."

Sergeant Calvin resents James for being held in such high regards with the General. 'If I would have met Sophia first, I would have had her first and you would be defining me that way, General,' the Sergeant deduces. 'I would have married your daughter.'

The General excuses himself from his study. Sergeant Calvin sits down in one of the study's chairs, remembering how he and his cousin conjured the plan for Colonel James's demise.

One night the two cousins sat on the deck of Captain Taller's ship. They were complaining about how unfair their lives had been and how hard they had to work for little reward. Cousin Taller mentioned that the General was sending his daughter's husband, a Colonel, for passage on his ship to Portugal. Cousin Calvin said he knew of this husband. He had just attended his and his beautiful wife, Sophia's wedding. He told him how the General's daughter was alluring and he could only imagine how ravishing she looked under her wedding gown. The more the alcohol flowed, the more the cousin's plan involving disposal of the Colonel, with the end result of the Captain becoming rich and the Sergeant marrying Sophia and inheriting her wealth. It was the perfect plan.

The General returned to his study, finding the Sergeant with a daydreaming look on his face. "I trust you will continue to care and guard my daughter during these times, Sergeant."

Still daydreaming, and not quite certain what the General was referring to, he promptly responded.

"Yes, sir, you can be assured I am perfect for your daughter, General."

The General shakes his head and wonders why the Sergeant seems so odd. Nonetheless, he was recommended for the duty and so he will be the one for the job. The General dismisses the Sergeant.

Sergeant Calvin exits the house and walks to the stable to retrieve his horse.

Galloping off, Sergeant Calvin continues thinking that 'it would appear mine and my cousin's plan is working well.'

Taking a short cut over a stream in order to return to Sophia's home more quickly, the Sergeant canters through the stream. Suddenly, he feels his saddle loosen. As he exits up the stream's tall embankment, the saddle slides under the horse's belly, throwing Sergeant Calvin backwards and deep into the frigid stream. He

struggles for air. His boot remains caught in his stirrup as the startled horse begins to gallop, dragging the Sergeant like a rag doll
through the rocky stream. With what little strength he can muster,
he reaches for his knife, pulls his body upward and cuts the stirrup, freeing his leg. His head crashes against a large rock, as he
falls into the flowing water. Holding his hand to his head, he can
feel warm blood seeping down the back of his neck. His horse runs
off, leaving the Sergeant alone and bewildered, shaking from the
wintery water soaking his body.

While working in the barn, William sees the Sergeant's horse
riding toward him. The Sergeant is nowhere to be seen.

"Easy boy, easy," William said, grabbing the horse's reins and
trying to calm it down. The horse continues trying to buck the
saddle off, throwing its hind legs high into the air. William quickly
releases the girth strap in order to relax and calm the anxious
horse.

Guiding the gelding to his stall, William picks the saddle up
from the ground. He notices the stirrup has been cut off. He
smiles. The previous day, while picking up a load of hay at the
Colonel's estate he had the opportunity to talk with Horace about
the Sergeant. William chuckles to himself. The stablemen had
formed a union and conspired to protect the Colonel's assets from
the Sergeant, who they both believed was a devious rogue. They
wanted to protect Lady Sophia from this scoundrel.

Horace was very fond of Sophia. He was almost like an uncle to
her. He taught Sophia how to ride her first horse. Horace was very
loyal to the General and his family. He was also devoted to the care
of horses. Many ill horses had been saved because of the care and
affection Horace showed these animals.

During their last visit, the plan had been set into place to loos-
en the Sergeant's strap, allowing the horse to be spooked and run
for safety.

As William stood outside the Langston's barn, he could faintly
hear Sergeant Calvin moaning in the far distance. One could only
hope he was in a great deal of pain and suffering, William thinks.
'My intention is to protect Lady Sophia, at all costs,' William repeats to himself, jumping into the seat of a wagon and snapping

the reins, motioning the horses to move. 'I will head out and see just how injured the Sergeant is. Perhaps wishes do come true,' he reflects.

About one kilometer from the barn, William finds Sergeant Calvin lying on the ground. His face and hair are covered with blood. Jumping down from his wagon, William calls out. "Sergeant Calvin, it is William, I am here to help you." This statement could be no further from the truth, William considers.

Looking up at William, the Sergeant moans, "I cannot move my leg."

William uses his large, strong body to grab the Sergeant under his arms and pull him up to a standing position. He helps the Sergeant to the wagon and loads his limp, pain-ridden body into the wagon. William is aware he could have been more helpful and inflict less pain upon the Sergeant with this maneuverer, but he had no interest in doing that. Snapping the reins again, William directs the wagon back to the barn and expresses his commitment.

"Ein Deutsch ist treu und ich werde Dame Sophia schützen." '*A German is loyal, and I will protect Lady Sophia.*'

Chapter Twenty

It had been four weeks since Grace had stitched up James's wounds. Despite his continuous pain and fever, he decided today he was ready to begin the one-day's ride to the Lisbon port. James knew the journey would not be easy, especially given his condition. He hoped good fortune would be on his side and that it would be easy to secure passage back to his homeland of England. His thoughts moved to Sophia. He could only imagine how she must be feeling over his extended absence.

It was against Grace's better judgment for James to travel, but James insisted. With Grace and Byron outside preparing the horses for travel, James remained inside to complete one more important task. He reached into his leather pouch filled with precious coins and removed three gold coins. Setting the coins on the table, he begins to write one last letter.

Dear Lady Grace and Byron:

Thank you for helping to save my life. I am aware of the awkward position I have placed you in, compromising your life in Portugal while caring for a British soldier. It is clear to me that without your assistance and tending to my wounds, I would have died. I want you to know I am forever indebted to you. I hope these coins can help express my gratitude and perhaps assist you with your finances, from one British citizen to another.

I would like you to know that if you ever decide to return to your homeland, England, you will always be welcome in my home.

Fondest Gratitude,
Colonel Abraham James Langston
January 29, 1734.

James folds the paper into thirds and writes Grace and Byron's name on the front. He places the coins in the letter and leaves the letter in Grace's darning basket. He knows the value of the coins will assist in remedying the financial woes for Grace for a very long time.

Walking outside, he sees Byron and Grace waiting with their wagon, which is hitched to two horses. James is confused by this sight, as he believes he was riding into town alone.

Grace could see the perplexed look on James's face.

"James, I believe it would be much too dangerous for you to make this trip alone. You are wearing a British Army uniform and still have not gained full strength after your injuries. For those two reasons, you are a vulnerable target on these country roads. I have decided it would be best for Byron and me to transport you—covered, in the back of my wagon. I am also aware of a shorter route to the port, which would be much less conspicuous and re-duce the possibility of you being detected."

James looks at Grace and smiles.

"I am starting to believe that British women are strongly opin-ionated and it would be futile to argue with them once they have made up their minds. For that reason, and because I believe your suggestion is correct, I agree to travel like baled hay in the back of your wagon," James said, smiling.

"Although, as part of this agreement, I would like to present you with these reises as payment for transport to the Lisbon port, and to simply point out that British men are equally stubborn and opinionated."

Grace smiles and gladly accepts the coins.

"Thank you, James. This money will go to good use, I can assure you."

Byron cracks the whip and snaps the leather reins. The two horses pull away as James lays covered with cloth and bales of hay in the back of the wagon.

Halfway through their journey, they stop by a creek to water the horses.

It is almost sunset when they reach a spot in the road, just outside the port of Lisbon. It was decided to park outside of the port for James to exit the wagon, since exiting in the middle of the port would have created quite a scene and perhaps cause more problems for Grace.

Tired and sore, James climbs out of the wagon. Approaching Byron, he shakes his hand and removes one of the Medal of Honor pins from his lapel. His body moves slowly. He realizes that possibly his health may be worse than he had previously assessed.

James pins the Medal onto Byron's jacket. The blue, red and white ribbons accentuate the importance of this gold Medal.

"For your bravery, Byron. And for helping to save my life," James said, saluting to Byron. "I also want to give you and your mother my address; that way, if either of you ever need something, or decide to travel to England, you can write me a letter and I can host you in my great country of England. Will you do that for me, son?"

"Yes, sir," Byron responds, suddenly feeling very important.

"Thank you, James," Grace said, seeing the impact James has had on her son. "I wish you safe travels and safe healing. Please tell England I say hello."

James cannot believe his good fortune of meeting this British woman and her son. 'God must have been watching over me,' he thinks. 'Now I need God to help me get home to my precious wife.'

As James walks down the hill into the town of Lisbon, he realizes he is one step closer to home. 'I hope I will be able to get a room at the inn where I had agreed to meet Captain Taller. Once I locate Taller, I can board his ship and be on my way.' James was pleased that after all that had happened, he was able to remember the name of the quaint inn where he was to meet the Captain. The inn was called Pousada do Marinheiro, Portuguese for Seafarer Inn. Walking down the hill, James could see Captain Taller's ship moored in the port. Relieved good fortune is on his side, his step quickens.

Passing one of the locals on the road, James asks, "Onde fica o Pousada do Marinheiro" *'Where is Seafarer Inn?'*

"Quarto blocs." *'Four block's'* the older man said, pointing down the hill and then with his hand making a waving motion to indicate it is on the right-hand side of the street. 'The man must know I do not speak much Portuguese,' James thinks. 'No doubt my British uniform was his biggest clue.'

"Obrigado." *'Thank you,'* James replies, hoping he said the Portuguese words correctly. The man nods and continues walking.

The closer James walks toward the inn, the more he can smell the fresh salt air.

Looking up, James spies the weathered sign reading 'Pousada do Marinheiro'. He also locates the tavern next door, just as Captain Taller had described. The tavern had an interesting name: "Taverna Furo do Cohen" *'Coxen Hole Tavern.'* '

The Coxen Hole Tavern was named after the famous 17th century Spanish pirate, Captain John Coxen, who terrorized Spain and was a famous buccaneer of the 'Brethren of the Coast.' James could only imagine why Captain Taller enjoyed this tavern.

Entering the Seafarer Inn, James secured a room for the night. He then requested of the innkeeper, "If anyone comes looking for me and I am not in my room, please direct them over to the Coxen Hole Tavern next door."

The innkeeper agrees and James proceeds to the tavern in search of Captain Taller. Entering the tavern, James was immediately struck by the smell of heavy smoke, alcohol and stagnate urine. Walking across the wood plank floor, he can see Captain Taller sitting in the corner, his back toward James. Approaching the Captain, he taps his shoulder without saying a word.

"Who goes there?" the Captain asks, with a slurred voice and a tone of familiarity, as if he knew most people in this tavern. Captain Taller slowly turns his head and is instantly sobered by the sight of Colonel James standing next to him. He was certain James would have been dead by now, given the injuries he had acquired during the ambush.

The Captain's mind immediately leaps from shock to panic. His plan had failed. The Colonel was supposed to be dead, the Captain was supposed to be rich, and his cousin, Calvin, was supposed to be able to marry Sophia.

"Hello, Captain. I am glad you are still here, waiting to return me to England. I was delayed because I was ambushed." James said, pulling up a chair and joining the Captain and the others at the table. The Captain smiles uncomfortably, perhaps from shock, perhaps from disappointment. Fortunately, the amount of alcohol in his body made it so it did not matter. He nodded at Colonel James and continued to ramble on with tales of lies.

James listened, wondering if the Captain realized how ridiculous and roguish he sounded. The conversation then moved on to the Colonel's ambush. The Captain turned to James and innocently began asking about his ambush. As the Captain drank more whiskey, he became more relaxed and the questions became more specific. At times the questions were so specific, only a person who was personally aware of the event would have been able to ask them.

"How were you able to attack a man so tall in height?" the Captain asked.

There was something about the shocked look on the Captain's face when James first appeared before him this evening, along with the way the Captain asked about the ambush, which caused James to deduce that the Captain was a drunk and an unethical and conniving human being. 'I am certain he has a connection to my ambush. After all, the Captain knew of my whereabouts and my value to the General. Perhaps the Captain assumed correctly that I was carrying gold and silver as part of my business with the King.'

"Where did you go after the ambush? I had no idea where you were or what happened to you. What life-threatening injuries did you sustain? How did you get away from the one remaining highwayman's friend?" The Captain asked questions rapidly with a slurred speech and a slight swaying in his chair. "I decided to stay in Portugal and wait for you and enjoy the women and the alcohol at the Coxen Hole. I also enjoyed spending the money I made from transporting you here."

James was now completely convinced Captain Taller played a role in his ambush. What James needed was more information for a court of law to charge the Captain with treason. To get that information more whiskey for Captain Taller was required. The drinks and the conversation continued to flow.

As the three other men at the table noticed the more serious tone of the Colonel, they excused themselves, saying they had too much to drink for the night and must get home.

The Captain and James now sat alone at the table. When James ordered another round of whiskey, he watched the Captain drink as he nonchalantly poured some of his whiskey onto the floor. James was not interested in getting drunk; he was interested in breaking down the Captain, causing him to become defenseless because of alcohol.

The level of alcohol consumed by the Captain had indeed weakened him. His eyes were glassy and his words were flowing freely.

"Colonel James, continue your story. I want to hear all the details about how the highwaymen did not kill you. I am surprised they did not kill you."

"After I left King John V, the carriage traveled quite far and then stopped suddenly. I could tell we were under attack. I grabbed my sword and jumped out of the carriage and began to engage in battle with the highwaymen."

"What about the dead carriage man?"

'Funny,' James thinks. 'I did not mention anything about the state of the carriage man.'

"I was able to cut the reins lose with my sword and I mounted one of the horses, making it easier to fight. I charged them head on."

"Well done. Cheers to that," the Captain said, raising his glass and drinking another shot of whiskey.

He slams his empty glass onto the table and calls out for more. "Leave us the bottle!" Taller demands.

James nods at the owner, implying it is all right and he will pay him later.

Captain Taller raises his glass. "Here is to killing the bandit's amigos."

'I have said nothing of a second man, nor of killing a man, nor their relationship with each other,' James deliberates. Deciding to not yet respond to the Captain's slip-up, James continues.

"I charged after the man. He retaliated, catching me in my chest and causing me to fall off my horse. I was able to fight the man off his horse and cut the side of his face with my sword."

The Captain takes another drink of whiskey. James is amazed the Captain is still able to sit upright, based on the enormous amount of alcohol he has consumed.

"Did you kill the bastard?" Captain Taller asks, happy James was doing most of the talking since he was beginning to loose controls of his faculties.

"No, I did not. I decided I would allow him to live and endure the pain and guilt of what he had just caused."

"I wish you would have killed the bastard. It would have been easier since his plan had failed. How did you survive his sword lashing deep into your chest?"

"I was carrying a leather pouch inside my jacket, which prevented his sword from going in deeper than it already had."

"So you were carrying a pouch of gold and silver coins?" the Captain asks, unaware his questions indicated he knew more about this robbery than he would have liked James to know.

James, looking directly into Captain Taller's face said, "Captain, I said nothing about having gold and silver coins, nor did I mention there were two men. I also did not mention the two men were friends."

"I am drunk, Colonel James. I must be imagining things. You will have to excuse my embellishment of your story."

"Captain Taller, from your comments and responses, I am not inclined to believe your excuse. If there is something you wish to tell me about your involvement with this ambush, then I suggest you say it now."

"What makes you think I have something to say, dear Colonel?"

"As mentioned just minutes ago, you indicated to me you know more about my ambush than you are letting on. If you are involved in any way regarding a British soldier being ambushed in Portugal, then you should know His Majesty would consider that treason, a crime punishable by hanging."

No sooner had James said these words, than five British soldiers, those sent by the General to locate Colonel James, entered the Coxen Hole Tavern. The soldiers had arrived first at the Seafarer Inn, as they were instructed by the General. The innkeeper, following James's request, advised the soldiers they could find the Colonel next door at the tavern.

As the soldiers entered the Coxen Hole Tavern, they looked across the room and spotted Colonel James sitting with Captain Taller near the rear of the tavern. They walked toward Colonel James, saluted him and stood next to him. James, pleased to see these soldiers, stood to address them.

"Colonel Langston, we are here on the behalf of General Cartwright, sir. He has instructed us to accompany you safely back to England. We also have a letter for Captain Taller, in the event we could not find you. The letter informs Captain Taller to continue waiting for you and once found to transport you safely home.

The very drunk Captain Taller looks at the soldiers and panic washes over his inebriated body. He is conscious enough to know the only reason these soldiers are here is because the General suspects foul play, and now after his conversation with the Colonel, he

is guessing the Colonel does as well. Their plan has failed misera-
bly. How could he have been so foolish as to believe his cousin's
get-wealthy scheme of ambushing Colonel James? The gravity of
this failed ambush attempt for wealth causes the Captain's head to
spin and he collapses face first onto the tavern table. Colonel
James motions for two of the soldiers to take the Captain to his
room at the inn next door. Colonel James walks to the inn with the
other three soldiers, requesting updates from England and giving
them specific instructions regarding the Captain.

"I want you other three soldiers to stand outside my door. We
will leave at the first sight of dawn."

"Yes, sir."

"And may we say, sir," one of the soldiers speaks out. "It is
good to know you are safe and alive. I know the General will be
very pleased with this news."

"Thank you, soldier. Mark my words, after what I have confirmed this evening, Captain Taller may not be happy I am alive,
because he will never forget who I am for the rest of his eternal
life."

Captain James does not rest well in his room. The pain from
his hand-stitched wound and the feeling of consternation overwhelms him. 'Captain Taller is a traitor. Who else was part of his
scandalous scheme? Justice will prevail, of that I am certain. For
now, I must focus on sailing safely back to England. Then, I will let
the General know of the atrocious actions of the Captain, and I will
once again be with my Sophia.'

The sun had not yet risen in the sky when James awakes. Still
wearing his uniform from the day before, he walks to the Captain's
room and orders his men to continue standing guard. Turning the
brass doorknob, James walks into the room and stands over Captain Taller's bed.

The soldiers have ensured the door remains left slightly open.
They are curious about what might occur. Colonel James has a
reputation of being a kind and fair man that you do not want to
cross. Those who have crossed him have witnessed his wrath.

Captain Taller is snoring and the room reeks of stale alcohol.
James removes his sword from its metal scabbard and presses the

cold blade firmly against Captain Taller's neck. The Captain opens his eyes, still groggy from his drunkenness the previous night. He looks at James, bewildered as to what is happening. James slices the sharp sword's blade across Captain's throat, making a very deep, yet not fatal cut from one ear lobe to the other. Warm red blood rolls down the Captain's neck, as James begins pronouncing the Captain's verdict. The soldiers stare through the small opening and quietly gasp.

"Captain Taller, loyalty in the British military is paramount to those who serve. You, sir, are a treasonous disgrace to the British military, of that I am certain. I am unaware what the Provost Marshal and the British Crown will decide to do with you regarding your deceitful acts. As for me, you will wear a massive scar on your neck for the rest of your life, reminding you of the shame you should feel when you use your throat to agree to criminal acts. I will make certain everyone knows why it is there. Your throat speaks evil and your mind is heinous. You should be happy I am a decent man and have decided not to do damage to your brain as well."

The soldiers, standing outside the Captain's room, listen intently as their level of loyalty to the British Crown increases instantly. They have all resolved, never will they cross Colonel James Langston.

"And now, Captain Taller," James continues, with his sword still on the Captain's ear. "Are you going to tell me the truth regarding your involvement in my ambush or shall I do more damage to the rest of your body?"

Captain Taller stutters. "It was not I. I swear."

James moves the sword tip to the Captain's heart and presses down with significant force.

"Captain! I demand honesty!"

Fearing for his life, the Captain begins to spew information.

"Here is the honest truth, Colonel. Two Portuguese men stopped me as I left my ship. They noticed your arrival and your carriage. One man held a knife to my throat; the other held my hands behind my back. They said they would slice me like a pig if I did not tell them who you were. I told them you were here to visit their King. The one man said, 'I bet he has gold and silver with him. Why else would he visit our King?' I knew I could not get word to you and I knew you were with the King. I could not interrupt your important meeting. Beside, you would be safe in the King's palace," the Captain fabricates.

"You are a liar, Captain!" James shouts, pressing the tip of the sword deeper into the Captain's chest. "You could have told those highwaymen any location for me. Yet you said the palace. You knew the path I would take back from the palace and yet you did nothing to assist in my safety. It was as though you wanted me dead. You are a soldier in the British Navy and you looked out for yourself. When were you going to tell me this part of your story?"

"I was a drunken fool. I was about to tell you when all those soldiers appeared saying they were going to protect you."

"Captain Taller, if I gain additional information that emphatically proves your role in my ambush, you will wish for the Provost Marshal's sentence, in that I can assure you, because my sentence for you will be far worse and much more painful. Do I make myself clear?"

"Ye- ye- ye- yes, sir."

Colonel James removes the blade from the Captain's chest.

"Now pack up your belongings and my soldiers will escort you to your ship. You have thirty minutes Captain. Get moving."

With those final words James walks out into the hallway. The soldiers salute. James nods, salutes and smiles.

"I suggest you all remain loyal soldiers as well, gentlemen," James said, aware the men have heard his entire interaction with Captain Taller.

"Yes, sir," the soldiers reply together, with serious looks on their faces.

"Now let us depart for England. I would like to get home. I have a new wife waiting for me and I expect she is waiting for an 'I am home' embrace."

The soldiers smile. They had heard of the Colonel's personably style. It had become a reputation of his and one of the characteristics which made his men so loyal to him. Today, they experienced that personable style first hand.

Arriving at Captain Taller's ship, James gathers his men before boarding the ship. "I believe Captain Taller wanted me dead during this trip to Portugal. There is most certainly more to this story. Stay alert men. Captain Taller cannot be trusted. He and his bandit friends wanted my coins and wanted me no longer alive. For whatever reason, I hope this is a lesson to all of you. The value of your training as a soldier is critical to every mission you are on. Remain vigilant, gentlemen. We are not home yet. Who knows what this voyage has in store for us as soldiers?"

While the group boards the ship, James sees a newspaper on the dock. The day was January 30, 1734. James was immediately struck by how much time had passed since he had first landed in Portugal.

Captain Taller assumes his role as commander of the ship and greets the soldiers as they walk onto his deck. James nods to the Captain, pointing one finger to his eye and then to the Captain, signaling he will be watching him. Captain Taller offers a weak smile in return.

The ship sets sail and James looks back at the Lisbon port declaring, "A deus Portugal," *'Goodbye Portugal,'* "I am happy to leave."

Holding his pocket watch from Sophia tightly, he calls out to the sea from the starboard side of the ship. "I am sailing home to you, my love. I love you madly and I will prove that to you when I return."

~~~

Concerned for Sergeant Calvin's health after his fall from his horse, Doctor Hadley is called to the house. The doctor completes his examination and determines the Sergeant required stitches on the back of his head.

"There is also a good possibility the Sergeant has experienced head trauma and strained some muscles in his leg. The good news is the leg is not broken," the doctor announces. "The Sergeant must remain still and get lots of rest."

William carries the Sergeant up to the unfinished guest bedroom.

Sophia waits downstairs for the doctor to return.

"He will need care, Sophia. Do you think you will be capable to provide such care?"

"Of course, Doctor. I will ensure he is cared for very well," replies Sophia, recognizing the irony that it was the concerned Sergeant who was to care for her and not vice versa.

"And how are you and your growing bairn?" Doctor Hadley asks.

"I believe I am well, although it is hard to correctly say. I am very tired all the time. If I could have my choice, I would sleep every minute of the day and then wake up, eat and go back to sleep."

Doctor Hadley chuckles. "That is to be expected, my dear. Especially during your first three months of pregnancy. You will simply have to come to expect it and make sure you do not strain or stress yourself, for that could harm your unborn bairn."

"I will be sure to do whatever is necessary to give James a healthy son or daughter," Sophia said.

The doctor waves goodbye and walks out the front door.

Sophia walks upstairs to the guest bedroom. Turning the crystal doorknob on the bedroom door, she sees Sergeant Calvin lying on his back.

"Did I wake you?"

"No, Lady Sophia, please come in."

"How are you feeling?"

"I am in a great deal of pain. Most of the pain is because I am a soldier at this moment incapable of protecting you."

"You must not worry about that now, Sergeant," Sophia said, hoping to comfort him.

Taking full advantage of this perfect opportunity to be alone with the love of his life, the Sergeants continues. "I am weak, Lady Sophia. Would you be so kind as to sit on my bed so I do not have to strain my voice talking to you?"

"Of course, Sergeant," Sophia replies, carefully sitting on the bed as to not cause more pain to the Sergeant.

"Mmmm," he moans. "To be near you is healing," the Sergeant lustfully comments, staring directly into Sophia's captivating eyes.

Seeing a bowl of water and towel beside the bed, Sophia dampens the cloth and gently wipes a large area of dried blood and dirt off the Sergeant's forehead.

"It would appear you brought most of the field home with you," Sophia said, smiling and hoping to lighten the mood and change the subject.

Rinsing off the cloth, she returns it to the Sergeant's face, then continues to gently wash down his arms, cleaning some of the small pebbles from his deep scratches. Grabbing her hand, Sergeant Calvin holds it tightly and thanks Sophia for her care. He does not release his grip. He is aroused by the feel of Sophia's young, silky skin. She does not pull back. Instead, she believes that perhaps her kindness will somehow help with the Sergeant's healing. Besides, 'He is a man in pain, not in his own home and could probably use an extra dose of comfort,' she reflects, justifying her actions.

"You are going to be just fine, Sergeant Calvin," Sophia said, patting his hand. "You will be up and moving soon without effort, I am certain."

With that, Sophia removes her hand from the Sergeant's grip and rearranges a curl of hair off her face.

While attempting to dislodge her hand from the Sergeant's grasp, the Sergeant notices Theodore enter the guest bedroom, carrying a serving tray of venison, fresh fruit and sweets, along with a pot of tea.

"Your supper, sir."

"Thank you, Theodore. Please leave the tray over on that small table," Sophia requests.

Theodore quietly leaves the guest bedroom and Sophia goes over to the table to pour the Sergeant a cup of tea.

"I had Theodore prepare you a meal. Hopefully, this food will help you to regain your strength. I shall leave you alone now Sergeant to eat and heal."

"Please do not leave, Sophia. I find your company assists my healing," Sergeant Calvin said, sitting up in bed and propping his pillow behind his back.

Sophia walks to the curtains to draw them closed. Sergeant Calvin finds himself completely mesmerized by Sophia's light almond skin, seductive bosom and long, flowing curls.

Walking to the table, Sophia bends over to pick up the plate of food. Lying in bed, with his knees bent, Sergeant Calvin's hand grips his swelling penis and he begins to squeeze and then to rub it up and down. 'I must release from the arousal Sophia has caused.'

Seeing Sophia's perfectly round voluptuous breasts, Sergeant Calvin releases himself, squirting his wet juices into his hand.

Sophia walks back to his bed.

"Are you hungry?"

"More than you can imagine," the Sergeant replies, not longing for food, but rather wanting to devour Sophia.

"I suggest you eat this and then you should start to feel better soon."

"With you in this room, Lady Sophia, I most certainly feel more spirited."

Sophia leans forward to touch his shoulder.

"You certainly do sound like you are improving quickly," Sophia said, smiling.

With her hand still on his shoulder, Sergeant Calvin reaches for the rose-gold locket hanging from the necklace around Sophia's neck.

"What is this fine piece of jewelry you have?"

"It is a wedding gift from my husband. It is an extension of his heart. It makes me feel closer to him when he is not at my side; that is why I never remove it from my neck."

Sophia moves the Sergeant's hair away from his forehead, ensuring all the blood has been removed and he is no longer bleeding.

"It looks as though you are beginning to mend, Sergeant. It is time for me to depart. Sleep well."

"And to you, Lady Sophia. I hope you have pleasant dreams. I am certain I will, as I lie here in this bed."

'What a strange response,' Sophia thinks, exiting the Sergeant's bedroom and entering her own bedroom next door.

Lighting several candles, Sophia sits at her powder dresser and removes the ivory hair barrettes, causing her long, black, curly hair to drop down her back. She begins to brush her hair with her silver brush. The bristles on her scalp are welcomed. They seem to draw out the stresses of the day and the woes of James not waiting for her as she climbs into bed. Sophia bends her head forward, rubbing the tensions out from the back of her neck.

During this time, Sophia is completely unaware that Sergeant Calvin is peeking through the large skeleton key hole in her bedroom door. Her every move hardens him.

After finishing brushing her hair, Sophia walks behind the room divider. She unbuttons her gown, slips it over her shoulders and drops it onto the floor. The candelabra's light captures her silhouette. She is perfectly positioned for Sergeant Calvin to enjoy watching the curvy outline of her body as she removes her gown. Sophia begins to untie her white tight corset and removes it as well. Sergeant Calvin is even more aroused, particularly since he believes he can discern the outline of her nipples, now that her corset has been removed.

Sophia stands sideways looking into the mirror. She tries to determine if her stomach is growing bigger. Sergeant Calvin begins to stroke himself, watching Sophia present her naked body to him.

"Your father will be home soon little one," Sophia said out loud as she slowly rubs her stomach. "He will be so happy you are growing inside me." Sophia is ten weeks pregnant and her pregnancy is barely noticeable. She hoped for a little bump soon.

Staring through the keyhole, Sergeant Calvin found himself obsessing over Sophia. His desire for her takes him to his darkest desires and beyond his human control. The Sergeant strokes himself harder. His up and down movement cannot satisfy the persistent stimulating itch he feels. He releases his tight grip, but it did not stop him from continuing to stare at Sophia's perfectly beautiful naked body.

Sophia decides that tonight she will wear her wedding night nightgown, the one with the lavender flowers embroidered on it. She reaches for the gown and pulls it over her head. Wearing this gown somehow makes her feel closer to James. 'Oh how I miss my lover and now father to my unborn bairn.'

Exhausted from the day and her first trimester of pregnancy, Sophia walks over to her bed, pulls the covers over her shoulders and falls into a deep sleep. Sleep comes easy as she is lulled into dreaming by the sound of sea and the smell of the midnight air.

Sophia awakens as the bright morning light blankets her face. She gets out of bed and walks to her window to enjoy the scent of the salt air. 'Oh how I long for the sound of James's voice greeting me in the morning. I want him to return home safely so I can tell him the wonderful news of carrying his first bairn.'

Along with the wave of sadness Sophia feels, she also feels a wave of sickness. Doctor Hadley had warned her about feeling this way and suggests some dry toast might help the feeling pass. Heeding that advice, she gets dressed and goes to the porch to wait for service from Theodore. Looking out to the sea Sophia releases her anguish and calls out. 'My love, come back to me. Please James, come back to me! God, I beg of you, bring my husband, the father of my child, home to me.' Sophia places both her hands over her face and sobs.

Lady Stephens walks onto the porch and immediately rubs Sophia's shoulder to comfort her.

"I promise you, Sophia, all will be well. James will be at your side very soon. You must stay strong. He would want you to do that for him."

Looking up at Lady Stephens, Sophia responds.

"I simply cannot endure this horrible, deep pain. I feel as though my heart has been torn out of my chest. I cannot bear to be separated from James ever again."

"And yet for now you must, my dear. Now gather your wits about you, because today is Sunday and we promised your father we would visit him. I also think this trip will do us both good. Theodore?" Lady Stephens said, turning to her loyal butler. "I shall take another cup of tea and please prepare one more for Lady Sophia as well. Would you also be so kind to tell Bernard we will require him to transport us in our carriage in a wee bit?"

Turning back to Sophia she said, "How is Sergeant Calvin feeling this morning?"

"I checked in on him briefly this morning. It would appear he is feeling better. He did indicate he would prefer to be performing his duty and stand watch for me. Poor thing. He took such a frightful fall yesterday. It is good he did not hurt himself more than he did."

Lady Stephens smiles back at Sophia. It was clear from Sophia's tone she was overly concerned for the Sergeant. Lady Stephens did not share the same compassion for the leech. She decided not to broach the topic again. Instead, she would keep her eyes on this soldier, a man whom she did not trust one speck.

~~~

Upon arriving at the General's estate, Lady Stephens excuses herself to go to the garden house first. "Please tell your father I will come in and say hello to him shortly," she requests of Sophia.

Sophia walks into the General's house and directly into her father's study.

"I thought Lady Stephens would be joining you today," the General observes.

"She is going to your garden house first, to pick a few fresh roses for us. I hope you do not mind, Father."

"Of course not. In fact, I think I might join her. I could use a bit of fresh air this morning."

As the General leaves his study, Sophia sits down at his desk. Sitting here reminds her of when she was a child. She remembers sneaking into her father's study and pretending to be her father. Sophia would give commands and write letters to her father with his quill pen. She would stuff them into his stationary and write 'Father' on the outside of the envelope. Sophia gazed around the room, admiring the expensive artwork on the walls and remembering the wonderful times she spent here as a child. Sliding her fingers across her father's leather desk blotter she notices, tucked into the sleeve, a letter. A letter with her husband's handwriting on the outside of the envelope! Why would James write her father a letter? When did James write her father a letter? Perhaps this is a recent letter. 'I would never dare open my father's confidential letters, but perhaps this one contains news of James's return.'

Willing to bear the consequences for her actions, Sophia allows her curiosity to dictate. With her heart pounding, she removes the letter from the envelope. Sophia stands to read the letter. Her eyes begin to jump around the page. 'I was ambushed by two highwaymen. A skirmish occurred resulting in my carriage man and one of the bandits perishing. I was also injured, taking a blade to my chest resulting in a deep wound.'

'Ambushed?' Sophia feels faint. The room begins to spin, as her body sways. She staggers back, crashing into her father's bookcase, causing several books to crush down onto the wooden floor, along with Sophia's body. She lies limp on the floor. Thomas rushes into the General's study, responding to the crashing sound. He sees Sophia's body lying on the floor, surrounded by scattered books. He calls out for Countess Elizabeth and Governess Abigale, who, without delay, come running into the study.

Thomas carries Sophia to the nearest guest room, accompanied by the two women. He places Sophia onto the bed.

"Send for the General," the Governess calls out.

Moments later, the General races into the guest bedroom and kneels at Sophia's side. Countess Elizabeth, busy patting Sophia's head with a cold cloth, informs the General, "She is still unresponsive."

"Thomas, what happened?" the General asks, looking at his butler.

Thomas explains how he heard a noise in the General's study and when he entered, books were lying on the floor, along with Lady Sophia. Suspecting there is more to the story, the General quickly walks to his study. Entering, he sees a spray of books on the floor. Also lying on the floor is the letter he received from the Colonel. Beside the letter is the opened envelope. Lady Stephens, who was slower reaching the house than the General, finds him in his study with a stunned look on his face.

"What has happened? Where is Sophia? Why do you look like you have just seen a ghost, General?"

"Indeed I have, Lady Stephens. I have seen the ghost of protection. Protection of my daughter from news I did not want her to learn about."

The General proceeds to inform Lady Stephens of the terrible news regarding James.

"And now this unfortunate news has just been made worse by Sophia's discovery."

"Oh, my, this is horrible and terrible for her and her bairn. It will be best you share the truth with her, General. She expects that of you. Let her know you have sent your best soldiers to respond to this situation. She is a wife of a soldier now. This tragedy will be one of the many life lessons she will have, forcing her maturity and wisdom."

"You are correct," the General admits, relieved by the suggestion and still anxious about his daughter's well-being.

Walking into the guest bedroom, he sees that Sophia's eyes are now open. Upon seeing her father, Sophia calls out.

"How could you? How could you hide this information from me? James is my husband. I have the right to know of his condition, Father."

Sitting on the side of her bed, the General shamefully responds to his daughter's questions.

"Sophia, my dear, all will be well. I did not inform you because I did not want to burden you or harm your bairn." The General leans down and kisses his daughter on her forehead. "I have sent five of my most elite soldiers to Portugal to escort James safely home to all of us. I can assure you, Sophia, I will have him home safely very soon."

"I am grateful you sent reinforcements to James's predicament. That still does not account for holding such valuable information for me. I am Colonel James Langston's wife. I know from living in your home you would have told the other wives of soldiers in this situation. Therefore, Father, I request that in the future you provide me with the same courtesy."

Everyone in the guest room remains quiet, unsure of how the General will respond to the forcefulness of Sophia's statement. The General was forced to admit that not only was Sophia just like her mother, today she exhibited the tenacity and conviction of a woman who would be an incredible asset as the wife of a soldier.

"Sophia, you make a fair request of me. Once again I want you to understand, I always have your well-being at the forefront of my decisions."

"I am aware, Father. Thank you. Now please let us get James home safely."

Everyone in the room that day was introduced to a new and stronger version of Sophia. Their surprise was accompanied by silence. Sophia decided it was time for her to travel home and get some rest, particularly after this fright.

Before leaving the house, Lady Stephens requests a private conversation with the General. She wanted to tell him what she believes is Sergeant Calvin's inappropriate familiarity and fondness toward Sophia. She also wants to inform him about the Sergeant's accident. Her intent is to ensure the General knows what is occurring in respect to his daughter. The conversation is short and the General is very grateful for this information, although he is certain there is nothing to be concerned about.

On the carriage ride home, Lady Stephens and Sophia chat about the scenery along the countryside. Greeting them, as they pull into the driveway, is Theodore. He helps the ladies out of the carriage as Lady Stephens hands him the roses she picked earlier from the General's estate. She asks him to place the flowers in the vase in her bedroom. Sophia, concerned for the Sergeant's health, said she will go to his room and see how he is feeling. She first decides to prepare the small vase of roses to help brighten his spirits.

Sophia knocks on the Sergeant's bedroom door and asks if she may enter.

"Most certainly," Sergeant Calvin replies, all too happy to have any amount of time alone with Sophia.

"I have brought you some flowers to help with your healing," she said kindly.

"Just seeing you in my room heals me, Sophia," the Sergeant asserts boldly.

Sophia is taken aback by this comment. 'His rudeness and lack of referring to me as 'lady' must be caused by the bump on his head,' she concludes.

"I do believe bed rest is truly needed to help with my terrible accident," the Sergeant responds, aware he might consider reining in his outward express of lust for Sophia.

Sophia barely smiles back; her mind seems somewhere else. This distraction does not go unnoticed by the Sergeant.

"Is something bothering you, Sophia?" Again the Sergeant intentionally chooses to use her first name, hoping to continue developing a closer relationship with her.

"I will simply have to be fine," Sophia expresses.

'Perhaps Sophia is saddened by ill news regarding Colonel James,' the Sergeant imagines.

"And what is this burdensome apex you seem to be needing to overcome?"

"It is about my husband and the reason you are posted at my home, Sergeant. Colonel James has not yet returned home. He has been delayed. I am most concerned about him and desperate to know when he will return home safely. I cannot imagine my life without him."

"You are a beautiful woman, Sophia. Many men would want to marry you, even if you were widowed. In fact, I myself would consider it an honor to care and provide for you."

'Are my ears playing tricks on me? Did I just hear the Sergeant say he wanted to marry me? What a strange comment to make as a guest in my home,' Sophia determines.

"Father said he is sending his most elite soldiers to Portugal to search for my husband. He gave me his word he would bring Colonel James home to me."

Sergeant Calvin was not pleased to hear that reinforcements had been sent to aid the Colonel. 'If the Colonel is found and returns home, my plan would be foiled. If, on the other hand, the Colonel is dead, it will be one of the happiest days in my life. Either way, one piece of the plan must occur in the next few days to ensure Sophia will be considered mine forever. I must bed Sophia. If I could be intimate with her, everything will work out well,' the Sergeant schemes.

"Your Ladyship, it pains me to witness you this worried and ill at ease. Allow me to escort you to your bedroom. You seem so very tired and I want you to know that although I am still recovering, your protection is of the utmost importance to me. It would also be encouraging knowing I still could do my duty and bring you safely to your bedroom. Would you allow that small gift to my self-esteem, your Ladyship?" the Sergeant pitifully pleads.

Exhausted from the day and hoping to honor the Sergeant's request, Sophia reluctantly agrees and allows the Sergeant to escort her to her bedroom.

Once in her room, Sophia walks directly to the window seat and sits down. Sergeant Calvin follows her, reaching for her leather suede book and handing it to her. His presumptuousness surprises her.

"Thank you, Sergeant," she responds, feeling uncomfortable and wishing the Sergeant would recognize he has overstayed his welcome.

Sergeant Calvin stares intensely at Sophia's bosom. She notices and quickly places her hand across her chest.

"Perhaps it is appropriate for you to leave now, Sergeant. I require my rest."

Still fantasizing about what wonders can be explored under her dress, the Sergeant reluctantly agrees to leave. "I am only a short distance away from you, dear lady. If you need anything from me, Sophia, you simply can call out my name and I will be at your beautiful side in moments."

"I suggest you continue to focus on getting well and once again assume your duties. Good evening Sergeant," Sophia said sharply, hoping to quickly end this very awkward moment.

Sergeant Calvin returns to his room, aware time is fast approaching for the possibility of Colonel James arriving home or being discovered as dead. He prays for the latter. 'Nonetheless, the time is now to secure Sophia's love for me. If I bed Sophia, she will realize she would want me as a lover. Even if Colonel James does return home, Sophia would easily choose me, the fit Sergeant, rather than the battle-worn Colonel. Once I take her body, she will easily give me her mind and her heart. When I have Sophia, I will own this house, have control of her wealth and command the servants. I will drink bottles of fine scotch with the General, and I will have an easier time advancing in the military with the General as my father-in-law. With Sophia as my wife, she will lose all her rights. I will own her and her wealth. My plan is simple and perfect. All I need to do now is bed Sophia. And it must be soon. My groin advises me it should be tonight.'

The more the Sergeant obsessed over these thoughts, a type of rage built up inside him. 'This is my home now and Sophia is mine. She will take orders from me and do as I ask,' his delusions spewed.

Sergeant Calvin calculates his moves and waits quietly in his room, ensuring the entire house is sound asleep before making his move. It was three am and the light from the full moon lit a path to Sophia's bedroom door. He very slowly opens the door, ensuring there is no creaking to alert Sophia or her sleeping puppy. He was grateful the little mutt played hard today and as a puppy required a lot of sleep. Opening the bedroom door wider, he sees Sophia sleeping on her side. Her back was facing him. Walking to her bed, he can feel the damp night air softly blowing in from the window. The room was faintly lit by the moon and a few embers were still burning in the fireplace. He removes all his clothes, exposing his plain body. He is impressed by how large his penis is. 'Oh how Sophia will enjoy having me inside her. She will have pleasures she never thought were possible.'

Slinking into Sophia's bed, Sergeant Calvin pauses to enjoy the shape of her body, outlined by her white bed sheet. He quickly hardens. 'I want her. I want her money,' he fantasizes. Sliding his body closer to her, his chest meets Sophia's back. He is certain he will explode with ecstasy. 'No, I must wait,' his mind controls itself with the little strength it has remaining. Sergeant Calvin's warm, hard erection touches Sophia's backside. She does not move. He gingerly slides her nightgown above her waist and moves his penis between her legs. All he must do now is insert himself inside her.

'Attack from behind, we would say in the military,' he joyously thinks.

Sophia slowly slips out of her deep sleep and becomes semi-conscious. She begins to rotate her hips on the bed. "Oh, James, how I have missed you. I am so happy you are home safely, my love," she said, imagining all will now be well in her life.

Sergeant Calvin said nothing. 'Think whatever you want Sophia, soon you will be mine and then you will always know who is in your bed.' He raises her top leg, trying to locate her vaginal hole in the dark.

Sophia gains more consciousness and suddenly realizes what is occurring. She becomes aware the person beside her does not smell like her husband. Instead, the person smells like Sergeant Calvin. Fearful, Sophia tries to turn around. Sergeant Calvin holds onto her arms. She is unable to loosen from the strength of his grip. Sergeant Calvin again tries to enter Sophia. He must get inside her. He must accomplish his plan.

"Take me in your hole now, woman! You will be my wife if I can bed you tonight."

'This man is delusional,' Sophia thinks. 'No time to think, only time to act. Act in the way my father taught me. Go for the groin, Father advised me.' With Sergeant Calvin's hip forward and his penis about to enter Sophia, she propels her lower leg back with all her might, clobbering the Sergeant's groin with her foot and causing him severe pain.

As the Sergeant lies moaning on the bed in the fetal position, Sophia jumps out of the bed, quickly grabbing the poker stick next to the fireplace. "How dare you attempt to touch me, Sergeant Calvin," Sophia yells, holding the poker stick toward him.

"How dare I? Lady Sophia, you have done nothing but indicate to me each day that you want me. You have even stooped so low as to tease me with your desires. We must accept your husband is never coming home. I am willing to accept caring for you and loving you. I am willing to make you my wife. I am even willing to offer you all the bairns you desire. From the moment we first met you displayed great fondness for me. It would only seem obvious we have this passionate moment together to become one."

"Are you a deranged man, Sergeant? My husband will return home soon to enjoy his first bairn!"

Sergeant Calvin looks at Sophia with a look of confusion on his face.

"That is correct. I am with bairn."

"For a woman with bairn, to tease me so, it is you I think is the one who is deranged, my Lady. Perhaps you express your attraction to me because you were missing and needing a man in your life to satisfy your desires."

"How dare you assume such a thing?"

"Your Ladyship, it would seem obvious to me, you are denying your love for me. Please put down the poker and come back to bed so we can enjoy each other's bodies and express our feeling of love for one another."

"Sergeant Calvin, the only feelings I have for you, sir, are feelings of disgust and contempt."

"How can you deny my love for you, Sophia? I did not come to your bedroom tonight to frighten you. Instead, I came to comfort you and love you and of course to give you what you wanted from me. I promise Sophia, you will have my word, I will tell no one of your fondness for me. I will not tell those in the house that you begged me to come to your bedroom. And that as your protector I climbed into your bed as you asked. The loneliness for your husband had become overwhelming for you as a young and lonely woman. You begged me, you pleaded with me to take you and satisfy you. As I recall, you regularly came into my room to ensure my health was improving and I was fit to make love to you. And as I recall Sophia, tonight you came to my room again and begged me for my caresses. I was the one who said 'no, your Ladyship'. I was the one who denied you of your wishes. In fact, as I vividly remember this night, I was the one who carried you back to your bed as you continued to beg me to touch you. I returned to my bedroom as the gentleman I am, leaving you frustrated in your bedroom. That is how I remembered tonight, your Ladyship. And I will make certain everyone remembers the events of this evening this way if you choose to ever breathe a word of this to anyone. My story will discredit you and even your beloved husband. If he ever comes home alive."

"You are insane," Sophia calls out, shaking with fear that the Sergeant just may be delusional enough to ruin her life.

"Oh yes, Lady Sophia. You are guilty of lusting for me and I am guilty for being completely and madly in love with you."

Sophia's hands tremble as she holds the poker in one hand and places her other hand across her belly to protect her unborn bairn.

"Now put that poker down and go back to bed. For now, this will be our secret, unless of course you decide to tell anyone what happened this evening. If you do that Sophia, I will be forced to tell everyone my truth about what happened tonight. I can assure you, the world will believe the protective honorable soldier of the British Army over some pregnant young woman who is missing her husband. A husband she has only been with, as a married woman, for two days. Your father would definitely not want to hear this embarrassing disgraceful story about you, Sophia."

Sergeant Calvin walks out of Sophia's bedroom and gently closes the door, careful not to wake the others in the house. He is angered he was not able to bed Sophia. 'My plan, my plan was foiled again,' he thinks, walking back to the guest bedroom. Climbing into his bed, he strategizes, 'I must assemble my thoughts and create a new plan.'

Sophia trembles as she runs to the door and locks it. She collapses on the floor with fear and begins to sob. 'James, are you out there? Will you come home to me or will I be left as a widow with our bairn? Should I accept the Sergeant's offer to ensure I am a married woman in society and accepted by the other aristocrats? Oh unborn bairn inside me, I will keep you safe. I will ensure you grow up with a father. James, I need you. James, I need a man in my life.' With these words Sophia falls asleep on the wooden floor. During the next several hours she has numerous dreams which make her even more fearful of the days ahead.

Chapter Twenty-One

James stands on the rocking bow of Captain Taller's ship. The only thing he can see is water. For days all he has seen is water. Oh how he wishes the wind would be in his favor to speed up this vessel and bring him sooner into his lover's arms.

As James looks up, he sees the downwind catching the sails and billowing them to push the ship forward in the sea.

James reflects and smiles. 'Is this ache in my chest from my wound or from the woeful void I feel from not feeling the warmth of Sophia's touch and hearing the sound of her sensual voice. I am a man who cannot humanly survive without the loving comfort my beloved Sophia brings to my being.' James visualizes himself lying next to Sophia and holding her tightly in his arms. The smell of her hair, the feel of her skin, the touch of her moist, soft labia. How he misses all the sensations Sophia brings to his body. 'Sophia fills a void in me, one I never knew existed.'

James's mind continues to wander toward feeling Sophia's soft, silky skin and looking at the radiant beauty of her face smiling back and comforting him. He realizes at that moment there is no greater nor powerful feeling in the world than the feeling of the enchantment, expressed through their undeniable love. It is at that moment, surrounded by the vast sea that James finds himself releasing his pent-up emotions as tears roll down his face. The reality of him nearly dying in Portugal becomes realization for James. 'I might never have seen my one true love again. Even worse, I might have left my new bride a widow and had no offspring to continue my family name and legacy.' James holds his hand over his heart. He touches his wound. 'If it were not for the love of Sophia and the strength she brings to me, I would not have had the brawn to hold onto that horse's mane and venture through the rain and down that dark, desolate road to safety. Sophia my love, you saved my life.' These thoughts raced through James's head as he retched over the side of Captain Taller's ship.

~~~

Sophia's legs trembled as she sat on the wooden floor with her hands holding her stomach. Sophia heaved into the bowl in her bedroom. This time her sickness was not due to her precious unborn bairn. No, this time, her illness was caused by the thought of Sergeant Calvin Gideon. Sophia rubs her stomach, making a circular motion where her unborn bairn resides. She knows now her main purpose in life is to protect herself and her unborn bairn. Frightened and terrified of Sergeant Calvin's words, Sophia fears the unconscionable acts and fallacious and intolerable words the Sergeant might convey to her father or her beloved James when he returns. She could never forgive herself if he ever spoke such words. Her anguish turns to panic. 'What would Father do if he believed the Sergeant? Would others believe I had relations with Sergeant Calvin? How would James react if he thought that during his absence I enjoyed the passions of another man? Would James ever love me again? Would he believe that the bairn inside me is his? Would they think it was Sergeant Calvin's bairn?'

Sophia continues to cry out loud, as the fear of Sergeant Calvin's threatening words has her believing he would tell this sordid lie to everyone. 'And what about the Sergeant's feelings for me? I am astonished he is in love with me. Has this man completely lost his mind?' Sophia wonders.

It is in the moment the feeling of illness leaves Sophia and the feeling of trepidation enters that she realizes she is in extreme danger. 'This deranged man, a soldier, has the ability to damage, or worse, destroy my life.'

Sophia's heart cries out, 'My beloved James. Pease come home soon. I require your protection and need you at my side. If you do not come home society might dictate I be courted by the Sergeant, and I can only imagine how torturous my life might become.'

These mere thoughts of the Sergeant's unforgiving attempts to pleasure himself beside her sickens Sophia. She realizes, 'If I had not stopped him, he would have entered me and continued to please himself. This is a man, hired by my father to protect me, and instead he has done the opposite; he has scourged me. Will people believe me if I tell the story my way? Lady Stephens warned me of him. She warned me to be leery of his fondness for me. I did not heed her warning and did nothing to discourage him. Instead, I felt pity for the Sergeant, as he lay on his bed so feeble after his horse accident. I only tried to be kind,' Sophia mourns.

"Lady Sophia? Lady Sophia?" Theodore calls from the opposite side of the bedroom door. "It is Theodore, your Ladyship. I am here with your morning tea."

Sophia rises from the floor and reaches for the pewter skeleton key sitting on the side table, the one she had used to lock the door to protect her from Sergeant Calvin entering her room again uninvited. She walks over to the bedroom door, while at the same time wiping her face with her hands and pushing away the damp hair stuck to her face. She unlocks her bedroom door and is greeted by Theodore, who has a very concerned look on his face.

"Is everything all right, your Ladyship?" Theodore asks, holding his serving tray, which balances a porcelain cup and saucer and matching teapot.

As Sophia begins to respond, Sergeant Calvin walks directly up to the two of them in the hallway. He greets them good morning.

"Sophia. Are you all right?" the Sergeant asks, staring directly at her.

Startled and intimated by his gaze, Sophia chooses to make light of the situation.

"I am sorry, Theodore. I must have accidentally locked my bedroom door," Sophia said, trying to create an excuse to hide her fear, the fear of being violated by the Sergeant and sharing twisted information.

"It is wise to keep your door open, your Ladyship. My duty is to protect you and to keep you safe. I cannot do my job if I do not have access to you," the Sergeant instructs.

There was something in the way the Sergeant spoke the words "do my job," which made Sophia feel that he was implying something else. Something intimate. Something that made Sophia feel even more frightened by what he might do.

"I will remain by your side at all times, your Ladyship. Please call on me whenever you require me to service your every need."

This time it was Theodore who thought the Sergeant's response might have another meaning. Sophia feels a sense of relief when Hannah comes running over to her, wanting to be petted. At least I have a dog to guard me from the man who has been hired to keep me safe. Sophia rubs the top of Hannah's head for comfort while Sergeant Calvin returns to his bedroom. Sophia turns to Theodore to continue her conversation.

"Theodore, I will dismiss having my first morning tea in my room. Instead, I will enjoy the rejuvenating fresh sea air outside."

"As you wish, Lady Sophia," Theodore complies.

Sophia proceeds downstairs and sits in her favorite wicker chair on the porch. Hannah lies by her side.

"Good morning, your Ladyship," William greets her while passing by the back porch.

"Good morning, William."

"I notice you are a little late coming out to the porch this morning."

"I did not sleep well last night, William. There were many things on my mind and bumps in the night that stole my sleep."

"Your Ladyship," William responds, sensing there is more to her Ladyship's comment than she is stating. "I wish to remind you,

I have given Colonel James my solemn promise to care for you and keep you from harm."

Just as William finishes these words, Sergeant Calvin walks onto the porch. He glares at William, and in an overly commanding voice said, "As for our Ladyship, she is perfectly fine. The 'only' reason for that is because I am protecting her and not you."

Sophia notes the Sergeant's authoritative approach toward William. She is taken aback by his rudeness and more fearful at the superior nature the Sergeant assumed.

"William," Sophia said addressing her groundskeeper and stableman.

"Yes, your Ladyship?"

"I want you to know you do a fine job for Mr. Langston and myself. Please excuse Sergeant Calvin's poor manners. That is not the way I want our staff to be addressed. On a lighter note, could you please bring me some fresh roses and place them in the kitchen? I will cut them and place them in my music room and here on my porch."

"I most certainly will, your Ladyship," William said, giving a quick glance to the Sergeant. A look that could easily be interrupted as saying 'you sir, are not the person in charge of this household.' The Sergeant tries to ignore William's look and casually sits down beside Sophia.

At that exact moment, Lady Stephens walks onto the porch. She instantly senses the tension in the air.

"Hello, Lady Stephens. It is a lovely day, is it not?" Sophia asks.

"It is indeed, my dear. Did you sleep well?"

"I am afraid I did not," Sophia responds, conscious of the Sergeant's presence at her side.

"I am very sorry to hear that. With your current health condition, it will be very important for you to have quality rest at this time. I must also say I was confused by some information I heard moments ago. Theodore informed me your bedroom door was locked this morning. That seems unusual. What caused you to make such a choice, Sophia?" Lady Stephens pries for more information, believing it was important to do so.

Sophia shyly lowers her chin preparing to respond. Sergeant Calvin abruptly answers instead.

"I was equally surprised, Lady Stephens, especially since I am right next door to Lady Sophia's bedroom and here to protect her. There should be no reason for her to lock her bedroom door, particularly at night. Am I not correct, Lady Sophia?"

"Perhaps being with bairn has caused me to act differently," Sophia responds, looking at Sergeant Calvin and again bowing her head. "I am simply feeling a bit of morning flutters."

"I see, my dear," Lady Stephens replies, well aware there is more going on with this situation than 'morning flutters.' "And Sergeant Calvin, when will you return to your post? By the sounds of your voice this morning, you seem to be back to your old self and prepared to begin your duties once again. I, for one, would feel relief and much safer knowing you were back outside at your post. Do you not agree, Sophia?"

Lady Stephens looks at Sophia in a way that indicates she is aware there is trouble afoot with the Sergeant and does not want Sophia to be in harm's way.

"Sergeant Calvin," Lady Stephens said, looking at the Sergeant with contempt. "The General was inquiring about you just yesterday. I informed him you were almost completely healed and ready to continue performing the duties you were assigned."

Sergeant Calvin is angered by Lady Stephens's tone and presumptions. 'I am the person in charge here, old witch,' he thinks.

In what only could be considered a bold move, Sergeant Calvin continues to sit down between the two ladies while they continue carrying on their morning conversations. He does not listen to what they are saying; instead, he sits impatiently and fantasizes how close he came to penetrating Sophia and enjoying how wonderful it must feel to be inside her.

"Sergeant Calvin?"

"Yes, Lady Stephens," he responds, annoyed at being pulled away from the most wonderful and fantastical daydream.

"I was saying, I believe you have overstayed your welcome here on this porch. Mrs. Langston and I would like to discuss private matters—without you. Matters concerning Lady Sophia, Colonel James and myself, as their trusted confidant."

The very sound of Colonel James's name makes the Sergeant ill. He needs the Colonel not to return from his mission.

Lady Stephens notices Sergeant Calvin's entire body become tense at the sound of James's name. 'Is this demon of a man aware that I would never permit anything nor anyone to harm either James or Sophia—and especially not their bairn?'

"I hope you ladies have a lovely chat," the Sergeant said, intentionally rising from his chair very slowly, as if to stall the ladies from speaking and annoying both of them as punishment for asking him to leave their conversation.

Once the Sergeant had left, Lady Stephens turns to Sophia and asks, "Shall we go for a walk on the beach, my dear? I suspect being closer to the sea would do you well. Perhaps it would give you the opportunity to share what is on your mind."

"That would be lovely," Sophia replies.

After some time walking down the beach, Lady Stephens casually turns to Sophia and asks, "Is everything all right, my dear child? I noticed you were not well this morning. Is there something more you would like to share with me?"

Sophia looks up and down the shoreline. She cannot see Sergeant Calvin anywhere. Unsure how to brooch the subject, Sophia simply begins with the question.

"What is your opinion of Sergeant Calvin, Lady Stephens?"

"An interesting question. Is there a particular reason you are asking this question of me Sophia?"

"I noticed he and William did not get along well this morning. I do believe William has ill feelings toward the Sergeant. I must remember to ask him as to why this might be so. Lady Stephens, I have come to agree with you and believe Sergeant Calvin has strong feelings for me."

"You must be careful, Sophia, his head is not wrapped on too tight. There is something about his mannerism and interaction with all of us that concerns me deeply. He has the eyes of greed, Sophia, and that concerns me the most."

Lady Stephens continues to engage Sophia in conversation, in hopes of learning why Sophia locked her bedroom door last night.

Having walked a good ways down the beach, Sophia finally feels safe to share her anguish with Lady Stephens. 'I want to tell someone about my petrifying fear. I believe my reputation and the safety of my bairn depends on it.' Turning to Lady Stephens, embarrassed and fearful, Sophia begins to confess what occurred last night with the Sergeant.

"Last night while I slept," Sophia begins.

Barely had Sophia said these words, when Sergeant Calvin approached the two women from behind and asks, "Mrs. Langston, is everything all right? You seem disturbed. Do you have concerns for your safety? Well, have no fear, I am here. I will always be here to watch your every move and ensure what happens to you is suitable for a lady of your status in society."

Sergeant Calvin said these words while staring directly at Sophia. He spoke as if to warn and remind her to keep their secret or she will be the one who wished she had not said a word to anyone.

Sophia becomes instantly flushed in front of both the Sergeant and Lady Stephens. A reaction that once again does not go unnoticed by Lady Stephens. The disturbing way the Sergeant spoke to Sophia about watching and guarding her also created great concern for Lady Stephens. 'What on earth happened last night,' she wondered? 'I am not a woman who is known for not knowing, and this matter seems very serious. I shall get to the bottom of this right away,' she resolves.

"You ladies must stay close so I can watch and protect you. If you wander off too far and go for long walks without me, then how will I be able to insulate you?"

"Insulate us?" Lady Stephens retorts.

"Sergeant Calvin, you are here to secure the grounds and protect the Langston's home from intruders. You are not here to 'watch over' Lady Sophia and observe her every move. You sir, seem to be over-stepping your bounds and expanding upon your duties."

"Lady Stephens, my duties were defined by the General and are not to be interrupted by you, dear Lady. Perhaps, it is you, as the guest of the Langston's, who has experienced the misunderstanding. Even now, with these loud sea waves crashing onto the shoreline, you did not hear me approaching you and Sophia."

'Of all the gall,' Lady Stephens ruminates. 'The Sergeant is clearly terrorizing Sophia, but how? I can see it on the poor girl's face. It is more than his words that are causing Sophia to worry. What is it? What has this deplorable demon done? I must act swiftly to outmaneuver this disturbed soldier. I must be the one to keep Sophia safe.'

"Sophia, shall we return back to the house and prepare for our visit to your father's this afternoon," Lady Stephens said, winking at Sophia, since no such arrangements had been made.

"And Sergeant, since you are in need of knowing our every move, we will also be spending the evening at the General's estate as well. Perhaps that will provide you additional time to survey the grounds, which as we both agree, are part of your duties."

Sergeant Calvin becomes infused with rage. He is unable to maintain composure. Grabbing Lady Sophia by her arm as they walk, he squeezes it tighter and whispers, "Sophia, you neglected to inform me of your plans for this evening."

Sophia winces with pain. She did not want to tell the Sergeant she had just learned about this trip to her father's minutes ago. She was, however, pleased Lady Stephens suggested it, as Sophia wanted to be free from the Sergeant's presence.

Lady Stephens, immediately struck by the Sergeant's brawn and brashness, responds after overhearing the Sergeant's rude words. At the same time, she observed him removing his hand from Sophia's arm.

"Sergeant, this type of behavior will not be tolerated. Not only does Lady Sophia not have to share with you her whereabouts, you are never allowed to touch this young women in the way I have just witnessed."

"With all due respect, Lady Stephens. I am here to protect Lady Sophia on the direct orders from the General. You, dear Lady, are interfering with my duties. Duties that do not concern you."

The torment created by Sergeant Calvin causes Sophia to tremble. 'Lady Stephens appears to have antagonized him to a breaking point,' Sophia observes. Sophia cannot imagine what the Sergeant will do if he becomes so angry that he feels vulnerable. She can only suspect he will lash out and accuse her of arousing and enticing him. 'What if he speaks of this? What if he destroys my reputation? What if he tells James?'

With these questions whirling around in her head, Sophia collapses with affliction to the ground. She loses consciousness, as her body protects her and her bairn from the misery she is feeling.

"Look what you have caused, old woman! You frightened Sophia to the point of collapse!" Sergeant Calvin screams out, whisking Sophia into his arms and running quickly along the beach toward the house.

"All will be well, Sophia. I am here to guard and protect you. I am in love with you and I want you safe because I want you."

Sophia awakens from the bumpy movement of being carried down the beach. While running, Sergeant Calvin is still able to kiss Sophia on her lips. Sophia turns her head. 'What is happening? How can this be? This man is possessed.'

Sergeant Calvin reaches the porch and calls for Theodore.

"Hurry, Theodore. Bring some cold cloths and some water. Lady Sophia has fallen ill. I will take her upstairs to her bedroom and meet you there."

Shocked, Theodore does as requested.

Moments later, Lady Stephens enters the house, desperately trying to catch her breath.

"Where," she pauses to breathe, "is Sophia?"

"Sergeant Calvin has taken her upstairs to care for her."

"No," Lady Stephens said forcefully. "She is not to be left alone with that man from this day forward. He is a diabolical demon and not to be trusted by anyone."

Theodore is stunned. In all his years of working for Lady Stephens, he has never heard her speak so ill of a person.

After laying Sophia down on the bed, Sergeant Calvin sits next to her and begins stroking her forehead. Sophia is now awake and tries to move to the other side of the bed. Sergeant Calvin presses down on her shoulder with great force, to keep her in the same spot.

"No, Sophia, may I remind you of our little secret. The one where you undressed in front of my eyes and begged me to make love to you as you fondled my privates and watched them grow larger. I was in my bed as a wounded and weak soldier and yet you continued. Shall I describe the birthmark on your lower back, my Lady? And the one on your lower stomach as well. Yes, I can identify your naked body, if, of course anyone—especially if your husband—asks me about it. Or perhaps instead of waiting for him to ask, I should just tell him first instead. Mmm, yes, I did so enjoy seeing you undress for me, Lady Beautiful."

Sophia's eyes fill with tears as Sergeant Calvin removes his hand from Sophia's shoulder and moves it onto her thigh. He begins to rub from her knee up to her groin. He leans down toward her ear and whispers.

"This is one body I will thoroughly enjoy exploring." His hand now moves onto one of her breasts.

Hearing footsteps approaching down the hall, Sergeant Calvin sits up, looks directly at Sophia, who is sobbing and shaking with fear.

"I shall take what should be mine, Sophia. You will give me bairns, and you will give me the type of life I desire."

Theodore and Lady Stephens enter the bedroom and see Sophia in tears and the Sergeant standing upright beside her bed.

"Thank goodness," he said. "Mrs. Langston needs these placed on her head. Lady Stephens would you like to assist with that?"

Lady Stephens approaches the bed, and looking down at Sophia, all she can see is a petrified young girl who has been tremendously traumatized.

"Sophia, all will be well. I am here to help and as soon as you feel able, we will get you out of this house and to your father's."

Sophia forces a smile with all the strength she can muster and responds, "Thank you."

Lady Stephens turns to Theodore and asks, "Theodore, please have William prepare the carriage for our journey."

"Dear Lady, I suggest Lady Sophia not travel today. Rather, she should stay here in bed where I can help tend to her needs," Sergeant Calvin proposes.

"Sergeant Calvin, you may leave this room and not enter it again. Lady Sophia will be fine and the trip to her father's will do her good. It is time for you to take your post outside, Sergeant. That is where you belong." Lady Stephens said these words with a stern look in her eyes pointing directly at the Sergeant.

Although the comment was directed at the Sergeant, everyone in the room felt the power and tension her message brought. As for Sergeant Calvin, he agreed to leave Sophia's bedroom, angered by being embarrassed by Lady Stephens. Walking away, he pauses one more time when he hears his name called.

"And, Sergeant Calvin," Lady Stephens begins with a strong and controlled voice. "As for your comment on the beach, the one about me being an 'old woman.' I can assure you, sir, I may be a woman of advanced years, but I am also an extremely wise woman, one that is well aware of deception when she sees it. So, soldier, I suggest you keep guard outside and stand down while inside this house."

Sergeant Calvin looks directly at Lady Stephens, raises his chin and walks out the door.

Theodore turns to Lady Stephens and said, "And that, dear Lady, is why I have enjoyed working for you for so many years."

Sophia rolls over on her side with her face buried into her pillow. 'I cannot live through this tension and conflict.'

After a few hours, Sophia regains her composure and the two women enter the carriage and travel to the General's estate. The entire trip was made in silence. Sophia could not bear to talk more about the events of the day with Lady Stephens.

The General enters his music room after learning from Thomas that Sophia was waiting for him there. Lady Stephens had chosen to visit the General's garden house to enjoy the flowers.

"I did not expect to see you this early, Sophia. Why the long face, my darling daughter?"

Sophia instantly drops her face into her hands and begins to sob. Her father, confused by what is occurring and hating the thought of his daughter in distress, immediately presents her with his monogrammed handkerchief, with the initials CRC, embroidered on the corner. The letters represented his name. Craig Richard Cartwright.

"Why do you cry? You are with bairn, you have a beautiful home and you are protected. My dear, a woman of your stature and notoriety has nothing to be sad about."

"Father, I would like to request a new soldier be posted at my home."

The General is taken aback by Sophia's comment. This was the last response he would have expected from his daughter. Her request begins to open up a whole series of questions to explore.

"I am surprised by your sudden request, Sophia. What has caused you to make this plea?"

Sophia is hesitant with her response. If she shares the daunting truth of the fact that the Sergeant attempted to intimately attack her, then she risks the Sergeant telling his erroneous story, the one where it was her, a young forlorn woman, who enticed and desired him. Should she risk telling her father, who may or may not believe her as a women? Could she live with the risk of James, her only true love, ever learning of this demoralizing occurrence? What information should she share with her father to have Sergeant Calvin sent as far away from her as possible?

"Father, I believe Sergeant Calvin's horse accident is more serious than we might first have thought. I do not believe he is suitable or capable to stand post and guard and protect myself and my home."

"I see," the General responds, still confused why this reason would cause Sophia to weep in such an intense manner. "Your protection is of the utmost importance to me Sophia. Your observation and reasoning makes good sense to me, my daughter. I shall have Sergeant Calvin removed from his duties at once and have him return to his infantry."

"Thank you, Father, I am most appreciative of your decision," Sophia said, finding her shoulders instantly lowering and her chin rising higher in the air.

She is comforted knowing she will finally be safe from the villainous rogue called Sergeant Calvin Gideon.

"Might there be anything else bothering you at this moment, my precious daughter?" the General probes, still believing there is more to the story as to why she wants Sergeant Calvin removed from her home.

If there is one thing he has learned in all his years in the military, it is to dig deeper. The more you can learn, the more you can become aware to combat the enemy or build the alliance. The more you are aware, the better you can defect and—or—align with your enemy and protect what belongs to you.

"I am just happy that Sergeant Calvin will be able to recover somewhere other than my home, Father. Thank you."

"How kind it is that you are thinking of his well-being, Sophia," the General said, again hoping his daughter might share more information about the situation, the 'situation' which he is now certain she has.

'A few days ago Lady Stephens updated me on details from what she and William witnessed in the garden house. Today, Sophia requests the Sergeant be removed. There is indeed more to this story that I need to understand.'

"I will leave you here, Sophia, as I have some other matters to attend to."

With that, the General leaves his daughter and immediately walks outside in search of Lady Stephens. It is time he uncovers more information about this 'situation'. He finds Lady Stephens sitting amongst the flowers in the garden house. The aroma of the roses lingers in the air.

"Do you have a moment, your Ladyship?"

"Of course, General," Lady Stephens responds, somewhat surprised by the concerned look on the General's face.

"Sophia has requested of me that Sergeant Calvin be removed from his post. As she stated to me, her reason is that she believes his accident has caused him to need additional rest and makes him unfit for duty. I suspect there is more to this story and I would hope you might help me assemble all the facts."

"I am afraid, like you, General, I have limited facts. As mentioned prior, I have found Sergeant Calvin to be overly fond of Lady Sophia. He becomes easily agitated and even angered if anyone tries to trifle with him in regards to your daughter. I do not believe I am exaggerating when I say Sergeant Calvin has become overly obsessed with your daughter."

The General's concern for his daughter increases. He does not take well to hearing this unsuitable news, particularly since it is in regards to the actions of one of his recommended soldiers.

"This is an outrage and completely unacceptable from one of my soldiers. My apologies, Lady Stephens. How long has he been displaying this behavior?"

"He has recently begun always wanting to be in the presence of Sophia, to the point where he will not want to leave her alone, even when she is with me. He insists constantly to know her whereabouts. When I confronted him, as I did today, telling him that what Sophia did in her home was none of his concern, rather his concern was to guard the exterior of the home, he snapped back at me stating his orders come only from you, General. Just today, Sophia had another fainting spell on the beach. It was after a tiff occurring regarding his duties. The Sergeant immediately whisked her to her bedroom. Before he left, he first stated, 'Look what you have done, old woman.' His aggressiveness has been most recent General, as well as his increased display of fondness for Sophia. It would seem he has become more attentive to her after his horse accident. He has always presented himself as a very charming soldier, one quite fond of your daughter even from the first day he came to her house. After his bad fall, he began to stay in the guest bedroom upstairs, next to Sophia's bedroom. It was then, if I might be so bold to say, that his obsession with Sophia began to be even more possessive. I believe, General..." Lady Stephens pauses to hold a rose, being careful to protect her hand from its thorny stem.

"You believe what, your Ladyship?" the General asks, anxious to hear what he suspects will be a fair and intelligent assessment of the situation from a woman such as Lady Stephens.

"I do believe Sergeant Calvin means to harm Sophia." At the exact moment of speaking these words, Lady Stephens pricks herself on one of the thorns of the roses' stem.

"Harm? What kind of harm?" the General asks, extremely unsettled by this comment.

"General, my comments are made by that of an older, wiser woman, with instincts developed and acquired over the years. Obsession can bring a man to become delusional and take ownership of possession to that which he has no rights. In this case, Sergeant Calvin has transformed his duty of protecting Sophia into one of controlling and acquiring her. He has converted his caring for her into an inappropriate obsession. These attractions have caused Sophia to become fearful. So fearful that last night she felt it necessary to lock her bedroom door. It was Theodore who had to convince her to open it. Once she did, Sergeant Calvin quickly emerged from the guest bedroom to remind Sophia he was there to 'guard her'."

"How dare anyone bring any level of fear or discomfort to my daughter? How dare he think he can control my daughter! As her father, I have a duty to protect her. She is a bright young woman, not a prisoner. She does not need to be owned through protection. I am the person who assigned Sergeant Calvin to the post at my daughter's house. Such unscrupulous behavior must be stopped immediately," the General announces with immense fury.

"General, once again you and I are in complete agreement. We both share a common interest in Sophia's safety, particularly at this time when she is with bairn."

"Lady Stephens, this type of behavior is also not tolerated in my military. I apologize, and I am sorry for the Sergeant's offensive behavior toward you and my daughter."

"I am certain all will be well, General. Sophia is fortunate to have a caring and loving father to protect her. You have done a wonderful job raising such a distinguished and gracious daughter, General."

"I will never truly forgive myself for that unsettling day when her mother passed away. I swore from that moment on I would always ensure there would be someone there for Sophia. Sadly, Countess Elizabeth and Governess Abigale could not fill the loneliness Sophia felt from the loss of her beloved mother. Lady Stephens, you might not be aware, but through your character and wisdom, you have managed to fill that void in Sophia's heart. A void created by her mother's passing. I can tell that Sophia looks up to you as a prudent sage with profound wisdom. I am forever grateful to you, dear Lady, for the joy and comfort you bring to my daughter. I know your companionship is especially important to her at this time."

"Thank you, General. I have developed a deep affection for Sophia. If I may be so bold, she is like the daughter I never had."

Lady Stephens lowers her head as deep sadness consumes her body. She is reminded by the one pain she has always felt, the pain of never being able to bear a child.

In light of the current revelation of facts and needing to search for additional truths, the General orders Sophia and Lady Stephens to remain at his home while he rides off to James's house to confront Sergeant Calvin.

~~~

In the guest room, next to Sophia's bedroom, Sergeant Calvin paces the hardwood floor.

"I would have to be a fool to think Sophia and Lady Stephens will not speak of my actions to the General." He speaks out loud to the emptiness of the room.

"It would seem I was too hasty in my attempt to implement a plan that would make Sophia love me. Now I must create a plan that does not cause the General to court martial me."

Sergeant Calvin continues to pace the floor in complete silence, while his mind plots and schemes.

A solution appears to him in a flashing moment, and the Sergeant walks over to the table by the bed. On the table are several bandages, rolls of gauze and a container of ointment. The Sergeant begins to cut the bandages into specific lengths. He then cuts several lengths of gauze.

Working quickly, Sergeant Calvin walks over to the wooden mantle of the fireplace, and in one swift move, smashes his head against the mantle. The pain is excruciating. He walks over to the mirror and looks for any sign of blood. No blood. Again he walks over to the mantle, and this time he bangs his head even harder onto the wood. Walking over to the mirror, he is pleased to see a great deal of blood oozing out of the newly formed wound on his head. Grabbing the newly cut strips of bandages, he begins to wrap his head.

"Perfect," he said to himself.

Taking the scissors from the table, the ones he had just used to create the proper length of bandages, Sergeant Calvin cuts through the top of his left wrist. More blood pours out of his body. Again he begins to wrap his wrist with the recently cut pieces of gauze.

While applying the last strip of gauze, the Sergeant can hear a horse in the distance, galloping toward the estate. He looks around the room, ensuring it looks proper and shows no evidence from what has just occurred. Sergeant Calvin climbs into bed, with a bandage on his wrist and a bandage on his head wound, which now has blood seeping through the cotton bandage. 'Now I wait,' he thinks.

Theodore greets the General at the front door. He is surprised the General is alone.

"Where is Sergeant Calvin?" the General asks sternly.

"I believe he is resting in the guest room, sir."

"The guest room? Why is he not at his post?"

"He indicated he was not feeling well today, sir."

"Then please send for Dr. Hadley, Theodore. This soldier should be at his post. I am not paying him to rest in the guest bedroom of Sophia's house. There are some issues we need to sort out. One of my soldiers up in my daughter's guest room is the first thing on my list."

"I believe you are correct, sir." Theodore nods, going off to find William, whom he will ask to retrieve the doctor.

Theodore can only assume Sophia and Lady Stephens have shared their concerns about the Sergeant and have remained at the General's home for safety and comfort.

General Cartwright stomps upstairs with his shoulders thrown back; there is a military forcefulness to his step. Arriving at the guest room door, he knocks. His knock can be heard throughout the house.

"Sergeant Calvin. Are you in there?"

'Now is the moment of truth,' thinks the Sergeant.

"Yes, I am here," the Sergeant said weakly. "Who is it?"

"It is General Cartwright, and I am entering this room."

"You are more than welcome to do so, sir," the Sergeant said, attempting to appear feeble.

The General opens the door. Upon entering the guest bedroom, he sees Sergeant Calvin lying on the bed, his head wrapped and blood seeping through the bandages.

"Sergeant Calvin Gideon," the General begins, ignoring the appearance of the Sergeant lying in bed. "It has come to my attention you are acting in a most unscrupulous manner toward my daughter and toward her guest, Lady Stephens."

'So those two ungrateful wenches have been weaving tales during their visit, with you, General,' the Sergeant summarizes and affirms his predication.

"Is this allegation true, Sergeant Calvin?"

'It is time for me to be convincing.' Sergeant Calvin prepares himself for his performance.

"General. I am honored you have come to visit with me. Unfortunately, I am unaware of what might have been mentioned to you to cause such acquisitions. As a soldier of the British Army, I am committed to my duty and to the Crown. Sir, I have carried out my orders for you, General, with the upmost level of honor and respect," the Sergeant said, seeking to be persuading.

"I have been informed you are exhibiting a somewhat inappropriate fondness toward my daughter."

"Sir, there is no question your daughter, Colonel Langston's wife, is a lovely woman. With that said, my assigned duty was to protect her and not intimidate her. I believe I have carried out my duties to the best of my abilities, sir. What I can say, is that my mind seems to have taken a turn after my accident. I have badly injured my head. Since then, my thoughts have not always been clear. My memory seems delayed. I have also begun to wonder if I am losing my sense for clear thinking. I have found these changes in my mind trying my patience and causing me to become agitated at times. Perhaps these are the conditions you have heard about," the Sergeant said, designing his accident to be the perfect excuse for his behavior of lusting for Sophia.

The General is pleased the Sergeant's story is consistent with that of Lady Stephens. Believing the Sergeant's recent behavior has been caused by his accident, the General feels more resolved by the possible motives of the Sergeant. With that resolution, the General notices bloodstains on the bandages wrapped around the Sergeant's head.

"Sergeant, I can see by the bandage wrap on your head, your injury has still not healed."

"That is correct, General. My fall from my horse was quite bad. It was amazing I even survived. Perhaps it was too much to disclose, but there are times I am not even certain of my own name, the name of others, or even where I am at the moment." Sergeant Calvin lies, impressed by his own fabrication of the state of his health.

"Sergeant, these are serious symptoms indeed. I have asked for the doctor to come and inform us on your condition. I am certain he will be equally concerned when he hears this news."

"Thank you, General. I truly appreciate your concern." The Sergeant is thrilled by the General's sympathy. 'And General, I am thrilled you believe my falsification. It would appear I am even more clever than I thought I was. You, General, have been duped by a Sergeant. A Sergeant who is obsessed with your daughter,' the Sergeant happily recounts.

The two men sit quietly in the guest bedroom waiting for Doctor Hadley to arrive. The General reviews the events of the last month—James, sent on a mission; the announcement of Sophia with bairn; and now the health of a man who was supposed to protect his daughter. 'Oh, how I long for my wife during these times. She always brought me great comfort.'

Sergeant Calvin pretends to sleep during the silence. With his eyes closed, he passionately fantasized about Sophia—the woman he was determined to marry.

Doctor Hadley arrives at the door. He recognizes he has been called more to this house in the last few weeks than to the home of any of his other patients. 'I hope this does not become a habit,' the older physician ponders. The doctor immediately begins to examine Sergeant Calvin. After asking a series of questions to assess the Sergeant's mental state, all of which the Sergeant intentionally failed, the doctor begins to slowly remove the soiled bandages from the Sergeant's head. He applies medicine to his wounds, stitches the wound and rewraps his head.

"I am surprised I did not stitch this wound the first time I saw you, Sergeant. It must have been from all the commotion occurring and the amount of dirt on your face."

"That must be it," Sergeant Calvin said, smiling.

The doctor wraps the Sergeant's hand, allowing the bandages to offer more support and relief. How strange, the doctor thinks. 'I was certain I properly stitched up the Sergeant's wound after his accident. And I do not recall his hand being injured. Very strange indeed. Perhaps my old age is catching up with me.'

"Rest now, Sergeant. I am going to talk with the General for a bit."

"Thank you, sir," the Sergeant said weakly, believing his deceit has been solidified.

Doctor Hadley leaves the guest bedroom and meets the General, who is waiting for him in the hallway.

"I suggest we go to the drawing room to discuss this matter, General."

"Certainly," the General said, with a concerned look on his face.

Once in the sitting room the doctor begins. "I believe Sergeant Calvin's head injury has worsened, General. I am convinced he has a serious concussion, one which requires hospitalization. I suggest you transport him to our newly founded hospital, St. George. He will receive excellent care from that facility. There is a possibility, if we do not move him, he may fall into a more serious state of health, perhaps a stroke, or a coma, or other symptoms resulting from a brain hemorrhage."

"As a general in our army, I had no idea it was that serious, Doctor.

"I'm afraid it is, General. He has suffered a very serious head injury. From all the fresh blood I saw today, I believe it has worsened, particularly since my last visit with him."

"A question, Doctor. Is it possible such a serious head injury could cause aggression or strong inappropriate behaviors toward others?"

"Most certainly, General. We are just beginning to learn about the function of the brain, but what we do know is this, when the brain swells it applies pressure to all areas of the brain. This pressure can strongly impact a person's behavior."

"Then I shall have him transported to the hospital immediately. Thank you, Doctor, for your time today. I am aware you are beginning to become a regular visitor to this home."

The doctor smiles. "I am always pleased to serve you, General. Good day."

Theodore escorts the doctor to the door and watches him pull away in his carriage.

Upstairs, Sergeant Calvin has gotten out of bed and is listening to the General and the doctor's conversation through a small opening in his door. The conversation has ended and he hears the General walking upstairs. Sergeant Calvin quickly and quietly moves back to his bed and waits for the General to open his bedroom door.

"Sergeant Calvin, it is General Cartwright."

'How different the General sounds from the first time he came to my room earlier today,' the Sergeant reckons.

Entering the room, the General announces the doctor's evaluation.

"After receiving the doctor's assessment of your condition, it has been determined it would be best for your health to transport you to the hospital."

"Sir, I am certain I will heal quickly and can resume my duty of caring for your daughter soon. Perhaps as early as this evening."

"I do appreciate your commitment, soldier. I am now ordering you to continue to heal in the hospital."

"I swear on my life, General, I meant no harm to your beloved daughter and to her guest, Lady Stephens. Her kindness toward me has been most appreciated during my time of healing. Sophia came to visit me day and night to ensure I was well. She is a very wonderful woman. I am sorry, General, if I offended anyone at this time. If I acted poorly, then I own up to my wrong doings and accept the consequences," the Sergeant said in a voice of innocence, wanting his theatrical abilities to benefit his cause.

"Sergeant Calvin, after speaking with Doctor Hadley, it would appear your head injuries are serious. Your injuries have the ability to affect both your mental judgment and your physical health. As we take you to the hospital, is there anyone you would like me to contact, perhaps a family member?" The General is saddened he does not know much about the Sergeant's personal situation. It has always been one of his disappointments as a high- ranking official in the British Army, not to be able to become closer to his men.

Sergeant Calvin, knowing the only local family he has is his cousin, Captain Taller, is resolved he will certainly not share this information with the General, in fear of him deducing his connection with the failed ambush.

"None that I can remember, General," he lies.

Both the General and the Sergeant are relieved to hear the sound of the hospital's carriage arriving and preparing to transport the Sergeant to St. George Hospital. The General prepares himself to return to his estate to inform Sophia and Lady Stephens regarding the health and relocation of the Sergeant. William walks up the driveway with the General's horse.

"Thank you, William. I have a question to ask you, and I would appreciate your honest and frank response."

"Of course, sir."

"What is your assessment on how the Sergeant has been interacting with everyone at this estate?"

"He was quite charming on the first day he arrived. During his time he continued to become more fond and familiar with Lady Sophia in a way I believe was unacceptable in his duties as a soldier."

William pauses, aware he must carefully respond and not express to the General the full repulsion and distrust he has for the Sergeant.

"Well sir, he continually wanted to be near Lady Sophia, while she was in the garden house and even when she was in her home. He demanded not to leave her side. It was his suggestion to stay in the guest room after his accident. He would demand that he must always be at Lady Sophia's side. Even before his accident, he would briefly stand at his post and watch and talk with Lady Sophia at every opportunity he could. He would even follow her to her bedroom."

"Her bedroom? What would be his reason for doing that?"

"I am not certain, sir. What I do know is that all of us in the house have been concerned with his actions, and we have all been keeping a watchful eye on Lady Sophia."

"Thank you, William; that brings me great comfort. Have you ever known of Sergeant Calvin to harm Sophia?"

"No, sir. What I can say is this, I did not like the way the Sergeant stares at Lady Sophia and how he touches her."

"Touches her?" the General responds with tremendous concern in his voice.

"I have seen him kiss the top of her hand in the garden house and stroke her face with the back of his hand on the beach."

"It is clear this matter with the Sergeant's inappropriate behaviors is not over, William."

"Yes, sir. Der Sergeant ist ein damon." *The Sergeant is a demon.*'

The General mounts his horse and travels toward his estate. It would seem Lady Stephens's view of the situation was correct in believing the Sergeant's behavior toward Sophia was inappropriate. And it would seem Sophia's fear of the Sergeant has been correctly formed based on the improper actions he has taken toward her. Even William's assessment of what he saw in the garden house and on the beach was correct in his mind.

'Now I have a soldier who has said he did not mean any harm to my daughter and a doctor who claims the Sergeant may be ill because of an injury to his brain. All of us have formed different views. For this reason, I cannot punish one of my soldiers who is behaving badly due to a head injury. Sophia may be my daughter, but as a General in the British Army, I must do what is just and fair.'

Chapter Twenty-Two

The phone rings in the kitchen and I race over to answer it. "Hello?"

"Hi, my little peanut. How are you?" my mother asks from the other end of the telephone line.

"Mommy? I miss you and love you, Mommy."

"I miss you too, darling. I cannot wait to see my baby girl. Are you having fun at Gramma and Grandpa's house?"

"Oh yes. Gramma and Grandpa are treating me great. I do lots of different things with them during the day and we usually play cards at night. I have also been reading a lot while I have been here. I have also been journaling, just like you told me to do. And I have written you tons of love letters, even though you didn't ask me to."

"You are too sweet, little one. You have always had a good way of expressing your words, Sarah Marie. You are the writer in our family."

"Thank you, Mommy."

"One day I am certain you will become a writer. I can see this as your calling in life."

"Where is Daddy?"

"He is working hard as usual. That is how it is when you have a family business. He told me to tell you that he loves you and misses you a lot."

"Tell him I love him more. And what about your hair dressing customers, how are they doing? I miss the ladies."

"They are all good. They have been asking about you. In fact, yesterday Barbara reminded all of us about when you were little you would sit on the customer's laps while I did their hair. Do you remember that, peanut? They would often read you storybooks. Oh how you loved to hear those stories."

"I was fascinated by storybooks. I remember, Mommy."

"Have you been to Uncle Johnny's farm lately?"

"Not for a while. Gramma has been taking me shopping and she bought me some new hair barrettes and a new pink dress with matching shoes. And I've been selling vegetables with Grandpa. Wow, he has a heart of gold!"

"He sure does, peanut. If he had one last piece of bread, he would give it to someone else if they needed it."

"I know, Mommy. I have seen him give vegetables away for free. I can tell he feels bad taking people's money, even though we worked hard for it. I love him so much. He is a special Grandpa."

"Yes he is, Sarah Marie. Well, I am calling to let you know that even though I planned to pick you up tomorrow, I am afraid I will be two weeks late. Daddy hurt his ankle. He will be fine; he just needs time to rest it and I need to help him get better."

"Will he live?" I immediately ask, thinking instantly about James and his injuries.

My mother bursts out laughing.

"Live? Of course he will live. Why on earth did you ask that question, Sarah Marie?"

"Ahh, I don't know. Sometimes when people delay their trip, it is because they have been badly hurt and cannot travel." I responded with the memories of James and Sophia fresh in my mind.

I began to ponder on this news. 'What if I won't see my Daddy again? What if he meets bad people?'

"Sarah Marie, your father is fine and I am fine, and Gramma and Grandpa have said it is okay if you stay a little longer with them. They are here to help take care of you and protect you."

'Protect me?' Sergeant Calvin was supposed to 'protect' Sophia.' Again, I become worried.

"Yes, they are good protectors and caregivers. They can teach you about the importance of family and certainly about living in the country and farming."

'Oh, protect me like the General, Lady Stephens and William,' I consider.

"I need to go, little one. Big kisses coming through the telephone. And please tell Gramma and Grandpa I will see them soon. And you will see me soon and will see your daddy when you get home."

"Okay. I love you, Mommy." I begin making smooching sounds through the receiver.

"Bye bye, little one."

After talking with my mother on the telephone, I run outside. My Grandpa is pulling weeds in the garden and my Gramma is hanging the wash on the clothesline. 'This is their estate,' I reflect. 'They may not have a garden house, like Sophia and James, or a porch to look out onto the sea, but their home makes them happy. I wonder if they are happy because of their home or because they love each other?' As I stare out on the horizon, I imagine if it would it be very different if they had a butler and a stableman?

"Sarah Marie, what do you see up in the sky?" Gramma asks.

"Oh nothing, I was just thinking about your and Grandpa's estate."

"Our estate?" Grandpa said, as they both laugh. "Oh yes, our estate is filled with lots of love and so much more," Grandpa said looking directly at Gramma.

"Yes, like weeds," Gramma said, smiling.

I look over at the two of them shaking their heads as though I had just said the oddest thing.

"I was just talking on the phone with Mommy. She sends her love to both of you. She also said she will pick me up in two weeks because Daddy hurt his ankle."

"Yes, we know, little one. Your daddy is very brave."

'Very brave. I wonder why Gramma thinks that?' "I am going to miss you very much when I leave."

I run over to my Grandpa, who is closest to me and hug him as hard as I can. Tears begin to roll down my face. He picks me up and holds me in his arms, squeezing me tightly.

"Oh, don't you worry, little chic-chic, we promise we will be right here waiting for you. You can count on us."

"I know, Grandpa. I just love being here with you and Gramma. You make me feel special. Plus, I am going to miss all the new farm animals on Uncle Johnny's farm."

"Uncle Johnny always has new animals coming along. That's just how life works, little chic-chic."

Grandpa wipes my tears with his blue and white checkered handkerchief. It is the one Gramma had given him as a Christmas present last year. Gramma embroidered his initials, CAA on the handkerchief as a joke. She said, "Now he will have the classiest, most aristocratic, Yankee handkerchief of anyone in the whole country." All the adults thought the gift was hilarious. I did not understand why it was so funny. The only thing I could figure out, after reading Gramma's book, is that every man should have their initials embroidered on their own handkerchief.

"Little chic-chic. I could use some help with all these darn weeds in my garden. Can you help me?"

"Okay," I say, with a sniffle.

I weed the garden with my Grandpa for a little while. I then announce, "Gramma and Grandpa, I am going to go play up in my room for a while and get out of the sun, if that's okay?"

"It certainly is, little chic-chic. Have fun," Gramma said.

I have no intention to play up in my room. What I want to do is read Gramma's book again. A lot has happened in the last few chapters and the suspense is starting to keep my eyes glued to every word while I am reading. I cannot imagine how this story will end and what will happen to James and Sophia. I have begun to hate Sergeant Calvin and I really like Lady Stephens.

It is funny how people in books can become like the people in your real life. William reminds me of my Uncle Johnny and the

General reminds me of my Grandpa. I think my Gramma is like Lady Stephens.

Walking past the living room on the way upstairs to my room, I sneak two chocolates from Gramma's chocolate box. I immediately pop one in my mouth, chew it quickly and then pop the other one in my mouth. My hand has melted chocolate on it and I wipe it off on my shirt without any thought of the consequences. I head upstairs. I walk over to the green shoebox and retrieve my book. I jump up on my bed, remove my bookmark and get ready to read. Taking a deep breath in through my nose, I can smell the scent of the old books. It has become a smell that relaxes me.

My eyes begin to read until I reach the final word in the book. I am surprised and saddened by the ending. Some parts made me very happy, but I thought Sophia started to act kinda different at the end. As if she had grown up and gotten stronger as a woman. Maybe because she had to. Disappointed that the book has come to an end, I turn the book over. It is then I see the letter 'I' on the back cover, next to the book's title. I am confused. There is only one person I can ask to find out what this means. Except the person I need to ask is not the person I want to ask. It is Gramma, and how can I ask her about something regarding her own books? I will have to be brave like Sophia was and just ask for help.

I walk downstairs, plotting how I will ask the question to get the answer I need. My Gramma is rocking in her rocking chair, reading her book.

"Gramma. You know I like learning about books, right? And how you teach me new things all the time. Well, I have a friend and she is reading a book, and after the title of her book there is the capital letter 'I'. What does that mean?"

"Well, I am also happy to help you learn, little one. Sometimes a story is too long for just one book. And sometimes there are different parts of the story and the author decides the story should be written through a series of different books. To deal with this problem, one option is for the author to use Roman numerals to let readers know the order of the books and the sequence of the story for reading. It also tells the reader how many books are part of the story or the series. The capital 'I' your friend saw is the Roman numeral one. Now she has to look for 'II'—Roman numeral two. In fact, this book I am just finishing right now has 'III', or Roman numeral three," Gramma said, only showing me part of the book. She makes sure she covers the picture on the book with one of her hands. In that way, all I can see is the III and the author's name, Anaed Eiram.

'Wait. Anaed Eiram is the author of my book.' My mind begins talking to itself. 'Hurry up and finish reading that book, Gramma. I want to make sure I have all the books in the set to read. I realize it is a good thing Mommy won't be picking me up for another two weeks, because I have a lot of reading to do before then.'

"Is that helpful, little one?"

"Oh yes, thank you, Gramma. I will tell my friend. I'm going back upstairs to keep playing with my horses."

I race back upstairs. I have to find the other book. The one with Roman numeral II. It will be exciting to read the whole set. I dig through the bookshelf trying to find the other book. I start to take each book off the shelf, one by one. I cannot seem to find the book. I begin to get very discouraged.

With an entire bookcase of books spread across my bedroom floor, I am disappointed that I am missing the most important piece of my puzzle. Frustrated, I slowly put each book back onto the shelf, checking each one before placing it into its spot. My arms begin to tire as I contemplate moving over one hundred books and Roman numeral II is nowhere to be found. Then I realize, 'If Gramma catches me with all these books spread out all over the floor, I will be scolded for sure. And worse, if Gramma knew I was reading her books I would be dead for sure. Well, maybe just grounded for weeks.'

As I continue putting each book back onto the shelf, I notice one of the books has an image on the front that looks like Sophia. There, next to the title, I see the Roman numeral II. I look for the author's name. It matches perfectly—Anaed Eiram. I had found the second book. I rejoice with relief. I lie on my back, with the wooden floor underneath me and rapidly kick my feet in the air. 'I found it, I found it, I know where the whole set is.'

After all the books have been put back onto the shelf, in what I believe is the correct order, I smile. What a great summer this has been. I pull the blankets off my bed, lay them on the floor, lay on my back and begin to start to read my second book.

~~~

After two weeks of reading, visiting my Uncle's farm, selling vegetables and playing cards with my grandparents, the day has come for my mother to pick me up and take me home. As summers ends I will begin the next grade level in my school. The good news about the delay in my mom getting me is that Gramma has finished her book and placed it into the bookcase in my bedroom. I was quick to notice it and snatched it away from the other books.

Before going downstairs, I sneak books I, II and III into my suitcase. I place my clothes on top of them to make sure they are not discovered. This is one story and series I definitely want to read to the end.

Hearing my mother's voice, I run downstairs and greet her with a big hug.

"Mommy! I missed you so much. I love you. You should have been visiting here too. I had so much fun with Gramma and Grandpa."

"I bet you did, and oh yes, little one, I wish I could have spent all this time with Gramma and Grandpa too," my mother said, smiling at my grandparents and mouthing the words 'Thank you' to them. "I love you so much, little one. I can't wait to get you home so you can have more fun with your brother and sister too."

"I doubt that," I say innocently, as the adults all laugh.

I lift up my suitcase to walk out the door.

"Can I carry your bag for you, little chic-chic?" Grandpa asks, trying to take the bag from my hand.

"I'm fine, Grandpa. I can carry it on my own. I am much stronger and have more muscles from all the farms chores we did this summer."

Again, all the adults laugh.

"You know what, little chic-chic?" Grandpa said, feeling my biceps. "I think you are right."

With that comment, Grandpa bends down, picks me up and gives me the longest and warmest hug and kiss I can ever remember him giving me.

"Boy, I am going to miss you, little chic-chic."

While still in my Grandpa's arms, Gramma walks over and gives me a big kiss on my forehead.

"I love you too, peanut. Now you be a good girl for your mommy and remember to keep reading and writing."

"Oh, I will," I say to my Gramma. "I will. Sometimes when a book is really good I just can't stop reading it."

Gramma smiles as we walk to my mother's car. As the car drives away, everyone waves. I also notice everyone has tears in their eyes, even Grandpa.

For the first hour of the car ride I am the one doing all of the talking. I tell my mother every detail about selling vegetables with Grandpa and learning to shoot a BB gun and helping on Uncle Johnny's farm. My mother listens and smiles, keeping her eyes on the road as she drives us home. When I have finished telling all my stories, my mother turns to me and said, "Sarah Marie, can you go into my purse and hand me the white jewelry box I have in there?"

"Okay," I say, with a confused expression.

Holding the jewelry box in her hand, my mother said, "Gramma wanted me to give this to you. It is very special. You have to promise to always take good care of it."

"Okay. I promise," I answer, intrigued by what might be in the box.

I open the box slowly, stunned by what my eyes are seeing. From inside the jewelry box, I pull out a long, rose-gold chain. Hanging from the chain is a heart-shaped locket with a ruby heart placed in the center. This is the chain I was playing with in Gramma's bedroom. It is also just like the one James gave to Sophia on their wedding night. I slide the necklace over my head. The pendant sits just under my forming breast buds. I grab the red heart and hold it into the palm of my little hand. I think of Sophia. 'We now have matching necklaces.'

"Mommy! I love this necklace; it is very special to me. And Gramma is very special too. She has taught me so much this summer. More than she may ever know. I have to make sure I call Gramma when I get home and thank her."

"That is a good plan, Sarah Marie."

As usual, my mother and I started talking about what she believes is the right way to go through life.

"Never forget what I taught you. You are my 'MVP' daughter, which means you have high morals, values and principles. Remember what Daddy and I taught you, my little one."

"I promise with all my heart. I won't forget, Mommy."

"Also, there is a love letter I wrote you inside my purse. It reads: *We have a very special connection, a bond like no other. I want you to always feel me in your life because I will always feel you in my life. Always know this in your heart, Sarah Marie.*"

"I hope that heart on the necklace helps you to remember the special connection you have with the important people in your life," Mommy added. "You have a special bond with Gramma and Grandpa and with your dad and I and your brother and sister. Those special connections are precious gems in life, Sarah Marie. They are connections within your heart."

The car pulls into the driveway and I immediately bolt upstairs to find my dad. The heart pendant swings and bumps against my chest as I run. My dad is sitting at his desk; he stops what he is doing, stands up, grabs me and picks me up in the air.

"There you are, my little one. I missed you so much. I love you, peanut. How was your summer at Gramma and Grandpa's?"

"I loved it, Daddy. I learned so much, I ate so much. I even played cards past my bedtime. It was so much fun. Fluffy slept with me every night."

"Well, I am glad you had a lot of fun. That was the plan. It was been pretty quiet around here without you. It will be good to hear your voice in the house again. Did you remember the three important life lesson I taught you before you left?"

"Yes, I did, Daddy."

"Tell me what they are again, peanut?"

"You told me that when your dad raised you, there were three important things to remember in life. Three words. You told me to never forget how important it is to stand behind these three words for the rest of my life."

"And what are the three words, Sarah Marie?"

"Your name, your reputation and your word."

"Good job, little one. That is correct. And how did you show the three important things when you were visiting Gramma and Grandpa?"

"Ahhh," I say, pausing, I was not quite ready for this quiz as soon as I got home.

"For my name, I made sure I introduced myself properly to the people I met at the vegetable stand. I shook their hand and I tried to find out their name too."

"Good job, peanut. And the second one?"

"For my reputation, I tried to make sure that Gramma and Grandpa always thought I was polite and grateful."

I hoped that my dad would not press me about having a reputation about being honest, because I think I might have told a few 'white' lies about saying I was going upstairs to play with my horses when I was actually going upstairs to read more of Gramma's book.

"And, the last and third one?"

"For my word, I would always do what I promised to do, like set the table or brush my teeth."

"That's my girl," my father said proudly. "These three important things define you as a person in this world, Sarah Marie. They are always important to remember. Hold on to these words and they will carry you far in life."

"I will, Daddy, I promise. I will never forget them."

My mother joined my father and me upstairs. As I see her entering the living room, I say, "This was the best summer vacation I could have ever asked God for. Thank you for letting me stay so long with Gramma and Grandpa."

"You are welcome, more than welcome, my little one," my mother said.

"How long until dinner?" I ask.

"We will probably eat in a couple of hours. But before dinner I need you to unpack and put away all your things," my mother kindly said.

I walk down the hall to my bedroom, hurry and open my suitcase and frantically tear through my things, looking for my three books. I see my red fringe bookmark sticking out from the side of my book. It is time to start the second book. I cannot wait to finish these last two books and find out the ending of this great love story. I want to find out what happens to all of the characters. I jump on my bed and for some reason Roman numeral "I" book is still on my mind. I decide to once again read the last chapter of that book. I wanted to remind myself what happened before I start on the second book. More importantly, now that I am wearing a heart-shaped pendant like Sophia's, "I want to feel like her, as I lie cozy in the safety of my own bed in my own house." I say this out loud, holding my heart-shaped pendant tightly in my hand.

"Sophia, Sophia, your love story has changed my life forever. I learned so much about being a lady and how a man should court me in life. What becomes of your life, Sophia? I will have to finish reading these books to find out."

Chapter Twenty-Three

The rough seas jolt the massive ship as Captain Taller carefully maneuvers his ship into London's port, giving the other vessels a wide berth. The Captain directs the seamen to drop the sunbleached sails as they begin to wrinkle and fall. He then commands the seaman to furl the luffing sails.

It had been almost eight weeks since James had first left his home port. It seemed longer since he had last seen his beautiful wife Sophia. It was now February 13, 1734, and next to his wedding day, arriving safely into port today had become the happiest day in James's entire life.

The seamen drop the kedging anchors from the side of the ship opposite of the wharf as the ship rocks up against the fenders. 'Funny,' James ponders, while bobbing on the ship as it reaches the wharf. 'That wallop against the dock is not nearly as strong as the pummeling my heart has taken from missing Sophia. My soul needs an angel's touch, and Sophia is my angel.'

Looking down at his pocket watch, he said out loud. "My darling love, I will be home soon, I promise."

The seamen throw the lines to the men on the wharf as they attach the lines to the inverted cannons now used as bollards to secure the ship. James gathers all the soldiers together in an effort to bring closure to this intense experience.

"I want to commend all of you for the fine job each of you have done to protect my wellbeing. All of you have carried out your direct orders from the General flawlessly. Thank you for bringing me home safely."

"Here! Here!" the men say in unison before walking down the plank together, off the ship and into a carriage waiting at the port.

"The General will be pleased with your service, gentleman. Upon consideration, it is clear someone wanted me dead during this mission. I intend to find out who that person is. When I do find them, they will be punished appropriately. You can be assured of that."

Each soldier was pleased when the carriage reached their home in the village. James was the last soldier remaining in the carriage. The next stop would be his estate.

The ride up the gravel driveway seemed to take as long as his entire trip from Portugal. The carriage pulled up to the back door of his home, a door carefully positioned so the front of the house would overlook the sea. James exited the carriage, paying the driver handsomely for his service. Walking toward the door, James sees William tending the garden.

"Colonel James, it is so good to see you! We have all been extremely worried for your safety." William sounds surprised and relieved at the Colonel's arrival. This is a man he had come to admire, respect and depend upon. Not having his presence in the home would have created another void in his life.

"I, too, have been worried for my safety, William," James said, smiling despite how fatigued and frail he looks and feels after his journey. "Is my beautiful bride home?"

"She most certainly is, sir. I have no doubt Lady Sophia will be extremely happy and relieved to see you home. It has also been a busy time here during your absence."

"I will look forward to sitting down, having some tea and hearing all about it, William. I trust you are well."

"Yes, sir," William replies, overly impressed the Colonel would care to ask questions about him, especially upon just arriving home.

'This action speaks well of Colonel's character,' William summarizes upon this observation.

James walks toward the wooden screen door, and with a weak grip, one caused from limited food from his fourteen-day journey home on Captain Taller's ship, he enters his home. The first thing James sees is Sophia, sitting in their front drawing room. He walks toward her. His footsteps alert her that someone is in the house. She looks up automatically, responding to the sound and lowers her head back into her book. Then, as if her eyes had just registered who the figure was in the hallway, she quickly looks up again and calls out.

"James? James is it really you?"

"Yes, my love, tis I," James replies, as the two lovers run toward each other and embrace with a long kiss.

Tears of joy and sobs of relief prevent the two from talking. Finally, Sophia gathers herself and confesses to James.

"Oh, darling, I was beginning to believe I would never see you again. The thought caused me enormous torment, beyond what your mind could ever imagine."

James kisses Sophia warmly on her forehead.

"There were moments during this journey I had thought the same, my beautiful and sweet Sophia. It was my love for you, along with my sheer desire to be with you, that has provided me with the strength to return to you this day."

Sophia weeps after hearing these words. Holding each other tightly, the room seems lost in time.

"The horror of your absence, James, was further compounded by some joyous news I have to share with you."

"Joyous news? I am intrigued. What is this news you speak of? Could it be you have recently located another estate sale for us to purchase more furniture for our home?"

"Well, this news may require new furniture, but not for the reasons you think. What would you say Colonel James Langston about someone else living in this house with us?"

"Someone else? Someone other than Lady Stephens? My darling Sophia, I know we have a beautiful home, I am just not certain that I want to create the Langston Inn, especially when I want to spend all of my waking hours loving you."

"The someone I speak about is very different from Lady Stephens."

"Sophia, my dear, I am not certain this is a good time to discuss this option. Perhaps this discussion is something we can decide upon at another time, once I get settled from my trip."

"I am afraid this is not an option, James. The decision has already been made. We will be having a new person living with us."

"Sophia, my darling, I am very tired and very concerned by what you are speaking about. Please my darling, I am so happy to be home and elated to feel your touch. I simply want to wallow in that pleasure for a bit."

"I am with bairn. You are going to be a father."

"A father? But how?"

"Colonel Langston, I suspect you are aware of the how," Sophia said with a bit of a smirk.

"Oh, of course," James said, elated by what he has just heard. "This is wonderful news. A father! Oh Sophia, I love you! We are going to have our first bairn. When did you find out about this news?"

"I found out the day you departed, James. That is what has made your absence even harder for me."

"I am sorry, my love. I cannot even imagine how you managed through these days, Sophia. Fortunately for us, I am here now and we will all be together as a family. Thank you, Sophia, for this magnificent welcome home gift."

The couple continued to embrace until James suggests they go and greet Lady Stephens and Theodore. Their timing was perfect, as Lady Stephens had just walked out of her downstairs bedroom, as the couple entered that portion of the house.

"I thought I was dreaming when I heard your voice, Colonel James. Now upon seeing you, I am still certain I am dreaming as to what I see before me."

Completely out of character for the lovely refined Lady Stephens, she approaches James and hugs him with all the strength of an older woman. James, who was at first surprised, received the embrace and begins to pat Lady Stephens on the back in attempt to comfort her.

"Yes, I am home safe and ready to care for and protect my beautiful wife and our first bairn."

Lady Stephens looks up at James, smiles and announces, "Sir, you took the words right from mind and my mouth."

The two smile at each other and then James turns to Sophia, who has tears rolling down her face, and swiftly wraps his arms around her.

"It is true, Sophia. I am home now. Home to be at your side, to live our life together and enjoy playing with our bairn, whom I am anxious to meet," James said these words smiling, while wiping the tears from Sophia's beaming face.

Theodore joins the group and shakes James's hand.

"Sir, I am not certain I have enough words in my vocabulary to express how pleased I am to see you back home safely."

"Thank you, Theodore. Your simple comments are enough for me to understand what you mean."

"I have prepared tea on the porch for everyone, and William has ridden off to alert the General you are home."

"Oh my, it is glorious to be back with such a welcoming and responsive staff. Thank you, Theodore."

The group enjoys their tea and speaks about the garden house and the lovely views of the sea from where they sit. The conversation is intentionally kept on the lighter side.

Once the General arrives at the house, Theodore escorts him to the porch, where James stands to greet the General with a salute.

"Thank you, sir, for sending your elite soldiers to Portugal. It was those reinforcements that helped me be here with you today."

"James, I would do nothing less for one of my finest soldiers. But for the rest of this visit, I suggest we consider our relationship that of a father-in-law and a son-in-law."

"That would be excellent, sir. But first allow me to present you the signed letter from King John V of Portugal, as was my mission and duty to the Crown."

James retrieves the letter from his jacket pocket and hands it to the General. Strangely, at that moment, he experiences an overwhelming sense of relief, as though the time has come for him to finally be allowed to rest.

"Theodore," the General said. "I see James is drinking tea. What is this type of nonsense? This man needs a proper drink. A scotch—as does his General."

"Yes, sir," Theodore responds, while everyone on the porch laughs, including Theodore.

"Scotch will be the perfect medicinal welcoming remedy, sir," James said.

"For you and for me," the General replies with an uncharacteristic wink.

When each person has their appropriate beverage, the General rises from his chair.

"I wish to propose a toast. A toast of gratitude. First, I am grateful for the safe return and successful mission of one of my finest soldiers, Colonel James Langston."

"Here. Here." Sophia, Lady Stephens and even Theodore respond.

"Next a toast of gratitude to my daughter, for her ability to supply me with my first grand bairn."

"Here, Here." The group responds again as James kisses Sophia on the cheek.

"Next, a toast to Lady Stephens."

"Oh my," said Lady Stephens as she instantly blushes.

"A toast of gratitude to Lady Stephens, who has welcomingly become my daughter's surrogate mother. This is a gratitude I can barely measure."

Sophia rises from her chair, walks over and hugs Lady Stephens.

"Thank you, Lady Stephens. Without you I do not know how I would have been able to manage through this long period of time without James."

"You are more than welcome, Sophia. You have indeed found a special place in my heart."

James watches the interaction between the two women. He is surprised by how close they have become while he was gone. 'And to think it was all because of a doorman at the opening of a library who suggested we attend an estate sale together.'

"And a toast to Theodore and William." The General beckons to William, who was tending the yards. He motions him to join them on the porch.

"A toast of gratitude to Theodore and William for their service toward my daughter and the comfort they have provided me in knowing Sophia was in safe hands."

"Here, Here." The group responds, in what now has become a very festive scene on the Langston's porch.

James looks over and notices Lady Stephens with an extremely sad face.

"Is everything all right, Lady Stephens?" James asks.

"I am sorry to dampen the festivities. It would appear I am having another moment of immensely missing my late husband. I yearn for him every day. It saddens me that he is not here to share this joyous moment. He would have loved you, James—and your adoring wife."

Sophia can see the pain in Lady Stephens's eyes. She rises from her seat and again walks over to comfort her.

"It must be the return of your husband that has brought out all these unsettled feelings within me. I still mourn for my dear Henry. This is why I had to find the right home for Theodore. He knew Henry and me so well," she said, looking over at Theodore and smiling. "I know Theodore will be a marvelous fit for the two of you in the future without me."

"Without you? Oh, Lady Stephens, I cannot imagine or ever want to think about anything ever happening to you. It is our wish you will be here to cherish these splendid times as we bring a new life into our family. Please do not speak of your departure. We hope you can stay with us or visit us as often as you wish," Sophia recants. The conversations and gaieties continued for a short while until the General then proposes to Lady Stephens to join him at his estate for the evening.

"Perhaps this young couple, who have just reconnected, might enjoy their house to themselves this evening, Lady Stephens, and as you well know, I have always welcomed your company at my estate."

"I agree with your presumption regarding this young couple, General. I graciously accept your offer—and thank you."

The General and Lady Stephens then depart the house after everyone, once again, expresses to James how thrilled they are that he is home. With the house empty of guests, James and Sophia walk upstairs to their bedroom and sit down at their window seat that captures the exterior views.

"I have cherished this day being back at your side, Sophia. You are my strength, my angel of hope. You are what has kept me a whole man."

Upon saying these words, James looks up and notices a lunar eclipse. The movement of the sun, earth and moon are aligned at once; it seemed a fitting metaphor for this evening. Pointing out the eclipse to Sophia he adds, "My love, the alignment of these celestial beings is a sign that we, too, have once again become aligned. You, me and our bairn."

Sophia, who looks radiant from the blood moon shining upon her, smiles with the innocence James has missed.

"Sophia, you are the only woman I shall ever love. You have my heart until the end of time."

"I shall love you for all eternity, James."

Looking up at the moon, Sophia turns to James and continues, "I love you to the moon and back, my darling."

James finds himself stimulated by the fine curves of Sophia's shoulders. His hand glides slowly along her slender neckline. He seductively lowers one of the shoulders of her gown, exposing the curves of her bosoms. James enjoys slowly caressing Sophia's plump breasts. They seem to have increased in size from the image he remembers. He gently pulls back her long, wavy black curls from her shoulders. Reaching his hand further into her gown,

James enjoys the touch of Sophia's soft nipples. She pulls back with a slight moan.

"What is it, my Sophia?"

"Oh James, the midwife warned me of this. It would appear that our little bairn is beginning to change my body and my breasts have become overly sensitive to touch."

"Well, I will just have to become more careful. And you will have to help me understand what feels sensual and arousing for you."

Stimulating his lover further he removes her gown.

"Oh James, I love you so."

"And I love you," James said, rubbing his hand over the small bump on Sophia's belly. Sophia moans with joy. James gently lifts Sophia from the window seat. Cradling her in his arms, he then walks over to their bed. He lays her down onto the blanket, laying his hand down onto her stomach and around her rising belly and then into her warmth. He lowers his head and kisses her belly.

"Hello, little one. I am your father. It is so nice to meet you."

Sophia laughs gently. James continues to kiss Sophia, now moving down between her legs. He spreads her legs further apart and licks her tenderly with his tongue, penetrating his tongue in and out of her moist vagina, Sophia lets out a loud moan. She begs James to make love to her.

"I need you inside me, James. I want you. I have missed your touch. I have missed the safety of you being next to me."

James is surprised by this comment. Sophia has never referred to the need to be safe beside him. 'How strange,' he surmises; however, his mind goes elsewhere. It goes fully to the beauty of Sophia's entire body.

Removing his uniform pants, James kneels down, again giving Sophia a pleasurable experience with his two fingers lightly circulating her clitoris as he gently licks her moist labia. He has always enjoyed arousing Sophia; however, tonight after a dangerous and almost deadly mission, a night of lovemaking will help to heal all of his wounds.

"I so needed to taste you, my love," James said, looking up from Sophia from between her legs.

Sophia begins to weep.

"Please James, let us once again be joined as one. I need you inside me and I need you close to me for protection."

James is still at a loss by Sophia's use of words the safety and protection. 'Perhaps this is due to her being with bairn,' he deduces. Nonetheless, his throbbing penis aches to be inside his wife. Holding back from entering her and hoping to increase her desire even more, he gently taps his penis onto the outside of her vulva. This is intended to be a tease for the prize they both are about to receive. Her tender lips rejoice with her wet juices. Then, without warning, James enters his lover. He gently moves his hips with hers as they glide to the beat of their body's rhythm. James climaxes deep inside Sophia, begging for her to join him. She obliges. Their two bodies combine as one. Sophia lets out a loud moan, loud enough for the entire world to hear and for all her fears and anxieties to be released. As the two of them collapse in one another's arms, the midnight air blows in from the window and against their naked skin.

After a short rest, James awakens, finding Sophia staring out the window.

"I love you, Mrs. Langston."

"I love you too, Mr. Langston, and although I have said this before, I am so glad you are home safely."

"Sophia, I am afraid to tell you, I almost did not come home from this trip. I am lucky to even be alive and be here with you."

Surprised and then shocked, Sophia sees the redness and swelling of the wound on James's chest. She places her hand over his scar and begins to weep. That is when James sits down next to her and begins to tell Sophia the entire story of his experience in Portugal.

"I am blessed. The Lord has saved me to be with you this day. The Lord could have taken me, and yet I am here with you. If it were not for those valuable coins stopping the sword from penetrating my heart, I would not be alive today."

Sophia continues to quietly weep. She is made speechless by the story she is hearing.

"Sophia, I heard an inner voice right before the ambush. It is this voice which caused me to move the coins to the inside pocket of my uniform jacket. Perhaps the voice could have been the Holy Spirit. It was that simple action which saved my life. During my healing, it was the thought of you and our love which kept me alive as I traveled in the darkness. I begged God to allow me to see you again. I knew I could not leave this world without being with you again."

"Your life was spared for a reason, James. I am grateful you returned home safely, especially after hearing all these tales. Our one true love is a special gift, and from this day forward I shall cherish each day I spend with you."

The two lovers return to their bed and fall asleep in each other's arms. Their rest is peaceful.

In the morning, James is awoken by the sun shining onto his face. He rises from the bed and looks out the window at the distant sea. Captain Taller enters his mind. A Captain who brought him to Portugal and whose ship brought him home. He thought of Captain Taller, the devious man who he is convinced played a role in his ambush. James kisses Sophia on her forehead while she sleeps soundly and quietly exits their bedroom. Walking into the kitchen for some morning tea, he is greeted by Lady Stephens.

"Good morning, Colonel James. I trust you slept well."

"I am surprised to see you here, Lady Stephens. Did you not spend the night at the General's?"

"I did and I have already returned back here. I know you had scheduled to see him this morning and I wanted to allow you two your privacy."

"Thank you, your Ladyship. We do have a great deal to discuss this morning. Some are rather important and urgent matters."

"I hope you and Sophia were finally able to rest well. I suspect you both required a good deal of sleep. You, from your trip, and her because she has not slept well during your absence."

"I thought as much," James confirmed.

As the two sip their tea, Lady Stephens decides to broach the subject about Sergeant Calvin's indiscretions and behavior toward

Sophia. She had determined it was her duty, as someone who was to care for Sophia in James's absence.

"Colonel James, yesterday, did the General or Sophia speak to you about Sergeant Calvin?"

"No. Neither one did, your Ladyship. In fact, with so many soldiers I am afraid I do not even know who Sergeant Calvin is."

"Sergeant Calvin is the soldier the General assigned to guard Sophia and your estate after you had not arrived home at what was assumed to be amble time to complete your mission. The General was not certain the details for your delay and he wanted to ensure Sophia's safety."

'Sophia's safety. There are the words I heard Sophia use last night,' James recalls.

"I suspect I would do the same if I were the General," James responds.

"The decision for a soldier is not my concern, Colonel. What has become my concern is his behavior while posted here."

"His behavior?"

Lady Stephens begins to share the events of the last few weeks with James. He cannot believe what his ears are hearing. His anger rises and his face becomes flushed.

"Theodore, William and I did not, and do not, trust this man's intentions. I would suggest you be very leery of Sergeant Calvin. He is not a man in a solid state of mind. I am certain he can, and will, harm us all, given the opportunity. He has trifled with William and myself on several occasions, and his temper is worth watching. William has not only observed this *behavior* you speak of but has also experienced it."

"Experienced it?"

"Yes, Colonel. This has been a constant behavior—even after he moved into your home."

"Moved into my home? When on earth did that occur?"

"After the accident," Lady Stephens answers.

James's internal anger intensifies. It is one thing for Captain Taller to try to harm me on a mission, but it is quite another for some sergeant to cause my wife to feel unsafe.

"It was determined Colonel, that the Sergeant's head injury caused his intense affection toward Sophia. Theodore, William and myself think differently. We saw his actions before the accident. Even then, they were not admirable."

"Where is this Sergeant now?"

"The General immediately dismissed him once I informed him of the scope of the circumstances. Doctor Hadley came and determined he should be admitted to the hospital, thinking it was his injuries which were causing his behavior."

"One can only imagine how much worse this situation might have been had you not been here, Lady Stephens. For that, I am forever in your debt."

"Nonsense, Colonel. I am a woman of my promise. Besides, I am very fond of you and Sophia; you two are like family to me. If my dear Henry was alive, he too would have never allowed this behavior to occur under your roof. Just know I am concerned by this soldier. He is dangerous. These are the instincts of a wise old woman talking, James."

Lady Stephens suddenly becomes ill, causing her to lay her head down on the table. In complete shock, James quickly rises from his chair and asks.

"Lady Stephens? Lady Stephens, are you all right?"

"I feel a wee bit weak. I am sorry. I have held on to this information for so long. I suspect I must have become worried about how I was going to share it with you, Colonel."

"Shall I help you to your room so you may rest?"

"Yes, please, James. I would be most grateful if you do."

"Theodore," James calls out.

Theodore rushes into the kitchen. Seeing Colonel James walking a very frail-looking Lady Stephens, he quickly takes her other arm as James informs him of the situation.

"Lady Stephens has become ill and we are going to escort her to her bed."

After getting Lady Stephens situated on her bed, James makes a suggestion.

"Your Ladyship, with all due respect for your well-being, I suggest we send for Doctor Hadley to come and determine what might be ailing you."

"I will not have that, Colonel James. I am fine. Thank you for all your concern; however, as I am certain Theodore will attest, I am both a very stubborn and resolved woman. There is nothing wrong with me that a good rest will not fix."

"Lady Stephens, I have also been known as being an extremely stubborn Colonel, but something tells me in this matter I may have met my match. I am also known as being a strong negotiator, so for that reason, here is what I am prepared to do, I will go and meet with the General. If, after I return, you are not feeling better, I will personally go and retrieve Doctor Hadley, whether you agree or not."

"Colonel James, I agree with you on both counts. One, you are a good negotiator and two, you may call for Doctor Hadley."

"Thank you, Lady Stephens." He pauses. "For your compliment on both counts." James smiles at her as he walks out of the room.

"Rest well, Lady Stephens. Otherwise, you will be seeing Doctor Hadley soon."

Lady Stephen smiles. 'Oh my. He is so much like my late husband, Henry.'

Leaving the room, James next turns to Theodore.

"My wife and I care very deeply for Lady Stephens and we know you do as well. It is my utmost duty to protect her as a guest in my home. Let us be sure Lady Stephens will be watched carefully during the next few hours."

Theodore agrees.

"Theodore, on a second subject, did you find anything odd about this Sergeant Calvin who was working at my home during my absence?"

"I beg your pardon, sir?" Theodore asks, very surprised by the question.

"Allow me to rephrase the question and be more direct for the sake of time. Did you witness Sergeant Calvin display any rude or strange behaviors toward my wife?"

"Sergeant Calvin was always very polite with me, sir. He seemed very helpful toward Lady Sophia. Although I did find it strange one morning when I found Lady Sophia's bedroom door was locked."

"Her door was locked? Why was that?"

"I am not quite certain, sir. I came to bring Lady Sophia her morning tea and found the door locked. This was very unusual for her. She seemed very tired that morning. When I asked if she was all right, Sergeant Calvin quickly appeared from his room next door and answered for her. He also dashed into her room several times that day to ensure she was fine."

"He entered my wife's bedroom? Several times?"

"Yes, sir. He was taking care of her and he guarded her very closely. He asked me to bring him anything she needed. He insisted on attending to her every need. He informed me that the General requested he watch closely over her, protect her, guard her and keep her safe."

"Safe. I seem to be continually hearing that word since my return home, Theodore."

"Lady Stephens and I did not believe this is what the General requested of the Sergeant. We did our best to watch out for Lady Sophia, without the Sergeant knowing we were watching him as he watched Lady Sophia."

"Thank you, Theodore. I can assure you, Sergeant Calvin overstepped his duties and boundaries. Wounded or not, he should have never attended to my wife in this manner."

"I agree, sir."

James leaves the house, making his way to the barn to retrieve his horse. This is the first time he has been to the barn since his return home. His horse lets out a loud whiny as James enters the barn.

"I see someone has missed me," James smiles.

"He has indeed, Colonel," William replies. He then walks James's horse over to him.

"William, before I depart for the General's estate, I wish to speak with you about something."

"Of course, sir."

"I have recently heard the most disturbing news this morning from both Lady Stephens and Theodore. This news is in regards to Sergeant Calvin."

"The man is a filthy rogue, sir. I warned him to stay away from Lady Sophia. If the General had not dismissed him, he might not yet be alive today, for I would have killed him. Even if it would have cost me my job on this estate. I knew he was trouble from the first day he set foot on these grounds," William immediately responds, blurting out his disgust for the Sergeant.

William continued to provide James with specific details on the Sergeant's behavior.

"Colonel James, I gave you my word I would protect all your prized possessions, and sir, I am a man of my promise, even when the situation began to worsen."

"Worsen?"

"Yes, I could tell the Sergeant was becoming more familiar with Lady Sophia after offering to move into the house to offer further protection, but Lady Sophia would not allow me to stay in your home. I asked her every day if she needed anything. Each day she would say, 'My husband will be home soon,' and for me not to worry. Sir, I did not like or trust the Sergeant. I am even willing to confess to cutting the leather on his saddle and bridle to bring him harm. Unfortunately, my plan failed. After his fall, he guarded Lady Sophia even more closely. I am even willing to go so far as to say he became more obsessed with her. He was happy to be sleeping in the room next to hers; although the maids are not convinced he was doing much sleeping in that bed."

"Why is that, William?" James asks, wrinkling his brow in bewilderment.

"When they went in to tidy his room each day, his sheets were moist and smelled of 'his self-gratification wetness.' Those were their words, not mine, sir," William assured him.

Enraged, James calls out, "He intimately stimulated himself in one of my beds! While my wife and staff cared for him?"

"That is what I was told, sir. The maids were quite disgusted. Soon after that, Lady Stephens noticed Lady Sophia becoming more withdrawn, almost tense and anxious when he was in her presence."

"I agree with your assessment of this man, William. He is a filthy rogue. I might also add, he is a fiend."

"I agree, sir. My concern now, Colonel, is that I wonder if the General is hoodwinked by this 'fiend,' to use your words."

"I am coming to believe you are correct, William. I will personally see to him myself, after I complete my morning meeting with the General. If the General cannot see how this fiend may have brought harm to his daughter—my wife—then I will rectify the situation myself. Thank you, William. I am very grateful I had you here. I requested you to protect all my prized possessions, and indeed you have."

James gives William a solid handshake, slipping a gold coin into his jacket pocket.

"Thank you, Colonel," William said.

Pulling the coin out from his pocket, he notices it is solid gold. It is certainly a rare and extremely valuable coin. "Sir, I cannot accept this."

"Yes, you must, William. That is a direct order from this Colonel. You may no longer have a wife due to terrible circumstances, but you realized how precious my wife was and is to me, and you did what I would have gladly done for you. For that I am forever grateful," James said with a bow and a smile.

Climbing onto his horse, James swiftly rides off to the General's house. After his discussions with Lady Stephens, Theodore and William, he has much to talk about with his new father-in-law.

Arriving at the General's estate, Thomas escorts James into the General's study. He impatiently paces, waiting for the General to arrive. James, assuming his role as soldier and not son-in-law, salutes when the General walks into the room.

"General, it has been brought to my attention that Sergeant Calvin is far worse of a man that you might have been led to believe. If it were not for the actions of my staff and my guest, your daughter would have been in worse harm and more fearful than she already is."

"Colonel, I was made aware of the situation you are referring to. I have investigated all of the details which have caused Sophia to be fearful. I am pleased to announce, I was able to resolve the matter before you returned home from Portugal. As part of my investigation, I spoke to Doctor Hadley. The doctor believes it was the Sergeant's horseback riding accident which worsened his health. This is why we determined it was best for the Sergeant to be in the hospital. He has a very serious concussion. There is even a possibility he may go into a coma."

"General, I can assure you, he will not have to worry about going into a coma. I will personally put him there myself, once I confront him with what he has done to my wife."

"I agree with your deep frustration, James. I had a similar reaction when I learned the Sergeant was not of sound mind. This is quite likely a permanent condition. I am certain he will not be able to return to duty. There is very slight possibility his health may improve; however, I suspect it will not."

"General, with all due respect, he may not be allowed to return to duty, even if his health does improve. From what I have learned today, I will not have him working amongst my men and certainly I do not want him anywhere near my wife."

"James, he has been given strict orders to never set foot on your property again. At this point, we must see what the doctor tells us about the status of his health before we proceed with any other action. I would like you to consider this matter now closed. On another topic, please tell me more about Captain Taller and the tavern incident. You indicated in your letter you have some concerns about him as well."

"Sir, I will be happy to share that story and about my meeting with the King; however, please know the issue with Sergeant Calvin is not closed for me."

"Understood, Colonel."

After the lengthy meeting, James sets out and rides home. The rhythm of the trotting horse allows the thoughts in his mind to wander. He can hear the words of Lady Stephens in those thoughts. 'These are the instincts of a wise older woman talking, James. I know there is something not right about Sergeant Calvin.'

James decides to detour from his ride home and head to the hospital to make a personal visit to Sergeant Calvin.

Walking into the two-story hospital, James looks very official wearing his Colonel's uniform. He stops at the main desk and inquires as to what ward Sergeant Calvin Harvey Gideon might be on. Armed with this information, James goes in search of the filthy, roguish fiend, who was once living in his house. Entering the ward, it is easy to deduce which patient is Sergeant Calvin. He is the only patient with a bandaged head.

James stands tall as he walks up to the foot of the Sergeant's bed. Sergeant Calvin immediately recognizes James and is certain his fear will cause him to soil his bed. As is proper protocol, the Sergeant sits up and salutes James.

"At ease, soldier. It is good to see your mind is still working and you are aware of how to perform proper military protocol."

Sergeant Calvin takes a large gulp in his very dry mouth.

James approaches the Sergeant, leans down next to his ear and whispers.

"I am aware of everything, Sergeant, including your masturbating in my home. You disgust me, soldier. You had better hope this head trauma of yours kills you, because if it does not, I am going to kill you myself. You think you like to touch my wife? Well I have a desire to touch your head and rip it from your shoulders."

The Sergeant tries to move away; however, James's strong hands on the Sergeant's shoulders pin him in place on his bed, as James continues to speak to him.

"I can promise you this, Sergeant. Your actions will not go unpunished, by the General, myself and the devil, because the devil is who you will be meeting after you die."

A nurse approaches the two soldiers. James slowly steps away from the wide-eyed Sergeant and the bed.

"There is no need to leave, Colonel. I was just going to check on our most charming patient."

"I best take my leave now, Nurse Ruth," James said, observing the name stitched on her uniform. "It is best the Sergeant gets well, so he can walk out the doors of this hospital. I will look forward to meeting him in town, one more time."

"You seem to care about the Sergeant, Colonel."

"Oh yes, Nurse Ruth. I most certainly care what happens to the Sergeant. More than you might ever know."

With that, James leaves the ward and Sergeant Calvin turns to the nurse.

"Nurse, I think I am going to be sick."

Lying alone in his bed, the Sergeant comes to accept that his 'brilliant' plan has been foiled. 'Now I must wish the Colonel does not learn of the entire plan, the part that involves my cousin, Captain Taller. I must ensure my drunken cousin does not divulge any information about the ambush in Portugal. Currently, I have the General believing I am innocent, due to the result of the accident with my horse. Since a General trumps a Colonel, I cannot allow the General to learn of my plot to have Colonel James killed so I could live out my remaining days as a very rich man with a beautiful wife.'

James walks down the very sterile-looking hospital hallway. To his amazement, he sees Captain Taller walking toward him.

"I am surprised to see you, Captain."

The smell of heavy liquor dominates the Captain's breath.

"I am here to visit a relative. I received word after my ship had landed in port that he was ill."

"I wish your relative good health, Captain. Good day."

Continuing down the corridor, James pauses. His internal instincts take over. He specifically remembers the Captain telling him on the journey to Portugal that he did not have any relatives in the city. James steps into the next hospital doorway and watches where the Captain walks. Captain Taller pauses at Sergeant Calvin's ward. James becomes astonished when Nurse Ruth comes out to smile and talk with the Captain.

On the other side of the door, the ward nurse approaches the Sergeant again.

"You appear to be a popular man today, Sergeant. You have another visitor. He is waiting in the hallway. Are you strong enough for another visitor?"

"Who is this visitor?"

"He said his name is Captain Taller."

"Oh yes, I would very much like to visit with him."

After the Captain enters the ward, James returns to the ward's door and peers into the window. What he sees shocks him. Through the window, he can see Captain Taller and Sergeant Calvin embrace, followed by lots of laughter.

James turns his back to the door. 'Visiting a relative? The drunken Captain and the scandalous Sergeant are related. I must inform the General.'

James mounts his horse and quickly gallops to the General's house. Dismounting his gelding, he hands the reins to Horace, requesting that he water and brush the horse, who has been galloping a great deal today. Entering directly into the General's house, not waiting for Thomas, James walks directly into the General's study. He finds the General sitting behind his desk, writing several letters, as determined by the number of pages scattered over the desk surface.

"General, I am sorry for this intrusion. I must speak to you at once," James said, haphazardly saluting the General.

"Certainly, James. I am surprised to see you again so soon. Indeed, come in."

"What I have to tell you could not wait another day."

"Should this information be preceded by a glass of scotch?"

"This information is critical to the safety of my wife, the integrity of your military and the inherent reason as to why I was ambushed."

The General suddenly changes his demeanor; sitting up straight in his chair, he becomes very attentive toward James.

"By all means, Colonel. Please tell me what this foremost information you have for me is."

"Sir, upon returning to my home, I decided to pay Sergeant Calvin a visit in the hospital."

"You did what?" the General pronounces harshly while standing up and raising both hands into the air and making a swift chopping motion with each hand.

"Please allow me to continue, sir. What I discovered is most valuable."

"Continue, Colonel. You certainly have my attention now."

"While walking down the corridor I came across Captain Taller, who was walking toward me. When I conversationally asked why he was there, he stated he was visiting a relative who had fallen ill."

"A relative? The Captain does not have any relatives in this city. He specifically told me that himself."

"He shared the same information with me, sir. This is when I became suspicious. I decided to remain in the hospital and placed myself in a doorway so as not to be seen. I wanted to see which ward the Captain visited."

"Not only do you have my attention Colonel, you have piqued my curiosity. Who was the Captain there to meet?"

At that moment, Thomas enters the room with a tray of tea. "Tea, gentleman?"

"Out!" the two soldiers shout in unison.

Thomas turned around and left the room providing an 'as you wish' before he left.

James and the General returned their attention back to each other. Again, the General asked, "Who was Captain Taller at the hospital to meet?"

"Sergeant Calvin."

General Cartwright falls into his chair.

"I believe it is time for that scotch I originally offered you, James," the General said, promptly pouring two glasses of scotch. "In God's name, what is going on here? Lady Stephens warned me about this soldier. She is indeed a wise woman."

"My concern now is, how in the devil did these two military men hide their relationship from us?"

"Better yet, Colonel, why did they do it?"

~~~

"What a lovely day it is, Lady Sophia," Lady Stephens said, smiling.

"I do enjoy the smell of the blossoms and the richness of the petals' colors on such a clear day," Sophia said to Lady Stephens as they walk through the garden house. "I am so grateful you are feeling better, Lady Stephens, and that you decided to join me on what I believe has become our traditional daily tour of my garden house. Before we continue, shall we stop and have some tea?"

"I agree, Sophia. Spending time in this garden house with you has become a special time for me as well. If I may be so frank, I have come to think of you as a daughter. Perhaps my comment is considered inappropriate since you lost your mother; however, I most certainly feel a special connection with you."

"Oh, Lady Stephens, those are beautiful words to hear. I, too, feel a special bond between us."

Sophia places both hands onto her stomach.

"I wish my mother was here to see the birth of her grand bairn. I am comforted to know you will be here and I will have the wisdom of an older woman to help me manage through life as a mother."

"I will enjoy that very much, Sophia."

Theodore brings the ladies their tea as they sit at the bistro table. They both smile as the butterflies fly gracefully through the air, landing on the flowers, especially those planted to provide them nourishment. As the two women's eyes enjoy the beauty of the flowers and aroma surrounding them, a monarch butterfly lands on Lady Stephens's shawl.

"Oh my, look at the vibrant orange and gold colors on such a delicate creature," Sophia comments.

"It is beautiful to watch."

William, who had been working in the garden, notices the women admiring the butterfly perched on Lady Stephens. He approaches the two women and asks, "Would you like to take a closer look at this majestic species, ladies?"

The women look puzzled.

"We most definitely would, William. But how?" Sophia responds.

William approaches Lady Stephens and places his hand near the butterfly. He then makes a request. "May I?" Clearly asking permission to place his hand on her shawl.

"Of course," She replies.

William places his hand on Lady Stephens's shawl and waits. After a few seconds pass, the butterfly climbs onto William's hand, much to the amazement of Sophia and Lady Stephens. The two women 'ohh and aww' over the beauty of the fragile insect.

"How on earth did you learn to breed, develop and communicate with butterflies, William?"

"I attribute it to you, Lady Sophia. Each day I watch you read. I decided to go into town and locate a book on the subject. Unfortunately, our town's library is not very well stocked with books. The librarian directed me to a very simple children's book. From that limited information, I taught myself how to raise and care for butterflies."

"William you have done a brilliant job, and I am sorry the local library is not well stocked to enhance your education," Sophia said.

Lady Stephens then asks, "William, would you mind taking these yellow roses into the house and have Theodore place them in a vase for mine and Sophia's rooms?"

"Most certainly, Lady Stephens. It pleases me that you want to enjoy my flowers, even in your room."

"William, I have come to depend on the beauty of these flowers," Lady Stephens said, smiling.

William leaves with the roses and Sophia turns to Lady Stephens and asks, "Lady Stephens, a query. I am afraid I am not aware of your first name. I have often wondered what it might be."

"Oh dear. How funny I did not share that with you. It is an old name, for certain. It is Henrietta. As a young child, I quickly adopted the nickname, Hettie. Henry insisted on calling me Henrietta. Sometimes he would say he was the Henry with the 'y' and I was the Henri with the 'i'. He would only call me 'Henri with an i' when he felt I was being bold and unladylike, or the times he thought I was behaving more like a strong, confident man."

As the ladies continue to sip their tea, Lady Stephens raises her teacup into the air, as if it were a wine glass. "Cheers, my dear, let us wish for the safe return of Colonel James."

Sophia politely smiles and looks at her with utter confusion.

"Lady Stephens, James has already returned home."

"Oh, yes, of course he has. How silly of me."

"I adore you both and look forward to the birth of your first grand bairn."

"Do you mean my first bairn?"

"Yes, I am certain that is what I said, your first bairn. Henry and I cannot wait to meet your little one. Is that not correct Henry?" Lady Stephens said, staring at an empty place at the table."

Sophia's confusion transforms into concern.

"Lady Stephens, are you all right?"

"I am perfectly fine, my dear. While the sun is warming my face, this garden is warming my heart."

Sophia is struck by the ray of sunlight shinning down on Lady Stephens's entire body from the pitched glass ceiling of the garden house.

"My dear, this moment is beautiful. It is as though hundreds of angels are singing in harmony and warming my body with light. And there is Henry. He is asking me to join him."

Lady Stephens then becomes completely silent. She gracefully receives the light from the angels above. In that instant, Sophia noticed the complete look of peace on Lady Stephens's face.

"Lady Stephens?"

Lady Stephens lowered her head to her chest and took her last breath.

"Lady Stephens? Lady Stephens!" Sophia yelled louder, calling out her name over and over again.

Theodore and William, hearing their employer yelling, come rushing into the garden house. They, too, become shocked by what they see.

"Please help her! Help her, please!" Sophia cries out, holding Lady Stephens's hand as it continues to grow colder.

After several minutes of trying to awaken Lady Stephens, it was determined she had departed from this life.

"I am sorry, Lady Sophia, I am afraid we have all lost a kind and generous lady today. We can only be comforted knowing she is with her dear husband, Henry."

Sophia sobs uncontrollably. "No-o-o!"

Before leaving the garden house Theodore turns to Sophia.

"Lady Sophia, Lady Stephens would not have wanted you to feel this way about her passing. Just this morning she shared with me she believed her time had come. She had dreamt of her dear Henry all night. She said they had danced on the ballroom floor of the Grand Lux Hotel. He held her in his arms and they glided across the floor as the music played their favorite songs."

"She told you this today?"

"Yes, Lady Sophia. I am afraid so."

"I cannot fathom she is gone. Lady Stephens is gone. I will not see her in this garden house with me anymore to enjoy the flowers and the butterflies with her."

"She will always be in the garden house, Lady Sophia," William said in a comforting voice. "You can be comforted that her memories will live on within you. As a man who lost his wife much too soon, I am comforted each day knowing that the memories of my wife are a part of me, and your memories of Lady Stephens are now a part of you."

The three of them walked with great remorse back to the house. William carried Lady Stephens in his arms as Theodore comforted the sobbing Sophia, who followed behind. Once inside the house, Lady Stephens's body is prepared for viewing.

Theodore requests that he stop the clock in the parlor, as is the custom. "My mother taught me to do that. She was very superstitious and perhaps I have picked up some of those traits."

"As you wish, Theodore," Sophia said.

Throughout the rest of the day the mood in the house was somber and sorrowful. Lady Stephens's body lay resting in the parlor and everyone donned their black clothing as a symbol of the mourning. Sophia sat in her library room, staring out the open window, while the icy cold air blew in from outside. The feeling of the air sent chills throughout Sophia's body.

Theodore knocks on the open door, hoping to bring Lady Sophia back to the present moment.

"Lady Sophia. As someone who has known Lady Stephens for a very long time, I would like to provide you with some comfort and suggest she is now at peace. She had lived a full life. She also cared deeply for you. So much so, that she wrote you and Colonel James a letter and handed it to me today, along with this hand-carved, walnut wood jewelry box. She asked me to present it to you at the right time. I do not know when she wrote these letters. All I know is that her final instructions to me were to see to it that I handed the letters directly to you and Colonel James. If there is one thing I can say about Lady Stephens, is that she was a very wise and insightful woman. I admired that most about her."

"Thank you, Theodore. I suspect this is a letter James and I should read together. Sadly, I cannot bear to read a message from Lady Stephens at this time. I will hold on to this letter, and James and I can read it together later this evening."

"As you wish, Lady Sophia," Theodore said politely.

James arrives home filled with anger and uncertainty over his recent discovery of Sergeant Calvin and Captain Taller being related. He knows once he joins Sophia in their home, the majority of his tension will be eased. Unfortunately, upon arriving home, quite the opposite occurs. James enters his house and discovers Lady Stephens's body laid out for viewing in his parlor. After stories are exchanged and grief is expressed, James and Sophia sit in their drawing room. They stare at the two letters from Lady Stephens. The first addressed to Sophia, the second to James and Sophia.

"How strange this is. Lady Stephens lies in wake in our parlor and yet her words are alive in front of us."

Sophia shakes her head in disbelief at the entire situation. Upon opening the envelope, a heart-shaped locket on a chain moves in the space. Sophia is puzzled, as this locket is similar to the one she is wearing, the one given to her by James on their wedding night. Sophia begins to read aloud the first letter addressed to her.

My Darling Sophia:

From the moment I met you and Colonel James, I could sense an instant bond connection between us. As I have said throughout our time together, you remind me of a younger version of myself. You and James remind me of the love my Henry and I shared for each other. My belief was further confirmed when

James presented you with a heart locket on your wedding night. My Henry presented me with the exact same gift on our wedding night.

I chose to not inform you of this unique similarity, in that I did not want to take away from the special meaning the locket held for you, especially since James was away, and later missing, and you did not know when he would return home.

Now I present you with my locket. Perhaps you may enjoy the continuation of our entwined life. I trust these letters under your care.

With much love and admiration for the woman you are and the woman you will become.

Lady Henrietta Stephens

February 23, 1734

Sophia tried hard to keep her tears from falling onto the linen paper of Lady Stephens's letter. Looking over at James, he, too, is wiping off several tears rolling down his face.

James takes the second letter, addressed to the two of them, and he begins to read it out loud.

Dear Colonel James and Lady Sophia:

It is my wish you become heirs to my entire estate. I am of solid mind as I write this letter today on February 23, 1734.

James and Sophia Langston are to receive my entire worth of near 300,000 pounds. The exact amount can be retrieved from Mr. Donithron, Bank Manager at the Bank of England.

Sophia Langston is to receive all my jewelry. It is my wish for Theodore Gribble to receive his share, as addressed in a separate letter enclosed.

James and Sophia, I want you to know, you have both brought me much love and kindness in my final days and months. I had lost hope after my dear Henry passed, and when you arrived into my life, my sense of life completely changed.

I wish you both many more bairns and all the fond memories they shall bring the two of you. It is my honor to leave my entire estate to you.

I know you will deeply cherish it and use the funds wisely. Sophia, might I also suggest, as an avid reader, that you contribute some of my money to the local library, so William, along with others, can continue to learn and enjoy time reading wonderful stories.

With Fondest and Everlasting Love,
Lady Henrietta Stephens
February 23, 1734

Sophia and James lean back in their chairs in complete and utter shock. They cannot believe what their eyes have just read. While still recovering from the blow of the letter's contents, there is a knock at the door. Answering the front door, Theodore greets the post-boy, who hands him a letter. The letter is addressed to Colonel Abraham James Langston. He thanks the post-boy and immediately walks over to Colonel James, who is sitting next to his wife, who continues to sob in the drawing room.

"Excuse me, Colonel James. You have a letter," Theodore politely interrupts the two of them.

"Thank you, Theodore, and as part of the late Lady Stephens's estate, she would like you to have this gift," James said, presenting Theodore with the letter. "I am sure the loss of Lady Stephens has not been easy for you. We are all experiencing her loss."

"Yes sir, it is a great loss. I am keeping myself occupied with chores in order to manage my grief."

"Understood," James said empathetically.

James stands and indicates he will read this letter in his study. Upon entering his study, James sits down and opens the letter recently delivered. Instantly, he notices it is written by Grace, the woman who cared for him in Portugal. Surprised, he reads the letter, and he cannot believe what he is reading. This letter confirms the reason as to why Sergeant Calvin and Captain Taller chose to keep their affiliation a secret. James continues to read. 'Does this devilish plot ever end?' he ponders. He is astounded by what he is reading, and although exhausted by the day, the adrenaline in his body has given him a new surge of energy to make things right and to make the wrongdoers pay for their despicable, vicious and selfish actions.

James calls out for Theodore.

"Theodore, would you kindly tell Sophia I must go to the General's house at once. It is a matter of urgency. I will return soon."

"As you wish, Colonel," Theodore responds, clearly aware this recent letter has filled James with indignation.

James's horse gallops toward the General's house. Rushing through the front door James walks directly into the General's study, aware he is barging in unannounced. Thomas sees James heading into the study. 'This storming into our house seems to have become a pattern for the Colonel today,' he said to himself while shaking his head.

"General, I have just received a letter from Lady Grace." The General looks puzzled by this rather rude interruption by Colonel James, and also to whom he is referring. Seeing the puzzled look on the General's face, James continued.

"Lady Grace is the British woman who nursed me back to health in Portugal. In this letter she shares how the highwayman, whom I allowed to live so he could feel forever ill about the death of his friend, showed up at her doorstep. He was begging for food and water. She refused to help him. He remained on her porch, weak, as he pleaded for nourishment. Lady Grace, who is a very plucky woman, later came out on the porch with her rifle and demanded he exit her property or his consequence would be the end of his life. The highwayman remained on the porch. Lady Grace, at a loss as to why this man was not leaving, asked the highwayman why he chose her house in the middle of the woods to beg. Here was his response.

James takes the paper and begins to read directly from the page.

"My Lady, I had a difficult encounter with a British soldier. He was harmed and I noticed his horse is in your coral, and I wanted to assure you were safe."

"A difficult encounter you say. From the story I heard, you attempted to rob that soldier and leave him for dead."

"We did exchange altercations," the highwayman responded, attempting to keep the appearance of the actual situation light.

Frustrated by the highwayman's story, Lady Grace sternly reacted.

"You are a thief and a murderer. Exit my porch at once."

"Kind lady, it was not my idea to rob the soldier. I am but a poor field man. It was my friend, who is now dead. He was hired by the Captain of the British ship. His name was Captain Taller. He said he would pay us handsomely if we would murder and rob the soldier. He said he and a family member were working together to devise a workable plot. He assured my friend the task would be an easy one because the road the British soldier traveled on would not be busy and the soldier would be fatigued from his long ship's journey to Portugal. His weakness would be no match for the two skilled highwaymen."

James looks up at the General. "Lady Grace was enraged by this highwayman's story. The scenario she heard reminded her of her own husband, a Portuguese soldier, who was killed out of treachery and deceit. The distain she felt for this highwayman lying on her porch, and the agony she felt for the loss of her husband, left Lady Grace no choice for resolution. She shot and killed the highwayman lying on her porch."

The General sat dumbfound in his chair.

"Sergeant Calvin's and Captain Taller's entire plan backfired. I am still alive and the Sergeant is not living in my house with my wife."

"On the behalf of the entire military, this behavior is intolerable!" the General bellowed, as he motioned his head left and right.

"It is time justice be served to these scoundrels, General."

"I agree, Colonel."

"Captain Taller reports to a different military commander. I will correspond with Captain Taller's Admiral immediately. I will see to it he is dismissed from all active duties at once."

"And, Sergeant Calvin? What will be done with him?"

"He has portrayed unscrupulous behavior. He will be court-martialed. His fate will lie in the hands of the military laws."

"Agreed, General."

"Sergeant Calvin is a mockery to our fine army. My expectation is for a court proceeding to provide public humiliation to this man. I want everyone throughout the streets of London to know this is not how we function in the Royal British Army."

~~~

The midwife signed the birth certificate as August 2nd 1734. James and Sophia were in utter bliss at the sight of their perfect child. Turning to the couple, the midwife asked the infant's name. Sophia immediately responded, "James Henri Langston. That is Henri with an 'i' and not a 'y'."

James looks over at Sophia in complete bewilderment. 'Has this woman lost her mind during childbirth? Why would she name our first son Henri?'

Seeing the look of bewilderment on James's face, Sophia turns to him and said, "James, if it is all right with you, I would like to name our beloved son Henri, after Lady Stephens."

At this point James was completely convinced his wife had lost her mind. Why give our son a male name after a female. It does not make any sense.

Sophia chuckles, seeing the baffled look on James's face.

"Lady Stephens's first name was Henrietta. Her husband, Henry, called her Henri, with an 'i', when she was behaving courageously—like a man."

"James Henri it is," James said proudly, now understanding the connection. "I cannot think of a finer name for our son. Named after his father, the soldier, and a wise, plucky and loving person."

Sophia gently strokes her fingers through the baby's dark curly hair.

"I am ever so grateful this day has finally arrived. I am a mother and I will enjoy watching our son grow up in this house and playing on our beach."

The midwife leaves the new family alone, as Sophia bends down and kisses her son on his forehead, who is now asleep in James's arms. The sight of her muscular Colonel holding this tiny, innocent infant brings a strange feeling of happiness to Sophia. 'My two James's. I love them both so much.'

James gently carries James Henri over to his wicker bassinet positioned next to their bed. He gently lays him down. Sophia feels a moment of joy and sadness as she remembers the day Lady Stephens purchased the bassinet for her.

Late afternoon soon becomes evening, and the sea's waves bring in the cooler night air into the bedroom. James begins to light a fire. As the fire grows, it crackles as the hot embers pop almost in celebration and announcement of James Henri Langston's birth.

"Tonight we may need our heavy blankets; there seems to be an extra chill in the night air," Sophia suggests, sitting at the window seat.

James walks over to the low, three drawer cherry dresser. Sophia had always enjoyed this piece of furniture, which was part of Lady Stephens's estate. She admired the craftsmanship and ornate carvings on the front of the piece. James cannot find the blankets within the dresser. He proceeds to search through his cherry armoire as well. He still cannot find their blankets.

"Theodore must have stored them away for the summer months, and he did not anticipate such a damp, chilly evening tonight," James said out loud to no one in particular.

James decides to hunt for the blankets in one more spot before disturbing Theodore to ask the whereabouts of the blankets.

He walks over to the wooden chest, decorated with leather straps. Unbuckling the brass latches, James opens the top of the chest and discovers the wool blankets he had been searching for. He removes the soft wool blanket from the chest.

"Sophia, my dear," James said, bringing the wool blanket over to her. "You will be surprised by what I have just located. Do you remember this wool blanket?"

Sophia turns her head, touching her hand to the blanket.

"Oh my, I most certainly do. This is the blanket we first saw in Lady Stephens's estate sale. The one I wanted you to buy for me. After being distracted by so many of her other treasures, we both forgot to ask her if it was for sale. I love this blanket, and sadly, now she is no longer with us and the blanket is ours."

James covers Sophia with the wool blanket and smiles.

"We will always be continually warmed by Lady Stephens's memories."

Sophia returns the smile, although her smile includes great sadness as it appears on her face.

James returns to the wooden chest, reaching down into the bottom of the chest, he removes a stack of weathered letters tied with twine. On top of the bundle of letters is another envelope addressed to Mr. and Mrs. Sophia Langston. He brings the pile of letters to Sophia. On his way to the window seat where Sophia is sitting, James hears something drop onto their wooden floor. He reaches down, picking up a gold chain and gold pocket watch. On the front of the pocket watch is engraved the inscription "Henry & Henri Forever Love." Sophia looks dumbfounded as James hands the watch to her. Sophia turns the watch around. On the back side of the watch is an enamel hand-painted miniature portrait of Henry and Lady Stephens. The portrait was painted later on in their marriage—after many years of marriage. Sophia was astounded she now had a lifetime memory of Henry and Lady Stephens's love. She also was intrigued by the image of Henry. This was the first time she had seen a portrait of him.

"Oh, James. I shall cherish this pocket watch forever."

"I imagine you will, my dear. Just promise me this. You will never call me Henry."

"Oh, James," Sophia said, throwing a pillow at him and appreciating James's ability to break the heavy mood in their bedroom. Sophia could imagine Henry using a similar type of humor with Lady Stephens. She understands why Lady Stephens thought their lives shared much in common.

The next day Sophia awakens and immediately begins reading Lady Stephens and Henry's letters, one by one, along with Lady Stephens's personal diary. She is astonished and moved by the intense love story between Henry and Henrietta. James looks up from beneath the warmth of his bedcovers. He sees his wife sitting on the window seat, wearing the cape he gave her for their wedding around her shoulders. Sophia has Lady Stephens's wool blanket around her legs.

Noticing James is looking at her and anticipating his thoughts, she responds, "Yes, my darling, I have been reading all of Lady Stephens's love letters and her diary as well. They have caused me to pause and devise a plan, James."

"And what might be this plan of yours, my wonderful wife?"

"I have decided to write a love story. It will be a story based on Henry and Lady Stephens's love letters. I believe the world could benefit from learning what true love really looks like. Would you not agree, James?"

"My darling, I think that is a marvelous idea, and I think Lady Stephens would be quite honored in knowing she has left a legacy. It would be a true testament to her and the type of person she was."

~~~

Months passed and the sun began to warm the plants, and buds could be seen on the trees. Sophia tucks James Henri in for his nap and continues to admire the sheer joy his angelic features stirs within her. 'How quickly he has grown in a year,' she marvels. She kisses his forehead as Governess Abigale assures her she will take good care of him while he rests for the evening.

Sophia is comforted by her words.

Walking to her master bedroom she finds James waiting for her.

"My lady, come sit down with me on our bed for a moment."

Sophia does as requested.

"You look beautiful this evening, my beloved wife."

"Thank you, James."

James hands his lover a glass of Bordeaux wine and proposes a toast to their first son, who turned one year old today.

"He is already growing up to be a fine son," James said confidently, in the voice of a very proud father.

"A fine person like his father," Sophia said with a smile.

James kneels down in front of his Sophia as he removes her night dress. She smiles with a nod of acceptance for what she assumed will come next. James takes his two hands and gently and respectfully spreads her legs apart. He begins to seductively kiss her inner thighs ever so carefully. He leans Sophia back onto the bed and continues to gently kiss her entire body.

"Mrs. Langston."

"Yes."

"Would you tell me a love story, please?"

"Of course, Mr. Langston," she said, smiling.

As Sophia weaves a love tale, James continues to kiss her, often stopping for a moment to say, 'oh yes and what else?' and 'oh no and what then?' At times he would spend long minutes sucking on her hard nipples, and at other times he would not kiss her at all and merely draw designs on her legs with his fingers. James would then bring his fingers closer to her aroused lips between her legs. It was those times she would stop telling her story and moan, instead of continuing with her story. James would continue his caressing for what seemed like a long time. Sophia could not contain her uncontrollable desire for James's touch. She continued to moisten between her legs until she could no longer think or develop a story line.

Filled with ungoverned passion, Sophia concludes with, "The End." She smiles, as if to imply her story was over.

"I think not, Mrs. Langston," James said emphatically.

With Sophia's legs still spread apart, James's hard expanded penis slides deep inside his wife. Sophia arches her back, moaning joyfully. She wraps her legs behind his back. She does not want him to ever leave this position.

James and Sophia climax together gracefully, in unison. He does not leave her. His throbbing warm penis remains inside her.

"James, I think this may be the greatest love story ever."

James smiles. He rolls over beside Sophia, holding her tightly in his arms. James whispers gently into Sophia's ear.

"Do you think we created our second bairn this evening, Mrs. Langston?"

"I do, Colonel Langston. I most certainly do."

About the Author

In her writing, D.M. Miraglia draws upon her inventiveness and the insights learned from growing up in a small town in Pennsylvania, along with living in the western and southern parts of the United States as an adult. Raised by what could only be described as old fashion, traditional values, by highly moral parents, her passion for writing has always been encouraged by her loving parents. D.M. Miraglia's defining moments included standing by her Mom, who has survived a two-time cancer illness. D.M. Miraglia's spiritual path of fifteen years was influenced by mentors, friends and family. Successfully owning two companies and current career experiences have inspired her journey for bringing real life events into her fictional stories. Her interests include jogging, mediations, reading, giving back to others of need and leading a life of inner peace and freedom. Her humble, compassionate and infectious spirit brings humanity to her fictional characters, allowing the reader to laugh and sometimes cry by what they read.